CONTENTS

THE SCREAMING ISLAND

"Are you sure there is buried treasure here?"

"Yeah, I have heard strange tales about this place. Ghosts and zombies and shit."

I resisted rolling my eyes as the small skipper boat we were on slid up against the sands of the island.

"It's not like a treasure map, Zach. There won't be a dotted path leading to x marks the spot," I told him as I surveyed the encroaching jungle.

It was exactly like my friend Will had described.

It was haunting how still the foliage was. Not even a sign of wildlife could be seen. Maybe the rumors of there being something supernatural on this island were true.

"Well, that ain't necessarily wrong though. I mean, if there is treasure here, it's not exactly going to be scattered about," Jack commented as he lit a cigarette and paid our guide.

"When should I return to pick you up?" the Egyptian man asked. His eyes betrayed his fear of the island, a clear danger that he was sure existed just beyond this line of trees. He was anxious to leave.

"Circle back near dinner time. We should be ready to go by then," Jack decided.

"You really think we can find something in just twelve short hours?" Patsy asked as she took out her camera. She was always so eager to capture everything on film. As we tramped through the overgrowth, it was beginning to look like there wouldn't be much to see though.

"According to Will, the crash site was near the north cliff-side," I said as I grabbed the heavy gear we would need for the eventual dive.

I knew my friends were likely expecting to find gold doubloons or medallions, but my interest was in antiques of a different kind.

"Just for clarity, remind me again what you said," the last member of our party, Anni insisted.

"If you weren't so busy wasting time making out on the trip over here…"

Jack gave me the stink eye, and I sighed, rehashing all the details that I felt were necessary.

"Okay, so a few years back, Will and his mates came out here on spring break. Said that they wanted to just get away from the hustle and bustle of the main islands and just chill with nature and shit. Well anyway, while they were here, they went for a few swims and stumbled across an old World War I bomber. He was able to dredge up a few cool things from the wreck before they returned to land," I told them.

"What exactly could an old aircraft have that we could sell?" Jack asked.

I pushed the jungle overgrowth aside, and we kept walking toward the north cliffs. I explained it to them. "These were probably the first of their kind. The findings of these artifacts could even reshape the history of the time. And they'd be priceless… if we can find them, that is."

"What about the rumors, though? Why is it called the Screaming Island?" Anni asked.

"Probably just to scare off any tourists. The place has been abandoned for a while, so I wouldn't be too surprised if a few legends came from here," I responded.

"Maybe there are howler monkeys somewhere inland," Jack joked.

***

"I have enough oxygen for about four hours of diving," Patsy said as we got to a clearing.

All of us paused for a short, tangible moment as we came across a pile of human skulls.

It was jarring and shocking, and immediately Anni spoke what was on everyone's mind. "Uh… Mark. I thought you said this place was deserted?"

"Well… now we know why it's creepy here," Jack muttered.

I swallowed a gulp of air and continued to push through to the next trail. "That's what Will told me… and that two years ago. Maybe it's changed since then. Maybe someone came to the island."

"That looked like more than two years' worth of skeletal remains," Jack snapped, grabbing my shoulder and shoving me against a tree. "What ain't you telling us? You keep mentioning you heard this story from Will, well… what about his mates? Why ain't any of them come forward with stories of treasure?"

I didn't know what to say… except that it was pointless to lie to them now.

"I'm not really sure what happened to them… Will never talked about that… but it's not like he was in the right frame of mind…"

Patsy's eyes sparkled with that sudden realization. "Wait a tic. Are you talking about William Carter? That guy that tried to commit suicide last year. I dated him sophomore fall semester!"

"Yep… that's him," I said, diverting my eyes. Jack was clearly more suspicious now than ever.

"So… we are following the words of a stupid crazy person that offer themselves?" Patsy realized.

"Why did he try to commit suicide?" Jack asked.

"Can we walk and talk? I don't like staying near that…" Anni commented as she pointed back toward the pile of bones. We agreed to that, but Jack kept a close eye on me as we arrived at the cliffside where it looked like some makeshift cabin had once stood.

It was clear from the ashes on the ground that it had also recently been burnt down. Probably within the last few months, I realized as I checked the perimeter.

"Something doesn't feel right about this besides the obvious," Patsy said nervously.

"Let's not overstay our welcome, okay? A lot of the info I got is probably old, so why don't we just dive, grab the goods and just hang out at the shore until Abdul shows back up to take us to the main island," I suggested.

"Suits me just fine. But don't think for a second I'm letting you off the hook about Will," Jack said as he started to strip down and get ready for the dive.

We had only brought enough gear for two people, and since he and I were the top swimmers from college, it made sense we would go. In the meantime, I told the girls to keep watch and tug on the line if there was a problem.

I prayed that my growing tension about the island was wrong and we could find the wreck quickly and leave.

We swam about to a trench that was about two kilometers from the cliffs and chose that as the spot to dive. I instructed Jack to stay near to me in case of sudden riptide, and the two of us soon found ourselves in a pocket of the reef that looked like it might be the perfect spot for debris to be scattered in.

To my surprise, though, it looked like it was an underground tunnel of some kind carved completely into the trench. The dive light on my scuba helmet barely penetrated the tunnel a few meters and from there it was complete darkness. For some reason though, I felt compelled to swim deeper. The ocean seemed to be calling me to search.

Jack was right at my side, motioning for us to go back. But something told me that a find bigger than any ruined aircraft was below. This was going to be groundbreaking, I just knew it.

Soon we found ourselves swimming up into what I soon realized was a chasm of some kind with an air pocket. I could even make out a distinct glow from the cavern walls. Something was hidden here beneath the island.

As we came up, I found myself staring at some kind of ancient wall. The carvings on it looked far more prehistoric than I imagined possible for this area, and it immediately sent images of the legends of Atlantis running through my mind.

Jack took off his helmet and rubbed his ears.

"I hate when they pop like that… we must be pretty far down. I don't see any sunlight anywhere," he commented as he checked around the exterior of the wall. Who knew when the last time humans had stood here, I thought to myself. The wall seemed to stretch for miles, dark and untouched and foreboding.

A strange, eerie sense of unease began to creep along my neck as we found an entrance to the other side, deeper into the labyrinth. A voice telling me that I should wonder, was this wall meant to keep us out… or keep something within? What had this place been built for?

The deeper we went, the more treacherous the path became. It wasn't exactly designed for people, the shapes were too oblong and nonsensical. It felt as though lightning had crossed through the stone and pushed its way into the crevices, even though it was clearly manufactured this way as if not meant for humans at all. Some strange unholy abomination made these, I thought as we arrived at a massive chamber that reminded me of a cemetery.

There were at least twenty oval shaped coffins standing in a row in front of us, each one of them placed in such a pattern to indicate their place in the hierarchy of this ancient society, or so it seemed. Jack whistled softly and took one of the lids off without even hesitating.

"What are you doing? That stuff could have some ten-thousand-year-old disease!" I shouted.

"Don't be a wuss, Mark. Forget the aircraft, this is where the money will be. Museums will pay through their asses for a fortune find like this. It could even reshape what we think about history," he said as he reached into the cylinder and took out a strange black stone. It looked like it was made of pure marble.

"This feels like a bad idea… something about this place reminds me of Will's trip. He said he ran into trouble… and that there were forces here that we couldn't understand. Maybe we should head back," I suggested.

"Not until we grab a few of these," he insisted, taking a few of the stone urns and then following me toward the entrance. All the while, it felt like we were being watched.

As we made it to the air pocket where we would need to dive again, I heard a strange whistling noise and turned back toward the tunnel instinctively.

There was something there. It was larger than any normal human and had eyes that covered its body. It looked like it had formed out of the shadows themselves. At first, I thought that I was seeing things. And then the monster slid against the wall the way a blob of jelly might.

I grabbed Jack to look, but in that split second the creature had vanished.

"What's wrong with you?" he snapped.

"I saw… I'm not sure what I saw," I admitted.

"Don't go crazy on me down here. I won't hesitate to drop your ass," my friend told me as he put his helmet back on and placed the black stones in his satchel.

I heard the whistling again but this time didn't look back.

We just need to leave as soon as possible, I told myself.

The tiny rocks shimmered with more intensity as they hit the water and I swam behind him, watching as it seemed like they were beginning to erode in the deep waters.

As we got back toward the trench, I realized that wasn't what was happening at all. The rocks weren't just dissolving. The urns were hatching. Some strange black tendrils were moving out from his satchel and wrapping around Jack's leg as I swam and I tried to catch his attention.

But it was already too late. Somehow this formless blob was expanding at a rapid rate and grabbing ahold of his appendages, making him sink the way a true stone would. I tried to grab ahold of him, but the creature was coiling into his skin tighter and tighter as he sunk into the depths and I knew I wouldn't have the power or the time.

I watched as his eyes bulged and he screamed in the deep, swarmed by the monsters and taken to their lair.

Instead, I said a silent prayer and crashed back toward the surface, calling out to my friends for help.

But the cliff side was silent, even as I tugged urgently on the rope. Anni and Patsy… would they be alive when I got there?

I frantically started to climb up, worried that some other unholy terror might be attacking them.

As I made it to the ridge, I caught my breath and saw a group of natives standing there with spears drawn. My friends were on the ground trembling and trying to surrender. It was clear that one of the tribal warriors had already injured Anni with a bloody knee.

There were at least twelve of them, all covering their bodies in a strange smelly copper paint with war designs and fearful monsters that reminded me of the creature that had just swallowed up Jack.

"Please don't hurt them," I tried to say. But it was about as useless as talking to a wall. A language barrier was there, and the natives were only interested in seeing us be punished. So, they grabbed me by the hair and tossed me into the center of their attack ring, a female group of musicians clamoring on the drums nearby as I was forced to make the decision to surrender as well.

It was the only chance I had to determine if we could escape and possibly get out of here alive.

One of the islanders shoved me to the ground. Another jabbed me with a pike. There was a bit of commotion among them as I began to bleed. As I looked up at our captors and got a better view of them, I started to understand why they were amazed by seeing us.

Beneath the war paint it was clear the natives were sickly, their skin a grayish green that was tight to their skin. Worse still, against the sides of their faces, I saw long gills that moved up and down as they breathed and fish-like eyes.

These people had been separated from society for so long they did not even resemble humans anymore.

They pushed us toward the jungle, motioning for us to listen or face more brutal treatment and Patsy gave me a foul look.

"I thought you said this island was deserted!"

"It's like I told you before; it's been a few years. Maybe something has changed since then," I remarked.

"Bullshit Mark! And where is Jack? What did you do to him!" she snapped. One native became angry at her heightened voice and shoved her again. I whispered, "Maybe we can talk about all of this when we get out of this mess alive?"

Soon we found ourselves at a very simplistic settlement. It was made of the same materials that we saw in the cabin but clearly was only made maybe a year ago.

We saw more skulls scattered about what looked like a crossover between a throne and an altar, and the natives began to chant as they tied us up and forced us on the ground.

Everything about their behavior and demeanor told me that we were about to be killed.

"Any bright ideas?" Anni whispered.

I was watching all of them, trying to figure out if there was really any chance they might be reasoned with.

Then from the front of the altar I saw a face that sent a shock down my body.

"Will??" Patsy screamed in surprise as her old boyfriend moved toward us, flaunting his strange bone jewelry like a king.

"You're dead… I saw you jump at the school," she whispered as he stood right over top of her.

"Of course I was. Before I came to this island, I was dead to the whole world…" he whispered. He seemed to be looking at us with amusement. And a bit of surprise.

"I honestly never thought you of all people would come here. My suicide was meant to stop you. Keep you away. I didn't think you would let greed cloud your judgement," Will said as he told the natives to pull us up to our feet.

"You came searching for treasure and found something Much more dangerous, didn't you?" he said with a sparkle in his eye as he looked toward me.

He barked another order, and a few natives came forward with what looked like a tomahawk.

"You've desecrated these people's holy land, Mark. For that, I'm afraid you're going to need to pay a price," he said.

I was still baffled by the strangeness of our friend being alive, but before I even knew what was happening, one of the natives was holding my arm still and preparing to chop off my hand.

"You don't understand! It was Jack!! He's the one that took the stones. I tried to stop him, I knew something was wrong with them. And then something under the water attacked him," I said desperately.

A few other natives closed in to watch this strange and sinister ritual, each of them holding a different tool or instrument I was sure would add to the torture.

"Your honesty is refreshing, but you were just like all the others. Couldn't steer clear from the call of the gold. And for that, you deserve this!" Will shouted and then motioned for the natives to enact his orders.

In one quick swoop, the tomahawk came down and smashed at my wrist, cutting at the bone. Since my arm was not resting on anything, the force of the impact was greater than I was ready for, and it sent me immediately into shock. But Will didn't even flinch when he heard my guttural screams.

He ordered the natives to slam the weapon against my arm again and again, severing the hand from my wrist until only bits of sinew and flesh could keep it together.

Immediately the native woman poured a fine coppery water on the wound, cauterizing it the way a laser might in surgery. It burned, but the shock of the initial pain had caused me to go completely numb. To my side, I heard Anni and Patsy screaming and crying, trying their best to not lose their minds as they imagined their own fate at the hands of our former friend.

Will took my severed hand and showed it to all the natives in triumph. They cheered, and he turned the hand over to let blood drain out, forcing me to have it drip on my face.

"Let the truth flow into your veins, Mark. Open your eyes and see the dark reality of the world around," he said as the natives forced my eyes open and the disgusting body fluids clouded my vision. It burned perhaps even worse than the amputation and I cried for him to stop.

Then they pushed me back to the sands and took the hand toward their nearest bone pile, tossing it on top and lighting it on fire.

I stood there; still transfixed at the reality of losing my hand and numb to the world when I heard the roar of the water and looked toward the horizon.

Something was coming up. Was it the same creature that had attacked Jack?

Immediately the natives dispersed like cockroaches, and I grabbed at the girls to hide even as Will lost his focus. He couldn't control their fear.

And apparently the amputation of my hand had been some sort of sacrifice that was meant to appease this blood beast.

We watched as Will approached the faceless creature, its formless body shrieking violently and towering two feet above his head, opening its maw and spewing toxic acid into his flesh.

Now it made sense how these people had lost their sense of humanity. They worshipped monsters… and as I watched Will get flayed alive like some dead cattle, I realized that it was their fervent desire to emulate these atrocious beasts.

With his face peeling off and his body being cut to ribbons by the monster, our old friend faced us.

"I am actually thankful you came. So you too could be granted the immortality I have. I had to leave the life I knew for this, but it was worth it. You'll see that the infinite wisdom they offer will have you strip off your humanity too," Will said, his voice shaking as he was attacked over and over. He was offering himself as penance for our crimes, confident the beast would resurrect him to a higher form of life.

I took the opportunity as a chance to run for the coast.

The girls followed behind as we heard screams from the natives. But nothing could deter us from trying to escape.

We made it to the shore where our guide was supposed to be waiting for us and I felt a gut-wrenching twist in my stomach as I saw the poor man on the sands torn apart like a beached whale. The creature had found him before we had.

Anni screamed again.

Then I heard Will whisper an offer of freedom.

"One of you must return to the world and tell them of this place. Tell them the danger so they too will one day be foolish enough to come to our shores," he snarled as his organs began to grow back within his collapsing body. He reminded me of a zombie, being powered only by the will of the mindless creature that was eager for more victims.

"We can pilot the boat, come on," Anni insisted.

Patsy hesitated for a moment, and it was that hesitation that killed her. A long, shallow hand from under the sand grabbed at her legs and started to pull her as Will pushed the boat out to shore.

"There is nowhere you can run from this!!!" Will screamed as Anni and I climbed into the boat. We tried desperately to reach for Patsy as she was swallowed by the undead monsters under the beach, but it was too late.

It was a miracle we made it off the beach.

As we pushed toward the open water, I activated the boat engine and didn't look back. We could still hear the shrieking even as we saw the last scrap of land fade away.

It's been almost a week since we were there. Anni and I made it back to the main island and got a quick rest before flying home.

At first, we agreed to not speak of what happened, to not even tell Jack or Patsy's family or friends. But such silence felt cruel.

So instead, we painted a picture of a terrible accident that happened on the way.

All the while, my anger and bitterness toward Will and the island grew. He had lured me there. But why? He had forced me to even lose a limb. And I still only knew that he wanted to satisfy a dark god.

His taunting haunted my dreams.

Until one day, I confessed to Anni that I needed to go back.

"We can't escape this," I told her.

She refused to accept our role in our friend's deaths and denied returning with me. But my mind was made up.

I have spent the time back to the island recording this to remember the fear and danger of my first excursion here. My hope is that now, with this new knowledge, I can gain answers.

But when I land, I automatically get the sense that nothing will be the same.

There are no skulls. No signs of a cabin or other structures. The island is simply barren and empty.

Only haunting laughter echoing in my head is now crashing into these shores. And the reality that my madness will one day consume me to take my life for having allowed greed to cloud everything I ever did.

Truly this is the screaming island.

INSTRUCTIONS FOR USING THE HARBORVIEW MOTEL MIRROR

So before we get started, let me get a few questions out of the way.

- It probably goes without saying, but I won't be providing the actual address of where the Harborview Motel is located in Texas; so don't ask.
- Like most urban legends of this nature, it's impossible to say for certain where it started or how it grew to be popular. So your guess is as good as mine on this.
- Although I will be providing you some step-by-step instructions on this ritual, please note that my experience is different than others and therefore if you do attempt this there is no guarantee you will fare the same.

The Harborview is one of those mom-and-pop owned motels that has survived the test of time thanks to its reputation for always having at least one room available.

Some say this is because the owners do a terrible job cleaning up after their guests and can never have all rooms ready in case of a surge of bookings. Others claim it's because their budget is tight, and the owners know that they don't get the usual clientele like other pit stops.

That's likely due to the reputation of the mirror, but let's not get ahead of ourselves.

The first thing you should know about the Harborview is that people don't come here for a good time or even a good night's rest. It's near to the highway and sits caddy corner from a 24-hour truck stop. Most business is taken over by the name brand hotels a few miles down the road.

No, people come here for a purpose. What that is will vary from person to person, of course, but for me it related to my wife Virginia.

Six years she's been gone, due to an overdose from drugs. Six years have I had trouble closing my eyes to go to sleep without conjuring up that last vacant stare she gave me when I found her. I've tried to figure out why she took her life, why she left me and the kids. I've blamed her job, blamed myself and even blamed God. But it doesn't provide any real comfort. Her departure left a hole in my heart, a void that needed to be filled.

I'm telling you this because of the first rule regarding the Harborview Mirror. You need to have a reason for using it. Don't be some daft fool that comes here and wants to try something for shits and giggles. It won't end well for you, my friend.

Of course, I can't say that with any degree of certainty either because I don't really know if anyone's experience is better than mine was. I'm only giving you the same advice I was told to heed based on word of mouth spread across the Internet.

That's where I first heard about the mirror, amid a menagerie of other articles about how to come to terms with grief by contacting the spirit of the one you lost. There's a multitude of them out there, but the mirror is the one that stuck out for me.

Perhaps it was because it sounded so plausible? So tangible? The way people described it, and the way it affected them… surely that couldn't all be for the sake of make—believe?

Six months is how long it took me to get the courage to give it a try. I knew that if I was going to succeed, I would need to follow the instructions given to the best of my ability… and well. That's the tricky part really.

There are at least 18 separate steps connecting to the mirror from what I have gathered, but some people put in a 19th or a different 13th step just to throw everyone off. Then another internet troll pops in and joins the bandwagon, distorting the original instructions more and more to the point where it's somewhat difficult to say for certain which are correct and which were simply tacked on.

I can only tell you what I did, so please; if your experience includes steps that are different than mine… share that.

First, you need to be from out of town. Easy for me since I lived up in Amarillo, nowhere near to where the motel is located. Some say it has to be that you have never been there before or even anywhere near to it. I can check that box easily too, but I suspect many truckers and travelers cannot.

Second, you should pack several things with you for the trip, the most important of which being a small pack of matches. This isn't for you, and you are not supposed to open them until prompted to do so. You can purchase them from anywhere, even from the truck stop across the road.

The other items are a change of clothes, a door wedge, a black ballpoint pen, and a bottle of water.

This next part isn't a step really, but I think it holds some significance, so I'm putting it out there for good measure.

It was around two in the morning when I arrived. (This is important timing for later on in step 5, so I would simply advise that you arrive about an hour or so ahead of time; just to give yourself time to finish your business and maybe grab a quick smoke or something.)

I walked into the truck stop to grab some Marlboros and beef jerky since I had been on the road for a few hours. (Like I said, I don't live nearby) and I was trying to find a good soda pop when the bright orange neon sign from the Harborview came to life in the reflection of the coke dispenser.

As I noticed the sign come to life, a few of the other patrons in the store did too; so I figured I should chat up the locals and see what they had to say about the motel.

"I'm surprised they have money to keep that sign on," I remarked to the cashier as I passed her my cigarettes and snack.

The young twenty something didn't make a reply at first as she rung me up, but for the life of me I swear there was something in her eyes that told me she had something to say.

"Isn't it run by just two people? Don't they ever sleep?" I said, hoping to goad her into a conversation.

"They come on when they're supposed to come on," she replied curtly.

"What does that mean?" was my next inquiry.

"Owners know when they have someone coming by. Don't ask me how. They just do. Must be a traveler out tonight needing a place to rest their head," she said as she passed me the change and then asked me, "What brings you here, stranger?"

Now, according to some blogs, this question is important to the ritual. Honestly, I don't see how. The cashier likely changes nightly and there's simply no way they could always ask the same question. But it did unnerve me that she asked, and I felt compelled to reply truthfully.

"My wife, I'm hoping to see her tonight," I told the young girl as I stared at the lights to the Harborview Motel. It was like they were meant for me.

"Good luck," she told me.

I went back to my car and checked the time. 2:24. Time to begin step 3.

You must leave your car parked at the truck stop and go by foot. Parking at the motel is bad luck and getting a cab to take you there is worse, or so people say.

There's an overhead walkway that links the truckstop to the motel, and the next step says you can use it to go to the Harborview or to return; but never both ways. It's up to you to decide. Even at this time of night, I didn't want to risk walking the 6-lane traffic, so I made for the overhead.

Once you are in front of the Harborview, it's time to wait. You should be there no later than 2:45 and no earlier than 2:40. (See I told you timing was important, and since every version of the ritual mentions this I'm doing it too) I arrived mere seconds before 2:45 hit, and I sat down on the second row of parking tape and looked toward the manager's office. The place seems abandoned. No one ever comes here except people like me, searching for purpose in their life.

This step is important (but then I guess all of them really are) and it's going to require you to remain undistracted by the noise. The sign will say CLOSED when you arrive, and you are to keep your attention on the sign until an unseen hand turns it over to OPEN.

This isn't easy, mind you. There's a lot going on. There are cars zooming by, some even get into wrecks while you wait. Police sirens going off, helicopters flying overhead, the occasional prostitute trying to get your attention.

Oh yeah, about that. This is a step I thought was fake, but since it happened to me, I'm including it. Some of the versions of the ritual say there is a particular prostitute that can appear while you wait and while descriptions vary from account to account, one thing that is consistent is that she is supposed to be asking for a smoke.

It happened to me about 3:09 as the minutes crawled by. I didn't hear her approach and when she stood beside me, I didn't smell any perfume. I was focused on the door, but in my peripheral vision I gathered she was wearing stiletto heels and fishnet stockings with a short turquoise skirt and a skimpy top to match.

The rules say she will be insistent on getting a smoke and you must refuse her. And you must also keep your eye on the manager's window. I did both, despite the fact that she was right in my ear, whining to grab ahold of my cigarettes.

After writing this, it has occurred to me that this is likely due to me buying them in the first place and hence her presence. So, if you want to avoid this distraction, just stay clean. I felt her tugging at my arm. She was very stubborn and wouldn't take no or my ignoring her lightly. Finally, I came up with an alternate solution and offered her my food instead.

"Mighty nice of you!" she said, snatching the jerky from my hand. At that exact moment, the sign in front of me moved, and I felt my heart race. I wonder still if it was kindness that allowed me to move on to the next step. All I know for sure is that I left her there and moved with haste toward the door. The instructions say you can't take longer than a minute to get inside. If you do, you might wind up meeting someone besides the owner.

I don't rightly know if I met that time since I didn't look at my watch, but I can tell you the manager's office was not at all like what I expected.

People say it appears to them in different ways. It's led me to think that maybe it's not simply the mirror that holds power, but the entire location. For me, it looked like a mash up between a Chinese restaurant and a video rental. Bland greens and bright yellows mixed. Old wallpaper peeled from the ceiling. Jazzy, scratchy music played in the background. Incense filled the air.

I couldn't really see the owner in the dim light behind the counter as he was busy grabbing something from under the desk, but he appeared to be short and stocky and of Asian descent.

He took out a guest book, slid it across to me and said in broken English for me to sign in.

"Room," he adds, pointing to the list. It is supposed to be a question, but for me it feels like a statement.

These next few steps are supposed to be the easiest in the process that I figured it's impossible to get them wrong.

Use the pen you brought with you.

You sign in under an assumed name.

You choose room 8.

I think for most people, the ease of these is likely what throws them off. Everything up to this part feels like you could easily get it wrong and ruin the whole ritual. But how could you possibly fuck up these three?

I didn't understand it until I was signing in, and you probably won't either.

It was this overwhelming sense of disturbance in the air around me. A compulsion to write something, anything, *anything* besides what the rules told me to put down. I had to practically force myself to forge a signature.

When I was done, the Asian man smiled in a queer sort of way and put the book away. For the life of me I wish I had seen how many other people had come here before, but in the heat of the moment I must have panicked. Had my name been the only one?

The owner told me to wait while he got the room key.

I couldn't help but notice the scratchy music had stopped. In fact, the office was dead quiet.

He returned a minute later with a large gold key tied to an even larger rusty copper plate that had an 8 scrawled on it with permanent marker. It actually looked a little like an infinity symbol, although I don't know why that correlation came into my mind.

The next step is supposedly optional. Like I said, some instructions don't include it; but others say you can tip him. Now the rules do say that you aren't supposed to bring any more than 44 dollars to pay for the room and that you must insist on paying that amount; but the rest is up to you.

I brought along about 100 bucks for gas, food and possibly HBO if it turned out the whole ritual was a dud, and this was all a stunt to boost their business. So I gave him a 10 dollar tip.

Per the script, the owner refused, and I insisted. Then I grabbed my key and made toward room 8.

It should be after 3:30 by the time you get there. Some people call this the witching hour and as I walked toward the room, it certainly felt like it. Where once there was noise and distraction from the highway, now everything seemed quiet. Now would have been as good a time as any to say fuck it and go home.

My purpose for coming told me I couldn't, though. So I used the key on the door and heard the lock grind as it unlatched from the hinges.

Room 8 looks like someone threw up in it everywhere. You don't come for the scenery. It has grey carpet with dark stains on it that some people claim are blood and two twin size beds, both of which are made with a peppermint on the pillow.

The instructions say you are to choose the bed on the left, so that's what I did.

I sat down and looked at the bed opposite of me, my heart pounding as I realized I was actually going to go through with this.

The door was still open, the rules don't specify whether you need to close it; just that you use the door wedge. But something about staring out into the world felt wrong. This place is separate from where I came, and I shouldn't let it interfere, I thought. So I closed it, placed the door wedge down and went over to the bed again, taking a few short breaths.

I told myself I was ready. People always do. I don't think anyone ever really is.

Then I went to the bathroom and turned on the light.

The mirror was waiting.

Now, from an outsider's perspective, the mirror inside room 8 looks no different than any other grimy, dingy motel would have. It takes up the whole wall, it's got a few fingerprints and dust on it and even a crack along the top like one sharp hit could shatter the whole thing.

I wondered how many people might actually come here for just a normal visit, stare into this mirror and go about their business without a care. It seemed unlikely. Because despite the fact that the mirror itself was ordinary, I felt an unease about it.

Something felt off. Don't ask me what. Maybe it was because I envisioned that the fingerprints were likely from the last person who came to perform the ritual. After all, the next step did say you were to sit in the chair in front of the glass and place your right palm against it.

According to the instructions, you must do so within two minutes of the first time you are entering the bathroom. So don't go in to potty or whatever, go in to get this whole thing started.

I sat and pressed my palm on the surface, feeling its cold resonate on my skin. You are to hold your hand there for another minute and, while doing so, you should look toward the right-hand side of the reflection. Wait until you see the flicker of a candle.

I must admit, I don't recall if there was a candle when I entered the bathroom. I was too focused on the mirror. I'm sure most people say the same. It's all-encompassing. Unyielding. Demanding of your attention.

But after a few short breathless minutes, I finally saw the candle ignited and I abruptly seized my hand away from the mirror.

The gentle flame from the wick lingered as I stared at it, my throat dry as I reached into my pocket and took out the matches. Getting this next part right was essential.

You are to stand up, burn a match and walk backward into the room. Keep your eyes on the flame and not on the mirror. My hands were sweaty when I struck the match against the box.

It only took one try. I got up from the chair and immediately started walking backwards. I didn't want to get anything wrong, so I was slow with my gait. I could see my reflection doing the same out of the corner of my eye. But again, that dreadful peculiar feeling lurched into my body. Why did it seem like the reflection was moving faster and I wasn't?

I stopped right in front of the bed opposite of mine. Then the match went out. At the same time the candle did too.

I stood there, looking toward the dark bathroom where my reflection had disappeared from sight and tried my best not to shake. Everything had gone exactly according to plan so far.

I knew I was to strip from my clothes and to change into the ones I brought with me.

Some speculators say that this is so the spirit you meet is fooled and doesn't haunt you from beyond the room. Others claim it's because you are trying to appear differently than the way you came, so as to symbolize some sort of transformation you are trying to make. Personally though, I wanted out of my regular clothes because I was soaked in sweat. Never had I been so nervous in all my life.

It took me less than three minutes to get into the robe I had brought. I figured something simple would be easier, but for some reason putting it on felt like I was slowly drowning.

All the while, I got the sense that the bathroom seemed darker than before. I was close to finishing all of the steps.

Once dressed, I tossed my used clothes in haste over to my bed and reached for the matches. There wasn't a moment to waste.

You are to start walking forward, toward the darkness, with the match ready. But you are not to light it until you are face to face with the mirror.

I took a tentative step forward. Then another. Then another. Finally, I was there. The bathroom was colder than before, I was certain. And despite the fact that the mirror was only a few feet in front of me, I saw nothing.

My hands trembled. I struck the match near to my chest and closed my eyes, saying the phrase I was told would provide me closure.

"Show me why," I whispered.

I held my breath for what seemed like an eternity, then I opened my eyes and slowly brought the match up to my face.

It was still me.

My mind panicked, thinking I had done one of the steps wrong. The ritual was meant to answer my fears, explain the loss I couldn't let go of. Was it all a hoax? Was this all a waste of my time?

Then, a smile creased across the features of my reflections face.

Silently; its free hand gestured toward the counter where somehow there was a bottle of water on its side of the mirror. It was the one I had brought with me, but I swear to you the steps do not say to bring it into the bathroom. Somehow it was there anyway. Across the void.

Then it took the cap off the water and gently poured it over the match that was illuminating us both. Mine was the only flame that went out.

In those few seconds of darkness, as I stared across at my illuminated reflection; I can rightly say that I forgot what I looked like. It was like staring at a stranger. The reflection did not move or waver. It just stared back and held my gaze for another few seconds.

It raised its mouth toward the glass and breathed gently, just enough to fog it up. Then it used its finger to write me a message. Slowly I watched as the letters unfolded before me, my brain trying to comprehend what each of them was as though I had never seen them before. It didn't seem to make sense until the word was spelled out in its entirety.

BECAUSE was all it said.

Then the darkness returned.

I sat there numb for a few long, lingering minutes. I thought back to Virginia and all the times we had argued. The last things I had said to her was cutting and harsh. That was why I had blamed myself.

So what did this message mean? This simple puzzle kept me awake the rest of the night as I laid in the bed. The rules say you don't have to stay until morning, but I have no idea where else to go.

I think I know what the mirror was telling me, and I think I understand now why the ritual is not recommended. Why my answer may not be so unique after all.

The morning light is creeping into my door, but it isn't welcoming. The roar of traffic is all that buzzes into my mind. I can leave whenever I want to. The ritual is over.

This is here for anyone else who is listening to these stories and searching for answers of their own to whatever is keeping them up at night. I'm telling you, if you are searching, you should stop doing so.

Because sometimes bad things happen and there is nothing you can do about it. And that's a hard pill to swallow. Maybe even impossible if you realize the deeper implications.

But maybe I'm wrong.

Maybe your experience will be different when you come to the Harborview Motel.

All I know is that I have to cross the highway.

And I can't go back the way I came.

THE HUNTER AND THE HUNTED

My head was spinning.

No… no it was the entire world. Everything is a blur.

Dizzying lights and jarring sounds filled me as I tried to stand.

Then I was yanked back down to the ground, my fog clearing as I got a good look at the person beside me.

Noah Hunt.

Noah… Hunt. My stalker. The boy that had been my living nightmare since freshman year.

"What the fuck are you doing here, you motherfucker??" I shouted as I tried to get up again.

Instead, I fell to the ground again, yanked down hard by his weight and as my vision cleared up more, I saw the reason why.

We were handcuffed together. The metal was bound so tightly against my wrist that I saw scratches and drops of blood against it as I tried to wake Noah up.

Flashes of memory sprang into my mind. I remembered going to a party. Gemma Angelson, her parents had a rental property near the lake.

I had gone to try and score a few packs of marijuana from a friend, and snuck out so that my parents wouldn't find me.

But it was hard to say for sure how long ago that was.

I tried again to wake Noah, but he wasn't breathing, and I began to fear the worst. Was he… dead? In the dim light of the canopy, I could see what looked like deep gashes across his chest and face.

Something had attacked him.

Instantly I was in defense mode as I scooted closer to his cold body and looked about the woods closely and cautiously.

The forest was curiously silent, and it unsettled me.

I took a moment to gather myself and tried again to stand. Noah weighed about 220 so the job wasn't easy.

"Help! Help!! Please someone!" I shouted at the top of my lungs.

It was eerily quiet, as if the entire forest was hiding from whatever had attacked Noah.

Dozens of questions filled my hand as I dragged his corpse to a tree. Had he lured me here? Was I a willing participant? And perhaps most important of all, what had hunted us and tracked us and killed Noah?

I needed to move and get to shelter if I wanted to gain any answers, so I used what little strength I had and pulled myself up to a hunched over position, my right side tugging downward to carry Noah.

Gemma's cabin can't be far, I told myself. I tried to spot the sun amid the treetops to get a sense of direction, wishing I had my phone with me. The only thing of any use was Noah's backpack, and it was on the other side of the meadow. It might have had a satellite phone in it, I thought as I began to crawl toward it.

It wasn't long before I heard the most unsettling noise come from the woods and I froze in place.

I've never been fond of the forest. When I was little; we lived close to a small patch of trees and my friends loved to go and play there but not me. I was probably the straightest arrow you could find, and I was worried that the woods would swallow me whole if I stepped foot in them.

At night, as I fell asleep as a child, the only thing I ever found remotely comforting about the forest was the ambient noises of crickets or the rustling of leaves. A calmness that descends over the trees as everything goes to sleep and it felt like nothing bad could ever happen to me thanks to this sense of ease that blanketed me.

There wasn't any type of calmness found here, instead the forest was eerily quiet to the point that it made me wonder if there was even a living thing nearby. And then the noise of the beast. I can't describe it properly.

I've never been good at identifying sounds, but it certainly didn't sound like any animal I was familiar with. Maybe it was a bear or a large carnivore coming back to check on its fresh kill? If so, I suddenly had even more reason to cross the meadow and try to get out of here.

Again, I tugged at Noah's corpse and crawled across the grassy clearing, stopping every few feet to catch my breath. This wasn't exactly the perfect time for me to realize I wasn't in good shape and Noah had to be at least two hundred and twenty pounds, if not more. I was starting to realize that if this became a fight of flight scenario, running wouldn't be a good option.

Pushing myself up again, I dragged us to as close to the backpack as possible and yanked it toward me.

I think I said a prayer and then I unzipped the pack to see what he had brought along for the trip. Instead of seeing anything useful, it made my heart drop to my stomach.

There were different hunting knives, at least six of them all looking like they were meant to skin game animals along with rope, twist ties and other things clearly designed to keep me from running away. Duct tape for my mouth, drugs to keep me sedated. But nothing that could help me in my current predicament.

I kept digging, trying to not make a sound as the howling in the woods got louder. Was it a pack of wolves? Was I about to be their next meal now that Noah was beginning to decay?

I froze in shock as I saw strange silver coins near the bottom of his bag along with a journal that was opened to a page filled with some kind of symbols that I didn't recognize. Was this like a code? And if so, for what?

I reached into the bag to pull out the journal, and just as I did, I heard a harsh rush of air overhead and I dropped to the ground, freezing in place.

I felt my chest beat rapidly against the ground as I heard the flapping of large wings and my eyes darted about the tree line. Whatever was hunting us was aerial, I realized as I kept as still as possible. I had no idea if the creature would be fooled by my attempt at playing possum, but it was my only chance at survival.

Above me, I heard branches crack and then another loud burst of wind as the beast crashed down on the floor of the forest and let out a shriek. I was too terrified to look, but just from the reverberation on the ground, I could tell that this thing was large.

I focused on the pool of blood that was near to Noah's abdomen where he had been intentionally attacked and saw little ripples against the still liquid as the creature got closer.

Long bony legs arched over his prone body, and I could feel a warm body against my own skin. It took every ounce of courage I had to not shake in fear as it dropped its head toward Noah and began to peck at his insides.

I closed my eyes and started to count backward from one hundred in the hopes that it would help, but instead all I could hear was the crunching of flesh in this beast's jaw. Saliva was dripping against my own skin.

And then, a few excruciating moments later, it was moving toward the tree line, and I convinced myself to open my eyes.

I'm not sure what I was expecting to see. It was gloomy and overcast and maybe my eyes were playing tricks on me, but the creature had to be at least nine or ten feet tall.

Perhaps most striking of all was that it looked like it was wearing clothes, a dark bloody red tattered cloak that reached down to its bony legs and obscured most of its body from view.

And it wore a mask. Not your typical mask, but one made of the whitest bone, like it had specifically crafted it from its victims and custom made to strike fear in new prey. I couldn't see its eyes but the fact that this thing which acted like an animal and yet stood like a man was now looking toward me with a sense of awareness, it made me want to shit my pants.

I told myself those were going to be my final moments on this planet and I was almost okay with that.

Then the creature shrieked again and disappeared into the woods, apparently too stuffed with Noah's intestines to bother with me.

I pulled hard on the handcuff that yoked me to his corpse; realizing that the beast likely felt confident I wasn't going anywhere anyway.

For the next hour, I tried to crawl toward the edge of the meadow, stopping to catch my breath and trying not to have a panic attack as darkness fell over the forest.

I told myself I couldn't give up. My family needed me to get home. My friends didn't have a clue where I was, and I needed to fight to live. But that was beginning to feel like it couldn't happen, not as long as I was stuck alongside Noah's body.

It began to rain about ten minutes later and I took it as a sign to rest. Surely the beast wouldn't return during the mild storm. I closed my eyes and retraced my steps.

Gemma's party had not been the smash I had been hoping for, but some parts of it had been pretty good. I remembered getting a chance to smoke a little weed, kiss a few cute senior boys, and even make a cool video with my best friends to go on Tiktok.

For some reason those random videos were spiraling through my head as I lay there on the grass and one in particular popped in my head about a couple that shifted their weight and carried each other.

I looked over at Noah's corpse, realizing that maybe I could find a way to lift his body and carry it rather than drag it, and decided to give it a try.

I can't tell you how uncomfortable it was for me to move and straddle his dead body. Noah Hunt has been nothing but a creep to me all year long, constantly trying to take unsolicited pictures of me or follow me home. I tried to even get a restraining order against him, but the police didn't take it seriously.

I wondered what they would say about current circumstances as his open wound mushed against my thigh and I held my breath and leaned in to wrap my arms around his waist. I used the pack as a way of tying a small makeshift bond between our bodies and zipped it up, carrying the load next to my body to keep his wound from touching any of my own.

Even with the handcuffs, I could get it done, and now the real question became would I be able to carry his dead body.

I made my grip as tight as possible and started to pull back, groaning against the shift as his arms came over me.

Next, I used my legs to push myself up and, in the process, doing the same to him. In a way, having the handcuff in the position it was in now, interlocking with my grip; was a good way of making sure he didn't slump over and we both fall to the forest floor.

Before I could anticipate what would happen though, his body started to tilt toward mine and I began to push up to lean it against my right shoulder.

It wasn't exactly a perfect balance like I hoped for, but now I could walk and it felt as though, with the way his arms were around me, it would be easier to drag him. His dead eyes were staring right down at my chest, and I did my best to not puke. If he had been alive, I knew Noah would be having a field day being so close to me.

Then I began to slowly move toward the forest, hoping that any sense of direction would come to me.

I don't really know how far I walked or for how long. All I could think about was that I needed to keep going. But I used the moon as a compass and kept it straight ahead, thinking that maybe I could find the lake and then weave my way around to Gemma's cabin.

As it turned out that actually worked. I found the shoreline probably half an hour later, and from there, I worked right, spotting a shady outline of a cabin in the distance. Maybe I felt a renewed sense of urgency because I heard something off in the distance again or maybe I was just so excited to get help, but those final moments getting to the cabin seemed to rush by and I wasn't even really aware of the fact that I had likely dragged Noah's corpse so far.

Loud music was still blaring from the cabin as I climbed the steps, a smile on my face as I shouted to someone inside to come out. But there was no response and as I reached the door I realized it was unhinged.

My excitement turned to dread as the door slowly opened and I saw a scene of carnage.

Blood was everywhere, even on the ceiling. There were bodies strewn about and tossed like dolls and most of them were torn apart with little left to recognize them.

The creature had come here and killed every single one of my friends, I realized as I slumped down on my knees and tried to hold back tears.

As I did, I realized too late that I was not alone in that cabin. The tall, cloaked creature was in the dim hallway, it's soft growl alerting me to its presence as it loomed nearer.

"Get the hell away from me!!" I shouted as I reached for some pots and pans nearby on the marble counter and tossed them toward the beast. For some reason it was like tossing a rock into a pond and the monster's body rippled and shifted. Unaffected by my outburst.

"What do you want from me? Why not just kill me too?" I shrieked as it kept staring at me. Given that I had lost so much already, at that moment, I did feel like giving up. I didn't really see a way that I could survive.

Then, as if acknowledging what I had just screamed, the monster opened its cloak and stretched out a long, charred finger toward me, pointing toward Noah.

I felt the air leave my lungs for a very long moment, immediately repulsed by the idea that the corpse I had been carrying around was what it was searching for. I didn't know what to think or how to feel.

I've hated Noah Hunt for months now, but I can't say that I ever felt he deserved to die. And especially not at the hands of a gruesome and disgusting humanoid creature.

I could only respond to keep myself alive and shoved his weight toward the creature, closing my eyes as its body reacted the way an ant mound does when you disturb it. My hand felt tight as I was yanked forward automatically, and it began to rip and shred apart what little was left of Noah.

But the carnage did not last long, instead its long bony mask was turning up toward me and sniffing the air, almost as if it was unsatisfied by what I had just offered it.

"What more do you want?!" I shrieked, too mortified to move as strange tendrils of flesh vined their way toward my chest. I was certain that I was now about to die.

But instead; it was the backpack that had been hoisted against me the creature now felt for.

The ratty old thing fell away as it broke Noah's arm and yanked it towards the empty holes of its mask.

I watched in fascination and horror as the fleshy tendrils of its body searched the bag and dug out the coins that I had seen near the bottom. It was looking at them the way a mother might a lost infant, or so it appeared to me.

I took the chance to reach down and begin to pull my handcuffed arm away from Noah. Thanks to the new wounds on his body, his arm was now dislocated from the rest of his corpse, and I actually could move freely. Having that bit of flesh still hang freely from my side was disorienting at first, but I couldn't let it bother me if I wanted to survive.

I began to run toward the open woods again. As I reached the porch of the cabin, I had second thoughts and looked to the carnage. Gemma, or one of the others might have had a cellphone on them, I thought as I slowly moved toward their bodies.

The creature was paying me no heed, but still I kept my movements slow and calculated as I reached toward one of the fresh corpses and checked for any sign of an electronic device.

Gemma was the one that actually still had a working phone and as much as I hated to do it, I had to break her fingers off of the device. Then I had to use her broken thumb as a way of unlocking it.

My first instinct was to call 911, but then an image appeared on her background as a screensaver that stopped me cold.

It was a casual shot of Gemma standing next to her lakehouse with Noah, and they were smiling and kissing as they looked toward the camera.

Gemma has always been vocal about her disgust for Noah as well, to the point that I was sure he wasn't supposed to be at this party at all.

Yet this simple picture painted a different point of view for me.

Instead of touching the phone icon, I began to read through her texts. Noah was the main one at the top.

We need to be able to contain it.

What's going on down there? Was the ritual successful?

I don't like how you are handcuffed to that thing. She could hurt you.

Wait. I stopped reading and realized that they were talking… about me.

What ritual? And why did she think I would somehow hurt Noah?

Out of the corner of my eye, I saw the beast crawling its way toward a wide gaping hole in the back of the room. A doorway to Gemma's parents' wine cellar.

A flash of memory came back to me as I remember asking her why we couldn't go down and taste some of the brews.

She had offered a flimsy excuse about her parents finding out about the party, but now I was beginning to see things in a different way.

Splinters of wood scattered around the basement door told me that the beast had once been scaled down here, and now it was returning…

I found myself stepping down the stairwell, following the creature like a lamb being led to slaughter.

It was moving its goopy body toward a stone slab that was centered in the room, placing the coins down on the slab in a precise, meaningful way.

All around I saw signs of wanton destruction from when the creature had apparently been released, and then my eyes focused on a video camera that had toppled over.

My mouth felt dry as I picked it up and rewound the tape.

Deep down, I knew what I was going to see, yet being confronted by reality was still a game changer.

The tape started with the stone slab front and center, and then I saw Noah's face brimming with life. With more purpose than I had ever seen.

He was rattling off the date and then claimed this the twenty-third attempt. Behind him, I heard voices. Then I saw Gemma and one of her close friends.

Carrying my sleeping body to the slab.

Noah was finishing up with the coins and placing them back in his backpack before encouraging Gemma to get back.

Once he was alone, He reached into the backpack and got out the handcuffs.

"A precaution to keep the monster from hurting anyone else," he said to the camera.

Then he began to chant some ancient words, something that made my insides shake. On camera, I saw my body do the same thing, and from within my body, the creature was starting to emerge.

He was doing best to not be frightened as its charred body grappled with him and lifted him into the air.

Everywhere the beast moved, my body was now its unconscious shadow. I heard the whispers of a word that told me it came from my subconscious nightmares.

I was the harbinger and cause of this evil being released on the world.

The camera ended with the masked creature looking into it, and I could see my own dark reflection.

I stared across at the stone slab where it now slept, mortified by these revelations, as I found myself stepping toward it.

I was a killer. A monster. An evil that Noah and my friends had tried to contain.

Tried and failed.

I turned my palm toward the fleshy tendrils with an open hand and waited as it snaked across the open air, wrapping itself tight against my skin. It had been running around the woods, scared and confused and hungry.

In a matter of seconds, it was now merging again with me, its host.

Less than a few minutes later, I was standing alone in the cellar.

I looked around at the blood and at the handcuff that now hung freely from my wrist. The last remnants of Noah were eaten by the monster as it came back inside me, I realized.

I took a few moments to catch my breath and then smashed the camera to bits as I took out Gemma's phone and finally dialed 911.

I began to walk upstairs, flashes of the shadow that lived inside me replaying the carnage. They had tried to stop it. Tried and failed so miserably.

Next, I stood out near the lake and looked down at the coins. These things that I felt were like offspring to me now. What powers did they hold?

I scattered them into the lake and walked away before the authorities ever arrived, including the phone I had just used to make the call.

When they arrive, I was sure they would assume it was a teenage drunk party gone horribly wrong, and I would be seen as the victim of a sick prank.

No one would know of the darkness inside me. The evil that was now whispering in my ear. It was fully awake, and our souls were symbiotic.

There are others, it said, like me that I needed to find. So I walked until I found the highway. I flagged down a friendly motorist.

"Where to?" they asked as I climbed into the back.

I looked into the rearview mirror and saw the bony mask of the beast where my face had once been. It was almost in complete control. My will was to follow.

This was how I would see myself now, for what I truly was.

"Anywhere," I said, my voice trembling.

"Everywhere." It added.

THE NIGHT LIBRARY

The downtown library was always a comfort to me as a young schoolboy.

Often getting picked on by bullies, I would hide away in the recesses of the stories I found there, imagining a lifetime of adventures I could never have.

Perhaps my favorite collection of works was one that never left the building at all. It was a large leather-bound volume of children's tales that was in the antique section of the archives, a place where most kids weren't allowed to go. Mister Newscome, the Head Librarian, knew me well enough to let me back there because I never took anything without permission. Besides that, as I mentioned before, the book that I loved was actually chained down to one of the reading tables.

Mister Newscome told me the reason for this was because the book was very old, dating back to the late 15th century and one of a kind, so I never really questioned it. All I cared about was sitting down and reading the stories and just getting lost in the pages as I went on adventures in my mind over and over again.

Eventually I got older, graduated and found myself in need of a job. I figured there would be no better place for me than interning at the library. I wanted to make books my life. They always kept me safe, and I felt at home when I was there, so it wasn't really a question of if I would do it but when.

Getting the position was easy. Mister Newscome was up in years now and needed the help and remembered me fondly.

I was told my job would be easy, simply restocking shelves and making sure no one made a mess. The library wasn't terribly huge, so I didn't think it would take much to do this.

On that very first day, my thoughts drifted back to my childhood escape in the archives, and I found myself wandering over there, just to be lost in a little bit of nostalgia.

As I touched the old copies of favorites on the shelves, my eyes wandered to the reading table where I would often read that one special book and I felt a pain deep in my soul.

The book was gone.

All that was left was the rusted chain where it had once been held.

At the end of my shift, I asked my new manager about it. His response was exactly what I expected. Someone had stolen the book a few years back.

Then he told me that he thought it was better that way; that the book was gone.

"How can you say that? I used to love those stories!" I told him.

There was something strange about that old children's collection, he admitted. He didn't know exactly what, but he always felt that it was not meant to be read at all.

The way he talked, he made it sound like the book was full of curses and magical spells, and it made me second guess what I had read all those years ago.

"Still, it's a shame that it's gone. If only there had been good security back then," I told him.

The conversation actually reminded him of something important and he asked me if I minded working as a guard for the library on a nightly basis instead of just being a stock clerk.

The hours wouldn't be too great, but the pay would compensate for it. Plus, he knew that he could trust me with his merchandise.

I told him I would do it even though I was exhausted from my first shift, I couldn't turn down the opportunity. Plus, it still made me so upset to imagine that my favorite childhood book was stolen, and this gave me a chance to prevent other irreplaceable classics from being snatched as well.

Although I didn't expect there to be any break-ins any time soon.

So, when he locked up the building, I grabbed a few stray magazines to keep myself awake and watched the television in his office as a distraction.

Not long after he was gone, the automated lights shut off, and the library was engulfed in darkness. I'm not sure why, but the feeling of being isolated in such a wide space made my skin tingle. It felt odd.

Still, the library was quiet and peaceful, so much so that it was difficult to stay awake. After about two hours of forcing myself to try, I decided to get up and drink a little water. I figured running to the bathroom would help with the situation.

About halfway there, I heard this strange low noise. The kind that you might hear when a house settles in the middle of the night.

Except I had to remind myself this building wasn't made with the same materials as a regular house, so it shouldn't have made such strange sounds.

Immediately I got up and grabbed my smartphone to shine a light down one of the carpeted aisles. Nothing. It looked just as peaceful as it had before.

At first, I tried to ignore it. I just went back to archiving the old books and trying to put them away.

It was strange wandering the aisles in the dark and trying to find things. Everything that had once been familiar was strange to me.

About every ten minutes, the strange groaning would return, and it would get louder. It was coming from the antique treasury.

I thought about the collection that had been lost and immediately started heading that way. Maybe it was another thief coming to steal a valuable manuscript. I didn't have anything to defend myself with. I didn't know what to do except that I had to protect these books.

I cautiously stepped into the room, using my tiny phone to illuminate the old leather bounds and paused as I saw the gleam of metal against the surface of one book.

Getting closer, I recognized the rusted chains and the table as being the same from my childhood, except that now suddenly the book I cherished had returned.

In fact, it looked like it had never left at all.

How could that be? I knew I hadn't seen it earlier in the day. Had I been in the wrong room?

I looked around again, second guessing myself and feeling confused. Was it simply so late that my mind was playing tricks on me?

For some reason, Mister Newscome's warning about the book popped into my mind as I touched its edges.

Was it possible this book could be affecting my thinking?

Impossible, I told myself as I slowly opened the pages. I would simply need to review just one story inside and it would show that this was nothing more than a children's classic.

I flipped through the volume and chose a tale at random.

The Midnight Shadow. One of my favorites. I remembered every detail as plainly as if time had never passed by.

The story was short and simple, but also elegant and powerful. A young boy was running away from home trying to find a better life, only to be confronted by a dangerous creature that lurked in the darkness and discover that the life he left behind was more promising than he realized.

For a young boy growing up, dreaming of adventure, it was a solid life lesson to discover.

Sometimes the grass wasn't always greener.

Just as I finished the story, I heard this strange rattling in the lobby and turned about sharply, worried that my initial suspicion of a thief was correct.

As I closed the book, I thought my eyes were playing tricks on me in the library aisles. The shadows looked like they were moving.

Slowly I stepped into the main auditorium, feeling suddenly uneasy in the same space that had once been my sanctuary. I felt I was being watched. Studied.

But I didn't know by what just yet.

I moved toward the open children's theater where readings often took place, telling myself it was just my lack of sleep and nerves.

That story had always been so scary for me growing up, because in the end the boy had to nearly die by the Midnight Shadow to learn his lesson.

And now, as I stood in the center of the empty library, I was sure that same creature was watching me in the darkness. I could see its eyes roaming the empty spaces of the dark, taunting me as though it was about to strike.

Was this a figment of my imagination, or had the story itself come to life?

I soon found out the answer as it stepped into the dim light and took form. It was at least twelve feet tall, with gleaming claws and sprawling legs. It had a wide mouth like a hippo and made a sound like a screech owl. It was even more frightening than my imagination had ever made it. And it was real.

It moved toward me the way that a predator hunted its prey, sliding in between aisles to confuse me as I stumbled toward the front desk.

My mind was fumbling to recall in the story how the protagonist defeated this beast. It was a simple solution, but at the moment, being confronted by this thing, my mind was blank.

I pushed furniture aside and toppled over stacks of books to try and slow it down, but the shadow just kept coming, undeterred. The only thing it cared to do was swallow me whole.

I don't want to die. I have too many adventures I still want to go on, I thought to myself as I made it to the front desk and hid under the counter.

The massive creature swirled about like a storm cloud, bellowing and reverberating the air to try and draw me out with incessant and confusing noise.

I blocked it out and thought of the story.

The main protagonist ran until it was daytime, the creature drowning in the daylight.

And then I remembered that the library had a basement generator.

I waited for a few moments until the living shadow changed its tactics and began to actively search for me again, then when I knew the coast was clear, I made a run for it.

The basement was not far from where I was hiding, just a small set of stairs that led into an alcove directly below. I was fortunate that Mister Newscome hadn't locked it. Once in the darkness below, I fumbled about on the wall to find the generator switch even as I heard the shadow getting closer.

As a living darkness, it could twist its forms to fit any place, and easily sniffed me out below. Its gleaming eyes filled with anger as I hurried to find the switch. Its eyes opened, and I saw millions of stars twinkling.

Then, at the last second, I found the generator and activated it.

Light flooded the basement and the rest of the library. Immediately the shadow dissolved, shrieking into the empty air as it was destroyed, and I caught my breath.

For a few moments, I wondered if what I had experienced was even real.

Then I heard a voice from above. Mister Newscome?

"You're already here?" I asked in surprise as I came upstairs and saw the mess of the library. The shadow had made sure to make my job look like I was slacking off. Especially because the night was apparently already over. My entire shift had passed by in mere moments.

I had experienced the story become reality, and it altered everything as a result.

Of course, the owner was curious about my explanation for the mess and I wasn't sure if he would even believe the tale, so before I responded, I went to the archives to check and see if the chained book was there.

Once again, it had vanished from sight.

It was then that I worked up the courage to explain the strange things that occurred while he was gone. Mister Newscome didn't interrupt as I explained how the story had come to life and tried to harm me. In fact, when I was finished, he admitted that he wasn't surprised to hear this would happen.

He reiterated what he had warned me of about the book before, and then admitted something that struck me as odd.

Besides me, as a child no other customers would ever bother the chained book. It was as though the mysterious fairy tales were calling out to me, tempting me to read more.

As long as I told their stories, they could continue to exist, Mister Newscome told me. I didn't understand what he meant. But the following night I would learn.

I thought about his words all day until it was time to clock in, wondering if the book would reappear in the darkness. I waited patiently, perhaps anxiously, to see if it was true.

Then I heard the strange noises and the hair on the back of my neck stood up. The book had returned.

I hurried to the archives and decided to see if another story would come true. I had to know if this book was taking a part of my soul.

The story I chose was called *The Stone Eyed Serpent*. A terrifying tale about a monstrous serpent that would make anything it bites turn to stone.

There was no way this could become reality, I told myself. I was convincing myself that these stories were just figments of my imagination. That's all it was.

Then I heard a rustling in the library. As though something ancient had suddenly been awakened.

I closed up the book hurriedly and went to look. Was it really the giant snake come to attack?

I didn't see anything in the shadows and for a moment; I was sure that it was all in my head.

Then I heard its vicious hiss, and it filled the air. The creature was here.

I stood still, watching as it slinked out of the shadows and towered over me. It looked like it could crush the entire building.

Its gleaming eyes told me that it was there to kill me, nothing more and nothing less. I had to run.

But where could I go? My feet took me to the other side of the library as fast as possible, but the serpent was faster.

It whipped through the aisles and began to coil around me, its fangs showing me that they were dripping with the magical poison.

I thought back to the story, knowing that I had to offer it something to defeat it.

But what did I have? I only had my body.

I stuck my hand out, trying to shield my face as it sprung forward and latched onto my fist.

It slammed its jaws closed, and I screamed out, kicking and screaming as the venom went straight into me.

Before I knew what was really happening, my hand was back, and I saw that it was turning to stone. The snake seemed to be laughing at me as it slithered back to the shadows, its job done to give me a reminder of what this powerful book could do.

I watched in horror as my hand turned to stone and I frantically wondered if it would spread to the rest of my body. I had to act quickly.

Moving toward the front of the library, I got my cellphone ready and called 911 as I prepared to slam the front door and take off my hand. It was the only chance I had at survival.

I closed my eyes, said a prayer and screamed as it shut, and my body was severed from the poisoned hand.

I blacked out shortly after that.

When I woke up, the hospital told me that I was lucky to be alive and I would be under psych evaluation for 72 hours because the injury was considered self-harm.

Mister Newscome came to visit me though and to my surprise he brought a gift. It was the chained book.

I actually recoiled in terror when I saw it.

"Get that fucking thing away from me! It needs to be burned. Destroyed somehow! It's a curse!" I screamed as he shut the door and we were alone.

He smiled and placed the book down, shaking his head and telling me that he had tried to warn me.

Then he explained how he knew of the book's power. It had been his curse, too. Many years ago, he had come to the library and been fascinated by the ancient collection. Not realizing that the more he read, the more he was bound to the library and forced to keep the stories alive.

He wondered if the curse would ever end. And then I came along. A young lad that had a curious mind like his. And now the curse could be passed on and he would be free.

As he finished telling me all this, I saw his body deteriorate and fade away. It was becoming ash. Or dust. A collection of stories now suddenly turned to nothing. Forgotten and abandoned, just like this cursed tome.

And now I am the one that must tell these stories. Despite everything that I knew was real. I did try to escape and never return to the library. But the book controlled me in ways I couldn't expect.

I am now part of this library, just like the previous owner was. Just like the others that come after me will become. We will tell these stories and make them reality, making nightmares survive for another generation.

The only hope I cling to is when I see eager, curious people come into the library and they read. Perhaps eventually the book will reappear and take one of them hostage next.

Maybe it will be you?

Maybe then you can be part of the story too.

THE DOLL IN THE WALL

Things were fine between Macie and I until we moved in together.

Not at first though, because the beginning was good. At least I can still hold onto that.

We had managed to sign a six-month lease at a duplex that wasn't far from our jobs for only a third of the normal price, which had us on cloud nine.

But soon we realized why we had gotten it for such a steal. First and foremost, the previous tenant had failed to remove any of their shit, so there was furniture, clothes and all kinds of junk just all throughout the place.

Then we had to deal with the fact that the power wasn't turned on yet.

"We can use candles," Macie said as we started to clear things out. The entire house felt so chilly it was hard to imagine it could ever feel like home.

It looked like it had been a single woman, probably just trying to survive paycheck to paycheck, I thought as I saw the ramen noodles in the pantry.

"She just up'n'disappeared one day, no notice, nothing. You can do whatever you want with her shit and the stuff you don't want, trash it," the landlord told us.

Once some of the furniture was out of the way, I used my phone as a flashlight to start taking down her family portraits and pulling nails from the walls.

Her life looked like that of a typical goth girl, trying to juggle social life with responsibility. Some pictures were her out having parties with friends, others where she was prim and proper for family. Reminded me a lot of myself, to be honest.

Next, I pulled the nails from the bedroom hallway, forcefully taking part of the plaster off in the process.

It tumbled to the floor, revealing something more than just a bare wall behind it.

There was some kind of closet behind the wall, I realized as I took my hammer and started to break apart the thin plaster.

Gradually the wall fell back, revealing a long thin closet that looked like it hadn't been used in years.

"Hey Macie… come take a look at this…" I called to her as I used my phone's light to get a better view of everything.

There were shoes on the floor covered in dust, all stacked neatly under organized outfits that matched them. Everything was perfectly in its place, but clearly unused for quite some time. I pushed the hangars aside to see what else was back there.

I kicked something on the floor, and it rolled behind the long coats, forcing me to look down as I slid them aside.

Then I saw its feet. And I screamed.

My flashlight traveled up the length of the body, a strange and eerie feeling rushing up and down my spine as I realized it was a doll that was about my height. It had pale plastic skin and bright blue eyes. Blonde hair and an hourglass figure. It looked like a life size Barbie doll.

As soon as I screamed, I heard a loud knocking on the other side of the wall and a man's voice.

"I said keep it down!!!"

I rushed out of the hidden closet, my heart pounding out my chest as I ran smack into Macie.

"Hey, I heard you in here… What's going on?" she asked.

Then there was a knock at the door. Loud and repetitive. Frustrated.

"Hold that thought," she said, grabbing a candle and we went to the den together, my nerves still jittery after what I had seen.

Unlatching the door just slightly enough to peek out, we found ourselves staring at a buff middle-aged man that was covered head to toe in tattoos with crumbs in his facial hair and bags under his eyes.

"You two new?" he snapped.

"Just moved in," Macie answered. I could tell the strain in her voice meant she was trying to be cordial.

"Listen, I work nights, so next time you start banging shit around I swear that I will come over here and slam my fist into your face. Ya copy?"

Macie's eyes flashed rage.

"Look you son of a—" I grabbed her arm and shoved her back, smiling politely through gritted

teeth. "What my partner is trying to say is… we will keep that in mind. Sorry."

He wiped snot from his nose and huffed off as I latched the door back and breathed a sigh of relief. Macie gave me a glare.

"What the hell was that? I could have handled that guy."

"And came out with a bloody nose or far worse," I said dryly.

"Whatever. So, what did you want to show me?" she asked, crossing her arms.

I tugged her by the arm, taking her to the hidden alcove I had found.

Using her smartphone to light the way, Macie gingerly stepped through the hideaway hole into the shadowy closet. A few more feet and she was right in front of the doll.

Immediately she jumped back, "Holy shit. You could have warned me!"

"What the hell do you think it is?" I asked nervously.

"How should I fucking know? What I do know is we are gonna get it out of here," she replied as she put her down and wrapped her arms around the huge doll.

"Jesus Christ, this thing is heavy," Macie complained. I tried to help her, but even with our combined strength, it would not budge.

"Don't throw out your back, you have work tomorrow," I told her.

She stepped back, rubbing her muscles sorely and remarking, "I guess we could call my dad. He probably has a dolly that can lift the thing."

We went back to the hallway, ducking through the hole again to avoid causing any damage and as we did, I asked, "Is there something we can use to… I don't know. Seal up this entrance?"

She gave me a teasing look. "Think Chucky will chop you up tonight?"

"Come on, don't make fun. You were scared too."

She chuckled a little as we went to the bedroom. "You're right, you're right. But the look on your face is still priceless," she said as we pushed one of our bookshelves into the hall.

Once in place, I felt a little more at ease.

Little did I know, the feeling wouldn't last long.

***

We spent the rest of the afternoon getting as much moved out as we could. I let Macie take it easy due to her back and did most of the heavy lifting alone. By the time dinner had rolled around, at least eighty percent of the stuff from the duplex was in the dumpsters.

Then Macie surprised me and ordered a pizza and we cuddled on our small couch and watched Netflix on her phone.

"Thanks for having my back today," I said as I snuggled a bit closer.

"You mean about the doll or the neighbor?" she asked, ruffling my hair.

I smirked, remembering how zealous she had appeared when the brutish man had threatened us.

"Both, I guess," I told her, giving her cheek a soft peck.

Eventually, I fell asleep to the sound of a Seinfeld episode, exhausted and hoping that our problems were just a fluke in our new situation.

It was a hope that I wish I could have held onto.

I'm not sure when it happened, but I woke in the middle of the night feeling painfully cold. Macie had already gone to bed, leaving me on the couch to freeze.

My bare feet touched the tile floor that was equally as chilly, and I walked over to the hallway to check the temperature.

We need to get that power on, I thought to myself as I realized it was too cold to get comfortable.

I reached for a candle to light my path to the bedroom, nearly jumping out of my skin when I did. I saw Macie standing with her back to me, right in front of where the hidden alcove was at.

"Jesus Christ, you scared me to death!" I shouted at her.

She didn't budge.

Suddenly the duplex felt a lot colder again.

"Macie?" I whispered, wondering why she wasn't responding to me.

I crept over to her, touching her shoulder to get her attention.

She pushed me away forcefully, mumbling something under her breath as she placed her palm against the wall. And began to scratch it with her fingernails.

"Macie… Macie, wake up!" I said, shaking her shoulders and pulling her away from the wall.

She was saying something, but I couldn't make heads or tails what it meant. It sounded like gibberish.

It sounded like some kind of foreign tongue.

She refused my attempts, this time shoving me down and again clawing at the wall. The sounds she was making were louder now, like she was calling out to someone.

It was like watching an animal struggling to free itself from a cage.

I scrambled up to my feet, ran to the kitchen, and poured a glass of water.

Quickly I splashed it in her face and my partner gasped for breath, her eyes frantically darting around the room.

"What the fuck," Macie shouted, looking down at her soaked pajamas.

"I could say the same to you. What the fuck were you doing?" I asked.

She looked confused and then saw the scratches on the wall and the shelf pushed aside.

"I'm not… I'm not sure… was I sleepwalking? I never sleepwalk. Not since I was a little girl," she whispered.

I took a cautious step toward her and then looked into the darkness of the closet.

"Did you go in there?" I asked.

"I'm not sure," she repeated, running her palm across her face. She looked so dizzy and sweaty, like she had just been on a three-mile run.

I used my smartphone to look into the hideyhole, just to be sure of something.

The light flickered back and forth across the dusty floor to where I had found the doll.

My heart dropped.

It wasn't there anymore.

"It's gone."

Macie's words echoed the thoughts in my head. Where the HELL had that fucking creepy doll gone.

I tried to not panic.

"Maybe you moved it while you were sleepwalking," I said, keeping my voice down as I pushed the clothes around in the closet. Even in the dark, I could tell that it was definitely not here.

"Are you kidding? That thing was heavy. How could I do that?" she asked as I climbed back out.

She was getting out her phone and about to dial 911 but I stopped her before she finished. "What are you doing? They'll think we're nuts."

She sighed in frustration. "At least let me call my dad. Maybe he can come tonight."

I passed the phone back to her, looking around the rest of the dark apartment. That thing could be lurking anywhere, I thought.

No. Fuck, get a hold of yourself. I was being crazy. There was a logical explanation for this. Macie sleepwalking could have given her the strength to move it without realizing it. There was no danger.

Still, I felt compelled to search as she dialed a second time.

"I swear that he could sleep through a bomb dropping," she muttered in frustration as it went to voicemail again.

I checked all the places I felt that her addled brain might have hauled the weird doll to like the bathroom and the other guest room, but found nothing. Just a chilly, creepy house where a doll was apparently hiding.

"Maybe we should just get some sleep," I advised, trying to calm my nerves.

We walked to the bedroom, and I opened the door. Behind me, Macie lit a candle, and I jumped out of my skin again.

We saw the doll's silhouette was there, sitting up in the bed. "Jesus Fucking Christ," Macie said as she walked in and saw it. Getting closer with the candle, I watched as my partner was brave enough to get a closer look.

Weirdly it also had clothes on now, a blue jersey that I recognized from my partner's wardrobe. And it seemed like the doll's hair had been combed. How could she have so meticulously done all of this in her sleep?

The way it sat there, just staring lifelessly into the void; it unsettled me. Macie squeezed my hand and backed out to the hallway, closing the door back.

"I am not going to be spending the night with that thing in the apartment," she insisted.

"Thank God we are on the same page," I said, a wave of relief coming over me.

Still, I knew I couldn't completely relax until we knew what the fuck was going on.

As we moved to the den, my mind fumbled to wake completely and think of what to do.

"This is such a fucking nightmare. We can't exactly go to sleep in the moving truck," I said as I unlatched the door and looked out toward the street.

It was nearly eleven, but only a few streetlights were on. The entire neighborhood felt eerie now, our little slice of it suddenly out of place. Then I noticed that the lights were on in our neighbor's side of the duplex and I tugged at Macie.

"We could ask him for help?" I suggested.

She gave me the stink eye. "I'd rather take my chances and sleep wrong in the truck," she remarked.

"Don't be like that. You can't risk calling into work. You just started and you need to make a good impression. Besides, maybe he knows something about the doll or the previous owner?" I said.

She rolled her eyes, sighing as we walked over to his door, and I rapped my knuckles on the panel.

"For the record, this is a bad idea," Macie commented. We heard him as he went to the door, opening it and glaring at us both like we were a pair of Jehovah's Witnesses.

"This better be fucking important. I go to work in an hour," he grumbled.

"Sorry, I guess we got off on the wrong foot earlier. I'm Trish and this is Macie," I said, gesturing to my partner. "I don't give a crap if you are Adam and Eve. Or is it Adam and Steve for gays?"

He laughed to himself and then placed his hand on the door hinge, getting ready to slam it in our face.

"I know it's late, but we were hoping maybe you could help us out with a favor?" I said as I saw Macie's eyes flare with anger again.

"We'll pay you!" I added.

He laughed again and started to close it. Just as he did, I shouted out. "Did you know anything about the previous owner?"

We stood there for a second and Macie huffed. "I told you this was a bad idea. I'm headed to the truck," she commented.

Then the door creaked open again, the man looking at me with a bit less suspicion.

"How much?" he asked.

I pulled out my wallet. "I've got forty-five dollars."

He bit his bottom lip and snatched the money, and for a second, I thought he was going to walk back inside and leave us out in the cold.

"The last girl… I knew her. Why you ask me that?" he muttered.

"She… left a lot of her stuff in our duplex. And we've been moving it all day. There was this, umm… one thing that we just can't seem to get out of the way and…"

He opened the door all the way, standing mere inches from my face.

"Is it that fucking doll?" he asked.

Now it was my turn to be surprised and shocked.

"Wait. You knew about that?" I said. Macie was speechless.

"Yeah. That thing is the creepiest shit I have ever seen. She would have full-blown conversations with it in the middle of the night. I can't tell you how many damn times I wanted to go over there and bash the thing to pieces," he snapped.

"Well, uh. No skin off our backs if you do that now. For real, the thing weighs like two tons and we want it out of the place," I commented.

He stood there for a moment, tapping his foot. Acting like a kid that was getting permission to raid the cookie jar.

"Yeah, all right, let me finish getting ready for work," he said.

He stepped back into his place and then paused, scratched the back of his head and commented, "Y'all can come in and wait if you want."

He walked off to the bathroom and Macie and I soon found ourselves loitering in this stranger's front room.

Everything about his place screamed a bachelor. Clothes on the floor, a beer next to the recliner, the television turned all the way up. It was a wonder that he found anything.

But then the pictures on the walls told a different story. I took a step nearer to get a look and realized that at some point this man had a family. A wife and daughter.

So where were they now? I wondered as I picked up the portrait.

Macie coughed in her hand softly and I turned to see he was back in the den wearing scrubs.

"Sorry," I muttered as I put the picture down hastily. "You have a lovely family."

"Had," he commented as he reached for the remote and turned the television off.

"Andrea ran off with some young hotshot a year back after our daughter died," he commented. Suddenly everything in his place didn't seem to exhibit the symptoms of a slob.

Instead, I realized it was all tinged with sadness. He was wallowing in grief of a life he couldn't have anymore.

"Anyway, let's go get that fucking doll," he commented. Macie stepped to the side and offered him a candle as he waltzed over to our apartment. We decided to linger in the door.

He was back in less than a minute.

"Hey. Where is the fucking thing?" he asked.

Macie and I came in, hurrying to the bedroom and finding no evidence the doll had even been there.

"It was right here," Macie whispered. She pushed past me to peer into the dark closet. It was empty too.

"You… you already moved it. Didn't you?" she whispered to the man. He was just standing there, a bit taken aback by her behavior. I actually found it odd as well. Disturbing.

Then she turned toward the neighbor. "Is this your idea of a joke? This thing is terrorizing us!" she snarled as she pushed him against the wall. I was surprised at how forcefully she did it. "What the fuck do you know about this thing??"

"Hey, watch your mouth you little bitch!" he snapped back, pointing a finger in her face.

I pulled Macie off of him as he adjusted his scrubs and started to walk out of the duplex.

"I knew it was a fucking mistake to come over here again. First it messed her up, now you too," he muttered.

I heard him slam our front door open, and I crossed my arms in frustration, looking toward Macie.

"Real smooth," I grumbled.

"The guy is a total prick. We don't need him," Macie said dismissively.

"Except for the fact that we apparently have a fucking possessed doll on our hands that nobody can find??" I shouted.

"It's not in the house. So at least I can get a little sleep!" she insisted.

We settled for bed, and I stared at the door, peering down the dark hallway. It was so damn cold.

"I don't really feel safe here tonight," I admitted as she finally got comfortable.

"Go sleep in the truck then," she grumbled.

I pursed my lips together, and then walked over and closed our door as tight as I could. Then I tucked in under the covers and sighed, watching as Macie fell asleep.

I kept still as to not wake her, and I was too worried about the doll returning to get a wink of sleep.

Instead, once I was sure that she was out of it, I moved over toward the large vanity in the corner and decided to scoot it to be in front of the door.

As I did, I heard Macie move about in her sleep and mumble something. Then I saw a glint of metal on the floor and reached for my phone.

It was a small screw.

I pushed the vanity a little further and saw that there was a ventilation shaft behind it.

I knelt down and slowly twisted the screw back in place at the bottom of the vent, then stood up again ready to push the vanity.

A plop on the carpet drew my attention back downward.

The screw had fallen out again. And it sounded like something was rattling in the vents. Something bigger than a rat. I made certain the screw was on tight.

This time, I watched as something inside the vents popped the screw out.

I woke Macie up immediately.

"What the hell Trish?"

"We're sleeping in the truck. No arguments."

***

There was an argument,

But we did wind up sleeping in the truck. We pulled our guest twin mattress out and laid in the back. It wasn't comfortable, but it was better than being inside.

Even in the back of the truck, I still didn't feel safe. Not as long as that doll was somewhere nearby. I slept facing the door, and barely got any rest at all.

Especially because we had a lot on our plate in the AM.

And it all went to shit anyway because Macie's phone died overnight, and she overslept and so our day started off on the wrong foot.

I opened up the truck door and heard her on my phone explaining to her boss she would be an hour late because of the issue and immediately knew she was going to take her frustrations out on me.

"Your dad was supposed to meet us at the truck rental place, yeah?" I asked as I dragged the guest mattress back to the front lawn and she finished her phone call.

"I'm texting him now," she muttered.

"Tell him to come here and get you to work. I can take care of the truck," I told her.

"And how are you going to get back here? It's halfway across town," Macie commented.

"I still have a bus pass," I told her. She whipped out my phone again and texted her dad, making the change. Immediately I saw her relax.

"Thanks babe," she said as she turned to me, and I shrugged my shoulders. Then she hugged my neck, which surprised me.

When it comes to affection, I'm always the one to initiate. This was not like her. But we had just been through one hell of a night, so I was glad to see she was letting her guard down.

"You should probably go," she said as she checked the time and passed my phone back to me.

"No, you keep it. I can charge yours when I get back. The power should be turned on by then," I told her. We hugged again, and I swung myself up into the driver's side of the u haul.

Truth be told, I could have just run in to grab a phone charger. But I didn't want to. I didn't feel comfortable going anywhere near the duplex again until I was with someone. Something was wrong about it, or rather… everything was.

Instead, I padded my time, taking the truck back and running odd errands. I didn't have a bus pass, I was making sure I didn't have to rush home. I was doing anything in power to make an excuse.

Eventually, though, I ran out of those, and I was getting hungry. Since I'd given the neighbor the last of my cash, going back wasn't avoidable any longer.

First, though, I went to the main office to grab our mail key. The landlord's wife snatched it from her collection on the wall and slid it through the service window, casually asking, "How are you enjoying our home?"

I thought about telling her the strange problems we were having. I even considered that she and her husband might actually already be aware.

But instead, I just smiled and took the key, telling her everything was fine.

I could tell from her blank expression it was the only answer she cared for, anyway.

Next, I went to the community mailbox and cleaned out everything that was still in there, skimming through it as I approached our front steps.

Then I looked up and noticed that our door was wide open.

Immediately my heart was pumping faster, and I thought about the doll. It was back.

I held the unsorted mail in a bundle, a makeshift weapon, just to protect myself as I stepped in our place and took a look around. Thankfully the power was on at last, but I still didn't feel completely at ease.

Placing the papers down, I listened and heard something coming from the bathroom. I reached for a kitchen knife and walked toward the door.

Squeezing it tight, I reached for the handle and then saw it turn by itself.

A flood of adrenaline filled me as I raised the knife in defense and then saw a woman step out, her eyes widening in shock as we both screamed bloody murder at each other.

I kept the knife in my hands and took a step back. "Don't come any closer!"

"Who are you? Where's Rose?" she asked frantically. She sounded even more scared than I did.

"Who the fuck is Rose?" I shouted.

"She lives here! I live here actually. I'm Sarah, her roommate. Now who the fuck are you??" she snapped back.

I kept my distance from the stranger, none of her story adding up.

"The landlord said the place hasn't been occupied for a couple of months," I said.

"Aye, I've been on holiday visiting family in Australia. Just got back," she muttered. "So wait. What the fuck? They sold the place?"

"Show me your itinerary," I whispered.

"What?"

"I said show me your fucking flight plan. You had to have had plane tickets or shit like that, right??" I snapped, still holding the knife straight at her.

"Okay, okay, calm down. I don't have that, but I have proof I live here, right here," she said, sliding her phone across the floor.

I reached down and picked it up, scrolling through the pics of her and the previous owner together. It suddenly registered that I had seen her face in the pictures.

"All right... let's say I believe you," I said, passing her phone back to her and relaxing a bit.

"When was the last time you talked to your roommate?"

"I don't know? A few days maybe. I booked a flight from Melbourne straight here," Sarah answered.

"A few days?" I looked over toward the pile of mail.

"You're sure?" I asked.

"Yeah. Now, can you please put that thing away?" she muttered.

I fumbled with the knife, placing it back in the drawer and then sliding my hands in my pockets.

"Sorry... it's just. Well, it's been crazy."

"Sure... I guess I would freak out too if I found a stranger in my place," she paused and looked around the house a bit. "And here I thought she redecorated. So you got rid of all of her stuff then?"

"The landlord insisted that she hadn't been here for a while, and the place looked deserted," I said. All of the mail agreed with me. There were overdue bills, collection notices, even a reminder to renew her license. Everything indicated that Rose had not been home in quite some time.

"Why would she lie to me?" Sarah asked as she walked to the bedroom. I followed, keeping my distance. Despite her story checking out, I wasn't ready to fully trust her.

"Did she say she was still here?" I asked.

"Yes... we talked almost every night, nothing out of the ordinary," Sarah paused as she looked toward the vent. The same one that had freaked me out the night before.

"Did you find anything... peculiar while you were moving in?" she asked.

Like a six-foot fucking sentient doll? I thought to myself. But no. I needed to play the long con and figure out what she knew.

"Like what?" I asked casually.

"It's... probably nothing," she said as she casually reached down and scooped up the loose screw.

"Your roommate is missing. That isn't nothing," I responded.

"And I guess I don't have a place to live," Sarah said with a smirk as she pocketed the screw.

"Well, I'm sure you could probably stay here a few days with us. My partner is always at work, so I could use the company." Damn it,

I realized that was a bad move to tell a complete stranger. Why was I always so damn trusting? I thought.

She smiled. "I appreciate the offer. But I saw that Mister Bill still lives next door, so I guess I'll pass," she commented and then added, "You know the guy killed his wife and daughter, right? Or did the landlord skip over that little detail too?"

I was speechless and stood completely still to see if she was joking. She wasn't.

Sarah whistled softly and commented, "Wow. I will take that as a no."

Then she clapped her hands together and remarked, "Got anything to eat? We can discuss it over lunch."

Too intrigued and terrified to know more, I accepted her offer.

***

As I made us sandwiches, Sarah told me the story.

"This was probably right after I moved in here. Rosie's old roommate had gotten married, and she couldn't afford rent alone. As it so happened, I just came to the states and needed a place to stay. Two peas in a pod, eh?"

I poured myself a glass of water and then she continued her story.

"Bill and his wife Andrea were always arguing. I mean fucking always. We could hear it. These walls are paper thin. We could hear them fucking when they made up to each other. And when he decided to go ballistic and knock her around," she whispered.

Slowly I spread Mayo on my sandwich, enraptured by her tale.

"Anyway, one night it's the same as usual. He's yelling. She's running. Their daughter Penny is crying. Rosie's had enough. 'I'm going to go over there and give him a piece of my mind, god damn it,' she said. We'd already called the police dozens of times before. Same old, same old. 'I tripped,' Andrea would say. Shit like that. It was a shame."

"She was a beautiful young lady. Probably better looking than either of us, if I'm being honest. And Bill was insanely jealous. He works nights. You know that. Always gone. Always sure she would have men over. She didn't, of course, but you couldn't convince him of that. Probably just projecting his own insecurity."

"So this night, this fucking fateful night; Rose goes over to talk to them. And she slams on the door at the exact moment that he was about to toss a lamp at Andrea. He said he was aiming for the wall. That fucking distracting knock? It made him flinch. And the lamp slammed right into Andrea's head."

"Rose saw it had happened just as the door opened. She had a key to their place somewhere. Andrea had given it to her. She told us how often she wanted to leave. Wanted to take Penny and just get out of there. We told her to. God damn, we told her to just run and never look back."

I had stopped spreading the Mayo. I was just listening now. Listening to the most tragic and frightening thing I had ever heard.

"So there Rose was. Standing there. Looking down at Andrea as she bleeds out, shards of glass in her face and neck and eyes. She reaches for her phone, but Bill snatches it away."

"No, he says. They'll lock me away. They'll take Penny from me"' he explains. He promises he'll call 911 the second that Rose leaves. Claim it was all just an accident. And Rose? She believes him. I wish I knew why, but she does."

"The next day comes and goes, and Rose decides to check on Andrea. Make sure everything is okay. Bill invites her over, tells her Andrea has made a full recovery and takes her to their bedroom to see for herself."

"And Andrea is there all right. Same blue eyes. Same golden blonde hair. Same hourglass shape. Human perfection is what she is. But she isn't a human at all. Not anymore. What Rose is seeing is a doll. A life-size replica that looks exactly like Andrea."

"A doll," I repeated as my voice cracked, my mind going a mile a minute as Sarah finished the story.

"Somehow, he got it done at work. That stuff they use for embalming corpses? Yeah. Keeps the skin fresh. And he made a fucking doll out of her. Rose wasn't the same after that. Truth be told, neither of us were."

The room was dead silent as I mulled over everything she had said.

"You... you said his daughter was killed, too?"

"As far as I know. I mean, she literally disappeared the same night, so two plus two equals four. Of course, because Rose didn't call the cops the second it all happened, there was no case. Everyone just assumed Andrea ran off and took Penny with her," she said.

"That's… that's insane," I admitted. My body felt numb. Her story explained a lot, but there were still so many holes. Things that didn't make sense.

"That doll was here when we moved in, in a closet behind a fake wall," I told her.

Immediately Sarah's eyes widened in alarm. "Shit, it's here! Where?"

So she knew something about it, I realized as I reached for the charger and plugged in Macie's phone. Now we were getting somewhere.

"I think Bill moved it last night. We asked him to help get it out and I haven't seen it since then," I admitted.

"Wouldn't surprise me if he found a way to get it back to his place without you realizing it. Bill was obsessed with that thing. Probably used it as a sex toy if I'm being honest. He treated it like she was alive," Sarah said.

"Funny. He said that Rose did the same thing. Made it sound like she was the crazy one," I commented.

"He would do that, eh? Fucking jackass," she scoffed.

"But it was here, though, sealed away in this apartment. Why would he do that?" I asked.

Macie's phone began to buzz urgently as soon as it gained power.

"Must be your babe," Sarah commented. It was Macie's dad. I let it go to voicemail and commented. "And you asked me earlier if we found anything peculiar here. You had to have meant the doll, right?"

"Look, Trish. I didn't realize this was twenty questions and I would be grilled," Sarah said nervously.

The phone buzzed again.

"If there's something you aren't telling me, I swear to god!" I said as I glanced at the caller id. It was her dad again.

This time I picked it up.

"Hey Chuck," I said as I turned away from Sarah for a second.

"Trish, I'm sorry to bother you, but have you heard from Macie?" he asked.

"Not since this morning. Why?"

"Well, I got a call from her job and they said she never showed up for work today."

That dread was sweeping over my body again.

"What? But you dropped her off right?" I asked.

I turned back to confront Sarah.

But she was nowhere in sight.

"I thought you dropped her off," Chuck responded.

Then I noticed something at the top of the mail.

My mouth was dry. My palms, shaky.

"Chuck, I'll call you back, okay?" I said as I reached for what I had seen.

It was a missing persons poster. Someone had stuffed it into the mailbox and it was crumpled up.

It was a poster for Sarah.

I called out her name.

No response.

The knife was back in my hands in less than ten seconds.

Then I dialed 911 without hesitation.

"What is your emergency?" the operator asked as I saw the bedroom door open on its own.

"I need to report a break in at my address," I said as I saw Sarah's silhouette standing there in the doorway.

I rattled off my information and hung up, slipping the weapon into my sleeve as I announced, "That was my partner. She's on her way home."

Sarah was tracing the outline of the photo frames that had hung on the wall, nodding to herself.

"Home. That's a funny word, isn't it?

"I mean, I called this place home for almost two years. And then woosh, life happens. *You* happen. And well, then it's just all taken away in an instant, hmm?"

I kept silent, wondering if she even guessed that I knew she was not the woman she claimed she was.

"When I was a kid, I used to live in this big five-bedroom house. It was a dream. So much space to run around. And stairs too. As a kid, I just loved running up and down the stairs. One time I fell down the stairs, though. Broke my leg. You could actually see the bloody bone sticking out. I screamed, my dad ran over to see what had happened. I remember him saying it was going to be okay. That he would fix me right up. But when I woke up in the hospital and I saw my leg was whole again, it didn't feel like I was fixed. Do you know why?"

I cleared my throat.

"I think you should probably go," I said. Cautious to keep a distance from her as she started down the hall.

"Because my dad sold that house. Because my mom couldn't bear to see me struggle to walk again and popped a bottle of pills just to make it all go away. So how the hell was I ever going to be fixed?"

She was at the entrance to the main den now, looking around the place and saying, "This is the first place that really felt like it was home to me. The first fucking place in a very long time."

I leaned back on the counter, keeping the blade ready as she gave me a quirky, yet unsettling smile.

"This was actually just one big house once too, you know. Four bedrooms, two baths. Absolutely almost perfect. Would've been everything I wanted if it included stairs," she laughed as her fingernails traced the wall next to the temperature. Then she began to turn it down and make it colder.

"I used to dream of stairs. Running up and down them like I did when I was a little girl. Sometimes I would close my eyes and I was sure I could hear myself on them, sure they were real."

"But I guess that doesn't matter anymore now that you're here." Her voice was colder now too.

"You need to go," I said, trying to keep my voice calm and firm.

"Sure. I wouldn't want to disturb my home," she said as she turned toward the front door.

Her nails were still scratching against the wall as she started toward it. I let my guard down. I shouldn't have said a word. I shouldn't have.

"It's not yours anymore," I responded.

In a flash, she moved like lightning, shoving me against the cabinet.

Her hands were in my eyes and mouth as I swung the knife and stabbed her in the side.

She screamed as I shoved her back, scrambling to find another weapon as she grabbed at my feet. I hit the floor with a crack, kicking at her face as she tried to scratch at my ankles.

Then she pulled me toward her. She had this strength that felt like I couldn't escape. She grabbed my wrists and held me now, smiling like a wild woman.

I struggled to move as her spit dripped on my face and she started to scratch at my face, whispering gibberish as she attacked me.

I saw the knife still plunged in her side, and bit her arm, forcing her to let go. In the next split second, I grabbed the knife and pulled it out. Then I stabbed it in her again. Again and again and again. Toward her chest and her neck, anything to get her off.

Sarah pushed away, crawling toward the wall as I squeezed the knife harder, looking down at my blood covered clothes.

Sarah started to talk louder, speaking like a damn demon as she crawled up against the wall, reaching for the temperature gauge again. Making it as cold as possible.

"Get the fuck out of my house!!!" I shouted as I waved the knife toward her.

She responded by crawling over toward me like a fucking spider, catching me off guard and throwing me to the top of the table. The knife slid onto the floor by the bathroom door as she started to slam her fists against me, again pushing her nails into my skin to draw fresh blood.

"My house. My house. My house. MY HOUSE." Sarah screamed as I used every ounce of energy I had to throw her off. She tumbled backward and hit the wall by the hallway as I jumped across the table and got the knife. This time I was the one that didn't hesitate. I grabbed her hair and slammed her against the fake wall, her head smashing through. Then I stabbed the blade straight into her heart.

Sarah's eyes widened in shock as she looked down at her open wound as I watched her crumple to the floor.

Then her body began to twitch, and she began to cough and shake. It looked like she was having a seizure.

I couldn't tear my eyes away from her. Watching as she began to shake even more violently. Her back was spasming as I heard bones breaking. Then she began to lock up, her legs pushing together and her hands freezing in place. Her eyes became huge, and she gasped a final breath as something slowly crawled its way over her skin.

It looked like plastic.

No, it *was* like plastic.

Sarah now resembled a doll.

I stared down at the lifeless thing, shaking and trembling as I looked down at my hands and feet covered in blood.

What the fuck had I just seen.

There was a knock on the door, and I jumped.

I had completely forgotten that I had called the police.

When I opened the door, two officers were speechless, staring at my bloodsoaked silhouette.

"I could have used you five minutes ago."

***

Twenty minutes later, they finished taking pictures of the scene and I gave the best damn lie that I could to explain what had happened. I claimed that I'd had a break in, and that the perpetrator had run.

They asked a few questions about the doll, but it was clear they were more weirded out by it than anything. And it's not like I was about to explain what really happened and wind up in the loony bin.

"I uh… don't suppose you could get rid of it for me?" I asked them as they finished taking a statement.

"Ma'am that's not our business," the first officer commented and then let me know that they would keep a car parked out front until the evening.

After they were gone, I couldn't stop staring at Sarah. Or rather, at what she had turned into.

I kept replaying the moment over and over in my mind, wanting to make sense of it. Always coming up short.

Once I managed to calm my nerves, I called Macie's dad back using her charged phone. I didn't tear my eyes away from the doll.

"Trisha, what's going on?"

"You wouldn't believe me if I told you," I said.

I told him that Macie had my phone, and he admitted he'd already tried to call it but it just would keep ringing.

"Is everything okay? I can swing by if you need."

I was staring at the doll lying on the floor, unsure if I wanted to get him mixed up in this horror.

"Everything is fine. I'm sure Macie just turned the phone off and took the bus to work. I'll have her text you the second she gets off," I said. I wanted him to believe me. I knew I didn't believe me.

But thankfully he let it slide. "Take care, okay?" Chuck said.

I put the phone down on the counter, realizing that I was still in clothes covered with blood.

I needed a fucking shower.

I slid off the barstool and walked over toward the hallway, keeping the knife with me in case the doll suddenly decided to resurrect itself.

Gingerly I stepped over it and went into the bedroom, grabbing some clothes and then carefully crossing back over to the bathroom.

I kept my eyes on the doll at all times, briefly wondering when the police finished running the blood if it would show two different types or just my own.

Had Sarah even bled when I stabbed her? My fractured mind couldn't remember. I started the water and kept the curtain open, putting towels down and choosing to shower with the doll in my

peripheral vision. I wasn't about to let it out of my sight until I could get rid of it for good.

As the water washed away the blood, I looked down at my trembling hands, praying that Macie was okay. I can't lose her. I just can't.

I shivered despite the hot water. Too much had happened in a short amount of time.

I closed my eyes, letting the shower wash over me, listening to the sounds of the dripping faucet and trying to make myself feel whole again. Trying to make sense of the world again.

It didn't.

A thump made my eyes bolt open, and I stared at the doll again.

Slowly, something unseen dragged Sarah into the hidden alcove behind the wall.

Fuck me.

I stepped out of the shower, quickly drying off and walking toward the front door.

I opened it a smidge and looked out toward the street corner where the police car was sitting, wanting their help. But I couldn't exactly walk out naked. And truth be told, I wasn't counting on them to do much given how they had responded before. If this turned out to just be my mind playing tricks on me, I didn't want to cause more trouble and wind up without a place to stay.

Instead, I grabbed another knife from the kitchen and gingerly crept toward the hallway, peering into the closet cautiously. But I couldn't see anything. Whatever had grabbed the doll, it was gone. But I could see something just beyond the clothes. A dark opening into some kind of tunnel between the duplex.

Quickly I went to the bedroom and grabbed some shorts and a shirt. I didn't want whatever had taken it to disappear. It was time to get to the bottom of this, I thought as I went back to the kitchen and grabbed Macie's phone. I didn't want to be without a means of communication.

Then, using the light from the phone; I stepped into the closet and looked into the strange dark space between our home and the neighbors.

Sarah had said that this building was once a single residence. Had she been telling the truth?

I stepped into the darkness, trying to get a good feel of my surroundings as I saw what looked like a similar door lingering open that led into the neighbor's closet.

He was probably sleeping right now, I realized as I checked the time. I thought of the strange story Sarah had told me before she attacked.

What if it was true?

Was he the one behind all of this, turning people into dolls? It sounded like some kind of black magic that I didn't want to mess with.

But now Macie was missing, and I knew the truth had to be somewhere inside. So, inside I went.

As I stepped into his bedroom, I dimmed my flash just a smidge on my phone and listened to his snoring. He was napping on the opposite side of a kingsize bed, unaware of my presence or doing a damn good job of faking it.

Still, it didn't look like he had been awake anytime recently. So, if he hadn't moved the doll… who did?

I took a step out onto his carpet, pushing the closet door a little further to make sure it stayed open.

Instead, it immediately slammed close, and I heard the neighbor make a soft snort in his rest. I cussed to myself as I tried to open it back, but the door wouldn't budge.

Fuck.

Nervously I moved across the carpet to his bedroom door, keeping the knife ready just in case he woke up and attacked. I had no idea what this man was capable of.

He seemed to be a bit restless, but ultimately undisturbed by the noise. I opened his bedroom door and stepped out into the dark hallway, second guessing even being here. This isn't safe. This is the beginning of a fucking horror movie, I thought.

No Trish, you're in the middle of one already, I realized as I looked toward his guest room. There was a light on.

I reached for the handle and jiggled it a little, but the door wouldn't budge.

There must be a key, I thought as I walked toward his den. But it was so pitch black, because of his curtains that I couldn't see anything. I adjusted my brightness again and slowly moved my phone across the room, looking for anything shiny in the shadows.

I found it. The fucking doll.

Not Sarah, but the original. The one she had said was a replica of his wife. Her lifeless eyes stared at me across the room as I saw the doll just in a rigid position against the television.

Was this one alive, too? I thought to myself as I kept the knife in a defensive position and kept looking. My heart felt like it was about to burst out of my chest. There were no keys anywhere, and I was considering racing out his front door.

No. Macie. I have to find her, I thought.

Then her phone rang. Loud, obnoxious and definitely enough to wake the neighbor. It was her dad again. I answered it to stop the ringing just as the bedroom light switched on.

Hide, I thought frantically as I scrambled to his bathroom.

I climbed into the shower and pulled the heavy curtain, getting down on the floor and laying perfectly still. I heard him walking up as Macie's dad tried to talk on the phone. "Trish? You there?"

I kept him on mute and turned the volume low as the neighbor stepped into the bathroom, yawning to himself.

Shit shit shit shit shit.

I kept the knife right against me as I waited and anticipated being assaulted.

Instead, I heard the neighbor drop his shorts and listened to him piss, completely unaware of my presence. Chuck was still trying to talk, though, and I was certain he was going to hear.

"You need to answer me!" he snapped.

The neighbor froze as he finished using the toilet, his silhouette right over the tub.

"Andrea…? Is that you?"

He shuffled his feet to the den, and I kept still, letting Macie's dad hang up as I listened.

I heard the neighbor say something else and then heard the bedroom door shut.

Fuck this shit, I need to leave, I thought as I stood up and peered out slowly. The coast seemed clear.

Macie's dad was calling again, but this time thankfully the volume was down.

"Chuck, now is not a good time," I answered with a whisper as I clenched the phone next to my ear. I couldn't exactly stumble in the darkness to the front door.

"I'm sorry, it's just that I was just thinking to check online and locate your phone. You remember how we installed that feature for y'all before the move? Anyway, are you sure Macie isn't there?" he asked.

I stepped into the den, listening for any hint that the neighbor was still awake.

"What? No. What are you talking about? I told you I haven't seen her since this morning," I replied.

"Well, the phone is there somewhere. It says it's still in the house," Chuck answered.

I froze, looking toward the long hallway. Toward the guest room with the light on.

"Chuck, can you call my phone?" I asked.

"Sure, let me do a three—way call," he responded.

I waited. Then, from the other side of the guest room door; I heard it ring.

I hung up on Chuck just as the hallway light flicked on and I saw the neighbor standing there.

Immediately I ran. I don't know what I stumbled over, but I pulled open his front door and ran straight to the cop car down the street.

"Help! You have to help me!!" I screamed as the officers got out of their car.

"What's going on?" they asked, both cautious to be near me as I waved the knife I was holding frantically toward the duplex.

"My partner. He's got my partner in there! Fucking hell, he's holding her captive!" I shouted frantically.

Both of them pulled their weapons and moved toward the entrance to my neighbor's house. I stood at the edge of the street, pacing and trying to stay calm. This would all be over soon I told myself.

I should have known better.

Three minutes later, the officers reappeared, no longer in a defensive stance. Both of them looked tired and frustrated.

"Ma'am, please come inside the building," they ordered.

"Did you find her? Is she here?" I asked, my eyes darting about the room. The doll was still right next to the TV where I had seen it.

And the neighbor was standing there in pajamas, looking every bit like the victim here.

"Ma'am, I'm going to need you to explain what it is you were doing in your neighbor's side of the duplex," the second officer said.

My mouth felt dry.

"I fucking told you. My partner is here. In that very room. He took her and has been holding her here against her will!" I shouted.

The neighbor went over to the room and unlocked it, letting us all peer inside.

It was decorated as a little girl's room, with pink unicorns and tea party equipment. Stuffed animals on a bed. And on that bed as well, Macie's phone.

"I was planning to return this to you tonight when I woke up. I found it outside in the yard," he growled.

"What? No. That can't be right. This isn't right. Why the fuck is this room locked?!" I snapped.

"Ma'am we need you to calm down," the first officer said as he reached for his taser.

"Calm down? My fucking partner is missing, and this maniac is hiding her here somewhere. I bet there's a secret closet somewhere here too, huh! Where you hide all your damn sex dolls!!"

"Ma'am, that's enough! You're lucky that Mister Langford here isn't filing any charges. As far as we can tell here, you're the one that broke in and you're the one wielding a dangerous weapon. Now I don't know what kind of issues you are having, but if we get a call from this residence again, someone will be leaving here in the back of our patrol car. Is that understood?" the second man growled.

All I could do was nod and try to not shake. They muttered apologies to the neighbor and then escorted me out.

I stood there in my own side of the duplex, watching as they left for the night. Realizing I was alone again to deal with this nightmare.

Back inside our own place, I put my phone down and slumped into the sofa. Was I losing my fucking mind?

I know what I saw, I thought to myself as I replayed the conversation over and over again with Sarah.

Then, a slip of paper slid under my front door.

I walked over to the peephole, trying to see who had left it.

Then reached down and unfolded the note.

It was the neighbor.

"Meet me at my place if you want answers—Bill"

***

I held the note in my hands, rereading it a couple of times.

"Meet me at my place if you want answers—Bill"

This was an invitation that I should have rejected. I should have called Macie's dad, told him I wanted him to come pick me up or anything to get away from the duplex. I should have run.

Instead, I told myself that I needed to know.

That whatever Bill had to say would make the world start to feel normal again.

I knocked on his door ten minutes later, note in hand, like a courier.

"Trish, glad you came. No knives this time, right?" he asked. His house was still mostly dark.

"Turn on your lights and then I'll come in," I said. My voice sounded so numb. I was done with all of this shit. All I wanted was to find Macie.

"Sure," he replied, stepping back inside. A second later, the lights came on and he called out to me, "You can come in now."

I pushed the door open, my eyes immediately focusing on the dining room table in his den.

He was sitting there, fully dressed like it was a family meal and on the opposite side… the doll.

"Why the hell is this thing here?" I snapped. My instinct was to just bolt, but something in my neighbor's eyes said not to.

"Please. Close the door and have a seat with us and I can explain," he insisted. I did as he told me, walking over to the table; noticing that the doll was now wearing different clothes again, matching the nostalgic charm that Mister Langford had on. Yellow blouse. Black skirt. Short puce heels. Her blue eyes seemed brighter, her unchanged, emotionless face a little more lush.

"Thank you," he said with a strained smile.

I didn't respond. I was too uncomfortable being this close to the doll.

"I wanted to… apologize for lying to you," he began. I did my best to not laugh. But he noticed my body language and immediately gave a stern expression.

"Do you want to hear what I have to say or not?" he snapped.

I sat there, almost as motionless as the doll, as he started to talk.

"Anyway, I wanted to apologize because I wasn't truthful about Andrea. When you arrived, I didn't want you to judge me for any of my… lifestyle choices, so I had hoped that putting her in that closet would keep my secret. Seems fate decided to take a different course."

"I guess I don't blame you for acting the way you did about her. It would have probably freaked me out, too. But she's perfectly harmless. Just a reminder of my past. A sin I can't ever be forgiven for," he said as the left side of his face twitched.

Was that a lie? A poker tell? I said nothing, letting him continue his story.

"No matter what, I want you to know that I loved my wife, I loved her. And I still love her. That's why I did this. I couldn't lose her. I just couldn't."

"I see that on your face when you talk about your partner, Macie. That drive to do whatever is necessary to be with her and make things work."

"Don't think we should be comparing relationships, Bill," I whispered. His face twitched again. So I was catching him in a lie. Which part of this story was even true?

"The point is, we do a lot of crazy things for the people we love. Things we probably thought that we would never do until the moment arrives and we are forced to do them. In those defining moments, it ain't about what's right and what's wrong. It's about what has to be done."

"Was one of those defining moments when you murdered her?" I blurted out. I just couldn't hold it back anymore. I was tired of the bullshit.

I kept a steady icy glare on him, but Bill didn't even seem surprised by my accusation.

"I guess I should have figured you'd hear that from someone," he admitted.

I opened my mouth, thinking of mentioning Sarah's name. But then wisely closed it. I didn't want to feed him any information. I needed to know what he did and then form an opinion. I was tired of the lies.

"What happened was an accident. But you've met the police around these parts. If they saw what had happened, I would have lost Andrea that night and Penny too. I couldn't afford that."

Penny. So the story Sarah had told me was true. Or at least what he was saying matched up with the words of a living doll. Whatever the hell that meant.

"Where is your daughter now, by the way?" I asked. This time I kept my voice calm, trying to make him think that I believed him. If any of this would help me find Macie, that was what mattered.

"Not right now," Bill said mysteriously. "Please let me finish my explanation."

When I didn't respond, he took that as an invitation to continue.

"My neighbor Rose, there are a few things about her that I didn't mention," he said, clearing his throat. "I guess we get the big one out of the way first… she was, for the lack of a better term, a witch."

The look on my face must have told him that I didn't believe that horseshit. But yet at the back of my mind, a dull voice wondered if he was telling the truth. I remembered the pictures of her goth clothes and saw them in a new light. The dolls… were they the work of witchcraft?

"She must have been real fun at neighborhood cookouts," I said dryly as I crossed my arms.

"I didn't believe it myself either. She actually told me the first day she moved in. Said she didn't want to spook me. I told her that I didn't give a crap about her new age astrology shit. Yeah…"

He looked over toward Andrea and sighed deeply.

"That night I did care though. I asked Rose to save her. Anything, I begged; anything for my wife to not have to die."

The room felt suddenly much colder as his tone got darker. I could tell this was no fantasy. Every word out of his mouth was the reality of what happened.

"She said she could do it. But there would be a price to pay. I guess there always is with these types of things. I was so drunk, so shocked by what I had done… I told her I would pay for it. I didn't care."

"She took Andrea back to her place. Did whatever kind of magic Mumbo jumbo, and then when she came back… she was like this," Bill said, gesturing to the doll.

"That doesn't sound like you got what you wanted," I whispered. I almost realized it didn't match up with the story Sarah had told me. Was either version the correct one?

"No shit? I was fucking furious. I demanded that she fix it. But she said that Andrea would be fine. 'She's more alive now than she ever was before,' Rose said. She instructed me that in order for Andrea to be… human, someone else would need to take the place of the idol. Like a split shift. Sometimes Andrea would be human, sometimes not. That was the only way."

"The soul can be housed temporarily, but you have to watch it carefully. The soul also wants to leave and move on. That's why you have to keep it moving. The transfer keeps that from happening. In between you will need to keep an eye on it or keep it from moving about. Follow those instructions and you will never lose your family. I never forgot those words."

"I told her to prove it to me, prove this magic was real, and she said she would. She explained it would have to be someone related by direct bloodline to house the transfer," he told me.

His lips were trembling, and my neighbor looked like he was about to cry.

Then his phone beeped an alarm, and he stood up almost robotically and went to the door of the guest room and unlocked it.

A little dark-haired girl appeared from the room.

"I can come out now?" she whispered.

My head felt dizzy as I watched her dance into the den, and she looked toward the doll.

"Oh… I guess my time is up, isn't it?" she whispered.

She reached for a knife from the cabinet almost like it was instinct.

I moved to stop her, but Bill held me back. I wanted to scream. Immediately she cut her wrist and blood pooled out like a faucet. She held it against the lips of the large doll.

As she did this, I heard Bill talk.

"So I did pay a price. And I had no idea how fucking heavy of a price it was going to be."

I watched, too mortified to make a sound as the lips of the doll seemed to become flushed with color. Followed by her face, her eyes, and her hair. The doll began to transform and become mobile, suddenly looking like a human being.

Breath filled her lungs as the blood was lapped up into her now open mouth.

At the same instant, the little girl went rigid and cold. As stiff as the mannequin she had just resurrected. I stood up, too shocked for words, watching as the now alive Andrea smiled at me.

"You must be Trish. Bill has told me all about you."

"What the hell."

I stumbled backward as Andrea stood up as well, placing a hand on her doll daughter's cheek and then leaning over to kiss it.

Andrea picked her up, carrying the doll back to the room and closing the door, turning to me with eyes that seemed to show pity.

"I know all of this is very confusing to you," she admitted as we walked back to the den.

"I don't know what I just saw. And I don't want to know. Tell me where Macie is. That's all I care about."

Andrea gave her husband a look. Both of them looked sad.

"We don't know," he admitted softly.

Suddenly I was shaking again. My world was shattering. I sat back down because I felt like I couldn't stand.

"What?" I couldn't even hear my own voice. It didn't sound like me.

"I'm sorry… the reason that we called you here is that we wanted to offer our help. I didn't finish explaining myself about Rose…" Bill paused as his wife sat down and she now decided to be the speaker.

"When she did what did to me, I think it changed her. And not for the better. She wasn't the same person. She became more violent, lashing out toward others. And she became obsessed with the power she held, always wanting more. She was even able to possess other people, including her roommate," Andrea explained.

"I met Sarah earlier today… or rather, a version of her. She transformed into a doll the same way you do," I said softly.

"She was in love with Sarah, but Sarah rejected her. So Rose killed her, to make sure her lover was with her forever," Andrea explained.

"So that must mean Rose is alive," I realized.

"Well, she kinda has to be for the spell to remain working," Andrea said with a nod.

I suddenly realized that it must have been Rose that had dragged Sarah away so quickly… which, of course, led to the inevitable next question.

"Then where the fuck is she? The landlords said she disappeared months ago."

"I keep asking myself that. Rattling around in my brain the last conversation we had. It was about the spell. I remember asking her a question that bothered her," Bill whispered.

"Like what?"

He snapped his fingers together.

"I remember asking her if it was normal for the dolls to move on their own."

A shiver ran down my spine as I looked toward Andrea. She sat there so pleasantly it was hard to believe she had been lifeless only a few moments ago.

"And that bothered her?" I repeated.

"She said she would check her spell book and try to figure it out and get back to me," Bill explained.

"And that was the last time you saw her," I realized.

"I think so," he said with a nod. Andrea squeezed his hand. It felt like he was being coached to provide these answers. I wasn't sure if I completely believed everything they told me, but what mattered was finding Macie.

"I think that Rose may be trying to do us harm," she explained. "I have been feeling… less alive than I used to. Less than even when I was alive. So I think… something has changed and we are in danger."

It was strange listening to her sound so concerned. She wasn't alive. I kept telling myself that. She died months ago. But I kept my cool and focused on the story they were telling me.

"Why would she do that?" I whispered.

"I wish I knew. But maybe if we had that spellbook? It could hold an answer or two," Andrea suggested.

I tried to recall all of the things Macie and I had hauled off to the dump. I didn't recall seeing any book like that.

"I will find it and I will find Rose," I promised as I moved toward the door.

I stopped, feeling awkward to just leave. Even though I thought this entire situation was a one-way trip to the funny farm, I told them both, "Thank you."

Bill followed me out to the front door, closing it as Andrea continued to stare at us. Now alone, he drew in his breath and gave me a somber look.

"I know this is a lot to take in," he admitted.

"That's putting it mildly," I responded.

"Look… you should probably take this," he said, reaching toward a nearby garden gnome and showing me there was a spare key to his place.

"This is the same one Rose used on that fateful night," he said softly. It was hard to believe such a tiny object held so much significance.

"I'll be back before you go to work," I promised. "I won't stop until I find it."

"Fine. But just remember, it's there in case I am gone… and if you do return…"

He glanced back toward the closed door.

"Make sure Andrea and Penny don't try to leave."

I held back any judgmental words I wanted to tell him and just gave him a nod. Something about his tone told me this wasn't just their safety he was concerned about. Was he as much a prisoner as they were? Trapped in a fantasy to believe his family was still alive?

A moment later, I rushed back to my home, immediately rifling through drawers and boxes to see if I had overlooked the book they told me about.

But as I looked and tossed aside our clothes mixed with Rose's, I realized that it wasn't there.

That left the dumpsters.

I rushed outside, looking toward the closest one. As much as I hated to be dumpster diving, I knew that it was my only option if I could possibly help Macie.

I went to the first dumpster, pushing the cover out and staring down at the trash. It was truly impossible to be sure that the book wasn't there. I couldn't even recall which dumpsters that Macie and I had gone to. But there were three more nearby.

I walked over to the next one, noticing that the landlord was out walking their dog. The large Irish Red Setter looked toward me, barking excitedly as it tugged on its leash, and I awkwardly stood by the dumpster. I was sure I probably looked like a crazy person.

"Is everything all right?" the landlord asked, walking over. The Irish setter sniffed at me excitedly, barking and wagging its tail.

"Sorry, I think I tossed something out while we were moving in and I'm trying to find it," I explained.

The landlord checked his watch.

"Well, you might want to hurry, lass. The trucks come in about ten minutes," he commented.

I tensed up, realizing that it was likely if the trucks came before I found it the book would be gone forever.

"Is there anything I can do to help?" the landlord wondered.

I gave him a strained smile and told him no. The last thing I wanted to do would be involve someone else in this madness.

He nodded and tugged his dog down the lane, glancing back at me curiously as I reached the next dumpster. This one clearly had items from the duplex, so despite the fact that I knew he was watching, I climbed in and started to rifle through the garbage.

I heard the truck as it pulled into the parking lot. Suddenly I was scrambling and tossing stuff left and right. Out of the dumpster. It wasn't here.

I only had one dumpster left. Climbing out, I ran over to it, the landlord just blankly watching as I did. I was sure he was likely going to call the authorities on me from how insane I looked. But I didn't care. I had to find that book.

Slamming the cover open on the last dumpster, I saw a large rolled up carpet mixed around a bunch of other stuff and started to unfurl it, thinking maybe the book had somehow gotten wedged inside.

Instead, I found myself face to face again with Sarah. The doll's lifeless eyes stared up at me as I looked down at her body. I had been right. There was no blood on her.

Pulling the doll up, I tried to shove her aside; not even bothering to worry about it right now. What matters is the book. It had to be here!!

I heard the dump truck making noise as it lifted the first large container, and I started to dig, trying to see anything that looked like it might be the spell book.

As I pushed Sarah out of the way of more of the garbage, though, it began to sprinkle rain. Just more bad luck I needed.

As droplets of water fell on Sarah, the unexpected happened.

Suddenly she was gasping for breath like she was going to suffocate. Her facial features turned to normal, and her eyes frantically searched the dumpster, completely shocked by where she was at.

"What the fuck is happening?? Where is Rose! Oh god. I can't feel my body. What the fuck did you do to me!!" she screamed. I watched as blood stained her clothes and she started to gasp for air, but the rest of her body remained stuck in doll form. An incomplete transformation.

The dump truck was almost on top of us as she begged, "Help me!! Help me please!!"

Instinctively I tugged at her right arm, trying to pull her up out of the dumpster. But the parts of her that were still a doll were too heavy.

Her eyes were fluttering as she stared up into the sky, rambling about the past.

"Rose, are you okay Rose? You look hurt. Oh god what happened. What the fuck happened."

"Don't hurt me," she whispered as she stared at me. But I could tell she wasn't talking to me. It was as if she was reliving her final moments when she had actually been a real person.

"Please don't. I won't say anything. Please… please…"

Then I pulled as hard as I could and, just like a mannequin doll, her fake arm ripped from its socket.

I tumbled out of the dumpster onto the ground as the truck arrived.

The driver gave me a strange look as it started to thunder and then his coworker motioned for them to lift up the garbage.

"Stop!! Stop!! There's someone in there!!" I yelled. I watched as Sarah fell out into the trash compactor. The storm prevented them from hearing me as I banged on the door, but the machine was already doing its work.

I heard a crushing and grinding noise echoing with her last scream as Sarah was taken apart. The driver stopped it just as it happened, jumping out to look.

But now, she looked nothing more like a person. Just a discarded and forgotten thing that no one would bat an eye twice about.

The driver gave me a look, noticing my pale expression and probably concerned that it looked like I would faint.

"Do you need some help?" he shouted as the rain started to pour down.

I said nothing, just staring at Sarah and realizing that with her gone, the last chance of finding the book was gone as well.

"It's too late now," I whispered. Too late for anything.

***

I went for a drink.

There's a small bar not far from the rental properties I found on my smart phone, and I wore a sour expression for them to know not to ask questions.

I took some shots, watched cars drive by, and tried to drown my sorrows.

I didn't want to be ready to give up on Macie, but it felt like this was the end. Without that spellbook I wasn't sure where to turn.

I kept replaying Sarah's last moments before she was crushed to death. Not only had it mortified me, but it shocked me because I hadn't expected to see Rose toss her away so quickly.

Did that mean that Andrea and Bill had lied about their connection? Was I just running around in circles for a couple of mad people that were toying with me?

Eventually, as much as I dreaded it, I had to return to the empty duplex. As it turned out though, it wasn't so empty after all.

Two patrol cars had returned, lights flashing because it was almost dusk. And before I even had to guess who had called them, I saw Macie's dad's truck.

I wanted to be upset, but I was past that point, he didn't know he was causing more trouble. And as I approached the house, he was the first to speak.

"Trish, where the heck have you been?" he said.

The landlord was there too, having allowed the cops entry as they finished up their questions with Chuck.

"Dinner," I slurred. I was still too buzzed to really dare ask why the police had returned.

He held a hand over his mouth. "You're drunk. What the hell happened today? These two officers said you reported a break in. Why did you not mention that earlier?" he snapped.

The landlord chimed in too, "Yes, and where is your roommate? You've been acting very suspicious all afternoon, lass."

The officers gave me an icy glare.

"Remember our conversation last time?" the first cop said. I was fully expecting that he was going to cuff me, but thankfully Chuck spoke up for me and remarked, "I don't believe Trish would be involved. Besides... it hasn't even been 48 hours. We should wait and see if Macie turns up," Chuck admitted.

"All right. But we are going to take a few things from the duplex, to check and see if anything of Macie's matches the DNA we got earlier," the second man said. My addled brain understood immediately what they were implying. They thought I had something to do with Macie's disappearance! Immediately I panicked and blurted out, "You need a warrant to do that!"

"I gave them permission. Remember, this property still belongs to me," the landlord snapped back. I did my best to not look like I was worried. I knew the officers believed they were just doing their job.

"We should have results by the morning. Have a good night," the first cop said as he tipped his hat toward Chuck and left.

The landlord walked out next, looking at me with added suspicion. "If we had known you would be a problem, we would never have let you rent here!"

Then Chuck and I were finally alone. He crossed his arms like he was about to give me a lecture.

"Chuck please, I can explain…"

"I hope it's a good one, Trish, because I'm at my limit here. I've put up with a lot of things with Macie over the years, and always done my best to stand by her, even when I don't agree with her life choices. God knows if her mother was still around, she would be mortified at the thought of her living with…"

He took a breath and closed his eyes before he said anything he might regret.

"Look, I can understand why you thought you didn't want to involve me with the break—in. But why did you lie to those officers? They said you never even mentioned Macie to them. And then you caused a disturbance at the neighbors? And the landlord said you were looking through the trash earlier! Just what the heck is going on?"

"I didn't say anything because if I did, you would think I'm insane. That it's ludicrous," I responded.

He crossed his arms again. "Just try me."

I checked the time, realizing that the neighbor was likely already at work.

Then I remembered the spare key, and I realized that as much as I didn't want anyone else involved, I needed help now to return to sanity.

"Follow me," I said as we went to the neighbor's door and I found the spare key before saying, "It would be easier if I just show you."

***

As we unlocked the door and entered Bill's side of the duplex, I announced our presence to no one in particular. The house was quiet. Andrea was now a doll again.

The moment he saw it, Chuck's jaw dropped.

"It looks so life—like," he admitted as he stared at the colors and clothing of the doll.

"That's because it is… alive, I mean," I said softly.

Chuck looked at me and raised an eyebrow.

"Trisha, this isn't a joke. Why are we here and why are you showing me this creepy doll?"

Then he got dead quiet for a second.

"My god. You're serious."

He reached for his phone like he was about to call 911.

"I can prove it," I told him as I pointed toward their daughter's room.

"Behind that door there is a little girl that can show you I am telling the truth," I explained.

"A child? Why aren't they out here?" Chuck asked as he walked over to the door and tried the handle. Of course, it wasn't budging.

"You're telling me the neighbors are locking their daughter up? Why the hell didn't you tell the police this either??" he asked in exasperation.

"Because when I saw her earlier, she would be a doll. I know this is asking a lot of you. But there is a key around here somewhere. The girl can show you exactly how this doll comes to life," I said.

Chuck bit his bottom lip, trying to decide if he believed me.

"Just give me this chance. It might help us figure out what happened to Macie," I pleaded.

He sighed and gave in, allowing me a chance to look through Mister Langford's kitchen drawers until I found it.

"This should be it," I said, as I tossed it to him.

The door unlocked a moment later.

We flicked on the lights, and I quickly looked around at the empty room. It looked just like it had when the cops had come in earlier.

"Well, this is definitely creeping me out," Chuck admitted. "But this reminds me more like a shrine than any child's room. Besides, where is she?"

"I'm not sure… but she was here earlier," I commented as I looked about the room again. How could she hide so easily?

"Did you check upstairs?" Chuck commented. At first, I thought he was being funny. "There isn't an upstairs."

"I work in house construction, Trish. The way this house is built, it could easily have two more rooms upstairs. The attic is sloped in the front and wide in the back. Plenty of room," he told me.

I frowned, surprised that it would be sealed off, and then looked toward Penny's closet and remembered how there had been a secret in mine. It made some sense there might be one here as well.

I opened it, surprised to see that was exactly what was hiding there, a thin staircase leading east toward the attic. It was so dark I could hardly see a thing. I used my phone light and saw that Penny was standing a few steps up with back turned to us.

"Oh my god you were telling the truth about the girl," Chuck realized.

"Penny, there you are. Come down," I said. But she didn't respond. I walked up the steps, thinking maybe she hadn't heard me, and grabbed her shoulder.

Then I realized she was sleepwalking. "Penny, wake up," I insisted as I told Chuck to get me some water. She was whispering under breath, and it sounded like she was talking in her dreams. It sounded so unnatural.

When he returned with a glass, I dipped her fingers in it and the girl's eyes shot up, confused. Unsure how she got there.

"Is my time up?" she whispered. Chuck's eyebrows furrowed in concern as he saw the cut on her wrist. "Did you do this?" he asked.

"I just wanted to help," she answered.

He pulled Penny to his side and then started toward the den.

I hurried behind him. "Where are you going!" I shouted.

"I'm going to the police station and this girl is coming with me," he announced. Penny suddenly started to pull against him.

"No. I can't. This is my home!" she insisted as she tried to reach for Andrea.

"This isn't open for discussion! No parent should ever lock their child away!" Chuck responded.

He glared at the doll just as Penny slipped from his grip and hugged it tightly.

"And God knows what else this child has endured living with that!" he announced.

He pulled out his phone again to dial the police, and I was about to shout that he stop, but I never got the chance.

Andrea moved toward him, like a train hurtling down the tracks. Her hand was wrapped around his throat, and she slammed Chuck against the wall, dragging him against the plaster. Chuck's phone flew in the air, skidding under their couch as the doll continued its attack.

He choked and gagged as he looked down at the doll, too frightened and shocked to fight back as he lost his breath and the living doll prepared to snap his neck.

Immediately I reached for a glass from their dishwasher and hurled it at the back of the doll's head. Some of the water seemed to burn the doll, but other than that, it had little to no effect except to shatter into dozens of pieces. Andrea's doll—like head turned almost completely 180 degrees, her cold lifeless eyes staring at me as she prepared to pounce on me next.

She let Chuck slip to the floor as he gasped for breath, cornering me in the hallway as my mind raced for a way to stop this thing. This wasn't like Sarah when she was a human. The doll was like a living, unstoppable robot.

Then I realized there was one thing that would stop it. And as much as I hated to do this, I grabbed Penny and held her close to my body, using her as leverage.

The child screamed and kicked as I motioned for the doll to move and let me get to Chuck. Much to my relief, the lifeless thing obeyed and stepped aside.

Cautiously I held Penny as tight as I could as we circled each other, and I knelt down to Chuck's side.

I then lifted him to his feet as Penny pried herself free to be by the doll's side. It was blocking our exit. And I knew it could easily overpower us if it wanted.

Instead, it began to force us into Penny's room.

As we stepped across the threshold, I grabbed the door and slammed it shut.

I heard the doll scratch against the door for a moment as I shoved some of the furniture against the door to make a barricade. At the same time Macie's dad slumped to the floor.

"Mother of Christ," he said as he rubbed his neck.

I knew it was probably the worst timing, but despite how shaken up I was, all I responded with was, "Now do you believe me?"

We pushed the pink bed to the door, listening to the doll trying to claw its way into the room for the better part of ten minutes.

The rumble of the storm outside and the thought of impending dread as we waited had me on pins and needles as I checked Chuck's injuries and then looked at my phone. No cell phone service due to the rain and if I didn't get him to a hospital by morning… I didn't want to even consider losing him, though.

"It will be fine. Eventually, the spell will take effect, and they will be forced to switch. Andrea can be human again and then it should be safe," I said.

"I'm not going anywhere near that thing," Chuck stammered as he struggled to keep consciousness. The blow to his head was severe, and I knew it was likely he might blackout at any second. He was right, given how unpredictable Andrea could be as a doll; there was no guarantee that she was safe as a human either. We had to find another way out of here.

"Then we will go upstairs. There must be another way out," I told him.

His eyes were becoming heavy as he grabbed my arm and muttered, "Find Macie. Help her."

"You're coming with me," I insisted.

"Too weak. I'm… sorry…" he stammered.

I watched as he slipped into unconsciousness, and even though I knew it was inevitable, I still tried to fight it.

"Stay with me, Chuck, come on," I said, slapping his wrist gently. But it was too late. He was out, and I was alone.

I checked my phone again and then turned toward the cramped staircase to the attic. My only option was to find a way out and get help.

I placed Chuck beside the bed with one of the pillows to keep him comfortable and then walked toward the shadowy hidden steps.

I checked the wall for a light switch, unsurprised to see that there wasn't one. Just a bunch of scribbles of crayons from Penny drawing in the dark.

As I progressed up the stairs, it occurred to me the poor girl likely spent the majority of her time up here, trapped to play alone because her father was afraid she would escape and become a doll somewhere beyond the confines of this house.

That wasn't even really living at all, I realized as I came to the top of the stairs and peered down the hallway. There were two rooms and the hall itself was littered with old boxes that were covered in dust. I walked over to the first door, pushing it open to see the hum of a small television. There must be a generator up here to provide it power, I thought as I looked at the screen. There was a children's program playing, toys on the floor, including even a small antique doll with what looked like human hair. So this was Penny's other room, her prison for when she became human.

I looked toward the wall where scratch marks showed how she had grown over the years with measuring and wondered if her mother hadn't accidentally died, would she have ever had a normal life? Did she even age now because of the spell? How could her parents have ever thought this would be a good idea? Just seeing how the room reminded me of a padded cell made me realize there was no way they cared for her anymore.

I went back to the hallway, trying the other room but finding that the door wouldn't budge. Then I heard the soft sound of a mouse scuffling across the floor and turned to catch it with my flashlight. Maybe the little animal had found a way out, I thought as I hurried to find it.

I pushed the boxes aside and saw that it was crawling into a broken ventilation shaft that led down toward our duplex.

As the mouse moved along, I heard that familiar rattling and almost panicked.

But it couldn't be the dolls. They were downstairs, I realized.

I leaned down and used the phone to look down the tiny hole, realizing I could see what looked like a small journal on the far side.

Was that the spellbook?

I searched through the boxes of contents more for anything that might help to pop the lock of the second room, convinced more secrets were hidden there as well.

At the bottom of one of the boxes I found a toolbox and grabbed a hammer. Using it I slammed against the doorknob of the second room.

Eventually, the lock snapped, and the door slipped open.

What I saw on the other side will haunt me for the rest of my days.

Long black tendrils of webbing spooled around the edge of the room, clustering together to form a mass of ebbing sacks that appeared to be filled with glowing puss. The strange material swirled around to form a cocoon that hung from the ceiling, and in the middle of each capsule,

barely even looking human anymore; were a trio of corpses.

I recognized each of them immediately even though the color was drained from their bodies and their features were fading away.

One of them was Sarah. Her body was the one nearly consumed by the gigantic webbing and to the right was the human body of Andrea, the puss sacks seemingly draining her of life even now.

The next one was Rose, the original witch that had started all of this madness. And seeing her made me want to crumple to the floor.

I was holding onto the hope that finding her alive would break the spell, but now; I felt hopeless again.

Especially because in the midst of these corpses I saw the one person that I was trying to save stuck in their own cocoon. The only one still possibly alive.

Macie.

I squeezed the hammer and started to hack at the webbing, but it was a pointless effort. It was like cutting off a chameleon's tail, except the sack of living tendrils that held them there was clearly faster at healing.

I ran back to the boxes, thinking quickly as I tried to find a better weapon.

I tossed box after box aside, realizing there was nothing else useful up here. Just knick knacks and old items that hadn't been used in ages. Beyond the house, the storm raged, and the power flickered and died.

Fuck, things just got worse, I realized as I checked my phone. My battery was almost gone too. I saw that the light was still on in the second room and realized the generator had to be in there somewhere. But there was no way to reach that with the black webbing in the way.

Then a sudden thought came to me, the candles in our duplex. I could burn the webbing!

With the hammer in my hand, I dashed down the stairs to the girl's room, ready to use it to defend myself and get past the doll. But in the dark, it was impossible to be sure where anything was, including Chuck. I could, however, tell that the doll had stopped trying to scratch at the door, so I took my chances and fumbled to move the furniture, stepping out to the dark hallway.

The house was mysteriously silent at first as I moved around, clutching the hammer even tighter. Then I heard Penny humming to herself, and her feet pitter pattered across the cold floor.

I could just barely make the outline of the front door. Instead, as I pushed forward, I realized something big had been pushed in front of the door to prevent my escape. At the same time, I felt fingers playing with my hair. Andrea.

I reacted as fast as I could, swinging the hammer around and smashing it against her face. The doll's perfect features broke apart in the same place where I had splashed water earlier and a sudden thought ran through my hate.

Water… they seem to not like water, I realized as the now faceless doll screeched, and I used all of my energy to push her straight into the bathroom.

The doll tumbled backward, smashing against the mirror and glass scattering everywhere. At the very same moment, I reached for the hammer from her face, ripping it out and this time using it to smash apart the sink.

Water spewed out toward her arm and immediately the doll reacted violently, screaming and lashing toward me with even more rage.

I stood back, reaching for the shower curtain and ripping it from the pole, pushing it onto the doll. It fell forward into the shower. And I turned the showerhead on, watching as water fell overtop the animated monster.

I couldn't pull my eyes away as I listened to the doll shriek, the water melting its pristine features. A mixture of anguish, sorrow and vengeance came over me as the doll struggled to escape the bath, its features finally completely collapsing until there was nothing left but a mass of sludge.

Just a puddle of goop with what had once been fake body parts now slurping down the drain and clogging the shower.

As the sludge pooled into the drain, I took a moment to savor the short victory; reeling from the incident.

But this nightmare was far from over.

*****

I'm not sure how long I was slumped on that cold tile floor, looking down at the shards of glass from the broken mirror that were scattered about and mixed with my own bloody footprints.

Another of the dolls was gone for good, the one that had started it all; Andrea. And now, I realized that the only obstacle I faced to saving Macie might just be Penny.

I didn't want to hurt the little girl, but considering how the other dolls have acted toward me, I wasn't entirely sure she was even really human anymore.

I would do anything in my power to save Macie, that was what I kept telling myself.

Standing up, I grabbed the hammer from the bloody mess in the tub and walked out of the bathroom, probably looking like some kind of serial killer.

I didn't hear Penny anymore, and the darkness that covered the entire house felt even more foreboding as I walked down the hall.

Was she hiding because she was frightened or because she planned to strike?

Gradually I crept toward the bedroom, the secret door that led to our side of the duplex wide open. So that was where she had run off to, I realized.

"Penny… I am not going to hurt you," I told her as I stepped into the dusty closet.

Only silence answered back as I moved toward the hole I had made less than a few days ago. Such a small thing that has spiraled Macie and I into a living hell.

Climbing through, I paused for a moment and listened. The duplex was silent.

Don't worry about her. Get the book,

Grab the candles and get out of here, I decided.

I moved toward our bedroom, using the wall as my guide to avoid getting lost. As I opened the door, I heard something in the guest room and froze in place.

Was Penny trying to use that vent to reach the book?

I pushed the vanity to such an angle where I could stand on top of it and unscrewed it from my side as fast as I could. The metallic cover flopped off and fell to the carpet and I reached inside, stretching my arm as far as it could go.

At last, I felt the book, and I gently nudged it out, the heavy tome tumbling down below with a thud.

The noises in the guest room sounded louder than just Penny hiding. Was someone else here?

Cautiously I stood up, my heart pounding. I need to get back upstairs and stop worrying about phantom noises, I told myself.

But my journey was cut short as the power came back on. It would have been a welcome provision were it not for the fact that now whoever was hiding could easily see me as I passed the guest room.

I kept the hammer close to my body and crept toward the entrance, pushing the door open ever so slightly.

On the floor, I saw someone crouched as though they were looking under the bed for something. I recognized their body immediately. It was the landlord.

And I realized also what it was they were searching for as I managed to find my voice again and snap, "Looking for this?"

Their eyes darted toward me, and the landlord quickly crawled out, standing up and facing me.

"All I want is the book," the landlord told me.

I looked at the tome, confused as to how they were even a part of this, and held it closer to me.

"Not until you give me Macie," I said, realizing they had to be the one that had taken my partner.

Their face went from calm and reassuring to monstrous in a flash. Then they made a sharp whistle, and I felt something wrap around my waist.

Tiny doll—like arms. Penny. I shouldn't have hesitated. But that one second was all she needed.

Penny squeezed against me, knocking me down like she was giving the Heimlich. She then climbed over me and held me down, twisting my wrist and snatched the book as I softly screamed. The pain from the brute force she used made my ribs ache.

She walked slowly back over to the landlord, passing the spellbook to them.

"Now the ritual can be a complete success," the landlord said excitedly as they brushed Penny's hair. "No half measures."

Then they looked at me with disappointment.

"I suppose I should have guessed after you so easily took down Sarah and Andrea you wouldn't go without a fight," the man said as they skimmed through the book.

"It would seem that I underestimated you, lass; but that won't be happening again." They flipped the hammer about to use the blunt end and before I got the chance to scream again, slammed me against the wall; the whole world turning to darkness.

***

When I woke up, I was still in the dark and I soon discovered I had been placed in the secret closet between the duplex walls. I fumbled around until at last I found the candles, using them to light the enclosed space.

There was a doll near me, about the same height as the larger ones. Instinct took over, and I kicked at it, only to discover that it was dormant.

In fact, upon closer inspection, I realized that it was incomplete. There were no facial features or other distinctive markings to make it appear lifelike, it was just a bland model.

But staring at it there in the cramped space, I immediately realized who this doll was for.

It resembled me.

I tried the left side of the closet, pushing against the wall to budge whatever the landlord had wedged there, but it got me nowhere. Next, I tried the other side, searching for whatever secret panel unlatched the door. Claustrophobia was sinking in, along with a feeling of despair. The doll was the obvious truth about what they planned to do to me, just another part of their collection. I had to get out.

I banged against the wall, trying desperately to get free, but it was fruitless. I was trapped.

I sat there on the ground for a moment, hyperventilating as I tried to get a grip on my sanity. I was so close to ending all of this, I thought.

Then I heard the sound of feet in the duplex.

Frantically I pounded on the wall again, hoping to get their attention. And thankfully, it did. The secret entrance opened, and I was staring at Mister Langford. He looked confused and scared, likely from the destruction that was throughout his place.

"Trisha? What is going on? What happened to Andrea? And where is Penny?" Bill asked.

I stepped out to his bedroom, trying my best to summarize what was happening. "The landlords. They are upstairs, they have Macie. They are going to turn her into a doll!! We have to hurry!"

"Is Penny there with them?" he asked as he went to his bedside and opened a drawer to grab a firearm.

I nodded and rushed to his daughter's room, the dread I was feeling growing stronger as I saw Chuck was gone too. They had taken him upstairs, I was sure of it. To complete their sick ritual.

Bill loaded the gun and took the lead to the cramped stairwell, commenting as we went. "We were told to never disturb this part of their house. I was against even allowing Penny to play up here, but I had to do something to make sure that she wouldn't leave…"

Honestly, I wasn't paying much attention to his ramblings. I was focusing on finding Macie and Chuck. "They will be right in there," I said, pointing toward the door on the right.

Bill was distracted by the playroom, looking shocked and disturbed by the environment his daughter was constantly exposed to.

"The wife said… she said that she would make sure this was all taken care of. And I trusted her… but this looks like a prison," he whispered as he touched the wall where the measuring marks were at.

"I sometimes got the feeling that she felt Penny was her daughter more than mine," he admitted.

The pieces fell into place. This had been the landlord's house before, I realized. And just as that realization was dawning on me, Bill turned his gun toward me and remarked, "I also know they would never hurt Andrea. They trusted me to protect this house. And that's exactly what I have done, unquestioningly. So that just leaves you."

"Mister Langford put the gun down," I said anxiously as I tried to back up, waving the candle back and forth and hoping it would be a distraction. Then I felt a presence behind me. It was the landlord's wife.

"Trisha is right, Bill. There will be no more violence today…" she said coldly.

Then she grabbed my shoulder and gestured toward the other room. "Besides, it turns out we will need her after all."

I held a tight breath as I was forcibly marched to the next room, another nightmare unfolding.

The husband stood near Macie, a blade in his hand with blood dripping from it. And on the ground, Chuck was dragged in to be a sacrifice for their altar.

"His blood is not enough. Never enough," the landlord barked angrily as I was forced on my knees. Bill kept the gun pointed at me as I placed the candle on the ground, but the wife insisted that I was not to be hurt.

I didn't dare make a move until I was sure that I could.

"I suppose, given how far she went for her, it only makes sense that her love is stronger than that of a father." The wife commented. I felt my lips begin to tremble. Love? Bill had said blood was required. Maybe he had been wrong… my mind was frantically trying to find a way to get out of this mess.

"Whatever you are doing, it won't bring your daughter back," I told them.

"Shut your mouth," Bill said as he shoved the gun against my neck. "I should fill you with lead just for what you did to Andrea."

"Mister Langford!" the husband shouted.

"Need I remind you that we can make another copy of your wife?" he commented as he gestured to behind the egg sacks. I could see now, they had other faceless dolls like the one downstairs. More and more copies to be made of the corpses they kept here on display. As long as they have their bodies, they can make more, I realized.

And soon Macie was going to be added to that collection. He began to chant from the book again; the strange webbing taking on an ethereal glow. It reminded me of the way Macie had talked when she was sleepwalking. Now it made sense. Something had been possessing her.

"Always in pairs, the magick connected these souls. Rose understood this spell, made it work. Why will it not obey me?" the landlord asked when it seemed to have no effect.

"Her energy was strong… almost as strong as our beloved," the wife whispered.

My mind scrambled to understand their twisted plan. So they had hoped to use Rose to remake their daughter. But that hadn't worked…?

"You need my blood for Macie to be bound with your spell, don't you?" I asked.

"The magick is in the blood. Ties the golems from the spirit realm to this world. And it will bring our daughter back… a version of her that we can keep forever," the man said.

I thought about the other thing they said. Love was the key to the spell…

"I know what you did wrong," I answered. Truth be told, I wasn't sure at all; but something stuck out. "You said it had to be an act of love. Right?"

The husband looked down at me, curious to see what I was getting at.

"If it's going to be from the heart, it has to be willingly. Give me the knife," I told him.

The tension in the air was palpable. I could see the gears turning in his brain. He was honestly going to listen to me, I was sure of it.

"Like hell we will! The bitch doesn't know what she is talking about!" Bill snapped.

The landlord gave him the evil eye. "You need to learn to respect us, Mister Langford," he warned.

But the neighbor had clearly had enough. He walked over to the man, shoving the gun in his face and remarking, "I am sick and tired of being treated as an outsider! I've done everything you ask of me, and you still continue to treat me like trash!"

The landlord drew in his breath, and I knew what was about to happen before it even did. He made the sharp whistle and Penny shot out from the darkness, knocking Bill back. But not enough to make him lose his grip on the gun.

Bill's animalistic nature took over, and much like the night when his wife died; he accidentally fired straight at Penny.

The doll fell backwards, its plastic body crumpling under the blow from the weapon. And immediately Bill panicked, trying to put the pieces back together.

"No!! No no no. Not you too!!"

I had only a second to act. I knocked the candle over and watched as the fire spread across the webbing.

Immediately the dolls in the background writhed in pain, trembling to the floor as the fire crossed Macie's body. I pushed myself against her and then pulled her out, her unconscious form falling alongside Chuck.

"No!! You can't. We need her! We have to create our family again!" the landlord's wife said frantically.

I grabbed the candle, waving it toward the rest of the webbing to spread the fire and then looked toward Bill. I would need his help if I hoped to save both Chuck and Macie.

"Mister Langford… Bill. Your daughter is gone," I whispered. The landlords were both so distracted trying to save the dolls I knew that now was my only chance to get his attention.

"You have to let her go," I told him.

He let the pieces of the doll slip from his hands as he looked at me with dead eyes. Then he picked up the gun and pointed it toward me.

"I can't live without them…" he whispered as he saw that the fire was already beginning to spread rapidly. Time was running out.

"I… can't *live* without them," he added as he pointed the gun toward his head and added, "I should have died with them that day."

"Bill, listen to me! I know you feel guilty for what happened. But this is your chance to try again. My family needs you," I pointed toward Macie and Chuck.

"Your family would want you to move forward," I begged.

His hands trembled as he kept the gun there for another moment and I thought for sure I would lose him. But something I said must have broken through.

He dropped it and rushed to my side, pulling Chuck up as I grabbed Macie. Both of them were dead weight, but all that mattered was getting outside.

We lugged them toward the stairs as the webbing fell apart, crashing into the dusty attic floors and spreading the fire even further. Just a simple spark had caused so much.

Somehow, we managed to make it downstairs without incident, and Bill helped me drag them the rest of the way to the front yard.

From our spot on the front yard, we could see the silhouettes of the landlord and his wife as they tried to save the dolls, the only family they still had. "We can't leave them in there," Bill decided. Before I had the chance to stop him, he ran back in. I stayed in the yard with Macie and Chuck, trying to revive them as I watched the house go up in flames.

Then there was an explosion, likely from the generator I had seen in the attic and the roof collapsed, and the flames kept spreading. I watched in stunned disbelief, numb to everything we had just gone through.

Was it really over?

***

Sometime in the next hour, the fire department came and kept the inferno from spreading to the first floor. After that, they were able to search the premises and found the charred remains of the landlord and his wife, along with the melted goop that remained of the dolls. I told the authorities that the landlord and his wife had been behind everything, including the previous incidents where I had called the cops. It was a story that they easily bought, given the mounting evidence that the landlords had killed at least three people.

After it was all said and done, they retrieved two things from the blaze. Somehow, despite the intense heat, the spell book and the doll with the human hair had survived. I kept the book to learn more about Rose. Chuck advised we keep the doll for fear of it ever being misused, and I was too frightened by its survival to argue.

As I read the book, I discovered that she had been mastering the magick from the landlords all along, privately practicing the techniques that they struggled with, the journal a detailed diary of her obsession.

It also revealed how she was suspicious after the incident with Andrea that the landlord and his wife would hurt her and Sarah, and that was why she hid the book. Her last entry was a concern that the landlords would hurt them, and given what had happened, I guess that was true. They tried to force her to reveal the spell and kept her in suspended animation until they could figure out the magick.

"All this time, they were searching for something so small," Chuck said as I told him about it over lunch a week later.

He apologized a lot for what happened, and he thanks me often for saving him and his daughter… although I'm not sure if I can agree that Macie will ever be the same again.

Since being free of her egg sack, my partner has been nearly catatonic, and we have had to bathe her, dress her and feed her. Sometimes her lack of emotion or physical response reminds me of the dolls, and it makes me want to cry.

"One day, one day, she will come back to us. We have to have faith," Chuck said. He's being gracious to let me stay here in their house, but his second wife is not exactly understanding. She blames me for Macie.

He has said that I should be patient. But then I think of the magick that Rose held and how she was able to do so much with it.

I told myself when this started I would do anything to get Macie back.

Anything.

Anything.

I look toward Macie as she stares blankly into the void.

Maybe it's too late, I realize.

Then I look at the spellbook.

Or maybe I just haven't tried hard enough.

SCARECROW BLOOD

"Daddy… do scarecrows bleed?"

I was lost in thought driving to drop off my six-year-old daughter Angelia to her mom's for the week when she blurted out that show stopping question.

"Hmm? What? What do you mean, sweetie?" I asked, glancing back at her as she daydreamed out the window.

"I saw one in that field. It looked all icky and weird. And covered in blood," she said, her voice a mixture of fright and concern.

I looked at the side mirror toward the cornfields we were passing by and nodded absently.

"I'm sure it's nothing. It won't hurt you," I told her.

I should have paid attention, but my mind was on this separation.

I knew Marcie wanted a divorce, and I knew there wasn't much left for me to do to stop it. Getting a lawyer, trying to juggle two minimum wage jobs and handle a six-year-old was taxing enough, so we agreed to week on week off for Angelia until we could settle on things that would be permanent going forward.

Thankfully she was more concerned with her pet iguana and watching My Little Pony than the problems we were having, but her little comment about the scarecrow had me wondering if her worry was expressing itself in a different way.

When we got there, I had forgotten almost entirely about the incident and focused instead on the new car parked in Marcie's garage.

It didn't take me long to find it belonged to a new boyfriend, Todd, who was "just leaving" as I gathered Angelia's things. Had she deliberately made sure that he lingered just long enough to cement the idea in my head that we were over?

"Took you long enough. Did you get lost?" she said as she got up from the porch swing.

"There was construction. You don't need to jump down my throat," I muttered as I watched Todd drive off. "I see you didn't waste any time."

I was baiting her for an argument, but it didn't work. Marcie said she was tired and needed to rest for her next shift at the hospital, so I gave Angelia a hug and drove back toward home. I had to speed a little just to make it to work, my mind drifting to her inquiry about the scarecrow as I passed the cornfields. Maybe it was some prank. It was almost Halloween. Kids do crazy things. Or maybe she dreamed it up. Truth be told, I didn't really give it a second thought.

But then again, I haven't been giving much of anything a second thought lately.

It's crazy that even though Marcie is in the same town, it now feels like we are worlds apart. But that's what happens when something comes between you and your partner, I guess.

Although I wasn't sure I could even call Marcie that anymore.

That night, on my way home from my second job, she called in a fluster.

"What have you been letting Angelia watch on her tablet?"

"Hmm? What's wrong?" I could tell her tone of voice was mostly irritation, but there was an underlying level of worry there. Something was wrong.

"She woke up screaming and crying and said a bloody scarecrow was outside the house," Marcie snapped. I felt a strange chill run down my spine.

"I'm sorry… I should have said something earlier. She said she saw it in the cornfields on her way to your house… Jesus Marcie… I didn't even know it was a problem, just thought it was her weird imagination," I admitted.

"Well, you need to fix this. She won't listen to me."

I heard a soft rustling noise and a moment later my daughter's whimper on the other end of the line.

"Hey baby. Can't sleep, huh? You had a bad dream?" I asked softly as I drove down the dark roads.

"No, it wasn't a dream… It was in the backyard. I saw it daddy, and it was mad at me!" she said between sobs.

"Is it there now? Maybe it went away?" I asked, calmly trying to reason with her.

She paused, apparently thinking about it.

"What if it comes back?" she whispered.

"Well, I'm sure your mom will make sure it doesn't… but even if it does… maybe the scarecrow is lonely? Maybe it just wants a friend?"

I was hoping that by making her supposed monster sound nice, it would lessen the issue. But the plan seemed to backfire immediately as she cried. "But daddy it was covered in blood so much!!"

"Okay, okay, calm down. Maybe it got hurt? Maybe it needs help? I'm sure it's not going to hurt you, baby. I'm sure everything will be fine. Your mom is there, and nothing can get to you," I told her.

"You… you promise?" she asked.

"I promise. Now I want you to be a big girl and go to sleep, okay?" I told her.

She promised she would and passed the phone back to her mom, who did not offer a complimentary thank you.

I sighed, wishing that whatever dreams my daughter had that night were good, and hung up the phone so I could focus on driving.

I was almost at the fields where she had claimed to see the scarecrow and I slowed down just a bit to see if I could spot anything amid the corn.

I felt a little silly doing it, trying to rationalize the hyper imagination of a six-year-old as I looked out toward one field and saw the familiar silhouette of a scarecrow.

Even from this angle, I had to admit that it did look… strange. Rather tall and weirdly dressed even for a mannequin. Was there really blood on its clothes or were my eyes playing tricks on me?

At the same time, I heard a loud noise and looked up just in the nick of time to see that I had let the car drift into oncoming traffic.

Immediately I jerked the wheel back to my lane, my heart going a million miles an hour as I pulled over and slammed on the brakes.

I sat there gripping my steering wheel for a second as I realized that I had come inches from meeting my maker just because I wanted to get a good look at a damned puppet in the middle of a field.

Recomposing myself, I let out a breath and drove home, convinced that I was just being an overprotective parent and my daughter was letting the separation get to her in her own weird way.

It would be great if I could end it right there and say that I was right about everything, and we all lived happily ever after, wouldn't it?

The next day, I got a text with a picture attached. Angelia had drawn the scarecrow at school and her teacher, concerned, forwarded it to Marcie.

"Explain" the caption from my soon to be ex-wife said as I stared at the picture. The childish drawing was black and red and dripping little bits of blood on the ground, a long stream of red crayon squiggling over to a cartoonish rendition of Angelia herself. She looked happy, but behind her I saw what I guessed were two stick figures meant to be me and Marcie, both of us sad and lying sideways like we were under the ground.

I sighed and stopped by her after school dance class to get a better understanding. Apparently, it was my fault this was happening, since I had put the idea in her head the scarecrow was friendly.

"What does the picture mean?" I asked her as she took a break.

"Oh, you saw it? You were right, daddy, the scarecrow was lonely. But now we are connected," she said.

"What do you mean, sweetie?"

"I don't know. I can just feel it," she replied in a sing—song voice.

"Well, I guess that's good, but why are me and mommy sad in the picture?" I asked.

"Oh, that's mommy and Todd. Not you. Daddy, you are silly. You know you are taller than Todd," she said with a giggle. I focused still on the fact that they were frowning, and her answer gave me some clue about her state of mind.

"The scarecrow doesn't like them, so I can't be with them. That's why they look sad," she told me.

It was a childish explanation, but I told myself it meant that she longed to be with me rather than Marcie.

That night I tried to reason with my wife about it, "You work so much, and Angelia isn't getting the attention she needs when she is here."

Poor choice of words because that just fired her up.

"I can handle things just fine. You're the problem here, David. You're sticking these weird ideas into her head and making her scared of everything. I swear to god once I get a good lawyer, you will never get to see her again."

That really hurt to hear my wife lash out at me that way. I knew this was hard on her, and I knew I was an easy target and this time I didn't let it go any further and left. Maybe she was right, and this was my fault. I was the one that couldn't keep our family together.

Couldn't make ends meet and couldn't live up to the promises of our commitment. I wasn't a good husband and definitely not a great father but damn it I was trying. Maybe too hard.

Maybe that was the problem? I didn't know, and I was too tired for another argument, so I let it go that time.

The next morning, things escalated even further, and I was woken from bed with repeated calls from Marcie.

"Jesus, this better be an emergency. You know I worked late…" I muttered. "Please, for the love of God, David, tell me this isn't your idea of a sick joke," she said.

I was awake immediately when I heard the distress and panic in her voice.

"What's wrong? Has something happened?" I asked.

"That damned scarecrow Angelia has been harping about. It's in the backyard."

That tingling sensation of impending doom flooded me again.

"I'll be right over."

I hung up, grabbed some fresh clothes, and drove to her house.

When I got there, she was on the front porch smoking, and I gave her an odd look.

"Don't start with me. You better be glad I didn't call the police on your ass. I want that thing dismantled and out of my yard this second!" she snapped.

"Wait a minute, hold up, you aren't making sense. First off, it would be impossible for me to do anything like that. I was at work. And your backyard is locked, besides you're not exactly a heavy sleeper," I said as I followed her through the house to the glass sliding doors that connected to the fenced-in yard.

I was hoping my logic would provide some sense of control to the situation, but when I looked out toward the grass and saw the thing, all of it felt meaningless.

The thing stood about eight feet tall, lopsided, and made of decaying wood with tattered clothes that were clearly drenched in blood. I had no idea it would look so ghastly.

Immediately I pulled my cell phone out and Marcie asked, "What are you doing?"

"What do you think I'm doing? I'm calling the police. Someone is clearly playing a sick prank on us."

"Shit. So it wasn't you," she said, her voice quivering.

"Dear god no, I may not like this any more than you, but I'm not going to play mind games like this," I said as I dialed. "Angelia didn't see it, did she?"

"No, I got her on the school bus before I discovered it."

"Thank goodness. She doesn't need any more nightmares," I said. I made a quick report and gave the dispatcher my wife's address before turning to her with a fresh idea.

"Listen, this place is going to transform into a crime scene for a while. Maybe it would be a good idea for Angelia to stay at my place tonight?"

Marcie looked like she wanted to argue but seemed defeated and nodded in agreement.

I kept staring at the scarecrow, disturbed by its jagged body and wondering just whose blood had been used to give it such a grisly appearance.

I went to work, trying to put the issue out of my mind, and picked up Angelia around 2. She was thrilled to get out of school early and I treated her to ice cream.

It made everything seem right to see her smile, even though I wasn't sure what was happening.

That night, I tucked her in with a bedtime story and tried to not fret over the bizarre situation at Marcie's.

As I was about to drift to sleep, Angelia screamed, and I jolted to her bedside.

She was pointing at the window where the sliding panel had pushed up and the curtains fluttered in the wind. Had someone tried to break in? Was that what this whole thing was?

Instead, as I approached the window, I saw a dark silhouette in my own backyard.

The scarecrow had moved here.

As I stared at it, I slowly closed the window and pulled the curtains close, my voice shaky as I reassured Angelia everything was fine.

Once she had drifted to sleep, I grabbed my gun from my safe and stepped out on my back porch, confronting the thing.

As it stood there only a few meters away, I could sense an otherworldly presence. I knew its arrival here tossed out any logical explanation for this.

I was clearly dealing with an evil spirit of some kind.

Despite the fact that my mind came to this conclusion, I still thought my gun would protect me and I raised it toward the scarecrow, demanding answers.

"What do you want from us? You aren't going to hurt my daughter, so you hear me?"

Of course, the bloody thing didn't respond, and that only infuriated me more. I fired a warning shot, yelling at the apparition.

"I know you're listening! You need to leave us alone!"

A moment later, I heard a loud knock at my front door.

Cautiously I approached with the firearm and opened it, not sure what to expect.

Seeing two dressed police officers, there would have been my last guess.

"David Westin?" they asked, scanning me up and down and probably thinking I looked like a madman.

"There's been a homicide at your wife's residence. We need to bring you in for questioning."

My mouth was dry.

"What. That's not possible. What happened?" I asked.

"Sir, put the gun down. We can answer questions at the station," the first officer said. She was reaching for her taser.

Immediately I dropped the firearm, begging for them to listen.

"I called the police hours ago to go investigate an issue at her house. Are you telling me… are you telling me my wife is dead??" I shouted.

Behind me, I heard Angelia made a soft whimper from her room.

"Daddy… I had a bad dream. What's going on?"

"Sir. Your daughter is going to remain in police custody while you come down to the station to answer a few questions," the second officer said.

It was clear the discussion was over for the moment, and I kindly told Angelia to gather her things for a trip. I was staring out at the backyard, fully aware the scarecrow was now gone again.

It had come here to let us know its work was done, I thought as I drew the connection to Angelia's drawing.

Once she was out of earshot, I asked the officers, "Did you find two bodies?"

"Are you admitting that you are aware of something related to the case, Mister Westin?"

"Just tell me, please. Was my wife alone or not?"

The officer saw something in my eyes to trust me.

"No. There were two bodies. Blood everywhere. They looked like they were pulled apart, limb by limb," he admitted.

That ended the conversation until we arrived at the station where they fingerprinted me and got a blood sample. I was numb to all of it.

I didn't want my wife dead, sure I hated the fact that we were going our separate ways. But this was beyond my resentment.

The scarecrow had caused this, why I didn't know, nor was I sure if it would now leave us alone.

I answered the officers' questions as best as I could until they told me I was free to go.

When I did end the questioning, I asked them if they found anything unusual in the backyard.

"Was there a scarecrow?" I asked. Their confused faces told me the answer was no.

On the way home, I apologized to Angelia for everything and sat her down on the edge of her bed to explain about Marcie.

Before I could get the words out, she said, "Mommy is gone, you know. So is Todd."

"You know?" I asked.

"I saw it in the scarecrow's dreams. It was a horrible dream."

"You woke up screaming… Angelia please, what else did the scarecrow show you?"

"Nothing really. Just a bunch of blackbirds over us every night. They have been following us. I think they will report to him."

"Report what?"

"If you're taking care of me or not," she said simply.

Again, that odd moment of unease fell over my body. "Because you're connected, and you felt mommy wasn't being fair to you."

"Yep. And now she's gone. You were right daddy, the scarecrow does want to help me."

The implications terrified me.

"Daddy, can we stop for ice cream?" she asked sweetly.

I was looking toward the fields. The silhouette of the bleeding scarecrow watching me every time my eyes cast that way.

"Sure, sweetie," I said through gritted teeth. "Anything you want."

CHERNOBOG STATION

Chernobog Station was but a hollow reminder of the grim reality of what the Arctic Circle could do in a single night.

Hoarfrost and harsh winds tore apart equipment, covering everything in a slick sheet of icy gray and black. It gave the impression of a shine as our ship dipped near the main landing platform. Captain Alan Blayne let out a soft whistle and took off his hat. It was clear the facility had seen better days, but that wasn't why he was paying reference. Among the frozen landscape, we could see the remains of the researchers that had failed to escape the sudden onslaught of cold.

Their eyes were wide with fear, frantically climbing toward any measure of safety that was available. But nothing that this remote outpost offered would have been enough.

"Thirteen souls, that's a bad omen," Abdul, our Iranian guide, commented as we dropped anchor. The water was at least thirty degrees below zero, and not a sign of life flickered around our boat as I followed the Captain to the ladder.

"Everything about this place is bad luck," I agreed as I checked my portable laptop. Signal was gone, and not even my normal apps could function in this awful environment.

"Best leave that here. No amount of mathematics will be able to help you with what they uncovered." That was Chief Science Officer Seneca Castaigne; a Croatian that claimed to have been a survivor of a previous Arctic megastorm. He was the one that said there would be no way the crew here had survived when we had discovered they were radio silent for nearly three years.

Or rather, when we had learned that this place even exists.

"How long do you think their dark winter lasted?" I whispered as we climbed. Despite the heavy gear we wore, it seemed that each step we made caused sharp cold pains to shoot through my body. A dreadful reminder of the impossible climate I would be working in.

"Most likely only a few hours, if they were lucky. But it goes without saying that despite the evidence of imminent death, these fine men and women did us all a service by sending out that SOS," Seneca commented.

"Do we happen to know why it took so long for the Arctic Outpost to get the information?" Blayne asked.

We were stepping now onto what looked like a helipad of some kind with a massive drill attached that was pointed toward the iceberg they had been excavating. From this angle, I couldn't see anything that made the chunk of ice any different than the hundreds of others that darted up from the frigid sea.

But clearly the researchers here felt their discovery had been worth keeping their entire operation hidden from everyone on the planet.

To answer Blayne's question, Seneca was scanning the area for electromagnetic activity and his equipment was already at extremely high levels. Even with all of the protective equipment we were wearing, the spiking meter made me uneasy. "All of the activity here is off the charts. It likely kept any sort of communication from transmitting until there was a soft spot," the Croatian explained.

The final member of our team, a geologist named Edward Kant; arrived in the rear with all of the necessary tools to take samples of the ice.

"Walk us through precisely what happened," Kant told Seneca. The older man gestured for us to follow him to the south side of the station, where the command and observation center were located.

"At precisely 1300 hours on November 4th, a category 5 mega storm capable of producing winds up to 140 miles per hour was recorded to have emerged from this location. There were no factors to indicate that the storm was on the horizon, no meteorological data to provide us with a reason to believe this island was in any danger. Of course, all of this is somewhat speculative as the operation was hidden from satellite imagery until after the storm hit. Then, the research team sent out what little data they had on an unidentified object of massive diameter to our outpost in North Greenland. The rest... as you can see, is history," Seneca muttered as we climbed the stairs.

"All of this was filed with the United Nations and Doctor Parker, our Head of Operations. Did you not read the file?" he asked.

Kant looked a bit flushed, not wanting to admit he hadn't. Instead, he focused on the iceberg and said, "I have never actually seen a glacial mass of this size."

"We should begin taking down all measurements and determine precisely where they stopped their excavation," Blayne commented.

"Captain, I don't think that will be necessary," I said, my mouth going dry.

In the early morning fog, we stood nearly a yard away from a steel platform that reached across a gap of the dead winter to the ice dam itself, revealing a dark hole that bore into the ice like God himself had punched into the ancient cold mountain.

All of us wordlessly followed the platform into the depths of the iceberg, the chill in the air suddenly making me feel claustrophobic. There was a presence here, something I couldn't quite put my finger on, I realized as we climbed down the rope ladder to a clearing below.

I was the first to arrive, my eyes fixed on the form of a completely crystallized woman standing near to where the drill had stopped moving. The massive vehicle itself was actually small in comparison to the object that had appeared from beneath the wintry rock.

It was clear and polished, as wide as Lake Michigan and as dark as the starry sky. Not a crack or blemish broke apart the shimmering surface, but around the edges I saw what looked like beveled contours that were made of stones from what looked like every corner on earth. Perhaps the most striking about the object was what I saw within. Reflections of myself, the other scientists and the iceberg, a mirror image of our surroundings save for one detail. The iceberg itself was carved as though a part of a larger city, one made not of human hands.

The buildings were as clear as glass, infinitely stretching beyond what I could see toward a shadowy beach that spanned what should have been the reflection of the gaping hole above. And amid the chaotic city of up and down, strange creatures that I couldn't hardly fathom coursed back and forth near to the edge of the mirror.

"What in the hell is this…" Kant asked, his voice hardly a whisper in the chasm. He took a tentative step closer to the massive-looking glass, his breath catching in his throat as his own reflective image caught his eye.

It was then I realized that his mirror self was acting of its own accord, marching toward Kant as if they knew each other.

At the same moment, the geologist came to a complete stop, his face paler than the iceberg itself.

"I can't… I can't move…" he cried out frantically.

I turned toward him, wondering if the shock of the mirror was causing him to panic. Instead, I saw his lower body was turning to crystal in the same way as the woman that was to my left. In a flash of light, Kant screamed out and the strange limpid material covered his entire body, paralyzing him.

"Get away from it! Everyone retreat!" I shouted.

Seneca was the only one that hesitated. He was fishing for a camera to take a few candid images of our find, not even remotely concerned about capturing the horror of what was occurring around us.

Grabbing his arm, Abdul chastised him, and we did not need any more prompting to obey and escape.

As we hurried to the frozen tundra outside, Captain Blayne tried to get a grasp on what we had just discovered.

"I think I understand now why this facility was removed from satellites," he said, holding his hand next to his heart.

"It shouldn't be possible, that thing. It's not of this earth, is it?" Seneca asked.

"We have a legend, of a world that is laid out across a flat smooth surface. A mighty king created an underground sanctum, to hide from a terrible winter that reshaped the world. They crossed over into another world, to remain hidden and there they became gods," Abdul said. His eyes were mystified by what we had seen, and I wondered how much of his story could be true.

"The mirror should be worshipped and revered, for it has powers beyond imagination," he added.

I thought back to what we had learned about the weather and how suddenly it had hit the base. "That wall of ice came down with a single impact of the drill… revealing the mirror. When the team saw the object, it must have been what altered the climate of this area," I reasoned.

"It completely changed the structure of this entire region," Alan realized. I could see the gears in his head turning as the air around us grew stiff.

"We need to lock down this entire island. Maintain the satellite blackout, no one should be allowed near that mirror. Contact our Allies, we need more drills here from every military force that is available to donate their men for a full excavation. We need to dig this up as soon as possible," he decided.

"You must be joking. Did you see what happened to Kant? As soon as his reflection saw him, he was frozen in place. We would be risking too many lives if we attempted to move it," I argued.

"And it's that sort of power we need," Blayne insisted.

When the words fell dead in the air, I realized immediately what prompted his sense of urgency. This was no longer a scientific endeavor, but a military struggle. Whoever held the mirror would likely be able to declare itself the next world power, I realized as I nodded reluctantly.

"I can gather a team, but I can't make any promises," I told him.

My mind raced as we left the outpost, the sea below becoming tumultuous as if nature itself could sense the dark plans that had begun.

As we climbed aboard, I took a look at the massive ice sheet again, trying to imagine how much of the pallid stone the mirror encompassed.

"We don't need just drills. We need weapons," I told the Captain. I hoped he would not suspect the true reasons behind my request, and much to my relief, he agreed to it without hesitation.

I kept my head down as our ship struggled to push away from the forsaken island, my brain working double time to decide how many explosives it would take to sink the iceberg to the bottom of the Siberian sea.

Little did I realize the nightmares I would be unleashing.

***

We did not return to Chernobog until the warm season came, our team tripling in size to fulfill the military's desire to procure the gigantic mirror.

Our fleet was filled with Russian and Iranian forces, along with a few East—Euro elites that were here merely to observe and bark orders. Each was armed to the teeth based on the preliminary warnings I had given about our find. I wasn't sure even with the most advanced weapons at our disposal if it would be enough, for other matters had occurred to the rest of my team after we departed in the winter.

Seneca was the first to experience bad luck, his wife leaving him when he returned to Croatia with the developed photographs of the mirror.

He had phoned me one night, his voice filled with dread as he tried to describe what he had seen in the pictures.

"I… we… we can't go back there. The mirrors are a doorway, or perhaps a portal. Worlds beyond our mortal understanding! I saw… death. And life. It was beautiful and terrifying…"

He offered to send me a copy of the photo, but then changed his mind over and over again. The more he talked, I recognized he was losing his mind as we talked. This was a man of science and years of repute, and he was babbling the way an infant would.

"I cannot look at myself in any mirror any longer. Only the True World is what can give me solace. I need to return. I need to release my captive dreams," he whispered over and over again. It sounded like a chant at some times.

Then, after speaking to his wife, I learned that his madness descended upon their household much like the megastorm.

She said that he had smashed every surface in our place that even had the slightest glimmer of his face showing. Then, with the broken jagged pieces of glass, he began to ram them into his eyes over and over again. She said it took her full weight to make him stop from bleeding out.

And the way she described him, Seneca did not sound like a man at all.

"His face is covered in permafrost, paler than a ghost and flaky. Yet it doesn't peel, it hardens and solidifies the way icicles do as they drip from firmament…" she told me, her voice hollow and afraid.

I did not hear from them again, instead seeing an article on a news blog that informed me of their fate. Authorities had raided their house after hearing complaints from the neighbors of a foul smell. It was like crystallized poison wafting through the air, or so they claimed.

And within they found both the dead body of his wife and the shattered remains of what some described as a statue of a man that was completely glass. Yet I knew this had to be the result of what the mirror had done to poor Seneca.

Captain Blayne was next. He said he was haunted by the images of the mirror in his dreams. Each and every night, his shadow self would take a step closer.

Blayne said sometimes he could feel his reflection closing in on him and choking the breath from his lungs.

"It's impossible to describe, but it reminds me of when I thought I might drown at an early age," he admitted.

When he heard what happened to Seneca, he immediately resigned and sought treatment in the States.

Only our Iranian friend remained steadfast by my new team as we approached the island. The fog lifted as we scanned the waters, and I tried desperately to recall where the iceberg had been.

"You're certain the coordinates are correct?" the lead researcher asked. Parker was her name, and she had a steely gaze that told me disappointing her would cost more than just my career.

We scoured the waters for the next few days, our men growing anxious and frustrated as none of the advanced equipment would provide even a hint of where the iceberg had disappeared to.

"This should not be possible. We have traversed these waters for nearly a week now," one of the captains said as our resources became scant. We tried using satellites, but only received more blurry images. The island seemed to constantly be on the move.

Abdul had a suggestion, but it didn't seem practical from a scientific perspective.

"The wards of this gate are protecting it fiercely. If we wish to find it again… a sacrifice must be made. When the kings sealed it away, a pact with the other world was made. This is what our scriptures teach," he told Parker. He wasn't merely talking about the loss of more resources. He meant a human ritual.

"We'll take that under consideration," she promised.

I couldn't tell if she had lost her mind as well. The next day I found out how far past sanity we were.

Abdul volunteered himself, along with several Iranian soldiers that believed this would be the only way they could ever see their families again.

"The sea has turned against us, the same way the storm destroyed the others. The gods are testing our resolve and we must show them our loyalty, and only by blood can this be done," Abdul told them.

He managed to block off the entire south deck of the ship we were on as the air itself went still in the eerie northern sea.

"We have to stop them!" I told the captains as some of the soldiers blocked off stairwells and shot anyone who came close.

Parker crossed her arms and cocked her head as she observed the ritual.

"We shouldn't be hesitant to embrace unknown concepts, gentlemen. This may in fact be our salvation," she told us.

Blood was streaking across the entire deck of the ship by midnight.

And then, as I tried again to get the captains to sail back toward the eastern shores of Siberia, strange auroras rippled across the sky.

Colors that I recognized at first and then morphed into strange unrecognizable pigments that made my head hurt.

All of our equipment went dead, and the power shut off, completely darkening the already foreboding sea.

The cascading rainbow of strange and abstract colors became like a raging river, constantly flocculating back and forth over the sea as we watched in awe.

Then the entire sky seemed to split apart. Waters rose from either side of the boats, our massive warships being tossed about as though they were mere toys.

The waters were pushing toward the vortex that formed in the sea, pulling our ships forward into a whirlpool of roaring thunder and iridescent lightning.

"The entire ocean is falling into that pit!" the men shrieked as we all hurried to the inner hull. Our ship rumbled and shook, threatening to tear apart as we began to tip toward the waterfall.

There was no escape to be made, I realized as I looked through the fracturing glass windows to the void below.

We were plummeting into the unknown.

I closed my eyes, grabbing ahold of the rail as all noise and all sense of surroundings faded away.

The crewmen around me seemed to split apart into separate shadowy reflections of themselves, each wailing like lost souls as we kept falling.

Blood rushed through my head, and I closed my eyes, feeling a wave of nausea hit me as water struck us on both sides.

I collapsed to the ship deck, Parker at my side, and the crewmen tossed about like rag dolls. Some of them were fortunate to survive, the rest were torn apart by the constantly changing waves.

Then we heard nothing.

My feet were wobbly as I got up and began to climb to the outer deck, my skin tingling with fear as I saw what was before us now.

Cities of lights and angles unlike any made by man hung in the air. Twisting and smooth architecture mixed together to form a sprawling metropolitan maze of grey ziggurats, crystalline walkways and amalgamated structures that stretched over the sky and toward the familiar icebergs that I had seen before.

Except that instead of a single massive reflective surface, now I saw hundreds of them, all floating ominously in the frigid air, waiting for us to reveal ourselves.

"This is not our earth," Parker realized as we moved to the captain's quarters to see if any of the power would work.

"Nothing. We are sitting ducks out here," the captain commented.

Parker was not so easily discouraged.

"We have longboats and oars, is that correct?" she asked.

An hour later, with less than a dozen men in a dingy, we were rowing toward fate.

The water felt thick, as if we were trudging through sand and it was becoming more and more difficult. The darkness below seemed to stretch for eternity, and strange indescribable shapes flowed about the waters, reacting to our movements the way predators would if on the hunt.

"Seneca's speculation of this being a portal was well founded it seems. What do you suppose the connection here is?" Parker asked as we got close to one of the larger icebergs that touched the water.

"A portal to an alien world? I'm not sure if even the most intelligent and philosophical minds could conjure up a hypothesis, ma'am. This is beyond my scope. But the only thing I truly feel here is… unease. We don't belong. And there is an invisible force that seems to be growing heavier with each breath we make."

"You may be right… but it is also enticing. We are likely bait for a power that is beyond the reality we have comprehended our entire evolution. We are reshaping history. So let us not balk now," she decided.

The row came to a halt on the western side of the pillar of ice, strange carved stairs revealing themselves to lead to the mirror's edge.

"Someone has been down this path already, I see footprints," one of the soldiers warned. We kept our wits about us as we went forward. Not even our voices sounded like humans anymore as we reached the mirror itself.

I couldn't help but to notice that Kant was still in the same place where we had left him, except now he was merged with the woman that we had discovered the first time coming to this arctic wasteland. The two of them seemed to be tearfully begging us to not go further. And beyond the mirror's surface, I saw those same abstract forms wailing.

"We need to reach the other side. Determine how the portal works," Parker said as she ordered her soldiers to lay down landmines. "Without the proper drills, this will be the only way to remove the mirror safely. Make sure they aren't too close to the mirror, or it could damage the specimen," she added.

I peered toward the crystallized inhuman form of Kant, looking at the woman's face closer. A dark realization dawned on me.

"We need to leave this place, this is not a suggestion. This is a prophecy that we are fulfilling. An evil that is being awakened!" I told her as I pointed toward the victims of the mirror.

The woman wore Parker's face. And here in this strange history, she had already been fated to be trapped forever.

"Don't you see that we need to turn back now?" I told her.

Parker was seemingly unfazed by the revelation, instead ordering the others to begin blasting as she sought cover. I was one of the few that remained close to the mirror to observe.

One by one, the explosives went off, rocketing across the surface of the ice and the mirror.

I did not know what to expect, but the end result was more frightening than I could have ever anticipated.

The glass reflections of ourselves shrieked louder than a rumbling quake. And long dark tendrils of crystal snakes out from the mirror's surface as sharp as glass ripping through the soldiers as lightning bolts. They were consumed and dragged into the widening maw of the mirror like morsels for a lumbering beast.

The mouth of the mirror showed me the familiar platform of the Chernobog outpost, and I shouted for Parker to run toward it.

A final blast rocketed me toward the opened void, and I felt the shards of the jagged mirror close in on my leg as I fell through.

***

I awoke on a medical ship, time itself slipping away as I faded in and out of recovery. The madness of the mirror echoed in my memories.

My rescuers were part of the East Euro agencies that had chosen to wait beyond the Arctic circle, and found me lingering in the water alone clinging to life.

"We could not find any of the other vessels, or any other survivors. The entire island vanished before our eyes… a flash of light and then it merged into the sea as if watching a massive gateway close," the soldiers told me.

Given what I had seen on the other side, I believed him.

I filed a report, recommending the entire area remain closed off to all vessels for the foreseeable future, and resigned from my position not long after.

The excavation has ended, and the remains of the strange mirror are nowhere to be found in the search parties that have been authorized.

Of course, I can only speculate, as none of them have returned either. The ocean seems to swallow all that enters the zone. And perhaps, as gruesome as it may be, it is better that way than finding what else the mirrors hold for our world.

OPERATION AQUARIUS

Sharks have always had an evolutionary advantage when it comes to extinction.

They know how to beat it.

They know the value of patience.

They've survived the Meteors, the Floods and even the Ice Age. From a scientific standpoint, it would be easy to assume that a species which has withstood millions of years of change could likely handle anything thrown at it, and for the most part; this would be correct.

But nothing could have prepared them for the Drought.

Historians say that it started due to a shifting in the rotation of our planet during the early part of the 23rd century. Conspiracists, on the other hand, claim that an underwater anti—energy missile was tampered with. Environmentalists cited global warming, politicians blamed whoever was currently trending in the polls as an opposer, and atheists blamed God.

But one thing all of them could agree on was this; the oceans were receding. By 2347, experts claimed only 40% of the world would still be covered by water.

We needed a miracle. What we got was Jonas Scinto.

Jonas was born to an affluent family in New Detroit circa Oct 2365. From an early age, it was clear he was a savant and was on the fast track for greatness.

Then the accident happened. Jonas was three and a half and his parents had chosen to take him solar sailing near to the Alaskan Ridges. Everything was supposed to be perfectly safe, but a miscalculation in the firing sequence caused their sailor to crash near the base of the ridge.

A search party headed by the Alaskan Lifeguard found the remains of Jonas' parents and five other passengers about twelve days later. Jonas himself was presumed dead, likely crushed by the waves. But that is not what happened.

Instead, the Offlanders found him; a group of nomadic explorers that believed the world's future depended on saving the oceans. Some called them cultists, but they treated Jonas fairly over the next eighteen years.

When he did learn of his origins, the boy who fell to the sea did only what could be assumed natural for anyone in that situation and chose to honor his parents and his new life by creating the New Oceans Marina Research Labs in their name.

Most people who heard of the resurrected prodigy donating his fortune toward the research of astral aquatics scoffed at the very notion. There was simply no way that Jonas would be able to afford to create a working space station capable of housing millions of underwater life forms.

And they would have been right, had it not been for the long trust he had established with the Offlanders; it should have been unlikely to happen at all. But the nomads didn't care about fame or fortune. All they wanted was their faith to be restored. For the oceans to rise once more.

It took 10 years, 9 months and 13 days; but eventually the *Aquarius* was finished in 2398. Jonas made the announcement at the United Nations seminar that the station would launch at the turn of the century. For a world that had ravaged its resources to the point of global starvation and a drop in population by 19%, it was certainly the good news that everyone needed.

But whatever hope the Aquarius provided was dashed to pieces on January 7 2399. A group of terrorists calling themselves Extinctionists sabotaged and hijacked the space station, taking Jonas and 13 scientists who were on duty hostage toward the stars.

What relative peace that had occurred because of Jonas' promise was broken, causing wars to erupt across the planet once more. Worse still, a few weeks later, the station went dark. Rumors quickly spread that the Extinctionists had massacred the scientists before offing themselves.

That was twenty years ago and to most, it has become something of an urban legend. The ocean in the sky. A foolish dream to save our dying world.

But not for us. We see the dreams of one man as the only chance to make it into the next century as a species.—Ernest T. Valsetto, Chief Executive Officer of the Aegir Foundation

The following notes and experiences have been faithfully compiled by our Terran Historian, Doctor A. T. Dajan

***

DEPARTURE
July 13, 2422

Cape Canaveral, Florida, former headquarters of the North American Space Administration

Vincent Retland watched as the young cadet made another round in the simulated treadmill, increasing the gravity density from point seven to point thirteen. The artificial intelligence by her side made the adjusted calculation in mere seconds, but the human took considerably longer.

She is a poor replacement for Labanté, Vincent thought, shaking his head and checking the chronospheres again. Launch was in less than a week, there wasn't time for mistakes to be made.

The next time the young woman made the lap, Retland raised his hand for her to stop and shut the program down.

"Your datasheets betray your skills, Miss Stram; I was expecting more from you today," Vincent said as the woman left the simulation and caught on her breath.

"It's been a while since I won those medals," the twenty something former athlete argued.

"Even so, you should have made the adjustments in your resumé. Not that it matters either way, it's not like there are other Olympic swimmers available," Vincent grumbled.

"I'll practice three times a day if it means I can prove to you that my recommendation from President Dicrest is well founded," she said defiantly.

"I couldn't care less who allowed you to be a part of this expedition or why. What matters to me are the results. So up your daily regimen to six and show me progress by next Friday or I promise I will call your precious sponsor myself and see to it those medals are taken away so fast your head will spin," Retland snapped back.

He knew the words would come off bitter and sharp to the young woman, but this was not a time for coddling. The stakes could not be higher.

***

July 17

Dennis Allen needed to get his head back in the game. The launch was only a few days away. In the short period of time that he had worked for the coalition, everything had gone to pot as a result. Dennis was starting to think that maybe he was cursed. First, during the Carolina starvations, he lost his son; then he discovered that his accounts had all been seized by the New Foundation in their claims for repurposing the country. It was a load of crock, but so was most politics in this day and age. Power vacuums existed in almost every corner of the world thanks to the Drought.

In so many ways, Dennis felt that going to Aquarius would be a godsend in comparison to the madness he faced everyday on Earth.

Allen didn't quite understand how it was that Aegir Foundation had managed to gather a crew in such a short period of time, but as he made it to the bay on the day before departure; he was starting to get a clearer picture.

He saw scared and frightened individuals from all backgrounds mirroring the same sense of escapism that he longed for. These people were thankful for the American Coalition even managing to scrounge the parts together to get to *Aquarius* and it was clear by their determination and anxiety that each of them were prepared to do whatever was necessary to make this work.

That was because* Aquarius* wasn't just about saving the oceans anymore. It had lingered above Earth as a forgotten dream for too long. Dennis could tell that each of the crew felt the same way. They had to succeed. They had to save their dying world.

***

Mission report July 21, 2422

Acting Commander Reggie T. Kinsler, I have sent our departure stats to Control, and it appears we are on schedule to arrive at *Aquarius* in T minus 13 hours. The crew is lively, a group of nineteen men and women that, under ordinary circumstances, I am uncertain would be able to work together so cordially. But these past three months have been hardly conforming to what would be considered a redundant schedule. We have worked hard with the limited resources we had to finish this project in secret. We couldn't risk another flummox like what happened with Jonas.

It's interesting how I find that my thoughts turn to him as I watch Earth fade away. This world was on the brink of collapse and this lost child managed to bring hope again to millions of people. Even if it turned out to be false, it kept the species going long enough for this to be possible.

Aquarius.

I don't know much about the place except what Control has provided us. For all intents and purposes, we will be landing blind. I have provided the blueprints to Jonas' original model to my security detail (three men, one woman) and informed them that it is quite likely the layout may have changed since its original launch.

Our mission is two-fold, we scout out the entire station and also determine if any portions of the facility can still be used or repurposed for terraforming another world. Control believes that if one of these goals can be achieved by the fall solstice, then we can possibly begin a process of selecting people from earth to live here and make the Aquarius a colony of sorts.

It will become more than a vessel for sea life, but also an ark for mankind; to sail us toward the next frontier, whatever that may be. I just hope I get to play some part in it.

***

ARRIVAL

Picture if you will, a long tunnel, widening and brightening the way a roller coaster might before tipping off into a plummet. The very stars seem reachable.

This is how *Aquarius* presented itself to us. A quiet frozen paradise, capable of being awakened.

But some dreams should be allowed to sleep eternally. For when our ship managed to latch onto the eastern outer ring, I could not help but to run scans and notice several key systems still operating functionally.

We were expecting to find a dead world marred by the remnants of a long-forgotten story.

What we found instead was far worse.

Commander Kinsler asked for my team to be the first to scout the entry point. Hanis and Tala took the rear while Beckett and I scoured the north hangar bay.

To say that the place resembled something more biological would probably be an understatement. There was this constant regression that could be seen everywhere we looked, barnacles and anemones growing wild across scores of metal and steel. It had been encased in the underwater material for so long that the place resembled a trench more than a working facility of any kind. And yet, amid all of this natural chaos, a sense of technology also seemed to carry through. Functioning electronic equipment, computer systems and the like.

Aquarius was like a slumbering giant, covered in warts and waiting to be woken up.

We spent four hours searching the entire outer ring and finding more of the same, just abandoned terminals, overgrown hallways and a disturbing quiet.

"The place is a tomb," Tala remarked.

I reminded all of us that our orders were to keep the comm system quiet.

But that was hardly possible, since each step made the tension rise.

It was in our final hour that we finally found something that made me question everything. A massive, sealed door that led to the inner sanctum of *Aquarius*. According to Kinsler, it was designed where the space station had six outer nodes or rings that circled constantly around the main central ark, and so far, that seemed true.

But when I scanned the seal itself, I saw something on the other side. A heat signature like that of a lifeform.

Like someone was watching. After twenty years of isolation, I wondered what sort of creature this might be to greet our arrival.

It would be less than six hours later that I found out.

***

Captain's Log

Our first night aboard the station did not go as expected. We set up a base camp near a blast door the security team found. Some of my colleagues wanted to rest and adjust to the changing gravity, but the peculiar scratchings and biological takeover that surrounded me on all sides was too great a mystery for me to ignore.

It was here that I first met the beings we would call the Settlers of this strange place, for as I gazed upon the markings I started to understand they were of human make, the way ancient glyphs were designed to seal away a tomb. A careful configuration to be sure, but nothing our group of mathematicians couldn't solve in a matter of hours.

The seal opened with a hiss and a shudder, pushing out thick foam similar to what you might see rising on the edge of a lake. And on the other side, we were all shocked to see rows and rows of algae and other sea life growing freely in the dense corridor. One of the older professors, Vincent Retland, hypothcsizcd that the inner atmospheric controls have been adjusted to prevent the water from completely evaporating. It's as though we are walking at the bottom of the ocean as we explore these tunnels.

But the real discovery did not occur until approximately 0330 hours. Hanis, the heftier of the security team, was scouting ahead toward the first generator room when we heard a scream.

I remember the whole group froze as they heard what sounded like his organs being ripped from his body. Then I saw it standing there hunched over him like a bipedal piranha.

In some ways, the figure still resembled a human with the same bone structure and gait, but for the most part it was merely a shadow of a person that had undergone undoubtedly countless surgeries for the sake of survival here.

When it heard us approach, it turned its bulbous head toward us and stretched out its elongated eyes to stare at us the way a hungry predator might. Rows of torn flesh of the Security officer hung from its mouth of sharp teeth, and for a moment I wagered that the thing might attack us. Thankfully Kinsler had his wits about him to use a powerful beam of light to ward off the would-be attacker and for a moment we regained our senses.

I have decided that we will not go further until we fully determine the state of decay for the Aquarius, and send all our data back to the Coalition and to Control to await further instructions.

***

Mission Report July 24, 2422

We have been here a mere 48 hours and already two of our small crew have perished. We were not expecting to be welcomed by anyone here, let alone by hybrid machinations of sea devils. I have managed to get Stram to hack into what limited operations the *Aquarius* has for an assessment of what has taken place over the past two decades. Most of the data has been heavily encrypted, so it may take her some time to come to a conclusion. In the meantime, I have sent a dispatch to President Dicrest of the situation. Our assumption to repossess *Aquarius* as a terraforming colony is no longer an option, and I'm prepared to return to Earth and postpone this mission until we can come up with a plan to take out this threat.

UPDATE: Some of what the analysis from *Aquarius*' database makes absolutely no sense. Over thirty new lifeforms have been created here using some sort of mutating algorithm designed by Jonas himself. If I'm understanding my science team correctly, it appears Jonas intended for human evolution to alter along with marine life in some sort of new world order. Was this meant for us to return to Earth and outlive the Drought? Other data seems to imply that the mutations were tampered with by the Extinctionists who somehow managed to stay onboard during the initial hijacking.

Paslar, my chief physicist; has speculated that they developed the hybrid humanoids we saw as some sort of virus intended to wipe out the *Aquarius* crew but still provide new life to the surface. If this is true, it means that they have managed to create a new type of human based around adapting to an environment without need for oxygen. It would simply be ironic that the people who wanted to kill us all wind up being our saviors, but if I have anything to say about it; the history books will always remember them as traitors to our species as a whole.

SUBLIMINAL 7/26/2422: I am finding it difficult to keep the small crew's spirits up. Ever since the discovery that there is hostile life aboard the *Aquarius*, many of our team seem ready to depart rather than problem solve the new obstacle. I will admit that at first I was also thinking we didn't stand a chance at making it here, but lately we've come to see that the *Aquarius* itself has accommodated our needs in unexpected ways. The changed environment is making it easier for us to work and we aren't needing our supplies as much as expected. I estimate we could extend our stay for another two weeks if Dicrest believes there is still a chance for us to override the main systems.

Unfortunately, there is still a large portion of the data that has been corrupted and Stram told me the only way we can learn more is by heading deeper into the station. I'll be dispatching the remaining members of our Security Detail tomorrow to see what they can find.

***

STASIS
July 27, 2422

The ship is alive. Commander Kinsler has insisted that our success can be achieved by finding the primary controls of the *Aquarius*, but I am dubious. Because how exactly do you override a living creature? We made it up toward the central node. The largest concentration of marine life can be found here. This is when I first saw the new lifeforms that exist in this hellish abyss. Sharks the size of double-decker buses swimming around freely, devouring the skeleton of a whale and using its carcass as some sort of home base for literally hundreds of smaller sharks. The small ones in the species reminded me of a mix of hammerheads and spearfish with long sharp noses and twisted teeth. I think what scared me the most, though, was when we walked through the corridors. Most of them slowed their swimming pattern and watched us, intently curious to see where we were going.

Then we heard the voices. At first, I thought it was only in my own distorted thoughts and broken sanity that I was hearing the incessant chants, but as I looked about the group, I realized all of us were suddenly paralyzed by the singular word that kept ringing in our heads.

Food

Food

Food food food food food food

Stram looked toward the sharks. "It couldn't be… a form of telepathy…?" she asked nervously.

Before any of us got a chance to speculate, a scream pierced the air. One of our engineers, Janice, was taken by the creatures. I watched in horror as they dragged her toward one of the airlocks and pushed her into the open water alongside the myriad of sharks.

Kinsler ordered the guards to raise their weapons and Stram immediately volunteered to rescue her, but it was over in less than fifteen seconds.

Despite the lightning speed at which the hybrid sharks managed to pull apart Janice's body, tearing her arms and her legs from her torso as though she were a toy doll; I remember every vivid detail. Her dead frightened eyes, the cascade of blood as the sharks worked like a finely crafted singular unit, each one making certain to not get in the way of the other.

And above all of it was a throng of music that played out across the sound system of the *Aquarius*. The dangerous creatures that called this place home were singing praises to this massacre. A minute later, only Janice's skeleton still remained, and I wondered if some of the marine life on the surface of the massive chamber would clean that up as well. I felt my own partner squeeze my hand anxiously.

Kinsler announced about an hour later that he is going to make the suggestion that we leave this place again to the Coalition, but some among our group are already talking about revolting if the answer comes back negatively.

***

July 30, 2422

Doctor Retland has requested that I begin a psychologist evaluation of the remaining members after the trauma we were exposed to a few days ago in the main node. We have returned for now to the safety of our ship and only allowed the security detail to roam the *Aquarius*.

This is a hostile place, unlike any we have ever seen before. I remember questioning his motives on the surface for his strict training but given what we have dealt with so far, I think it's safe to say he actually didn't prepare me enough.

Commander Kinsler is preparing for departure, but we have met with a snag. Once we made it within the *Aquarius'* hold, it seems the gravitational pull of the rings will not allow us to break free unless we can find a way to shut off the generator. Retland speculates that the Extinctionists have likely been guarding the system for quite some time.

There are still myriads of questions I have about this entire ecosystem though, for despite its brutality I can see that *Aquarius* is a functioning environment. It thrives in fact and each time I venture out, I notice more life flourishing. How is any of this possible when the humans in charge have devolved into savage lifeforms?

I keep thinking the sharks must serve as a key part of their day-to-day life.

Of all the sea creatures we have seen so far, the sharks are the most evolved. The humanoids seem to worship them as gods. And the sharks have even achieved what Mister Allen called 'Supernatural' abilities.

I, however, believe there is another portion to this tale that we are not privy to, and I have decided that if we are leaving soon, I would like to test my hypothesis with or without the Commander's permission.

It will be risky, but Tala and Frank have already agreed to help me. The plan is simple, but should we not return, I will place this record here as a testimony for our actions.

1. We will travel under the hours of morning when the *Aquarius* seems to be at its most peaceful. I'm not entirely certain what schedule these beings seem to keep, but so far, the time here seems to indicate an 18-hour nocturnal schedule followed by 6 hours of rest. I believe this is partially due to the rotation of the *Aquarius* being misaligned with the equator resulting in longer periods of darkness, and the beings both marine and bipedal have adapted by being active during these periods.

2. I will be diving into one of the smaller nodes near the south portion of the core. The smaller sharks that have only recently been bred seem to be kept in quarantine here, and this will provide me what a chance to capture one without risk of danger from the adults.

3. We will dissect the shark's brain to determine how it has been able to achieve the abilities that it has obtained and what role of any humans played in their new evolution.

I plead to whatever God is still listening that we can achieve this goal... and until then; this is Mary Stram signing off.

***

DISCOVERY
Log of Doctor Vincent Retland

Our primary marine biologist has sacrificed her life to make an astounding find concerning the hybrids we have encountered aboard the *Aquarius*. After spending nearly two hours prepping and then another trying to lure one of the smaller hammerhead hybrids toward a portion of the tank that is meant for surgical operations, Mary managed to trap a male hybrid and two smaller females. During the process, she unfortunately lost her life. The larger adults saw through the ruse and, using their modified fins, managed to pry open the cage and free the two females. The young male died in the process as the adult also lodged a part of their spearhead into its lower abdomen.

Dennis thinks that the adult was trying to prevent us from salvaging the body. Stram insisted that we focus on saving the specimen rather than her as one of the other adults grabbed a hold of her leg and dragged her down toward the murky waters below.

I wish I knew how best to express her bravery. But I can say now that it was not in vain. Me and three other volunteers have succeeded in dissecting the shark's body fully and come to a startling conclusion. It would seem that these sharks are fused with artificial intelligence of a sort, designed to modify their brains and provide them with cognitive abilities superior to even their human hosts.

And their brains have been enhanced to triple their original size. Dennis says that he believes this accounts for the shark's telepathy and also why the humanoids seem to worship them.

"It's a hive mind mentality. They are the alphas here. The humans have become like worker bees."

It was a stunning and shocking revelation that made us all question God himself. Fear has gripped the few of us that remain.

With over half of our ship crew gone, I worry that we may not even be able to return to Earth to warn others of the dangers here. *Aquarius* is indeed a living, breathing world.

But from what I have seen so far, it is clearly in opposition to the restoration we are trying so hard to achieve.

It is Death Incarnate itself.—Vincent Retland, Chief Physician

***

Supplementary information

The chambers to the west of the docking bay were the first that began to flood. The crew of the small endeavor that had managed to survive for a few weeks aboard the *Aquarius* were still naive enough to believe that the incident was accidental.

They didn't want to believe that the creatures they had encountered which had ripped them apart and used them as fish food were also smart enough to end them all.

It was obvious that the flooding was meant to end the long stalemate between the two groups, and the sharks, which were normally sealed off, can notcannot,were allowed to roam free. Their sense of smell was increased, allowing them the chance to find any runners in less than a minute.

Commander Kinsler managed to set a few underwater charges that pushed back the larger species trying to attack. But it was only a temporary delay. The sharks were smart enough that they knew when to expect the charges.

The sharks could heal their wounds. Some would be stagnant for hours, drifting amid the flooded corridors like pieces of torn wood. Then slowly they would recover, even with the most brutal harm coming to their bodies. These creatures could adapt to anything.

All the while, the worshippers chanted and watched, pleased that the small sacrifices were enough to appease the larger sharks.

Kinsler sent out a final message to NASA and to the Coalition, begging them to blow *Aquarius* from the sky. Anything to prevent more madness from spreading.

Then the waters pushed in, covering him with a surge as powerful as fifty elephants, and those who came to the *Aquarius* were gone forever.

***

ASSESSMENT

The data we received from the *Aquarius* was perhaps the most frightening that I have ever read in my life. To imagine these poor folks struggling to breathe and fighting against what sounded like monsters, it was shocking, to say the least. In other parts, horrifying.

We planned a memorial service for the unfortunate victims on August 13, which was attended by well over three hundred family members and friends. And afterward, all of us listened to the emergency broadcast from the Coalition.

"I will see to it that their efforts to save our species are not in vain. Each and every piece of data collected from the Aegir Foundation will be assessed by a team of experts over the next several months. We're going to spend as much time as necessary going forward. Myself and the other members of the council still believe that the resources and technology available on the *Aquarius* are the best chance humanity has for a stable future. If that means that we must send up a dozen more operations to secure the facility, then so be it. We have full confidence that our men and women will do everything in their power to achieve this dream. We're going to do this. We're going to win."

Over the next few weeks, President Dicrest implemented several new policies to prepare those involved with the Foundation for attempting diplomatic procedures with the inhabitants of *Aquarius*. According to the charter he developed, the beings on board the space station were no less human than any other culture on planet Earth. This included the hybrid sharks that were discovered. Dicrest insisted that we needed to do everything in our power to either come to terms with the superior evolutionary society that was discovered on *Aquarius* or else further division would develop between the surface and that isolated abyss.

I cannot, in good faith, continue to support such action when people's lives are going to be sacrificed for something that could destroy us as being separate from the animals. My colleagues have countered that I am opposed to progress in humanity. Nothing further could be true.

But at what point do we concede defeat to beings from the depths? How many more volunteers will fight to take back *Aquarius*?

Instead, I feel that replicating the technology Jonas invented here on Earth is the key to our survival. So I will be taking my leave of this place, and pray in good faith they see my reasons are solely for the betterment of our whole species rather than wasting resources.

God forgive me for the dreams we are conjuring. For I fear that both are leading toward true extinction—Ernest T. Valsetto, Chief Executive Officer of the Aegir Foundation.

***

CONCLUSION

Private logs of President Dicrest, October 2422

My team has estimated by the year 2531 there will be no surface water remaining on Earth. Our options, such as they are, have become limited to one.

We must surrender to the *Aquarius* and beg they allow at least a select few of us to join their ranks. The ocean in the sky is the only viable choice for preservation of species. The announcement of our dying atmosphere and dwindling resources has already caused unrest in nineteen countries. At this rate, we might all die before even bowing down to these hybrids.

I cannot help but to feel guilty for the part I have played in this grand folly. I also fear that if the truth came out regarding the mutations on the *Aquarius*, and how our government had a role to play in the original hijacking; that at this point I would either be deemed a savior of mankind or become a martyr for further revolution.

I am uncertain now, as I review further communications with the newest team to arrive on *Aquarius*; if it scarcely matters anymore.

Whether we live or die, our species is doomed to be slaves to the powers of Mother Nature.

SHADOWS IN THE BASEMENT

Let me cut to the chase and just catch you up on what's happened so far:

1. This house is fucking haunted.

I don't know how the hell anyone managed to sleep at night here and call themselves a human being. We moved in just last Monday and I knew something was up. I've always had a sixth sense about this sort of thing. One time my wife and I spent an anniversary at a hotel, and we changed rooms four times because I felt something was wrong in each suite we stayed in.

Turned out I was right. Either a murder or some weird scandal had happened in each one of them.

This property was no different, but we didn't really have a choice in the matter. I won't go into too many details, but our finances have been very tight lately, so this was all we could afford.

Anyway, back to the ghost thing. Our youngest, Callie; is the one that first had an encounter. That was Wednesday.

She said that someone was in her attic. But we told her that there is no attic.

"Well, I hear someone walk around on my ceiling then!" she snapped. I decided to take her word for it and check. And wouldn't you know it, there was some residue from a shoe on the ceiling.

How the hell it got there, I don't know, but I was convinced that something was wrong. Especially because of what happened next.

2. My children had nightmares about the basement before it was unlocked.

When we got to the property, we were told there was a wine cellar. Nothing out of the ordinary, and actually it sounded like something that we had always wanted. There was a lock on the door, which the real estate agent admitted they didn't have a key for.

"I'm sure if you use something strong you can get it open though, just no one has ever really had much use for the space down there," they said.

I knew something was off. I could feel it. My skin was crawling as I looked down toward the basement door. There were about four steps that jutted downward and then ended abruptly in a short hovel. The door looked old. Probably older than the house itself. It did not look pleasant or friendly.

It looked like it was meant to stay locked.

My wife was immediately intrigued by it, though.

"I bet there is some great sangio or Syrah down there. I can borrow my dad's drill and get that open in no time," she told me.

I had a bad feeling. Especially when both Callie and Adrian had dreams about the basement.

Adrian was first. He has always had an avid imagination. After Callie had reported that she was sure people were walking on the ceiling, he couldn't sleep and came to bed with us. That resulted in a night where no one got any rest because he kept waking up screaming.

"What has gotten into you?" I asked him.

"I keep hearing something under the floor. It's getting into my skin!!" he would tell me frantically. He said there was something that was growing under the house. In one dream, it was a weed, the next it was an octopus. Either way, it was unsettling. He had never had strange dreams like this before.

Still, my wife was now even more curious because of the nightmares.

"If there is something about the basement, I want to know what it is," she decided.

Audrey has always been a bit stubborn. I told her to leave it alone. My hope was that maybe if we ignored the otherworldly presence in our house, it would get tired and move on.

That didn't happen.

3. Something in the basement doesn't want us to leave.

It was Saturday when Audrey finally found the way to open the door. I didn't even know she had gotten the drill. I had to go to work that day and by the time I had gotten home, she was already in the basement.

I remember walking in and announcing to the kids that I was home. Normal Saturday afternoon would mean they were either playing outside or on their Xbox.

But this time the house was empty and quiet.

I immediately felt the hair on the back of my neck stand up as my first thought went to the basement.

Sure enough, I saw that the door was slightly ajar. But I couldn't see anything beyond the fourth step. It seemed like it plunged straight into darkness.

I was just about to walk down there and see if she was maybe sorting through whatever might be below when I had second thoughts. That sense of foreboding overwhelmed my body and instead I decided to call her cell phone.

I heard it ringing below my feet. Then I heard Adrian make a giggle from the stairs and I turned toward the basement door and called out to them.

"Hey, don't scare me like that!" I shouted.

No response. It made me uneasy. I tried to call again, and it rang and still she didn't respond.

"Adrian, tell your mom to come up. And you too. Where is Callie?" I asked.

"We're all down here," he responded.

Something in his voice was off. It was chilling.

"Okay, well, are you coming up then?" I asked.

"No."

A Short and succinct answer. Something was wrong.

"Adrian, listen, I need you to come upstairs…"

"Why don't you come downstairs, father?" he asked.

That didn't sound like my son at all. I looked down into the stairwell and saw two glowing orbs, which I assume were his eyes. I couldn't see his pupils, just those white circles. I tried my best to not be frightened as I spoke.

"How long have you been down there?" I asked.

"Long enough," he responded.

I took a tentative step toward him.

"You really need to come up now. All of you. It's not safe down there."

He smiled and I could see his teeth. It made the rest of his shadowy face look inhuman.

"Are you sure it's safe up there?" he whispered.

I didn't take any more steps toward him. I knew this was wrong. I felt cold talking to him. Like it was just an empty void.

That was Saturday and I waited an hour before I was sure that they weren't coming back up. Then I tried again and told them to come up and got the same response, except this time from my daughter.

"Daddy. I like it down here. You will too…" she said in a hum.

I hardly slept that night because I was so worried about my family. I didn't know who to call or what to do. It's not like the police were going to come over something like this. I kept hearing scratching on the floor, and it would keep me awake. I have never felt so watched as I stayed in bed. Like there were eyes in the floor below.

Then Sunday came, and I went to work, trying desperately to ignore the sense of dread building inside me.

I would get texts from my wife every so often.

"When are you coming home?"

"The kids miss you…"

"I miss you too, of course. We need to be a family together."

"We have to stay together as a family."

That prompted me to respond. "Then stop this foolishness and come upstairs."

"It's you who is being the fool here, John."

I decided to stop reading the texts after that.

When I got home, the house was quiet again, and I didn't even go near the stairs. I grabbed some sleep meds and locked myself in my bedroom, hoping that the night would pass quickly.

Now it's Tuesday and things have progressed worse. A lot worse.

"We're hungry daddy. Can you please come feed us?" Callie whispered to me as I passed the stairs this morning.

I called a few people in the area, spiritual leaders and such, hoping maybe they could give advice. As you might imagine, no one wanted to talk to me.

They thought I was crazy.

Maybe I am? I didn't think that it would be possible for something so simple to be so sinister, but it is. And I'm terrified because I don't want anything harmful to happen to my family.

"Why don't you come up and eat, baby?" I asked my girl.

"We can't. It won't let us leave." As if I didn't already have confirmation that something was happening down there, this sent shivers across my spine.

"And you can't leave either," my wife added. I saw all three of them there. Three pairs of eyes in the darkness staring up at me.

"Just come down here," Audrey insisted.

I took a step toward them, my heart racing. Something was compelling me to go deeper. Take one more step. Just do it John. Just do it.

Then I heard this low growl as I reached for the door. It was like the house settling and preparing to swallow me whole.

I slammed the door and caught my breath, refusing to go a step further.

For a moment, there was silence. Then I heard a soft noise on the other side of the door.

tap tap

I ignored it at first.

tap tap

I bit my lip and whispered, "Who's there?"

There was a giggle mixed with that hellish growl.

"Daddy, it's me… please open the door. Please?"

TUESDAY

I really wanted to just break down and cry after what happened because I was about 90% sure that my family was gone.

They went into the dark basement below and they have refused to come back upstairs since Saturday. I've tried everything to see what is down there, flashlights, lanterns. But I haven't gone past the door. I can sense an evil there. And I know it's taken them.

In fact, I was so upset I did something I probably shouldn't have, but in a way, it's gotten the ball rolling toward some answers.

Full disclosure, some alcohol was involved in the decision making.

After a few drinks, I called the one person I thought might have answers to this mess, the real estate agent.

Truth be told, I felt ashamed that I didn't think of it sooner. But another reason I wanted to call is because my patience was gone. I demanded an answer when she finally answered the phone.

"John, John. You need to slow down. You aren't making sense," she stuttered.

Something in her voice told me that she fucking knew, and I was too drunk to care about her to let it slide.

"You need to fucking get over here and explain what the hell I need to do to help my family," I demanded.

"All right. All right. I will be there in a couple of hours."

I sat at the kitchen table, fidgety and afraid. Every so often I would hear the pitter—patter of bare feet below me. The sound of my children supposedly playing in the basement. Every time I heard them laugh or giggle, I nearly lost it.

In fact, right before the agent came, I was in a really drunken stupor and started to yell down at the basement, demanding it respond.

"I don't know what you want from me, but you need to let my family go. We haven't done anything to you, do you hear me??" I screamed.

Of course, the basement didn't respond. It was unnaturally quiet in fact. And that just made me even more upset.

I stumbled down the steps to the door and slammed my fist against it. "What the fuck do you want??" I shouted louder.

This time, I heard a low scratching noise and nearly jolted from the step as I saw strange lettering burning into the door from the other side.

It took a moment for the word to form, singed into the old wood permanently like a scar, and it made me literally gasp for air.

Then the doorbell rang. The real estate agent was here.

I fumbled back upstairs and went to the front door, glaring at her.

"About fucking time," I responded as she came in.

"John… you've been drinking. What the hell is going on? Where is your wife?" she asked nervously.

"That's exactly what I have been trying to tell you! They have been in the basement! And now they won't come up," I explained.

She walked over to the stairs and looked down at the door, commenting, "I see that you managed to take the lock off. So what was down there, anyway?"

"I haven't gone down," I admitted.

She gave me a puzzled look.

"What is that on the door?"

She walked toward it to get a good look and then asked me, "John… Did you do this?"

"No. How could I?" I asked.

She tried the handle, but it didn't budge. The door was stuck shut.

"And you're telling me that Audrey and the kids are down there? How long have they been down there??" she asked as she jiggled the handle with no luck.

I fidgeted with my feet, feeling ashamed and embarrassed and frightened all at once.

"About four days now."

Her eyes widened in alarm, and she pulled out her phone and announced, "I'm calling the cops. John, this is unacceptable. It's negligence! You should have called the fire department by now. How the hell are they getting food and resources down there?"

She pushed me aside and walked back to the kitchen as she dialed 911.

Then I heard this low rumble below our feet and a noise from one of the bedrooms.

"What was that…?" The real estate agent asked.

Then, as she was talking to the operator, a shadow appeared from the doorway, and I felt immediately cold and empty inside. Standing there in the hallway was my wife. Or at least, it was something that looked exactly like my wife.

"Oh, thank god," the agent said and added to the operator that it was a false alarm.

"Is everything all right?" Audrey asked softly.

I was at a loss for words, watching as my wife walked into the kitchen and stood alongside the sink.

The agent slid her phone back into her pocket and gave me the stink eye.

"It would seem that your husband here had the idea that you and your children were in danger… honesty, I'm hoping all of this was a great prank at my expense," she commented dryly.

Audrey laughed. It didn't sound like her laugh. I kept still as the agent walked over to her and added, "After this little scare you gave me, I think I deserve a drink. You did say you got wine from the cellar, correct?"

"I can get you something," Audrey answered, walking to the fridge.

"So what was it that my husband told you was wrong…?" she asked casually.

"You… you and the kids were locked downstairs. Or something. In the basement. Audrey, I heard you down there," I said softly.

She poured the wine and smiled at me. It was not the friendly look I knew from her.

"Well, I'm clearly not in the basement now, am I? And you believed that nonsense?" she asked the agent, passing her the wine.

She sipped it and chuckled softly.

"Well, to be honest, I've heard a few rumors about this property. It's been… somewhat difficult to sell. So the story sounded outlandish, but I guess I let my imagination get the best of me…"

"Rumors?" I said, keeping an eye on Audrey. She was watching the agent the way a lion stalks their prey.

"Where are the children, anyway?" Our guest asked.

"Excuse me?" Audrey said, seeming surprised by the question.

"I really should be going but before I do, can I at least confirm the children are alright?" the agent said.

"Oh. Yes. Yes, of course," Audrey said, fumbling for something. I saw it just as her fingers curled around the handle and I made a noise.

"Watch out!!"

But it was too late. She twisted the knife and slammed it straight into the agent's face. The woman screamed, dropping the wine glass and immediately scrambled to defend herself.

Audrey was faster. She grabbed the woman's hair and slammed her into the sink, forcing her under as she started the water.

"Audrey!!! Audrey, you're going to suffocate her!!" I screamed as I tried to pull her off.

She pushed me away and then turned on the garbage disposal, a grinding noise filling the air as I heard the woman scream louder and blood begin to splatter out in every direction. My wife didn't even blink as she kept the woman's face down until her body had gone limp.

Finally, when she was sure that the real estate agent was dead, she lifted her from the garbage disposal and tossed her to the floor. I did my best to not look at her mangled face.

Then she dragged the bloodied body toward the basement stairs.

"Audrey. Audrey, talk to me. What the hell are you doing? Talk to me, damn it!" I said, trying to stop her. She made a hissing noise and pushed me away from the stairs as she walked down and pushed the door open to the sheer darkness below.

I tried again to stop her, and she scratched me across the face, slamming me against the wall as she dragged the body down the stairs to the basement.

I listened as I heard the noise of bones breaking and growls from predators fighting over a fresh meal. It sounded so primal, so animalistic.

Then from the darkness, Audrey stepped out and closed the door, looking down at her blood splattered clothes.

"What have you done," I whispered, barely able to find my voice. I was in fear of what she might do to me if I got in her way.

She blinked; looking confused and surprised by my question.

"The children were hungry."

I clenched my fists.

"Those… those things down there aren't our kids…"

I looked at her with hate and anger. "And you are *not* my wife."

She made a low hiss.

"That's no way to talk to me, John… and I would be careful with what you think you are going to do next. Ask yourself carefully… how many people are going to get hurt because of your stubbornness?" Audrey snarled.

"The police will come, they're going to eventually realize that poor woman went missing. What the fuck do you want from me??"

She turned toward the door and opened it back before snarling, "I'm not staying up here to argue. I'm going back to be with our family… where you belong too, John."

"Don't you fucking walk away!!" I screamed louder. I was shaking. Convinced she would kill me in a second if she could.

She turned her head and gave me a curious look.

"The house already told you what it needs… I suggest you start listening to it."

Then she disappeared into the darkness and shut the door between us.

I went to the door, struggling to get it open again. But it would not budge.

I screamed in frustration as I touched the burnt letters.

Fuck. I'm such a wreck I forgot to mention what the message was.

'More.' It fucking said. This fucking house wants more. And I think I just gave it exactly what it needs.

WEDNESDAY

I won't be mincing words. My family is gone.

I know it, you know it. We all fucking know that they are dead.

But that doesn't mean whatever the hell this thing is that took them is going to win.

It's been nearly five days now. I lost my family over the weekend and now I see that this house has a force of evil that I wasn't prepared for.

That I don't think anyone was prepared for.

But I'm going to keep fighting. My family deserves that.

After my experience with Audrey, I decided to try to get the police again. A woman had just been brutally killed in our house and she had fed their corpse to the basement. I figured if that didn't pique their interest, the sheer amount of blood on the property would.

I recognized that the entity I'm battling doesn't want me to seek outside help, so I probably should have anticipated that my phone wouldn't work on the property. Instead, I drove down to the police station to provide a statement. I had no idea what sort of tricks the entity would play while I was gone, but I also felt so relieved to get out.

Guiltily, part of me wanted to keep driving. But no, Audrey and the kids need me to finish this.

I didn't tell them the full story, but just enough to convince them that an accident had occurred at my new house, and they needed to come investigate.

One officer said something interesting just as we were about to leave.

"What was the address again?" he muttered. I told him.

"Huh… wasn't that the place they found that kid a few years back, Tommy?"

"What kid?" his partner asked as we walked out of the station.

"Can't remember. The husband was an abuser and had kept the kid locked up in the basement for years, though. Then afterward the wife went insane and killed the son and the daughter. It was crazy," he said.

"I remember that now," the other officer said, and then the rest of the ride became weirdly quiet.

I tucked that little bit of info away into my brain as we drove to my house, and I prepared for whatever fuckery the house was going to throw at me next. Something told me that Noah and his family had not made it out of this house alive. And I didn't want to be next.

Honestly, I thought that I was prepared for anything by this point. But the house proved me wrong again.

As we got inside, I directed them to the kitchen, only to find it was completely clean from top to bottom. Not a speck of blood anywhere or any body tissue.

"Is this some kind of sick joke, son?" the second officer asked as he came back from checking the rest of the house.

"No… it's true. Here, let me get you the real estate agent's business card," I stammered as I fumbled through my wallet.

"What's in the basement?" The other asked, looking down at the closed door.

"I… I don't really know," I admitted.

"You got the key?" He asked.

"It isn't locked," I said.

"Well then, lead the way," the second officer told me.

I froze. I couldn't think of a good excuse to not go down into the basement, but every bone in my body told me something horrible would await us.

"I would really rather not," I said nervously. Then one officer sighed and pushed me down, muttering he didn't have time for this nonsense. They both flanked me to prevent me from going back upstairs and I reached for the door, hoping to god that it was locked.

It opened with a slow creaking sound, and I gestured toward the darkness. "I don't believe there's any electricity down here," I admitted.

"Where exactly is your family, sir?" One officer asked as they took out their smartphone to shine a light down the basement stairs.

I could just barely make out a brick wall. It was that dark.

"They aren't here. Wife took my kids to visit mom upstate, for the week," I lied. I really don't know why. I knew it was a mistake the moment I did but it was too late.

"Daddy…?" a voice whispered down below and I closed my eyes and prayed the officers didn't hear it.

Of course they did.

"What was that?"

Before I knew what was happening, the two men were taking me down the stairs to the edge of the basement. We couldn't see anything down there. Even the light was hardly penetrating the shadows.

But then amid the gloom we saw my little girl, standing amid a pile of what looked like human waste.

And I suddenly realized she was shackled to the wall.

"Holy shit," one officer exclaimed, running toward her.

"No… it isn't safe!" I shouted.

"Get back against the wall," the second officer snarled, pushing me away even as his partner knelt to check Callie for injuries. I could see her mouth was still dripping with blood.

"That's what I was trying to tell you. They attacked that woman," I insisted, but the two cops were no longer listening to me.

"Are you okay, sweetie?" the officer asked.

"That isn't my daughter!!" I said frantically.

"You better shut up before I make you regret anything else," the second cop snarled.

"Daddy, I'm scared," Callie said as she cried softly.

It sounded so much like my little girl. I wanted to believe.

"Leave her alone!!" a scream came from the darkness. The officer that was helping Callie jumped in surprise, turning to see faux Audrey standing there in the gloomy basement. There was hardly enough lighting to make out her face, but I could tell that portions of her skin were beginning to peel away around her nose and eyes. Beneath it, her skin looked like porcelain, new and young and different. Almost the way an insect might break out of a husk.

"They aren't ready," faux Audrey said as she stepped closer. I recognized now my initial guess was right. She looked like a new person, with dark red hair and paler skin. Not the woman I had married at all. Not even close.

"Ma'am, we are going to need to question you and your husband," the officer said sternly.

"He's not my husband," she said, confirming my fears. The house had changed her… but into what?

Before the officer had a chance to move, the stranger said, "These aren't my children either… not yet."

"What is going on here?" the other officer asked.

"I don't really care. All of you are going to come down to the station and clear this up immediately," the first man insisted.

"No. You can't take them. The house needs them," she snarled, blocking the stairway.

"Lady, if you don't move right now, I will tase you," the second officer snapped. I watched as the stranger's eyes turned completely black and then the entire house rumbled again.

"What the hell…" the cop said, looking down at his feet. I watched in shock and horror as his legs became bolted to the floor, transforming into wood. He struggled to move as the strange shapeshifting magic moved up his body and he started to scream in terror as it covered his body.

Before he had a chance, he was as stiff as stone, immobile.

The second man was no different, frantically running up the stairs only to have them act quicksand and begin to swallow him alive. He turned and tried to shoot the stranger, but it didn't do any good. Whatever had emerged from my wife's body was unfazed by the attack.

As soon as he was gone, she turned her attention to Callie and smiled in the most sinister way.

"Nothing will prevent our return. Our survival," she whispered.

"Daddy… I want to go. Please help me…" she whimpered.

I looked at the tears in her eyes and then looked toward the stranger, mortified, as I realized that I was wrong about all of my family being gone.

"Callie… daddy's going to save you. I promise," I said, reaching for her hand.

"She belongs to the house now, John. Audrey tried to tell you. But you wouldn't listen," the woman hissed as she blocked my path to my daughter.

"And you just took two men's lives. How the fuck are you going to explain that one away? This house will be torched to the ground once locals know it's haunted," I snapped back, my voice shaking in fear and anger.

"The house will keep them away. It has already grown stronger. Soon, it will be able to make things right," she whispered in a reverential way.

"I want my family back. They didn't hurt you," I told the demon. Her eyes blazed with fire.

"But the family before you did. A price must be paid! We will walk this earth again, and you will help us… or you will never save the ones you love," the stranger told me.

I realized in its own cold, calculating way, the demon that had taken my wife hostage and formed her body to suit its needs was now offering me a choice.

I could harvest souls for it, to save my children.

"Where is Adrian… show me my son before I make any deal," I said.

She stepped aside and in the darkness, I saw his weak, frail body. He was hardly conscious, a thick layer of some kind of strange plaster was covering his skin and he was struggling to breathe.

Seeing him there made me want to scream. To cry. To kill this monster.

But I knew I couldn't if I wanted to even get a chance to save my kids.

"I'll do it…" I whispered as my lips trembled.

"I'll gather the souls you need. But you have to let my children go."

THURSDAY

I fucking hate this house.

Sorry about my language. I'm just so frustrated.

Today marks it being six days since my family was taken hostage by a demonic entity in the basement. After three days, I started documenting everything.

I guess I really felt I was losing my mind.

Considering that after the initial incident, my wife killed our real estate agent and then two police officers were swallowed up by the house.

My hope had been to make others see what is happening here… but this evil is stronger than I realized. I feel like it's manipulating me and holding me and my children hostage.

I guess you could say I am mad. Especially because I agreed to go out and bring more souls for the demon in exchange for my children's safety.

Yes, Adrian and Callie are alive. For now. But the house is hungry. The stranger that emerged from my wife's husk explained to me, and I don't understand it but this is what she said.

I'm still reeling from the fact that my wife is likely gone forever, used as a shell for this new life form that is somehow able to communicate with the house.

"The real estate woman was a sinful body. I force fed your children because if I don't feed them, the house will simply consume them. Audrey did that to keep them alive, John. She was doing what was necessary to keep them alive. Unlike you."

I ignored the jab and said, "So the house must be fed sinless and innocent souls, is that it?"

"Yes, and you must hurry, John. Otherwise, I can't stop the house from feeding on them and they will be lost forever."

Some part of me told me that my wife's spirit was the one also making this deal with the devil. She knew she was doomed but wanted to do everything in her power to save our kids.

It's my duty to do the same.

I left the house that morning, promising to return in only a few hours.

I know some of you have suggested that I simply leave. But what good would it do? This thing would find a way to hurt others. And I would lose what little life in me I have left if I knew I willingly left my children.

I've been a coward. And it's time to start thinking of a way to defeat this evil.

As I got further from the house, my head began to clear, and I considered what I knew so far.

Something had happened here before we moved in, something that likely killed the family that had lived there. So that must mean that there is a record of it somewhere.

I managed to find the local newspaper archives downtown and requested a snoop. Thankfully the woman at the desk didn't ask any questions.

And soon I found myself going down a proverbial rabbit hole.

It took longer than I anticipated but I found two entries about the address, one only two years back.

>mother kills both children and then herself in a gruesome massacre that rivals the original tragedy.

That got me digging a little deeper and I soon found in the other article that one of her children was apparently adopted, and the son of a man that also claimed to have been attacked by spirits at another house over 8 years ago.

>woman adopts son of heinous criminal in shocking end to a dangerous case.

The article explained that she said her husband was charged with kidnapping the boy. But the original biological father was still in county lockup.

I did a search on him next and found an interview where he was attempting to warn others about an entity that had made him kill his son years ago.

>"There was evil there that I couldn't explain, it was compelling me to do things that I didn't want to. The house was alive! And it took my son! And I know that it will want to feed again!! You must destroy it!"

It made me wonder if it was even possible to destroy this evil. Where did it come from?

I knew my next stop would be the county jail. To talk to this estranged father.

I checked my watch, nervous and afraid that the demon would think I was taking too long. I needed to buy some time somehow.

The only solution I could come up with was to swing by a local church and convince a pastor to stop by for a baptism.

"And you said it's your children that need to be baptized?" the older man asked as I drove him to the house.

I figured a man of God would be the closest thing to sinless I could find. And maybe if I got lucky, he could even help defeat this evil.

I drove back to the house, trying to fend off any questions the pastor had. a sense of dread overwhelming me as I got in and headed straight for the basement.

"There is something evil about this house," he said as he entered. Then he paused at the top of the stairs.

"I know this place. People died here," he whispered.

I froze and looked down, wondering if the house might attack because of the man's realizing its true intent.

"Your children don't need to be given the water of God… but his spirit, take me to them immediately," the pastor insisted.

I couldn't even see the basement floor. We walked together and toward the wall, my mind reeling as I wondered if this man would even stand a chance against this evil.

It wasn't the darkness that scared me now, but what was happening down below that sent a shiver down my spine.

When I got down there I saw to my surprise that the faux Audrey, the stranger; was sleeping. She was in a fetal position in the corner, almost like an insect going inside its shell again, and it made me wonder if I had the chance to rescue my children.

Adrian was hardly moving, pale as a sheet and covered in the same goop as before, and Callie was actually asleep as well. Was the house working its magic on them, to change them the way it had Audrey?

"The demon is weakened… some time ago… I can feel its pain. It's anger. It's in the floorboards. The walls. The entire house," the pastor realized.

"What happened here?" he whispered, not knowing the full story.

"Father, that doesn't matter. We have to work quickly to save them," I said as I began to work on the locks.

He went to check my son, hardly able to get him to move.

Callie's eyes shot open.

"What are you doing…?" she asked in a groggy voice.

"I'm getting you out of here. We are leaving Callie. I'm going to save you," I responded.

Then she kicked at me and started to scream.

"Don't touch me!! Get away!! Get away!!" She kicked at me, and I frantically looked across the room to see Adrian was standing up now, looking almost dead to the world. He was grabbing the pastor by the throat and crushing the man's windpipe.

"You've taken too long, John. Your daughter is gone." His voice was almost completely monotone. "No… no, please god no," I said as I managed to break the lock and grab her hand.

"Callie, you come with me," I shouted as we moved toward the door.

"No!!!" Callie screamed. Then the pastor tugged at his cross on his collar and showed it to Adrian. He hissed in pain and dropped him, then the man shouted, "Run!!"

I obeyed and ran up the stairs, the house rumbling and shaking as I did.

As I made it to the ground floor, Callie tugged at me and finally pulled away.

"I don't know you!! Stop!!" she screamed. Then I looked at her and realized that her eyes had changed color. I hadn't seen it in the darkness, but her hair had too.

This wasn't my little girl.

The house shook again, and I turned to see the stranger push her away up from the floorboard, her naked and monstrous body snarling as I looked on in horror.

"You dare to go against our arrangement??" it snarled.

"No… no, I brought what you asked for!" I said desperately.

"You tried to attack us. And for that, you must suffer," the stranger snarled louder.

"John!!" I heard the pastor said as he managed to make it to the first floor.

"It's not too late for your family. You must undo the sins that have been committed here!!" he begged.

"Silence!!" the stranger screamed louder and then made the girl become her puppet, her hands featuring and forcing the child to comply.

I watched as the little girl screamed and opened her mouth in pain.

Then hornets began to swarm from her mouth.

I was pushed to the floor by the sheer force of them, watching as they moved toward the pastor, stinging him madly with the fury of a legion of demons. They were going to kill him before he could have a chance.

And it was giving me a chance to escape.

I crawled toward the door as I heard the child screaming louder and felt my heart drop as I managed to push my way out to the front yard.

I had to abandon my children there. The house had officially claimed them as its own.

As I managed to escape and heard the buzz of the hornets grow louder, I made up my mind that there was only one thing I could do now.

This place needs to be destroyed. It has taken everything from me, and I'll be damned if I don't make it pay.

FRIDAY

It's been a very long week.

Last Saturday, my wife Audrey and my two children were taken hostage by a demonic force in the basement.

I learned very quickly that Audrey was gone, but that if I played nice with the demon that I could save my kids.

I didn't play nice, and it kept them from me.

Nothing was left except for me to try and destroy the house.

I knew it wouldn't be easy. It's been clear to me this entity has great power with the ability to control people's minds and take their bodies as its host.

And I knew I would need help.

So I went to the one person that I thought might even consider helping, the man that owned this house eight years ago.

After the incident two years back where it was discovered that his son was saved by the family that lived at a similar house to mine, I learned that he was cleared of all charges.

That isn't to say his life was better though, because I soon discovered that he was at the local psychiatric hospital under careful watch.

Apparently over the past 24 months, he had tried suicide several times.

I don't blame him. I feel like I'm in the same boat, if I'm being honest. The demon within this house has used me the same way it did him.

I found him in the commons room staring out the window down at the grass. He looked like a broken and defeated man, with no sense of purpose anymore.

I was about to give him a reason to live again, even if it was for pure revenge.

I asked, extending my hand to shake his. He ignored the gesture.

"Who the fuck are you?" he snapped back.

"John. I… well, there is no way to make this easy, so I'll just say it. I think I am dealing with the same demon you fought eight years ago."

Noah's eye twitched. I could see that he was scared. But he could also tell I wasn't lying.

"So then it's starting again…" he whispered.

"I had hoped… when I told that woman the truth about what happened to Jasper… I thought when I saw the reports that she killed them both that meant it was over…" he shook his head and tried to not let his hands shake and tremble.

"But that was just the demon warming up, wasn't it?"

"No… I think she really did go insane and kill them both. It weakened the entity, until my family moved in just last week… it's been feeding off my wife and kids in the basement," I said.

"Feeding? It's still using their bodies?" Noah asked.

"My wife…" I paused as my own voice cracked. This was more difficult than I realized saying it out loud.

"Audrey is gone. The demon created a new body for itself. It's going to do the same for my children. And I think… after that it will spread and infect other homes," I admitted.

"Then why come to me? Just leave. Get away from here and forget about this place. Your family is gone," Noah insisted.

I held back a tear as I clenched my fists. "You think I don't know that?!"

A few of the orderlies looked at me in surprise, and I controlled my anger so as to not cause a scene.

"But you know as well as I do that running away solves nothing. Too many people have suffered because of this thing. I want to kill it…"

I swallowed a gulp of air and offered a proposal to him. "Eight years ago, you managed to wound it enough to keep it dead for at least this long. You must have done something different!" I said.

Noah looked at me like I was a madman.

Maybe I was. Then he laughed.

"You want to know my big fucking secret? Do you? It's the reason I went to jail. I killed Jasper. Yes, I killed my boy. He was six…"

He stood up and jabbed his finger in my face.

"Do you have any idea what it takes to watch the innocence fade from your child's eyes as you are holding their heart in your hand??"

"But I knew… I knew it was the only way to stop this evil. I had to stop it before others were hurt…"

I could see the anger there. It was the same passion that drove me now.

"Help me… please. You and I seem to be free of the influence this thing has… let us use that to our advantage and get rid of it once and for all," I urged him.

"You're joking, right? What's your plan? Nuke the place? And how are you gonna get me out of here anyway?" he asked with a laugh.

"You know the answer to that," I paused and leaned forward, whispering my plan to him.

He actually smiled for the first time.

"The house demon has powers to manipulate people, right? So it can certainly get you to be brought to it, if it so chooses. So if I made it believe you were offering yourself willingly… then there wouldn't be an objection from the staff.

"It's crazy… but it might work," Noah agreed.

"So then we just go and burn the motherfucker down?"

"Do you have a better method?" I asked.

He crossed his arms and laughed again.

"I have a bad feeling about this… but sure. Why the hell not?"

***

By afternoon, Noah and I were headed toward the house. It took little to convince the demon of his interest. It remembered the wound he had caused, and the entity made it clear that it wanted to exact revenge.

And from the way Noah was fidgeting, I could see that he was eager to do the same.

I was sure this would be the last time I set foot in this house. One way or another, it was ending here.

The door opened of its own accord as we stepped on the porch. Noah and I both felt a cold chill, and I knew. The demon was back at full strength again. It didn't really need us. Now it was going to dispose of us as obstacles so that it could go elsewhere.

As if to confirm this, I saw the stranger and two children I didn't recognize sitting in the den, waiting. To the side of the girl stood a life—like the husk of Callie and the same of Adrian was near the boy.

My poor children, taken and destroyed by this evil. It was pulling at my heartstrings, but I knew that it was too late for them.

Apparently, Noah recognized the stranger and the boy.

"Jasper… how dare you continue to use my son's body for your purposes, you monsters," he said as he clenched his fist.

It then occurred to me the stranger had to be the woman that had killed Jasper and this girl only a few years back. A desperate attempt to stop the evil from spreading that was now backfiring.

"He was the first one to awaken us. It seems only fitting he continues to be our primary vessel," the woman and Jasper and the girl all spoke in unison.

"That won't be happening. This is going to end. You arc going to die," Noah responded.

"You think I don't realize you came here to kill us? You will fail."

I shook my head. I actually had a different motive. One that I hadn't even told Noah about.

I remembered the pastor's words about undoing old sins and though it seemed crazy, I made a conscious decision to try something unorthodox.

"You want to spread and grow elsewhere? Then use my body. It's healthy. And it's not gonna be something that people question either. You can leave this place and go where you want. But if you do that, you'll have to give these souls back to the bodies you took them from. My family. Bring them back. I know you have the power to do that now," I said.

Noah looked at me in shock.

"You can't be serious. This thing will just use you as a puppet."

"It needs me. The same way that it needed you all those years ago. I'm not sure why, but I feel our roles as fathers serve a distinct purpose in its own evolution…" I saw the demon girl twitch, and I remarked.

"And it knows that it can't leave here with these three bodies. It fed on my family simply to regain strength. Now it needs to be able to expand," I offered myself again and swore to the demon.

"I'll make whatever oath you want, but my family needs to be freed of your grasp. They didn't hurt you. Honor them by letting them go," I insisted.

"No. I won't allow this!" Noah said.

He pulled out the knife that he had brought and snapped. "You think you are so god damn smart? But I've been willing to kill before to stop this thing and I will do it again!"

He pushed me to the ground and slammed his weapon into my shoulder, causing me to scream out.

To be honest, his response was part of my plan. But I saw that the demon recognized the potential it had to use me and immediately it lashed out toward Noah.

"You are the one that took our survival and freedom from us! You will regret ever stepping in our path!!"

I saw the moment of distraction and leapt at the chance.

I grabbed the knife and pulled it off my shoulder just as the demon pushed toward him in full force.

And then I tackled Jasper to the ground and jabbed him repeatedly in the chest.

Even as I completed the act, I saw the color in Adrian's cheeks begin to return. The plan was working.

The demon screamed at the realization that I was turning on it even as Noah took out his next weapon of choice, a simple match. He lit it and tossed it at the woman, causing her clothes to catch fire as I kept trying to make Jasper lose consciousness. I had to keep telling myself that this was not a child. It was a monster. And I had to stay strong. For Adrian.

Suddenly the house rumbled and shook with all its might. I saw bars begin to grow on the windows and the floor move and try to swallow us whole. The entire house was fighting back. The demon was using all of its resources to stop what would come next.

But I didn't hesitate anymore. I tossed the weapon next straight at the girl's back and shouted to Noah, "Do it!! Now!!"

He kicked the woman off and then ripped off his jacket, revealing a makeshift explosive he had made. It wasn't easy to get the materials without raising any red flags, but we had been cautious. And this would be enough to do the trick if he could get the demon back to where this all started. The basement.

"Surprise motherfucker," he shouted as he tackled the woman to the ground and they both tumbled toward the basement.

I crawled toward my children, grabbing their hands and pulling them as I raced toward the entranceway. I had only seconds to escape.

The door itself was beginning to close the way a lion's maw would, and the entire property creaked and groaned as I leapt out. My children in my arms.

Then Everything burst into flames.

I tumbled onto the front porch as I heard the screams of a thousand demons fill the night and the top of the house roof spilled off, debris tumbling in every direction.

I collapsed in exhaustion as I clutched Adrian and Callie and struggled to help them breathe.

As the last remnants of the house flew up in the air, they both started to wake up and I sobbed in relief. It was finally over.

***

The fire department was on scene in less than ten minutes. I provided the best statement I could of a home accident that had taken my wife and Noah. I claimed he had been holding them hostage in the basement and then finally decided to end things once and for all. They hadn't made it to the debris down there yet, but they accepted my version of events pretty easily given the man's track record of violence.

As I was given a warm mug of coffee, I laid my wife to rest in a nearby empty garden. I held Adrian and Callie close to me as they cried and tried to comprehend what had happened. Honestly, I'm not sure they ever will know.

I don't have much to remember her by, but I will do my best to live the rest of my life trying to find a reason to go on. I have never really been a believer, but I think I felt Audrey smiling down on me as I laid her ashes to rest. I did it. I saved our kids.

They insisted on taking us to a local hospital for an examination to make sure we were fine, and I accepted. I had a feeling I would need some intense therapy after this last week.

As I sat there in recovery and saw my kids get their own examination in a room adjacent to mine, I thought about Noah. How he was now at peace too with his own family. And I was doomed to be a guilty survivor.

Then there was a knock at the door.

"John?"

It was one of the officers that had brought me here.

"I just wanted to let you know that everything has been cleared up. We got a statement and you're clear."

For a moment, I was at a loss for words.

"I'm sorry, what do you mean?" I asked.

Then in the doorway I saw standing there a man in handcuffs that should be dead.

Noah Hunt.

"Mister Hunt has confirmed what you told us at the property. It seems he also had help from a few of our officers and the real estate agent. I'm so sorry you had to go through with this. We are putting this monster back where he belongs as soon as possible."

Noah looked at me with those same cold dead eyes and immediately I knew.

"No. No, you can't send him to prison…"

"John. He tried to kill his own son. He held your family hostage for a week before killing your wife. We're nailing this bastard hard."

"No, you don't understand!!" I screamed as I strained to get up.

"It's quite alright John," Noah said in that same monotone voice. The demon's eyes fired up as he added, "I've accepted my fate to return to the gallows…"

"Why, you could almost say it's like going home again."

THE LOVER'S LOCKER

Can your love survive our lockup? Provide an unforgettable Valentine's Day for that special someone with an evening at our exclusive escape room, where love is put to the ultimate test! Call The Lover's Locker today!

The place was brand new, so new that when I went in to get their brochure, I could still smell the fresh paint on the walls. It screamed extravagance. The kind of place that middle class socialites went to on a date night.

So what was a boy from the Bronx doing here with barely a dollar to spare?

Two words: Brandi Myers. We'd met only a month before on a dating site and I wanted to make the jump from swiped right to a relationship status, and this place felt like the right spot to do that.

When I texted her just days before Valentine's and asked her if she had plans, I had actually already booked us a room. According to the clerk, they were selling fast, and I didn't want to miss out.

"None so far," was her response, so I sent her the tickets and the next thing I knew, she was squealing in my ear over the phone.

"Babe! I can't believe you booked us that! It looks so classy! You really shouldn't have!"

"Well, I figure maybe it will finally give us a chance to really get to know one another. Make a decision about our future?" I told her.

"Is it going to be just the two of us or a group thing? How long will it last? I want to have dinner first, is that ok?" she had a few other questions that I couldn't answer, but I figured that we would just wing it and see where the night took us.

My reservation was at six that evening and I got there a little early with a bouquet of yellow roses, her favorite color. She came dressed in one of the most stunning tight outfits I've ever seen, and I wrapped my arms around her and leaned in for a kiss.

"Babe, you know how I feel about PDA. Come on, you're embarrassing me," she giggled. She smelled the roses, and we held hands as we went inside. A small group of other couples waiting eagerly to be told where they would be spending their evening.

"Cole and Brandi?" a bald man called out from the front desk. I raised my hand, and we shuffled to the front of the line.

"You requested the deluxe suite, right this way," the man said. We were led to a hallway on the left and followed a dark red carpet toward a room marked DXL, where the man provided a few rules.

"In case of a fire there is an alarm on the left side of the room behind the painting, and if at any point you wish for the experience to stop you simply need to profess your undying love for one another and we will open the door back before the timer is through. Do you have any questions?" he asked.

"What if we need to pee?" I asked, suddenly realizing that I should have done that before we got back here.

"Ah yes, of course, let me show you where the restroom is at."

"I'll wait," Brandi told me.

I went and did my business and hurried back as fast I could, but my date wasn't in sight.

Figuring she had already gone inside, I slipped out the key the man had given me before entering the room.

I'm not entirely sure what I was expecting to see on the other side, but it was certainly not this.

The room was covered in ultraviolet light, making every surface seem far more illuminated than normal. Rose petals were scattered across a concrete floor and long metallic chains draped from the ceiling.

The chains meshed together to form a heart, a box of some kind wedged amid the bundle and what looked like rows of knitting needles poking toward the center table from the bottom of the box.

On that table there were several books, all of which were opened, and some had ripped pages, most of which appeared to be arranged in an arrow diagram that pointed toward the left wall.

But that part of the room seemed blank, instead it was actually the opposite side of the wall that truly captivated my attention. Rows of one-way glass were lined up that reflected everything across the room. Except there was one distinction on the other side of the glass, and it made me gasp in shock as I realized Brandi was lying on the ground, covered with blood and petals.

Immediately I ran to the mirror, trying to bang on the glass and see if I could get her attention. Yet instead, the next noise I heard left me in a panic. It was the sound of the door locking.

Then a voice came over the sound system.

"Welcome esteemed guests to our deluxe suite!"

Immediately I started calling for help. "My girlfriend is injured! Get 911!" I shouted as I tried to dial myself, only to soon find that cell phone reception was blocked.

"You'll find that we have taken the steps necessary to provide you the most immersive experience possible connected to your personal love story," the voice droned on as I scrambled to find the picture that the man had said was an emergency release. Yet there was nothing. And the door itself had seemingly disappeared into the wall, as if hidden by another trigger. I was locked in, and Brandi was either dead or about to die.

"If you can unlock the mysteries of each other's heart, you can make it out a better person and a better lover. But if not, you may discover that Love itself may be that which tears you apart," the recording concluded.

I got down on my knees and tried again to get her attention and see if she was responsive, slamming my fist against the thick glass in frustration.

I glanced up at the ceiling and realized that one of the chandeliers above the chains looked like it was a security camera and I shouted, "Is this your idea of a sick joke, man? My girlfriend is in need of medical attention!"

There wasn't a response.

I went over to the table and tried to flip it in frustration, soon discovering it was bolted to the floor. And then I felt something taped to the bottom. It felt like some kind of tool.

Crouching down, I realized that it was a magnifying glass, and I quickly removed its tape before staring at the mix of papers on the table.

As I looked through the magnifier, I realized that some of the words on the papers were colored differently. I started to piece them together and try to form a secret message.

It felt like it was taking hours as I looked across the glass to where Brandi was lying. I had no way of being sure she was all right, but I knew time was of the essence. It felt like I was wracking my brain trying to figure out the scrambled message.

Then I heard the strangest noise coming from the other side of the glass. It sounded like tapping.

I stopped what I was doing and went up to it, trying to pay attention to a pattern. Was it Morse code? I tried my hardest to pay attention, but I honestly didn't know a thing about it. Even as it went silent, I suddenly realized that this could be a vital clue that I had just missed. Was Brandi going to be in mortal danger all because I couldn't solve these puzzles?

I felt trapped, both literally and figuratively, and in frustration, I went back to the books. Grabbing the first one off the table, I chunked it at the wall. It fell to the floor, and a page stuck to the wall. To my surprise, it was a cipher.

I grabbed it and studied the other pages again, realizing I could use it to unscramble the code.

S—A—V—E was one word. Panic set in as I tried to understand the rest.

Save her and you save yourself, it read.

Did that mean Brandi was still alive? And did that mean I was in danger, too?

A moment later, the tapping returned, and I realized I might be able to figure out what that meant as well with the cipher. It was a stretch, but maybe the two were connected.

As it finished, I managed to write down the one word I was sure that had been sent. Key.

There was a physical key somewhere in the room, maybe the way out of here or something else.

The question was where.

I got down on the cold floor and pushed petals out of the way, trying to see if maybe the object was hidden somewhere. There were literally thousands of them covering almost every inch of space in the tiny room, but I kept sweeping them aside.

Soft music began to play as I pushed more petals out of the way, and I froze when I recognized the song. It was something that Brandi and I had loved on the radio only a week or so before.

How the hell did they know that?

As the music kept playing and I pushed more petals out of the way, it began to get more and more distorted, until at last it was repetitively playing the same part of the song over and over.

Maybe it was another clue? I listened to the lyrics.

Never hit so hard in love

Wrecking ball by Miley Cyrus.

Immediately I reached for the chains, tugging on each of them to see if one of them might collapse.

The fourth one did and at the end was, in fact, a small key connected directly to the main chain.

The box, I realized as I looked up at the intricacies of the hidden puzzle. What else about this room was part of the game? Was this really just a test and none of it real?

I heard over the intercom Brandi beginning to gasp for breath and I saw through the mirror she was beginning to convulse from the shock.

"Hey! Hey I'm right here! I will help you! Just hold on!" I shouted as I tried to get the key loose from the chain. Instead, I realized I would have to carefully pull the chain toward the box, but it still wouldn't reach. The only way would be to dislodge the box from the needles, I realized.

Wrapping my hands with the ripped-up paper to protect myself, I began to push at the needles to reach the sides of the box.

Even with the added layers of paper, it felt like sharp cuts directly against my wrist and it took all of my power to not stop. Brandi's gasps were the only thing keeping me going. I know that it was my fault she was in this mess to begin with, and I could hear her now begging for my help.

"Cole... pull the alarm... get us out of here!" she demanded in desperation.

"I don't know where it is!! There's no portrait on my side!" I yelled back as I finally found the strength to push the needles deep into my skin and grab the box.

It tugged out rather easily to my surprise, and I managed to unlock it only mere seconds later.

I was expecting something inside to help us out of this hell, but instead as I opened the box, the lights went completely out, preventing me from even seeing inside it.

The sound was cancelled too, and I could not hear anything from her side as I scrambled to find my phone. Surely it was somewhere on the table? I fumbled down on the ground and blindly began to search.

Then I heard a roaring noise from below the table, what sounded like a growing furnace.

A song by Johnny Cash filled the intercom as I felt warmth beneath my feet and panic set in. Were they really going to burn us alive in here?

"Cole!!! Cole I can't move!!! Help me!!" I heard Brandi scream over the song.

I used the glow from the fire to make my way to the mirror and bang on the glass.

"I'm trying babe! Just hold on!"

The flames were shooting up and melting the table from underneath, causing my makeshift footstool to reach the ceiling to collapse. And the rose petals were acting as an extra flammable material for the growing blaze, I realized as I demanded to get let out.

But of course, there was no response.

"Brandi. I'm sorry about all of this. I love you," I admitted to her.

"Don't you fucking dare give up! I want to fucking live!!" she shouted with a whimper.

I stood up, braving the inferno and reaching for the box to try and grab whatever was inside.

Photographs. Of the two of us. Driving around and making out, trying to just laugh. Had we been stalked by this business?

What was all of this? Some of the photos showed either one or the other marked with black permanent marker, and then at the bottom etched into the box was a warning.

Save yourself or save her.

I had to make a choice. But how was I going to save her? I had nothing to give to her.

"Brandi, I need you to get up," I begged as I pushed my back against the glass wall. She couldn't see me, but I saw she was now scrambling to find a way out of her own prison.

"I don't understand what is happening Cole, what is this?" she whispered as I saw water was beginning to pour in from the ceiling on her side.

"Look… I'm probably not going to make it ok. I think I know what to do to make this thing stop… and I'm really sorry…" I said as I covered my mouth, unable to speak.

I ran toward the blank wall and started to claw at it. Anything to ruin this building. If they wanted me dead, I was going to take them down as much as possible.

Instead, as I ripped the wallpaper off, I found what looked like a portrait of myself.

I pulled the paper off more to reveal the rest of the painting, stunned by the details to my image.

The escape switch, I thought as I pulled it off the wall and I saw the way out was right in front of me.

Then the lingering question hit me. If I pulled it, did that mean Brandi would die?

A message came over the intercom.

"Congratulations! You've found your one true love, yourself. Use the escape lever to end the simulation and rediscover your life," it said in a robotic voice.

At the same time Brandi was desperate to stay above water on the side of her prison. And if I pulled it, I imagined she would likely drown.

There were probably a dozen excuses I could have used to save myself, to let her go. I didn't really know this girl. Didn't know if we were going to work out or not. Heck, after this hell, if I were her I would definitely dump me, I thought sourly.

But I told myself I had to save her instead.

"The wall! Rip off the wallpaper!!" I shouted to her as the flames licked against my skin.

She heard me and didn't hesitate, jumping through the rising water to scratch at the different wallpaper.

"Love is blind. And love cannot exist without first there being selfishness…" the intercom announced as Brandi gasped for air.

"You can do it! Come on!" I shouted. I saw bits and pieces of the portrait show up.

"Pull the lever!!" I told her desperately.

Both of us were moments away from death.

She turned toward me and demanded, "You do yours too. You're there too, right??"

I felt a chill run down my spine as I realized she was breaking the escape room rules. "They said either one or the other. We can't both go!" I insisted.

"Fuck it Cole. Fuck the rules! Pull the damn lever on three!!" she demanded.

One.

Two.

***

The next thing I knew, I was waking up on the ground in a back alley. It felt like I had been hit by a freight train. My clothes still smelled of fire, I knew that it had all been true.

I tried to call Brandi, but couldn't get through. I stumbled out of the alley and called a cab, getting to her house in about ten minutes. They had dropped me off on the south side of town, with little more than the clothes on my back.

I ran to her door and slammed my fist against it. She had already made it home and looked just as shaken as me.

"Brandi… I'm so sorry about all of this," I stuttered.

Her glare told me that any chance I had at a second date was gone. "I don't know what you did to provide that place all the intimate details about my life, but you are sick. That place was a nightmare, Cole. We almost died!"

"I didn't do anything! They must have been monitoring us!" I insisted.

"All the more reason to not be together. I can't live like that," she argued.

"You have to believe me that I didn't know this would happen," I admitted.

She crossed her arms uncomfortably. There was something that she wasn't telling me.

"When I went in the room, I wasn't alone, Cole, not at first," she explained.

"Someone stabbed you, right? Did you see their face?"

"It was you," she whispered. The air around us felt colder as she explained. "But somehow… I knew it wasn't you… I can't explain it, but I played along. This other you gave me a warning about the escape room. It's meant to be a representation of how our relationship will go… and… and if that's true… I just can't get hurt again," she admitted.

"I don't understand. What you are saying isn't possible," I said, my throat feeling dry. "Is anything we experienced tonight?" She snapped back.

"Just go home, Cole, leave me alone."

I tried to go back to the escape room today, to complain to the management and maybe get answers, but the building was already being stripped apart.

"Moving on to the next town," one worker explained. Or more likely covering their tracks, i thought.

I don't fully understand what we experienced or what was real about this hell. Was the escape room an illusion or a vision of my future with Brandi?

For now, I can only view her from afar, wondering if the game of love I played was worth it.

THE WINDS OF MARS ARE HOWLING

Approximately 334 days before this event, according to the Martian Calendar, NASA began to use the *Perseverance* Rover for research of the Red Planet. Thanks to the Rover, we have learned more about our distant neighbor this year than ever before.

But not all of it is for the betterment of mankind.

Two microphones aboard the Rover have been recording the winds of the red planet for quite some time, trying to determine the acoustic differences between our world and Mars.

Mars has an unusual atmosphere compared to this planet, with very different temperature, density, and chemistry. These differences have three main effects on the sound you'd hear:

The Speed of Sound

Sounds emitted in the cold Martian atmosphere take slightly longer to get to your ear. With an average surface temperature around—81 F (or—63 C), Mars has a lower speed of sound, around 540 mph (~240 meters per second), compared to about 760 mph (~340 meters per second) on Earth.

You probably wouldn't notice up close, but over longer distances you definitely would. Imagine trying to hear the roar of a fire, only to realize that the house you were getting to had already burned down.

The Volume of the Sound

The level you hear will also be automatically lower on Mars. The Martian atmosphere is about 100 times less dense than on Earth———

that is, there's just a lot less of it. That affects how sound waves travel from the source to the detector, resulting in a softer signal. On Mars, you'd have to be much closer to the source of a sound to hear it at the same volume as you would on Earth.

The Quality of the Sound

The atmosphere of Mars, which is made up of 96 percent carbon dioxide, absorbs a lot of higher—pitched sounds, so only lower—pitched sounds travel long distances. This effect is known as attenuation—a weakening of the signal at certain frequencies—and it would be more noticeable the farther you were from the source.

Put together, these three impacts change how you or anything would sound in the atmosphere of Mars.

Imagine then, the surprise felt when it was recorded only a week ago; what sounded like screaming.

I was at my station, reviewing the audio and barely drifting off to the ambience that was carrying through the microphones when this extremely high-pitched shriek pierced the airwaves.

Immediately I fumbled with my gear, snatching the headphones off as I felt my heart beat faster than it ever had before.

I took a moment to recompose and then placed the headphones back on to listen. The noise was gone, but it did feel like there were reverberations from it everywhere in the audio. There was this low thrill that filled the void from the shriek.

Hesitantly I rewound the audio, turning the volume to a lower frequency so it wouldn't hurt my ears. Ordinarily to get proper analysis we are told to not do this, but the situation was unique, and I figured that it would be easier to handle the screams if they didn't terrify me.

What I heard disturbed me beyond what mere words can describe.

The best way to offer an explanation would be to provide you with an anecdote from my childhood.

I had a dog named Brutus when I was little, a large Labrador retriever that could hold his ground against the toughest predators out there. One time I swear I saw him run off a bear. This dog was loyal. He would always go with us hunting and make sure that we were protected. It was like he had eyes in the back of his head.

One particular hunt, my brother and I decided to go out when it was storming and try to find a few deer that enjoyed grazing after a soft rain. Yet the storm hadn't quite passed us yet and I fell into this muddy ditch. Brutus came slipping and sliding right behind me.

His leg got caught by this gnarly thorny branch and he let out this yelp that pierced the rain. I got up and tried to help him, but it was like attempting to wrangle a fish as it flopped from the water.

Brutus was confused, terrified and struggling so much that it was only making his pain worse with each passing moment. We couldn't seem to pull him free.

I told my brother to go get our dad, try to find a rope, and we could perhaps snag the branch up and free Brutus. Meanwhile, he continued to whine and yelp, the thorns digging into his leg muscles the more he fought against the snare.

"Ain't no way to move that branch. It's too muddy. I don't have any good equipment," dad told us when he assessed the situation. He told us to leave Brutus there and he would figure it out.

But he didn't. Instead, as my brother and I went home, I could hear my dog's shrieks echo across the night air. The sound of suffering. Endless pain. And with each new yelp, it became worse.

The sounds across the airwaves of Mars reminded me of my dog and how he died that night caught in the mud. I was helpless to save him, as helpless as I was to find out the truth about these recordings.

I pulled up the location data from the rover to give me an idea of where the shriek had come from.

Near to one of the many wide craters that we have been studying to search for Martian water, I realized.

The data was still being transmitted, and it told me that the final compiling would come in the morning. It was difficult to wait, but I knew that there wouldn't be many more answers coming that night.

Still intrigued by the noises I heard, I decided to pull audio files from the surrounding area for the past week and see if I could determine any clues.

It resulted in a lack of sleep, and even fewer answers.

As I pieced together the audio on my home desktop, I noticed that a pattern emerged. The screams were there, every so often, amid the data.

But they were moving. I pulled out a map of the Martian landscape and began to chart a course where I heard them. As the rover moved and surveyed the area, the noise would sound as though it was following the river.

Was there a possibility something was alive on the Martian world and watching our rover?

The painful and anguished screams haunted my dreams. It sounded worse and worse with each new recording I found. Hearing the silence and the low thrumming soil of Mars in between the unexpected shrieks was a blessing.

My tired brain told me there was more to it, but I had to sleep. And of course, nightmares came when I did. I saw cities that didn't have shape. Metropolitan areas on mars from ancient times. It reminded me of the old science fiction stories from the 20s, an entire civilization living under the ice.

In the dream, something crashed on the surface of the planet. Something from a world unlike any we had ever encountered.

The dream didn't offer it any shape or form. It was just this abomination of noise that was surrounding the entire landscape. The martians ran and shrieked, the formless creature mimicking their suffering and spreading its awful noise everywhere. The ground shook and swallowed them all up. Leaving behind only vibrations.

I woke the next day in a cold sweat. It felt like that same noise had permeated my skin. I wanted so desperately to find out what was happening on the Red Planet, so I got to work and immediately checked the other rovers to see if they picked up mysterious signals. I wanted my dream to be nothing more than my fragile imagination.

But as I reviewed the traces of data we had collected, I saw disturbing evidence of something within the soil where the rover had surveyed.

Microorganisms, bacterial life that can exist anywhere in the universe. It was migrating through the ground and following the rover.

I began to check other data, photographs and videos from the area that had been downloaded and properly cleaned.

Yet I found nothing. No evidence of a life form near to the area. Or at least… not one visible.

As much as I hated to do it, I decided to present the data to my manager. I figured they could keep things under control and perhaps alleviate some of the worry I had. These screams were troubling me, making me lose sleep, and I wanted to find a scientific solution that wouldn't terrify me.

She promised to review the data but the next day when I asked about it, she acted like I had made the whole thing up.

"That has already been processed and cataloged. I want you to focus on the other findings from the crater," she insisted.

When I returned to my research, though, I found copies of the audio files on my computer which confirmed that I had truly heard these noises. So why was she denying their existence?

I tried to move them offline again to have someone outside of our facility review the data, but soon found that the information was now heavily secured.

"Someone didn't want this to get out," my close friend Stephen told me. I showed him the chart of the Martian landscape that I've been reviewing, and he began to trace a pattern from where the different noises had come from.

"And each time you said that it's a high-pitched noise?" he asked. I nodded, and he told me something that should have been plainly obvious: "This thing is getting closer and closer. Each time you record it, the pitch is decreasing. The wavelengths are traveling to you slower and slower as well. In other words, something may have gone terribly wrong on the surface of Mars and we don't even know about it yet."

"Do you believe it could be something dangerous?" I asked.

"What have the samples shown?"

I reviewed them again. The sudden findings of life that I had recorded were now gone, erased completely. Rewinding that trace data showed a shocking result. When the noise came, the bacterial life forms would shrivel as a result.

These screams were acting as a pestilence on the Martian world.

The next nightmare I had was more vivid. The extraterrestrial parasite which had crashed on the planet was now infecting the ground. I saw a lush and vibrant Mars transform into the wasteland we knew so well.

The civilization that named the planet home was killed in only a matter of weeks. And then the virus ate them alive. Devouring every part of their body and possibly even their soul.

I saw the invisible effects of the screams on the planet everywhere I looked in my dream. Scars that ran deep into the red core revealed wounds of dead soil, dangerous invisible parasites that eagerly cling to any life that passes by.

Suddenly, I felt my leg slipping into the crimson soil, being pulled under. Dragged down to this Martian hell. I found myself scraping and gasping for breath as dirt and soil was spilling into my throat and I was drowning on this alien world.

I woke up gasping and unable to breathe, and I ran to the bathroom and began to vomit.

What came out of my lungs were particles of sand and red soil. I looked down at my body, astonished to find that I was covered in the color of Mars from head to toe.

Swiftly I bathed and shook away the nightmare, disturbed by this sudden telepathic connection I had with the planet. Was it because of the infectious noise that I had heard? Was it trying to eat me alive the same way it had the old Martians?

I tried again to tell my supervisors of the potential threat, but instead of listening, she informed me that I was going to be relocated to a different department.

"There was evidence that you attempted to retrieve secured audio files recently and share them, which goes against our policy. You're lucky you have a job at all," she told me.

I was astounded at the sudden change in attitude, her behavior seemingly hostile when I brought up the recordings.

"I'll have the rest of the team review them. But I'm afraid I will have to ask you to clear out your desk and leave by the end of the day."

I did as I was told, but not before I created a small back door program to get into their network. It didn't take long, and I was certain that monitoring the noises would be smart for the future.

Once finished, I left for lunch and started to download the files to my own laptop, Stephen assisted me with it but told me that most of the files now seemed corrupted.

"I think your bosses are doing this on purpose," he said.

"I think it might be that this noise is affecting them subconsciously," I admitted as I fidgeted nervously with my fork.

"Have you tried to play the audio backwards?" he asked casually. The thought hadn't even occurred to me.

"Are you saying it'll be like a secret code or something?" I joked.

""No, but it could reveal something about the samples we are missing," he told me.

As we experimented with the corrupted audio again, I heard distortions and shrieks again and he immediately became tense.

"Jesus, that's a nightmare," he whispered nervously. His hair was standing up on his arm as we kept listening and I commented, "It gets louder every time the rover is obtaining samples."

"The samples that are transmitting data here… transferring whatever this is… to earth?" He asked.

Neither of us knew what to make of that implication, but he requested to review the data and try to hack it that evening, so I let him.

I called my boss that evening, begging her to listen to reason. Something about all of this was very wrong.

"You need to step out of the way of progress. These samples will show us how the entire planet of Mars has evolved into the Eden it is today."

"An Eden? Are we talking about the same planet?" I asked with a soft laugh, but she didn't appreciate the joke. Her tone was serious.

"What the planet is offering to our world is greater than anything you can imagine. Terraforming an entire world into a perfect environment, it would be a miracle for Earth," she whispered.

I found myself suddenly uneasy talking to her.

"But… the planet of Mars is dead. We've seen that it's deteriorating, perhaps even dying. How is that a blessing for us?" I asked.

The silence in the next moments were ominous.

"Death is the only consistency in the universe. Life sprung from nothing eons ago. It's inevitable that one day it will all be snuffed out. Our time here is for one purpose alone. To serve as fuel for the next cycle."

"What… um, what are you talking about?"

Then I heard this low thrill behind her as she kept speaking. "It's our every existence that is the problem. Life is meant only to feed death. And death, that's eternal. Perfect. Beautiful."

"Michele… Do you hear that?" I whispered, becoming terrified by the conversation. She sounded possessed. It sounded like the winds of Mars were bristling through her lungs.

"It is the warning of the future we must prepare for. The inevitable transformation of our own world."

My mouth felt dry.

"These samples that have been taken from the craters… what exactly happens to them?" I asked.

"I think you know the answer to that. They come here. They will find their way to our world, one way or another," she whispered. The noise in the background was making my ears feel like they were bleeding.

"Surrender to evolution. Death is the ultimate phase of all life."

I hung up the phone and frantically called Stephen, hoping that he was available.

Yet I got no answer. I grabbed my keys and decided to race to his house. These recordings were more than just a peculiarity. They were a threat to our world.

I tried to knock on his door, but there was no response. I shouted for his attention, yet instead I heard that same shrill noise. It made me want to cover my ears and get into a fetal position.

I pulled myself up and found a window I could crawl into. Inside his small one-bedroom house, the noise was deafening. My eardrums felt like they could burst as I stuffed wads of paper to soften the intense screams.

Then I found Stephen mutilated in his living room. It was clear the injuries were self-inflicted. He had taken one of his kitchen knives and sliced off his ears first, stuffing them into his mouth. Then he had sliced his wrists and let the blood drain out on his couch. Finally, even as his life ebbed away, it appeared that he had carved open his stomach, letting his guts hang out and dangle on the carpet.

Somehow, despite all of this madness, I saw that my friend had typed a message on his laptop.

A warning.

THEY ARE LISTENING.

I found myself wanting to pick up that same blade and harming myself. This invisible voice was urging me to kill. To let death take over my useless body.

The blade touched my own neck, cutting into my flesh as I struggled to escape the screams. I managed to get out before I was overwhelmed by that desire.

As I drove home, my boss called me again. I panicked and sent it to voicemail. When I later checked the recording, all I heard was more of the same howling.

Slow, methodical shrill noises that told me the strange invisible threat I had heard was now here.

I made it home, hardly able to think straight or even focus, then I managed to compose this wanting for others.

I have realized that the concerns Stephen had were even more serious than we first understood. The dangerous invisible evil is already on its way here.

And worst of all, we may already be too late to stop it.

THE FINISHING SCHOOL

I woke up with a pulsing headache, a throbbing pain at the back of my head. The world was dizzying for a moment, and I couldn't even properly make out any shapes or colors.

As I came to, I soon realized that I was handcuffed to what looked like a school desk. A quick study of my surroundings told me this was accurate. There was a man right alongside me also on the floor, cuffed to a desk and behind him another and behind him another.

I was in some kind of classroom, with at least a dozen or so people, all of whom seemed to be chained up.

My eyes took in the surrounding posters and artwork. There were children's drawings and safety reminders all scattered across the wall, most of them older than I was. Then my attention went to the front of the class, the blackboard where a teacher should have been to instruct. In its place was a simple, concise message written in chalk and large enough for all of us to read.

Tornado Drill: 8:05 AM.

I checked the clock on the wall. According to it we only had a few minutes before the event was supposed to happen, so I talked fast.

"Hey! Hey you! Where are we?" I asked, kicking the man's foot next to me.

His eyes flared at me suspiciously. "Like I would know? How should I know? We could be in Hell for all I know!"

I decided to not bother talking to him anymore and turned to my left. A petite young woman was there. "What about you? Do you remember how we got here?" I asked, yanking on the handcuffs. The sound they made as they rattled against the desk was echoing everywhere.

"I was in the mall, with my… boyfriend. And we were headed toward the food court when… I don't… I don't remember anything after that," she admitted timidly. I could tell by the look on her face she was more worried about the boy than her own safety. But something told me that pretty soon that would change.

The clock struck 8:05 a moment later and suddenly this shrill scratchy noise came on over the PA intercom. The system had to date back to prior than 1980s, I thought to myself as I tried to cup my free hand over my ear and hold my head against the desk.

"Attention class of 2021, please rise for the pledge of allegiance," a very strange voice announced. It was difficult to say for sure what gender it even was. It didn't sound quite human.

Then there was a sharp click, and a grainy old recording of the American flag pledge came on over the speakers.

As it finished, all of us looked at one another in confusion and fear. What the hell was going on?

"Attention Room 3, your tornado drill will begin now. Move to the hallway."

"How the hell are we supposed to do that?" I said out loud. Not that I expected the strange machine to respond. Instead, there was a loud rattling from above and it made me look at the ceiling of the room for the first time.

Above every desk there was an air vent and on cue, those vents opened. Then, abruptly loud noises and shards of glass spit out from the vents and straight toward us.

I reacted in a moment, yanking my body toward the floor as the broken glass sliced across the back of my neck. Using the top of the desk as cover, I did my best to huddle there, a portion of my thigh and right foot damaged from the sudden unexpected rush of projectiles.

Others in the class weren't so lucky. A man sitting two desks in front of me had a glass shard impaled straight in the neck. A woman had several hit her across her cheek. And the rain of sharp blades continued to come.

"The hallway!" the woman beside me shouted. "We can scoot the desks and use them for cover!!"

I nodded and slowly pushed my desk that was acting as a shield as the rest of the ceiling seemed to rumble and shake and the broken glass was now being replaced by more dangerous burning chemicals.

Those that weren't under their desks were given second-degree burns as we all shouted for them to take cover and then move.

The hallway felt like it was a lifetime away. I pushed the desk slowly, doing my best to try and time the pattern of the falling chemicals and glass. My hands were already burnt from the hot toxins and my shins were bleeding.

I just need to get out of here, I resolved as I pushed toward the door. Some of the others were fighting for the door, trying to shove through and pull their desks along. I knew there would be no way we could escape as long as we were shackled down.

Then I looked up at the burning acid and had a horrible realization.

"We need to let the chemicals burn through these cuffs," I told the girl. I held my arm at a specific angle and then scooted my desk toward the proper position.

I bit my tongue and held in a scream as the torturous acid hit my skin and the metal at the same time. It only took ten seconds for me to be free.

And at the same time I ran through the door, urging the others to do the same.

The girl managed to pull through with only minor burns and three others. Then we heard a strange clang and realized that the class door was sealed shut.

The ones that didn't make it out were now slamming their hands against the door trying to wriggle the knob, but it was pointless.

Next, we watched as the vents reversed flow and sucked the other people in the class toward the ceiling. It was like watching a real twister take up houses. All of them slammed against the roof of the classroom as we watched from the safety of the hallway.

And just like that, the nightmarish event seemed over, and I was standing in the hallway looking down at my burnt, shaking hands.

The other survivors were turning their attention to our new location, a long tile hallway that seemed to connect to at least a dozen other classrooms just like ours. And much like us, others had escaped hellish classrooms at the last minute and were trying their best to cope and recover in the hall.

We all shared the same beaten and confused expression. None of us sure where we were or how we got here.

"Attention class of 2021, please make your way to the main auditorium for a word from our principal," a voice said over the intercom.

Then the lights in the hallway came on fully to illuminate the path toward the right.

I looked to the others for ideas, uncertain what we should do.

There was an emergency exit nearby, but it didn't take one guess to assume it was sealed shut. So instead, all of us shuffled our feet down the hallway, following the guiding light to our next torture chamber.

We soon arrived at what looked like a cafeteria with long tables all arranged with simple school breakfasts. Packaged donuts, boxed milk, fruit bowls. At least thirty meals were all lined up and ready for us as we entered the room.

A couple of survivors went to check the exits, none of which had any windows toward the outside while the rest of us settled and I decided to eat.

Surprisingly the food was delicious and fresh.

"Our captors must want us somewhat healthy," I said as I carefully opened the milk. My hands were still shaking.

Then I saw a shadow cross the back curtain of the stage that overlooked the cafeteria.

Immediately I jumped up and pointed. A few others saw it too.

"Who goes there?" one man shouted aloud.

The shadow paused. It looked unusually tall.

Then we heard this strange obnoxious laugh.

A second later, the curtain pushed back and revealed a costumed mascot, a large stuffed animal costume that resembled a walrus, with a goofy cartoon smile and enormous floppy arms.

From the center of the stage came a microphone that rose up toward the walrus's mouth.

"Well what a squeaky clean group you are! Welcome class of 2021! Welcome to Final School!" it announced happily. I couldn't tell for sure if the thing was a robot or a person in a suit.

"Today has been fun, but don't forget here at Final School, the fun can only last until the bell rings! And then it's time to learn, learn, learn!"

"Are you for real? What is this?" one man asked. He abruptly jumped toward the stage, ready to attack the mascot.

A moment later, two children pushed their way out from the curtain and stood in the way of his attack. It made the moment pause in confusion, and that was all it took. One kid whipped out what looked like a cattle prod and struck the man straight in his chest with it. He flew back hard to the tile floor, coughing and wheezing. Then a few other children appeared alongside the mascot. All of them wore generic uniforms, and all of them looked like they were emotionally disconnected to whatever the hell was going on.

"Remember to play nice," the walrus chuckled.

Just as he finished talking, we heard a buzz and the doors to the cafeteria unsealed themselves.

"Recess!!" the kids all squealed as they ran back behind the curtains out of sight.

All of us that had survived the initial insanity gave each other a long stare. Then we bolted for the doors.

I could see sunlight. I was ready to taste fresh air.

But it was a mirage.

The moment we stepped out to the playground, I suddenly realized I wasn't looking at the sky at all. It was some strange reflective surface that covered the entire surrounding area.

"It's like we are trapped in a giant fishbowl," one man realized. I got a good look at the playground. There was plenty of equipment, all of which seemed to be in good working order. And a long, tall fence with barbwire that surrounded us on all sides.

Just as the last survivor came out, the cafeteria doors slammed shut.

"No entry until the bell rings," a sign said on the doors as we looked around and tried to get our bearings.

"This has gotta be some kind of crazy dream. What is this? Lord of the Flies?" a woman asked as she approached a tall juniper tree that was growing near the center of the playground.

There were names carved on it. Hundreds of them. And tally marks. Counting the days stuck in here, I realized as I saw that they covered the entire base of the tree.

Then we heard a strange whirring noise, and we watched as some of the equipment seemed to move on its own as if someone was using it.

"Something tells me this is going to be worse than before," the first man said as the ground below us started to shift from grass to sand.

One man was standing there watching as it did and then realizing he was sinking even as I climbed onto a jungle gym.

"It's quicksand!!" I shouted to the others.

Everyone frantically ran as the sand started to swallow people whole. Half of us made it to the different pieces of equipment, using them as lifelines until the strange sand disappeared.

Then we heard a bell from the cafeteria ring and saw the children standing and beckoning us back inside.

I cautiously touched the ground, looking at all of the different splotches of blood that were trailing the grounds, and swallowed my breath.

Something told me there would not be any graduating ceremony anytime soon.

***

We are lined up on a brick wall with bleachers facing opposite of us in what looks like an old school gymnasium. This entire place has been built to resemble the types of places we went to as children, but I know it can't be the same thing, considering all of the insane shit we have endured thus far. There are still plenty of us alive, but from the moment we stepped into the gym, I realized that probably wouldn't last long.

The children that seemingly were in charge of this place lined up on either side of the squeaky-clean tile floor. All of them are holding a bright and shiny red leather ball. I know immediately what we are going to play, even as one boy steps up to the middle and holds the ball up.

"P.E. will include dodgeball, jump rope, and then a physical fitness class. Remember to do your best."

I'm so sore from the other incidents that I wonder if I will even have the ability to make it through these unscathed, but I know I don't have a choice.

"We work together, we can make it out of here," the petite girl next to me said as a whistle was blown.

A second later, the spheres the children were holding changed from harmless ordinary dodgeballs to spiky, dangerous urchin type objects. I knew one hit from those sharp protrusions would likely kill us if it struck a vital organ.

Immediately the children began to hurl the dense weapons toward us, the heavy balls surprisingly bouncing and moving across the gym floor with ease. We had little chance to do much else besides run.

"Toward the bleachers!" one man shouted excitedly. A woman beside him was struck in the head with the spiky object, the full force of the needles piercing her face and knocking her down.

As soon as it did, I also noticed that the needles seemed to latch on to her cheek, preventing her from being able to remove it.

A moment later, as we ran, I realized why that was. We heard this soft rhythmic beeping noise coming from the dodgeball. It got faster and faster as I understood it was counting down. Then the latched weapon exploded directly on the woman's face, killing her instantly.

A man to the right of us was a little luckier. If you consider the loss of a limb better than dying; and his right leg was blown up from the force of another object.

As he hobbled and crawled toward the bleachers, he begged the children to stop their onslaught. They all looked at him with emotionless eyes and then raised their weapons, smashing it down on his pleading body.

We turned away before the explosion caused his innards to scatter across the gym.

"This is madness," a woman snarled as she rushed toward one of the children. I watched as the dodgeball struck her straight into the chest, but she kept running, tackling one of the children.

To my horror, the bomb went off, killing them both. Then a sharp alarm noise came overhead, and all of the children stopped what they were doing.

A moment later, the mascot entered, the ridiculous costumed creature waddling over to where the kid had died and examining the scene. It occurred to me that the children seemed to be in awe of the mascot, as though awaiting its orders.

Was it the one that was really in control here?

"Looks like all of you will be getting detention," it said in that same null voice. Was it even human?

"Enough of this! Who is in charge here?" one man snapped. He stepped toward the walrus boldly and I fully expected to see that the children might attack again.

Instead, the stuffed walrus held up a flipper and kept them at bay, remarking, "All class members who make it to the end of the day will be hearing an important message from the principal at our awards ceremony!"

"I think this thing is just a fucking robot," the girl commented.

I realized that I felt silly for not even thinking of that a moment ago and watched as the walrus left with the remains of the child, perhaps to go be cremated somewhere.

Whoever was running the show clearly cared a little about the kids that were here. But why none of them seemed to be remotely acting like regular children was beyond me.

And before I really had a chance to even ponder it, the main kid in charge announced we were beginning the next activity.

"Please choose a partner for jump rope," the children ordered.

I looked toward the girl, figuring that with her slim figure, it was a safe bet she could make it through to the next game.

"I'm John, by the way," I offered my hand out to her.

"What does it matter? We are probably going to die in here anyway," she said as she refused my friendship but added, "I'm only gonna partner with you to make sure I make it to the next activity alive."

The others that were still alive did the same and then we were placed in the center of the floor and the children brought out normal looking rope that they extended between our feet.

As an added challenge, they next bound our feet with chains and one older girl in the group commented, "We want you to act as a team."

As they came up to me, I got a good look at the boy that was chaining me down and saw that he had a tattoo on his ankle. "What's your name?" I whispered to him.

"Those sort of things don't matter here," he answered back. I tried to look for some spark of humanity left him and wondered briefly if any of these kids were even real either. Was the entire facility run by life like drones?

The whistle pierced the air a second later, and the rope began to move. Quickly my partner and I jumped, and I matched her rhythm, worried about what would happen if we missed.

A moment later, the rope caught on fire, the burning heat making me begin to sweat as the kids strategically made their rope move faster at a steady pace.

The girl and I did good for a short minute, but then as they began to speed up, the flames would hit our ankles almost every jump. It made me want to cripple over in pain.

Two women behind us both tripped from the rope and were burnt badly and fell down on the floor, begging the children to stop.

"Where are your parents? Why are you doing this??"

Thankfully it seemed as though death was not their immediate fate as the children moved on to other participants and started to perform double Dutch with their other members. Making it twice as hard to avoid the flaming rope as they sped up.

I could hardly keep going even after two minutes and the heat seemed to get even more intense.

Finally, after about half of our group was hit by the blazing weapon, they moved on to the next activity.

All of the remaining adults that hadn't been burnt were told to wait in the locker room for further instructions.

As we were huddled inside the tight space and the doors were locked, I realized that this was the first time since the playground we were all alone.

"If anyone has any ideas on how to get out of here, it's appreciated," the girl commented as she rubbed her sore ankles. I was in so much pain my entire body felt numb. I had no idea if that was a blessing or a curse, to be honest.

"That weird mascot mentioned an award ceremony later. Probably back at the cafeteria. But I think I saw a main office near the front of the building. I bet you anything there is a control room up there. Someone must be in charge telling these children what to do," a man said.

"And how do you suggest we get there? Seems every move we make is monitored," I asked.

"We will work together, just like I said. These are just kids. They can't stop us if we use force," the girl offered.

A woman next to her shuffled her feet uncomfortably. "I don't know if I can justify harming children. It's likely they have been brainwashed to obey. We shouldn't be hurting them even if they are doing this to us…" she admitted.

I felt the same, but didn't say a word. It was clear the majority was ready for this nightmare to end.

"If we can get the people in charge to end this idiocy, maybe it will save the kids, too. The needs of the many will he accomplished by just a few," the man argued.

"You're just speculating. We don't even know if any of this will work," another said. Soon the locker room burst into an argument.

The doors slammed open a second later and one of the older children gave us a glare.

"The physical fitness test will now begin," she announced, leading us back to the gym.

All of the adults that had suffered from burn injuries were gone and now in the middle of the floor I saw that, well, the actual tile was missing. I even rubbed my eyes to be sure I wasn't imagining things. It was in fact cut off by what looked like a bottomless hole. A chasm that cut through the whole area.

I tried to look down and see if there was anything below, but it seemed to stretch for miles. Perhaps into some furnace below. And dangling over the pit was a rope, which seemed to be covered with oil to make the climb even more difficult. Did the children even understand they were literally making us risk our lives?

I was placed in the front of the line and waited as the bell rang. The rope was only a few feet in front of me, but I still had to make a running start for it.

Leaping out above the pit, I gripped onto the slippery rope and quickly started to climb. Even with the oily surface, it was still possible for me to ascend, but not easily. I could hear the others actually cheering me on as I tried to not look down.

But just when I thought that I might make it, the game changed and something above me fell through the roof vents. Needles. Sharp pointed ends struck my head and against my hands as I clung to the rope and shivered in pain. It wouldn't be long before I lost my grip entirely.

My only chance was to try and swing back toward the edge.

I started to shift my body weight as I slid down the rope, my hands sweaty and the onslaught of falling needles making my nerves begin to stress and ache.

Just as I made the third swing I let go, barely grabbing the edge.

The others rushed to help, but the children blocked them. If I was going to survive, it would have to be on my own. Desperately I clawed my way up the side, gasping for breath as I collapsed to the ground and looked down at the pit.

"This is insane. I can barely even stand up from this torture," I moaned as I looked at my shaking palms. The needles had hurt more than I realized.

The children looked at me and then the oldest one in charge ordered, "Take him to the nurse."

Before I knew what was happening, I was escorted out of the gym by several larger kids. Toward the office that the one man had speculated we might be able to use as an escape.

A bag was placed over my head before they marched me down the hall, shoving me rudely as they moved forward.

Eventually, I was placed in a chair and my hands were bound with a zip tie. Then the bag was removed, and I found myself staring at another adult.

Someone that was running this hellish drama.

She gave me a fiendish smirk and said, "Looks like you thought you were going home early."

The nurse administered some kind of shot directly into my bloodstream without even bothering to tell me what it was for.

As I watched the needle press into my body, I was sure that I was about to die. Instead of a quick death like the other adults here, it would be slow and torturous, and this strange woman would revel in my suffering.

Immediately I started to sweat and feel faint, my lips clammy as I begged her to stop. The entire room felt dizzy and then at last, she tossed the needle aside into a sharps container and commented, "My, you certainly are a squealer, aren't you?"

I was panting, hardly able to see or speak coherently, but it didn't matter. She was going to make me listen to her strange ramblings.

"You have been brought here for a reason student 6091, and that is to prove yourself worthy of readmission to society. Given your skills so far in our school activities, you stand a high probability of being able to graduate from our program," she commented as she pulled a file from a nearby metallic cabinet and read off my life as though I had died long ago.

"John Reders, age 32, a single father living in the suburbs of Chicago. You have two children, David and Susannah, ages 8 and 4 respectively. You work as an auto mechanic and enjoy chess matches and hiking in your spare time," she commented as she slid the profile across to me.

"Does all of this sound accurate?"

Despite how parched I was, I managed to give her a whispered reply. "I have no idea what you want, but once I get out of these bonds, I swear I will kill you, bitch."

She leaned over toward me, smiling coyly before smacking me across the face with her gloved hand.

"You will learn that we do not tolerate insubordination in this facility of any kind. Do I need to remind you why you are here?" She snapped.

She turned the folder over to the next page, which showed photographs of me having drinks with friends, spending time at work at long hours and not coming home to be with my family. Things I had felt guilty for over the past six months, bad habits I was struggling to cope with.

And here they were on display as crimes, my sins that had landed me in this hell.

"You are fortunate that the charges aren't more severe, or we wouldn't even be having this conversation. You have forsaken your family, Mister Reders. You have fallen into a lifestyle of pleasure rather than responsibility. As a result, you squander what money you earn, and your children starve. You are a poor excuse for a father and therefore unfit to return to being a parent until you are taught a proper education."

I didn't fully comprehend what she was saying, but I gathered that this prison was a place for people like me to be rehabilitated, under whatever strict guidelines they enforced. A second chance, according to their standards, to be a better person. And if we failed to be strong enough, then a deadly fate awaited us.

I knew her logic about health and recovery and being a good parent didn't line up with the atrocities that I had seen here so far, but I was too frightened to correct her.

"When is this graduation ceremony?" I asked.

"Tonight, after the final period. We will gather our students together in the band hall for a celebration and announce the graduates. But to make it there, I needed to make sure you were on equal footing with the others. Hence the need for your vaccination," she commented.

I looked toward the needle, wondering what exactly she had dosed me with as a bell rung and the nurse stood up, pleasantly smiling.

"Enjoy the rest of your school day, Mister Reders. I hope to see you again tonight. I think if you apply yourself to your education, you will go far," she said.

I was marched by children back down the hall, confused and disoriented even without a bag over my head as we passed by what looked like class photographs of previous grads.

As I paused to look at the numerous alumni, it occurred to me this secretive program had been running for quite some time undetected. Who could be handling all of the finances and how did they even find people to be candidates for their experimental prison?

Another sobering fact was evident about the photographs. Less than half a dozen persons were in each picture, the rest of the seats empty.

Meaning the chance of survival here was slim, perhaps nigh impossible.

Still, I had to think of my own two children and fight to survive as long as I could. Even if it did mean against the others, I thought as I was escorted into an art studio.

There were perhaps only nine of us left, and as soon as I entered the classroom, each of them viewed me with new suspicion. It's easy to guess why. I had been given special privileges to not go through with the remainder of the fitness test, and that must mean they think I'm involved in whatever is going on, I thought as the children ordered me to take a seat near one of the easels.

Our teacher, the strange emotionless costumed walrus, immediately gave us instructions on the assignment.

"Each of you is filled with inspiration. Aspiring dreams that are waiting to burst forth. Here we get the chance to express ourselves and show our achievements on the canvas," he explained as the children locked the doors.

Whatever was about to happen, I knew good and well it was not going to be as pleasant as he claimed.

"Under your desk, you will find the tools you need to create a masterpiece. Something that truly speaks to us and helps us to see what type of artist and person you really are," the mascot said.

All of us reached down to take a small black bag from the underside of the desk, unzipping it to reveal razor blades and other sharp objects that typically people would use for self-harm and the costumed mascot explained.

"You have thirty minutes to put your sweat, tears and especially your blood into your work. Those that put in the most effort will get to move forward to the next class. So, try your hardest and work for a better grade than your classmates!"

Immediately a timer was started above his head and looked at the objects in horror, realizing that he expected us to actually cut into our flesh and let our own blood act as paint for the project.

The others hesitated and started to use the razors on their skin, wincing and shrieking in pain as their blood dribbled onto the paper.

One woman had a different type of masterpiece in mind though and immediately lashed out toward one of the other adults with the sharp weapons, stabbing them to the ground.

Surprisingly the costumed mascot did nothing to stop it and after she killed her art partner, the woman announced, "I found out that she'd been sleeping with my husband. So this is my artist's depiction of what I want to do to him."

She spit on the bleeding corpse even as the mascot nodded and announced, "You get a 90! Head for the music room and enjoy your extra recess!"

She dropped the weapon and stepped over the body, leaving the rest of us confused and befuddled but also no less suspicious of each other.

"What about you John. What did you do?" the petite woman I had talked to earlier asked as she held the blade safely in between her knuckles. I couldn't tell if she intended to harm me or the others as well. None of us could be certain what the others were capable of.

As I looked down at the bloody mess, though, I began to dizzy and stumbled across the room to vomit.

It must be the side effects of whatever the nurse gave me, designed to make me incapable of completing this task, I realized as I vomited in the trash can several times and felt the room begin to spin.

One man tried to approach to help, but I pushed him away, uncertain if those in charge would view it as cheating.

I needed to act fast, and the only thing I could think of was to use the blade against myself and threaten to hurt myself.

"If this is really supposed to be about rehabilitation, then let the rest live! Let us get out of here," I demanded.

The children actually seemed to show emotion for a split second as I held the knife against my wrist where I knew the most blood could be spilled. It was a bluff, but I needed to see if my guess was right about this demented facility. Would they allow me to survive simply because of their twisted moral code?

"That will be enough!" the mascot bellowed, motioning for everyone in the class to stop. He went from desk to desk to look at the artwork, supposedly grading each and everyone of us as though it really mattered. It felt like our survival was going to be the toss of the dice.

Myself, the petite woman and two others were told we could head to the music hall. I knew that meant the others would be executed and as the knife was wrestled from my hand, I considered trying to stand up for them.

I have to be able to make it back to my own family, I kept reminding myself as I felt the strange vaccine the nurse had given me start to take effect. If I don't push forward, it will all be for nothing.

Somehow, I got the impression the others that were told to leave had the same guilty conscience and we all reluctantly were led away even as the art studio doors closed, and we heard the ones left behind beg for their lives.

A roar of gunfire and paintballs filled the air, and we heard their screams grow higher, almost to a crescendo, until at last, everything became silent.

Then paint and blood mixed together drained from under the door, a sickening feeling in the bottom of my stomach as I realized that the four of us were the only ones still standing for this final round.

We were taken to a music hall where the children told us to pick out an instrument and I found myself hardly able to stand up from another bout of nausea.

Then, as I finally reached the flute stand near the middle of the class, I saw the playbook was opened to a song that told me my suspicion was right. We were nearly at the end of this mad game.

They were going to force us to play the ceremonial orchestra followed by a funeral procession theme.

Slow, soothing music began to play as all of us took our seats and watched the children line up against the wall. Despite the pretense that everything was fine, I knew good and well that only a few of us would survive this final test.

I didn't know the people alongside me in this class, but I still couldn't believe that all of them might be dead in a few minutes.

As the music got a little faster, the children ordered us to start playing, and we all did our best to keep up.

I have never even had talent for music, but I tried my hardest to appease them even as I felt the room beginning to move. Everything was suddenly shifting around as we kept playing, the room rotating as we saw behind the walls a row of strange small holes that had sharp spikes poking straight out.

I knew that if we stayed where we sitting at the moment, we would be impaled in only a matter of seconds so immediately I tried to stand.

Only for something to shock me and cause me to collapse back in my seat.

"The performance mustn't stop!" a child said as the room kept rotating. We all reluctantly played and as we did, I noticed that the room began to move the other way. Someone was actually getting the music right.

"Keep playing correctly!" I shouted to the woman. She had a trombone, and I could tell that she was exhausted, but we couldn't afford any mistakes.

One man was about to be hit by the deadly darts and tried to flee, only for the agonizing shock to cripple him and cause him to flail backwards towards the weapon. He screamed in pain as the spikes pierced him, but didn't kill. We kept playing to the end of the song to keep the rest of us alive.

As the chorus came to an end, the room stopped moving, and the children cheered. Some even suggested an encore. I could tell that the woman who had kept us alive those few minutes wouldn't have the strength to play again, and thankfully the encore was not required.

To my surprise, as we were moved from the band hall toward the mess hall, I saw the nurse that had tried to kill me was waiting for us with what looked like awards.

Since there were only three of us left, I was hoping this meant all of us would get the chance to make it out here, but I noticed that she only was carrying two awards.

One of us would be put to the test a final time, I realized as we were told to stand at the center of the stage.

"All of you have managed to come so far in this program, and we can't thank you enough for all of your hard work to reach the top of your class," the nurse announced.

As she was talking, I saw that the auditorium was filling up with children. I was surprised to see that there were so many of them. At first it was just a dozen, then I realized that there were hundreds of them.

Did they all live here in this underground hell? How did they survive?

"Before we pass out the awards, I think it's time for a quick snack for all of you," the nurse said as the doors at the back of the cafeteria opened, and I saw more adults rolling in carts. I held my nose as the stench of rotting meat overpowered me and I saw that they were actually being fed the corpses of all the other adults that hadn't made it this far.

The children didn't even wait for a serving bell. They growled and snapped at one another to grab a piece of the chopped-up bodies and chew it as fast as they could. I felt like I was about to throw up again by watching the cannibalistic display.

Now I knew what these children were being turned into. Monsters.

I didn't care to have any other questions answered, too sickened by the realization that if we had lost, we would be in that meal as well.

To my surprise, the petite woman that had been here since the beginning reached for my hand, her eyes filled with tears as we listened to the children eat the flesh of our competition.

"My name is Sam, by the way," she whispered as her lips trembled and the children finished the last bits of meat.

For but a moment there was a connection between us, a mutual understanding that we didn't deserve this treatment despite whatever issues we had in our real life. Nothing could even come close to this level of hell.

And then the nurse got out a raffle ball and started to spin it, the numbers clattering around as the hungry killer children waited to hear who would be crowned the champion.

I didn't have to guess what would happen to the loser.

"Our graduate in this class is none other than John Redars! Step up here, John!" she announced.

Immediately the children moved toward Sam and to the others, ready to pull down and eat them alive.

I tried my best to hold on to her for as long as I could, her screaming and kicking the entire time.

"You will forget about this place soon enough, John. I knew you would make it. Come, as we get you ready to leave, there is one final thing I need to show you," the nurse ordered.

I tried to keep from looking as the children trampled and attacked my friends. I was so traumatized by the event I found myself shaking as I moved toward the back hallway.

"I'm sure by now you recognize that this entire process was orchestrated to make you a better person. But we couldn't have done this without people that were in predicaments just like yours. Down on their luck, angry with loved ones. Scorned. We want to offer you the chance to be able to recommend a future student to us," she said, passing me a small pamphlet.

"You mean someone to send here to die," I realized.

"If they can survive our tests, they will be fine," she commented softly.

She soon led me to what looked like an old elevator that had a key code to prevent anyone from entering and as she got me ready to leave, she added, "Just think over all that you have learned here end I'm you will see the benefits to our program."

Then she injected me with another dosage, a strong sedative this time; and pushed me into the elevator. I couldn't even open my mouth to scream as the doors slammed shut, and I found myself getting dizzy.

The last thing I remember was the elevator rising toward the surface.

***

When I did wake up, I was in the middle of a heavily wooded area. It felt surreal to imagine that everything I experienced was real. The pamphlet the nurse had given me was more than enough proof. In addition, the wound on my wrist was all stitched up.

I walked for about a mile to the road and from there I hitchhiked.

"Where to?" A passing motorist asked.

They actually looked a bit nervous to help me and it was then I realized I still had the clothes from the prison underground. I probably looked like an escaped convict.

I told them to take me to the nearest police station.I told them my story from start to finish. I showed them the wound on my wrist. I also insisted that they could check my clothes for fingerprints and gave them my pamphlet.

There was nothing that matched any known criminals in their database.

It suddenly occurred to me this was likely why they had trained the children to be their foot soldiers. None of them would be traced. And likely all of them had been kidnapped at infancy.

I thanked the officers for their time and managed to get a ride home from one of them.

I was desperate to see my children again. Once I got home, I made a promise to them that I would be a better father. I can only hope that time will erase some of my awful memories of school.

REMEMBER TO SPAY OR NEUTER YOUR ANIMALS

I'm not here to be your friend. What I do is really fucked up.

But I'm not the villain here.

Every Christmas or birthday I see the same thing happen. People get dogs that they think they're ready for their kids to train and then it winds up being too much responsibility. Or the kid changed his mind at the last second and now wants a turtle instead.

Suddenly the dog is a burden.

When they bring the pups here to our shelter, the goal is to get them rehomed.

But we don't live in a world caked with butterflies and rainbows. There's a harsh reality that most people don't think about, and that's because we all tell ourselves we are good people.

Over half of the dogs we take in never get a good home. We try to keep them as long as we can, but honestly supplies are limited. Our budget is even more so. Typically, a dog or cat can stay with us for about four days and then we have no other choice but to put them down.

There is nothing worse than having to euthanize animals that just wanted to get a good home, but given the local population of strays is already overwhelming a lot of neighborhoods, we don't really have a choice.

I'm not a bad person for trying my damnedest to give these animals a second chance and this is why I often encourage people to spay or neuter as soon as possible. Anything we can do to curb the population is better than this active euthanizing. It feels like we are hunting and killing these innocent creatures.

And if you think that what we are doing is harmless, then my recent nightmare could make you see things differently.

I came into work to my shift after Christmas just like always, a fresh box of pups at our door with a hastily scribbled message on the side of the cardboard. "FREE TO GOOD HOME"

Of course, this was expected. Many people assumed that we would just post the dogs on Facebook or Instagram and get them rehomed before the day was done. Sometimes they view us as a charity, not bothering to even give us a return address. Part of that is likely due to shame for just dumping the dogs at our doorstep.

Either way, these four pups look healthy and robust, larger than normal huskies if I had to guess. I'm not an expert on those things. It looked like they had brought in a whole family because two of the dogs were larger than the others. I called out to my coworker to help get them inside to the cates. These animals looked scared and frightened, confused about what was happening.

Because of this and their sheer size, I kept my distance as best as I could until we could get them to a holding area. I can't tell you how many times I've been injured simply because of putting my hand in the wrong spot.

And these dogs definitely looked like they could put a hole in my hand.

Stanley, one of the other few sad saps that agreed to work after Christmas, helped me as best as he could as the dogs yelped and snapped at us.

"Blimey, these mutts are heavy! How in the world could they have just gotten them?" he asked as we finally got inside, and I grabbed one of the rope leads to get the larger male into a cage.

"I haven't the foggiest, but man, these dogs are full, like they just ate a full-grown person!" I said as I lugged the large male into his pen.

The others were placed in a separate pen each, and it seemed like the large female was the most aggressive. Likely a protective instinct for her pups. Thankfully none of them lashed out against me or Stan.

Once we had them separated, I took a breather and got a better look at the larger huskies. They looked more like wolves, to be honest. And the hair on the back of the female was starting to bristle. She was not too happy being separated from her pups.

"Let's get them some food and water," I suggested.

Once we were away from the dogs, my phone buzzed. It was my supervisor, Brent Easton. Brent had been getting on to us lately about the census and keeping our kennel at low population. Big surprise right after Christmas. He was singing the same song and dance.

"Listen Lance, I like you. I know you love those animals, otherwise you wouldn't be in this line of work. But I just got the New Years budget and they've cut us down thirty percent from last year. That means we aren't going to be able to play nice anymore," he told me as I followed Stan to the pantry.

"Are you kidding me? You can't be serious? We need to educate our community about this crisis. Killing more animals isn't the solution!" I argued.

"You think I don't know that? But this is all a numbers game and honestly, we have bigger problems to deal with than the shelter. The only way we are going to keep the place afloat is by doing what needs to be done. Besides, you know as well as I do these animals wouldn't survive on the streets, anyway. This is a mercy," Brent told me.

I reluctantly agreed and hung up, getting a big bowl for the dogs and heading back to the kennel. It made me hate myself to even admit that I knew he was right. We simply didn't have the supplies available to be able to make a difference. It was a sobering thought as I slid the bowl of food toward the pups. But despite how they had seemed hungry, both were now resting in the corner. Or at least pretending to.

For some reason as I offered them water, it felt like their eyes were on me.

Something about these dogs unnerved me.

I sat back and decided the next step was registering them into the system, otherwise it would do no good to even keep them here. And as I did, Stan rushed in with his phone against his ear, looking a little panicked.

"One of my kids fell off the trampoline I just bought them for Christmas! I have to go!" he announced.

I wished him well and told him a few fleeting words as I got back to work.

A few hours passed, and I got some other paperwork done, the dogs continuing to rest and watch me. Occasionally the larger ones would get up and test the strength of the kennel gate, snarling angrily as I offered them food again.

It was clear by now they were starving, yet they still refused to eat.

Something was off.

And then, just as I was about to head to the restroom to take a leak; something extraordinary happened.

The large female was pacing, panting and banging her body against the cage, circling the tiny kennel over and over. Then it began to spasm, uncontrollably shaking and hitting the pen as it began to howl loudly.

Every hair on the back of my neck stood up as the male joined in her howl.

The female kept convulsing, collapsing onto the floor of the shelter even as it began to spit up some white and yellow mucus.

Before long, I saw hair begin to shed off at an alarming rate and the howls were replaced with the sharp breaking of bones. The hound's body was beginning to change.

Its hind legs were straightening, and it's robust chest sounded like it was cracking and shifting to a small size.

Next, its snout and face drastically transformed. The long, haunched look of the wolf now resembled that of a starved older woman.

A human being with wild and scared eyes staring up at me.

"Holy shit!" I shrieked as I stumbled backward and realized the woman was almost completely naked.

What the hell had I just witnessed.

I kept my distance from the cage as I looked toward the others, watching as they began to transform as well. First, the male wolf shook and spat out strange mucus from his nostrils and mouth, his teeth cracking and his jaw breaking as it reformed into a familiar human face.

The two younger pups were the same. Their transformation seemed a little less violent, but in less than five minutes, I had seen all four of them metamorphosing into actual human beings. It was uncanny.

And yet they still seemed to have animalistic habits, snarling like the wolves they had just been and keeping their distance from me.

Immediately I offered my jacket to the woman to let her cover herself as the boys hunched in the corner. She was wrapping her arms around her body and insisting the focus be on her boys.

"If you have a hot meal? Or warm tea? Anything that is high in protein," she explained.

I was still taken aback by all of this and had a thousand questions, but I complied with her wishes and warmed up some toaster strudels for them.

As I gave the children their food, I watched both of them in stunned fascination as they lapped it up like animals. They were having a hard time reverting to normal human tendencies, I realized.

"How long… have you been…" I said stuttering as their animalistic behavior bothered me.

"Shapeshifters? Werewolves? Or just monsters in general?" the man said as he leaned against the bars.

"We don't remember. Each time we change, we lose a little more memory of our lives as humans. Eventually… we stop changing back all together," he muttered. He looked like he wanted to snap me in two simply for looking at his wife for even a fraction of a second.

"And you can't… control the change?" I asked.

"If we could, do you think we would spend our lives pissing on trees and eating skunk?" the man snapped.

"He simply means to help," the wife offered. Her children were becoming upset at the raised voice of their father. My attention focused on them.

"Let me get you some clothes. We have a donation center in the back of the building. These kids shouldn't be having to eat on the floor and be naked."

Surprisingly, the man seemed offended by this offer.

"You think that offering us some simple trousers and cleaning us up makes us like you? We will never be human again. The clothes you offer will simply be ripped to shreds the next time we change. And it's doubtful we will even remember the experience. This is our life now," he said.

The wife nodded solemnly. Then I watched as the family began to howl in unison. It was an eerie and ominous feeling.

But I wasn't simply going to brush aside accepting their curse as being fate.

I told them I had to go make a few phone calls after the family refused to leave the cages.

"If we get out and hurt people… I'm not so sure I could forgive myself for hurting others. Especially if we can't control it. Innocent blood shouldn't be shed," the wife explained.

To be honest, I didn't really know who to call or how to explain it, so even after making a few calls to nearby science institutions and such, I realized I was still at square one. I guess I shouldn't have expected anyone to believe this. Who would?

So I lied, and I called my boss and told him I had a bunch of very unique dogs that I needed help with. To hold them down so that I could euthanize them.

It was an awful lie. But I hoped that if someone else saw this family, it would make a difference. And I couldn't exactly just sit around and wait for them to change again. My shift would end soon, and I didn't want the next person coming in to just do the deed without being aware of what these people are. There was no telling when they might change.

My boss said he would get there as quick as He could, especially since Stan had unexpectedly left. But it wasn't fast enough.

The family began to revert back to their dog forms about a half hour after I made the call.

"No! You can't do this! I have to show them that this is real!"

I whipped out my phone to try and videotape the transformation, but the father lashed out from the cage and swiped it from my hand, cracking my screen.

I wasn't sure if he intentionally prevented me, or it was the beastly instinct taking over. Once they were transformed, though, it seemed that the werewolves were far more vicious than before. Did it make them hungry going through the shapeshifting process?

Kevin showed up about ten minutes later.

"Are these the mutts?" he asked. He was clearly half drunk, probably from a Christmas party and I doubted he would listen to my explanation. But I had to try.

"There's been a misunderstanding. These aren't normal dogs," I started to explain as he got the supplies ready.

"Damn right they ain't. Look at how big they are! What are they been feeding these things?" Kevin asked.

"No you don't understand. These are like… actual mythical werewolves, boss," I stuttered.

Of course, he looked at me like I was crazy as he approached the first cage.

"You're shitting me, right?" he whispered as he rattled the door. The large female reared its back and her hair bristled again. She wasn't about to go down without a fight.

"Grab that rope," Kevin ordered.

I considered my options. If I complied, I knew it was likely this entire family would wind up dead at my hand. Even though I knew they likely didn't want to kill innocent people in their wolf form, surely it wasn't okay to murder them? I felt lost in a dilemma that I never anticipated. But my reaction was almost instantaneous.

"No. I can't. These animals can't be harmed," I said as I pulled him away from the cage.

Kevin gave me a disgusted and disappointed look.

"What the hell you been smoking? Do your damn job. We can't have large vicious dogs in here when we open it for adoptions next week," he snapped.

I tried to reason with him, but he had already opened the door to the mother's pen.

I grabbed his arm again as he prepped the syringe and, in the same instance, the female leapt forward and bit at his ankle. The male rushed toward him as well, pushing the metal grating down.

"Holy shit!!" he screamed as he dropped the needle. He managed to pierce the father, and the dog yelped, hunching back as the medicine took ahead.

I acted quickly and opened up the other cages where the two young pups were waiting. I stood there, paralyzed in fear that they might attack me too, as the wolves surrounded Kevin and nipped at his skin. Covering him with scratches as they barked. Then they went toward their dying father.

They seemed to ignore me entirely. Or perhaps they respected me for rescuing them? They were watching as the medicine made the large male werewolf fall asleep, his mouth foaming and his body convulsing. It looked like utter pain. Endless agony. I had never seen it happen like this before, but it reminded me of when people said they saw prisoners get lethal injections.

"Get the damn rope, Lance, before they get out!!" Kevin screamed.

Instead, I opened the door and let the dogs run free from the shelter. The mother werewolf gave me a look that I understood to mean thank you, and then she and her boys ran off.

Meanwhile, my boss nursed his wound and gave me an ugly look.

The male was slowly turning back into human. He looked at it in abject confusion and horror, still not comprehending what he was seeing. Or perhaps refusing to accept it. Instead, he focused on me.

"You are done here. Do you hear me??"

I didn't really care. I couldn't even imagine the horror of letting them die. And it occurred to me that I felt the same about all the other animals in the shelter, too. This cruel cycle had to stop. I wasn't sure how he was going to explain the dead body at the shelter, but I wasn't going to be part of this anymore.

Later that Sunday evening, I wrote up this account and pondered over everything I had discovered. It was terrifying to have my entire world shattered. In fact, I was honestly reconsidering if the whole situation had even happened. Was I simply projecting my own anger toward the way that our society was tossing aside animals?

The answer came late that night. A slam against my door. I peered through the keyhole and saw Kevin standing there with hardly any clothes on. He looked distraught, confused. And his eyes were bloodshot and wild.

"You have to help me, Lance! You were right about those animals!"

He looked like he had attacked something. Maybe another person.

Was he regretful over his treatment of the wolves? "What happened to the body?" I asked.

He didn't know I was testing his response, but his answer sickened me. "I had it disposed of. And I managed to hunt down and get rid of those others as well! We can't afford to have bad press. Not now! But this has to be stopped somehow, right? Please help me!" he pleaded as I saw him beginning to transform again.

I felt my body go numb as he told me that the others had been harmed. My efforts to rescue them were snuffed out. It made my entire soul feel hollow.

"Sure… I will help you," I said as I got a chain and led him by the neck into my house. I locked him in the bathroom as the transformation started to finish and blocked the door as best as I could.

Then I made a phone call.

"Animal control? I have a wild dog that got loose in my neighborhood. I've managed to lock it in my bathroom, so it doesn't harm anyone else. I think it's already hurt one person," I told the operator as I listened to the newly created werewolf slash at the door frantically.

"In my opinion I think it needs to be put down."

ONE CALL AWAY

I had just sat down for my ride home on the late charter bus when I felt something odd under my seat. It was like sitting on a lump, it wasn't too big, but it was definitely uncomfortable.

Instinctively I reached under to try and remove the object and my hand touched something familiar. The small size and glint of plastic told me it was a smart phone but not a brand I was familiar with.

Someone must have left it here by accident, I thought to myself.

Since I had a little time until my stop, I unzipped my backpack and took out my portable charger. As luck would have it, the plug fit and immediately the phone began to charge.

I watched it the way you might a kettle, waiting for it to boil. I don't know why. I didn't really expect to be able to unlock it, but part of me was hopeful there wasn't a passcode.

Five minutes later, it powered up and made a grinding noise like an old modem would. I grabbed it up and waited to see what secrets were within.

The screen was completely black, no background at all; and the time was definitely off as though it hadn't been updated in some time. Even the year was wrong.

How long had it been here?

There was no reception, and it didn't look like I could unlock it, so I just set it back down and focused on my own phone.

Then I heard the distinct sound of a text message notification.

Coming from the older phone…?

But that shouldn't have been possible, I thought as I picked it back up and saw in short succession there were dozens of messages. All from the same person, apparently.

Immediately I did my best to read them in rapid response.

>Where are you?

>Why aren't you responding?

>Is everything okay?

>Don't go through with it.

That message stuck out to me as I kept reading and scrolling toward the beginning of the story to try and figure out exactly what was going on.

>Hey, glad we could finally exchange numbers. Call me anytime! Alice.

>Thanks for actually responding. I was beginning to think that no one actually saw me these days. Calvin.

Alice and Calvin. These two sounded like lovers, and I was about to get all the juicy details of their relationship, I thought.

This must have been Calvin's phone. And he kept everything about Alice on here.

I saw that he had no other contacts in his phone, which was a little strange.

Next, I decided to check pictures.

There were several taken at strange angles, all on the same day of the same person.

It looked like he had taken the photographs on his phone right here on this bus.

Did he frequently travel this route too?

It felt strange to imagine sitting where someone else had and knowing exactly what it was they had been doing.

Instinctively I glanced up to see if maybe the woman in the pictures was on the bus today.

I'm not sure how freaked out I would have been if that had been the case, but I breathed a sigh of relief when I realized besides myself and a few other riders, the bus was empty. And none of them resembled the woman in the pictures.

As I scrolled back in time on his phone, I saw that he took at least a hundred pictures of her, maybe more. This was bordering on obsession.

And then I saw in his notes things that he said about how he felt about her.

Even before they actually exchanged numbers.

This is what the phone's notes said:

***

I saw a woman on the bus today. Something about her stood out as different than any other I have seen before.

Have you ever heard of soulmates? I guess I got a funny feeling when I saw her and I'm wondering if maybe it's that. She's very beautiful, so much so that I doubt she would want to be with anyone like me.

I know that you would say I should take a leap of faith, but look where that got me. What if she rejects me? Or worse, decides to not respond.

***

I paused there in the notes, wondering who it was that Calvin seemed to have faith in. There was scarce else to find on the phone. It was too old for there to be social media or anything like that and besides the myriad photos of the woman, the only thing I hadn't really checked was his call log.

Of course, the thought of it made me feel like I was already invading this stranger's privacy too much. But something about this conversation was intriguing. I needed to know what had happened.

I pulled up recent calls and saw that the same number had tried to call him over and over.

Then it finally hit me how long this phone had apparently been sitting here.

Six years. It seemed impossible. But what happened next was even more so.

The phone let out a ping again. A new message? How could that be?

I slowly reached for it.

UNKNOWN
Do you think you know me?
Again, I felt uneasy even reading the message, or daring to respond. It was a private number, so I figured that it was pointless to do so and I immediately put the phone down, trying to ignore the next message coming in.

Maybe you should keep reading. See what happened with Alice.

I went back to the text messages. My eyes nervously scanning the bus. Was Calvin on the bus watching me?

The notes continued:

I finally worked up the nerve to get her to notice me. We hit it off immediately! I'm so excited. We exchanged numbers. This is exactly the lucky break I have been looking for. At last patience has paid off.

The text messages also seemed to show a story of a despairing man that didn't get recognized for anything.

>Hey Calvin, are you doing okay? I wanted to invite you to drinks, but I wasn't sure if you had the time.

I appreciate it, Alice, but I really can't go. I have a lot of work to catch up on.

But his notes told a different story.

How I wish that I could have a life with her. The things we could do together. But that isn't how it's meant to be. She won't understand the things I have to do. You would understand, of course. You always knew what I was capable of.

What exactly was Calvin planning?

Another message chimed in from UNKNOWN.

Please tell me you have seen where this is headed. I can see the worry on your face. You think I hurt her.

This time, I decided to respond.

If you didn't hurt her, then why are all these text messages sound so obsessed with her? And the pictures? You were stalking this woman! And if I didn't know any better, I would think you are stalking me!

Don't be ridiculous. You are nothing like her. True, you will be just as interesting to follow and watch, but Alice was special. She really wanted to help me.

"What are you?" I dared to ask. I knew there was no way this old phone should have been working or providing messages without service. But the texts had already convinced me this was not an ordinary conversation. Something beyond the realm of my worldview that was now creeping to the forefront.

I went back to the text messages. The more I read, the more disturbed I was by Calvin.

>I'm worried about you, Calvin. I always see you sitting alone on this bus. If it wasn't for that phone, I would think you were dead.

>You don't need to worry. I'm fine. But I appreciate the concern. It's been a long time since anyone really worried about me.

>You promise me that you are okay?

>Of course. I will be fine now that you are with me.

>The only time I'm with you is when we travel on this bus together! Why don't you ever want to come with me?

>I told you before that I can't. Why don't you just leave it alone?

>I'm starting to think you are trapped on this bus.

>If that were true, my only concern would be to get out of here. I wouldn't be wasting my time getting to know you.

A few more days of messages like that scrolled by, Alice growing more concerned, and then an awful truth started to come to light.

>*Calvin, how long have you been searching for someone?*

>What do you mean?

>*I was doing some research on this bus... trying to figure out why you were so familiar. I realized I read your story when I was a little girl.*

>Alice, stop. Stop talking about this.

>*No. I need to know. Are you... are you dead?*

I froze, rereading the message. Maybe she had misunderstood? Then he gave a reply.

>Of course I am gone. That's why it's been so difficult to explain things to you. I don't want you frightened.

The moment I read the message, a mirror image of that same message popped on screen. Calvin was repeating what he said to Alice.

I don't want you frightened.

Too late for that. I was terrified because of the fact that I was now apparently texting a ghost.

What do you want from me? I asked.

The same thing I wanted from Alice. I needed her to leave this place. But she wouldn't listen to me. Maybe you will...

I took out my phone and quickly did a search history on this bus the same way Alice had.

Specifically, I was looking for tragic events surrounding this route.

It didn't take long to find one from only six years. The same time as the text messages.

>*Local woman jumps from a moving bus.*

>*Alice Fitzgerald; a local real estate agent has been found dead near the corner of Fourth and Pine. Witnesses claim they heard her talking to herself or to an unseen person she frequently told to leave*

her alone before she leapt from the bus to her death when it was moving at approximately 75 miles per hour.

I texted Calvin.

Did you make her jump?

Of course not! I didn't want that. But once she understood that I was going to try to be with her… she overreacted. You were going to be with her… you mean possessing her body.

There was a long pause, and I got a chill in the air.

The phone was how he found his victims. I understand that now. He left it here for a curious passerby like me to find.

I stood up and pulled for the cord that would make the bus stop. The phone pinged again.

You can't leave me here on this bus… I won't let you. I have been here too long!

I tossed the phone down and tried again to get the bus to stop. It only sped up.

I felt something overpower my body. I knew it had to be the spirit of Calvin trying to enter my very soul. We were coming up to a curb. If I timed it right, I could jump and survive.

I moved toward the front of the bus as it began to slow down to pick up passengers. Now was the chance to escape. I rushed to get off even as the spirit overwhelmed me and I fell down, slamming into the concrete.

But somehow, I made it, and I was free from this strange encounter.

I stood up and wiped blood from my lip as I turned to watch the bus roll off. The passengers had all acted like they couldn't see me, likely a side effect of this demonic influence.

But as it turned away, I saw Calvin's ghostly presence standing there, glaring at me. Somehow, I was lucky to survive.

I saw him pick up the old phone in his hand and then slide it under another seat. Waiting for another victim to be curious enough to find it.

REMINISCENCES OF AUCTURN

We were never even supposed to be here.

48 kilometers past the Arctic Circle, the lone helicopter neared its target.

According to the classified reports she'd been graciously given, the facility wasn't even supposed to exist.

Even from this angle, it wasn't much of a surprise to see that the majority of the structure was still covered in ice and debris from an explosion.

Meaning rescue would likely take days, if not weeks, without the right resources.

Even with that added bonus, the chances were slim.

What were the odds that the scientists and other personnel below would even survive hours with limited oxygen?

Beverley knew better than to voice her concerns, though. Her employers didn't pay her to ask questions.

Take samples, catalog the findings and eliminate all damaging evidence. That had been her mission statement for the past seven years.

The pilot landed the helicopter near to where her envoy was waiting and she gathered her belongings, preparing herself for the harsh cold beyond.

Not many dared to brave this pocket of the world, and most who did would likely be considered insane.

"Doctor Warren! Welcome to Site Levichion," the rescue team captain shouted over the noise of the copter as she climbed out.

"How much of the survey have you completed?" she asked, holding her mask over her face and following him into the bowels of the earth.

"My team has just finished placing the beacons, which will relay the radar image to us here. I wanted to wait for you to arrive before we performed the scan," he explained.

She gave him a very condescending look.

"There are men and women that are struggling to survive below, Captain. Next time don't wait for an audience when considering their lives."

A few short moments later, the beacons activated, and the monitor lit up with all kinds of data.

Thankfully despite the weather, the beacons were able to pick up the precise structure of the facility and the geothermal activity around it.

"Have you been able to determine what caused the collapse?" Beverley asked.

"Initial reports tell us it was some kind of explosion near the north observatory tower. I believe most of the astronomical equipment was being kept there as well, so it's likely the Ulthar telescope has been completely destroyed."

That saddened her to hear, even though it wasn't unexpected. The entire Levichion facility was purposed for all kinds of scientific research, but she had always had an affinity for the stars.

When the UN had provided the funding necessary to give the group state of the art astronomic equipment, she thought it would be the first step toward new discoveries in the solar system.

Now it was looking like only frustration and destruction had been meted out by these loner researchers.

"Do you believe it's possible that there might have been a spy among the team?" Bev asked as she checked the data herself.

She wasn't sure if the Captain had simply failed to mention it as a test of her own skills, but even a cursory look at the blast analysis told her that this sort of collapse had to be manmade.

Someone inside the facility had deliberately sealed them in.

"We have speculated about that, but I think it's best to leave that sort of theory behind until we can attempt to make contact with any survivors," he responded.

She gave him a curt nod and passed the tablet back before remarking, "Then let's begin immediately."

1900 hours

Point of entry was determined by the scans to be viable near to the western entrance of the site. A long series of chasms ran through the ice split apart by a wide sloshy river that plummeted into the depths of the Arctic. The only obstacle that currently prevented the team from entering was already being drilled into by the massive rescue vehicle. It's loud thundering on the wall enough to wake the dead.

"Fifteen meters left," Operational Supervisor Yuri Sarkomand announced as they paused the drill to let it cool down. Despite the freezing temperatures, they could only use it in short ten-minute intervals to avoid overheating the battery.

"How many physicians do you have on staff?" Beverley asked as she stood on a nearby observational platform and looked down another one of the deep pits. It was dizzying to imagine that these miners went into the ice at least three times a week for all kinds of material, everything from geological finds to fossil fuels.

"All of my team is trained in proper first aid and CPR, if that is what you mean…" the captain answered.

"I'm not one to give up on human life," she replied curtly.

She put her safety goggles back on and watched the drill finish its work, the raw dark hallways of the site becoming visible moments later as the ice sheet fell apart.

An hour later; they were moving in.

"Western sector was for residential, recreational centers. Looks like all of this is in good repair," one commented as they checked the first series of rooms.

"Or never used at all.

As they arrived at the next depthmeter mark, the Captain raised a hand for them to pause and remarked, "Oxygen will begin to grow thinner as we get further in. It would be advisable if we remain together and keep communication to a minimum. Remember we only have six hours of breathable air, so moving fast from area to area will be in our best interest."

"Were most of the survivors near the northern tower?" she asked.

"As far as we know, the Levichion site was running on a skeleton crew at the moment. Full operations were meant to begin this October, but I'm guessing that won't be happening now," he said.

Once the entire room was depressurized, all of the team entered a freight elevator and Computer Specialist Anthony Maxland began working on getting it restarted.

"There were seven generators. Only one of them is currently online. Rerouting power might take a little bit of time," Anthony explained.

"Work your magic," the Captain reassured him as he placed his assault rifle down.

Doing so gave her a moment to inquire about it.

"Did the UN authorize weapons in the event of a hostile takeover?" she whispered.

He gave her a short but discerning nod.

"It's pointless to not bring up the obvious. We have been circling around the subject ever since you arrived, Doctor. Clearly, someone on the team did not want their findings to come to light and took it upon themselves to sabotage this entire mission. We have no way of knowing if that person is still alive or not. Protecting ourselves is my top priority here."

"Shoot first, ask questions later, hmm?"

"I will attempt to remain peaceful toward all of them for as long as necessary," he said firmly.

She considered another query when the elevator jerked to life and the freight doors slammed shut. They were on the move to the northern tower.

"No turning back," Maxland teased as he grabbed his own weapon. He was doing his best to not seem nervous. None of them knew what to expect up ahead.

2200 hours

There was darkness, foreboding, and even the scent of death. It also looked foreign, strange architectural designs that shouldn't have been made for any human run oblong down the side of the walls. As though they had simply repurposed a far older ruin.

The moment the elevator came to a halt, they saw a few bodies frozen on the ground; likely exposed to the initial blast. At least their suffering was quick; she thought as she followed the rescue team down the eastern corridor.

Most of the rooms were completely collapsed, piles of rubble pushing into the main structure.

It was already beginning to look like there weren't going to be any living survivors.

Soon they reached one of the main data centers, a row of monitors flickering on and off from the last little bits of power that were flowing through, and Beverley noticed that several of the displays were showing what appeared to be satellite readings.

"Does anyone happen to know what they were working on before the event?" she asked out loud.

It was at that moment she realized she had wandered off from the group. The room was silent except for her and the echoes of her fingers clicking against the dusty keyboard.

A few failed passwords later, she was into what remained of their findings.

It looks like someone tried to wipe this memory; she realized as she worked to decorrupt the files.

Then abruptly the power came on entirely.

"Doctor Warren! In here. There's something you might want to see," a voice from the next room over called to her.

Soon she was awestruck at the impressive planetarium that was on display. It was clearly far more advanced than any technology she was familiar with. But it also looked old, perhaps even older than all of them combined.

There were planets and stars that she did not recognize, and the holographic readings only further confused her.

"Am I reading this correctly?" she asked. The Captain took a look as well.

"You might as well be asking me to translate Greek," he laughed back.

"It's weird that this room was not destroyed, right?"

"Everything above us has totally collapsed. Structural integrity is holding at about fifty-eight percent," a soldier added after finishing his scans.

"So far, we have found six bodies from the manifest. That leaves Commander George Arwan, Chief Astronomer Howard Curwen and Chief Physician Marginy Lang as unaccounted for. How much more of the facility do you think is still intact?" Yuri asked as he returned from the eastern conference room.

"Spread out and search, Doctor. I take it you wish to remain here to gather clues?" the Captain asked.

She gave him a nod, waving him off.

After several attempts to simulate a cycle for the system on the display, she watched as the holograms circled around the star in question until suddenly freezing in place. Glitching because the data went back no further.

And then she saw.

A bold and white orbiting planet that fell into place from beyond. It was no bigger than their own, beautiful and isolated all at once.

Speeding the simulation forward, her eyes watched as the little planet seemed to flourish with life, changing from pale white to a familiar bluish green.

"They called it Aucturn, the Living Planet," a voice said from the shadows.

"Who are you?" she whispered, her hands shaking as she realized this had to be a survivor.

Down here with no food for nearly a week, she could see blood coating his hands and mouth; evidence of cannibalism in his crazed look.

"Curwen. And you must be, Doctor Beverley Warren… from the University," he said with a smile. He sounded almost excited to realize who she was.

"You… know me?" she asked carefully.

"I know of you. And I recognize why you are here and welcome it. Surely you've seen by now why I took the steps necessary to seal us in this icy tomb?" Curwen said, taking a step closer.

"You do realize that you just confessed to several crimes?"

He flailed his head back and laughed madly before pointing at the holographic display.

"And what about them, Doctor? Are you also going to charge them with crimes?"

She pursed her lips together.

"I'm not sure I follow you."

"Don't lie to me. Do not insult my intelligence," he said as he got right next to her. Then he activated the sequence again, and they both watched as the data showed what happened next. And Curwen narrated.

"The quiet planet was about to reach for the stars. They even designed this entire structure to communicate with the heavens. And what did they get in return?"

A dark moon appeared, hurling toward the planet like a bolt of lightning.

And then it was trapped in the cycle of the blue planet.

"I don't understand what I am seeing," she admitted.

"Aucturn society was invaded by an exoplanet. The newcomers took to their world, their technology. And they killed any survivors."

"This is not possible," Bev admitted.

"I think you will find that the satellite imagery is accurate. 66 million years ago, humans were the invasive species of this world. A parasite taking hold of their world and killing the original hosts," Curwen spat.

"If what you are saying is true, there should be evidence on the moon of its origins," she whispered.

Curwen gestured above toward the collapsed observatory.

"Why do you think I had to do that? If word got out that humanity was in fact alien, what do you think would happen? Our very existence would be shaken. The entire human race has been nothing but a lie," he laughed.

"If your goal was to make sure this information never got out, you failed. The whole world will know about this soon enough," one of the rescuers said as they entered the room from behind Curwen.

"What I did was an invitation for people like you, Doctor Warren. You see, before the blast, we uncovered evidence of the Aucturians still here on earth," the mad man answered.

"They have been waiting a long time to take back their home," he snarled.

Suddenly his body began to twitch as though something within was desperate to break free. She could hear bones breaking and skin tearing apart as he fell over in pain, a bulging mass of spores pushing themselves out of his flesh.

Then her team tried to open fire on Curwen.

It had the opposite of the intended result. The spores burst out, scattering strange black mists of toxic fumes into the air as Curwen let out what sounded like a scream of pleasure.

Beverley stumbled away from the shadowy fog, watching as the two men suddenly began to choke on it; their bodies actually withering as the strange material engulfed them. Immediately she sealed the room off.

Moments later, the Captain and the others returned from the rest of the facility, mortified at what they saw. Their companions were slowly being melted alive by the spores, their thrashing bodies fusing with the floor as a purple mucus oozed from Curwen.

It looked like it was filled with eggs.

"We need to leave this place, immediately," Beverley insisted.

"We've managed to discover what was left of Marginy's body. Do you wish to take it back to the surface for an autopsy?" Anthony asked her.

She went over to the gurney where the half-eaten corpse was laying and checked it quickly for any signs of possible infection.

"It's too risky… whatever this is, it's been trapped here for centuries and evolved to use our bodies as hosts. We can't allow any of the remnants to come to the surface," she insisted.

0200 hours

The journey back was silent, filled with melancholy. Their comrades dead, entering the freight elevator to return felt like it was giving up to some of the rescue team. But they didn't know what Doctor Warren had learned.

She gave a full report to them as the elevator moved away from the north sector, including the bold claims Curwen had made.

"The astronomers were likely able to make contact with these aliens somehow. This facility must have been their last resort for survival millennia ago."

"And Curwen, in a last-ditch effort to save mankind, impacted the tower," he said with a nod.

"I think not. I believe he wanted us to come here. It was an alluring trap. The survivors were the bait. I think the Aucturnians infected him first and hoped that by bringing others here, they could find a way to escape," she explained.

"If they wanted to spread themselves beyond this strange prison, why not simply do so in secrecy?" he asked.

"I'm not sure… Curwen claimed that he wanted people like me to know the truth…" she admitted.

"Do you suppose now that the world will be ready for the damning truth about humanity? It will change everything we ever knew about ourselves," he said.

"These reports will need to be classified. What was left of Aucturn died here today. We can't let the world crumble simply because our society has made mistakes in its past."

"But surely you must see that eventually this whole charade will crumble… if there are other things left from them that we have hidden. What do we do then? And what if the leaders of our world are all part of this grand conspiracy?"

Was it possible that Curwen knew the powers that were in charge of her own life would openly suppress this information? Was he appealing to her for another reason… hoping she would be a traitor to her own kind?

Unless…

She looked down at her own skin, a dreadful thought forming as she realized she had been the only one unaffected by the spores down below.

Was she… not as human as she believed?

Then she saw the captain's fingers slowly reach toward his weapon.

"We tell no one." She reiterated.

He relaxed, and the elevator moved them closer to the surface.

But slowly, as she caught glimpses of the sun and her mind wandered toward possibilities of alien children millennia ago looking up and basking in its rays, she realized that would not be the end of the story of Aucturn.

She looked at the fading shadow of the moon, the secret exoplanet the invasive humans had come here on and knew that silence would mean that the truth could not be spoken.

No, this world was once theirs. And by my hand, it will be again, she thought.

I will tell everyone of their songs.

And slowly we will remember what it was like to live.

THE SQUATTER

не сите куќи се домови————

I should have taken more notice to the graffiti when I arrived at the Highbrooks.

But the sad fact is that the strange scribblings on the complex were the least of my worries here.

Traveling alone is never something I would recommend when you arc in an arca you arc unfamiliar with, but my options were limited.

If my fiancée Peter was here, he could have translated the words, but he had still not gotten his green card when I bought the property in south Sussex.

That was just another item to add to the list of mistakes I made with him.

The building stood approximately thirty-three meters away from the rest of the cul-de-sac, a relic of a bygone era.

To be honest, when I first got the keys to go tidy up the apartments, I actually wondered if the place had been condemned at some point.

That's the problem with me though, I always dream too big. Where I saw potential others could look and see nothing but headaches and more debt.

Nothing about the place had been updated in well over ten years, thanks to the downturn in the local economy. Dust and cobwebs covered every surface, boards nailed down each window. It felt more like a tomb, and I was a grave robber intruding.

This was supposed to be an investment in our future, but instead the purchase was feeling more and more like a train wreck.

As I moved toward the second floor to inspect the wiring and floorboards, things didn't improve much. I used my phone's flashlight to illuminate my steps, shining it down the dirty hall like a beacon. Clearly no one had been here for years, I thought as I saw something in the distance, something stir, and I remembered the seller's warning of rats.

Cautiously I approached, trying to see where the vermin scurried off to. When I rounded the corner, though, I found myself face to face with something far larger than any rodent.

At first, I didn't know quite what it was, except that it had to be about the size of a grown ape. It was hunched over the way such a primate would do in order to protect itself, and from this angle, all I saw was long matted hair. That, coupled with the foul order, made me initially think it actually was such a great beast, escaped from the zoo.

When the light hit its features, it stirred, and I recoiled in fear; frantically grabbing my keys to search for my mace. While doing that, I dropped my keys in a panic, and I heard the thing make this low grunting noise like it hurt to even move.

As I reached down to retrieve my phone, I caught a glimpse of its face and found myself in utter amazement. This was not an animal at all, but a decrepit homeless old man. My weak light showed that his aged features had all the signs of starvation along with bruising. He likely had been hiding in this abandoned building for a while, using it to hide from the cold and rain that was common this time of year. I could see that he just barely had any sight at all, his eyes glistening curiously toward me as he tried to determine if I was friend or foe.

How long had it been since he bathed or had a proper meal? My heart went out to him, thinking of the hard childhood I had growing up in the States.

His naked body was covered in tattoos and scars, his muscles frail and his skin sagging everywhere else that his beard did not cover. Everything about him screamed an addict, a victim of this criminal society that had been seeping into Europe for well over my entire lifetime.

"I'm not going to hurt you," I told him, realizing that he was likely more frightened of me than I was of him. He tilted his head, clearly understanding the words, but did not respond. Could he even speak? Or had he been so far removed from his fellow human beings that he no longer felt it necessary?

"My name is Bernice. Bernice," I said, placing a hand on my chest and then gesturing toward him. "What is your name?"

He opened his mouth, trying to clear his throat and then in a low guttural tone he said with a thick Slavic accent, "Dom…"

"I'm going to help you Dom," I told him as I slid open my phone called Peter. I knew he was probably still on his flight in from Copehagen, but I figured maybe he could still help.

"Hello?" he asked as I put him on speakerphone.

"Peter… babe. I'm here at the apartments. We have a neighbor… can you help me tell him that I'm going to contact the homeless shelter?" I asked softly.

"What? What are you talking about? Is it a squatter?" he asked with his thick accent.

"He's just a harmless old man… he looks lost, babe," I told him.

"You wasted my time for this? Callpolice and get him out of there," he snapped and ended the call.

I sighed, and figured he was probably irritated from his long flight. We had worked so hard to get him into the country, and this whole thing of trying to renovate the Highbrooks was an idea he had never been onboard with.

I kept telling myself that I knew he would calm down once he got his green card, once he saw all the things that London could give him.

"Sorry about that Dom… I'm going to try and find some help… okay?" I told the frail older man.

All he did this time was nod.

I moved back down to the first floor, trying to use what limited internet I had to find the nearest shelter. It was about thirteen blocks away, not bad.

Pushing the door open, I went back to my SUV and decided that I would stop by and ask them to help Dom on my way to the airport.

I was confident that the good deed would make up for some of the other cosmic bad luck I had been receiving lately.

How little I knew…

***

Peter landed around 6 that evening, after a little delay waiting to get into dock. He looked grumpy, but smiled when he saw me. I brought him his favorite food and a sign in Russian that said welcome home.

"You misspell home," he whispered to me as he kissed my forehead.

I blushed and remarked, "I'm just glad to see you made it."

"Have you got a hotel for us?" he asked as we walked to the baggage claim.

I bit my nails, nervous to tell him the bad news. The fact of the matter was, I was dead broke. The recent expenses with the title for the property had set me back about forty thousand.

"Actually, babe, we are gonna have to stay with my folks tonight… it's just for tonight, maybe tomorrow," I hesitantly told him.

His eyes flashed frustration, but he didn't say a thing. Peter has always had a short temper, and I knew that the idea of having to stay with family was going to upset him. Since my folk are devout Christians, the chances of getting any alone time were relatively next to nothing.

But thankfully he was too tired from his flight to make an argument and just huffed in disappointment, grabbed his bags and marched toward the front of the airport. I slinked behind, wanting so badly to ask him about his trip and a dozen other questions, but my common sense told me he wasn't in the mood.

Instead, for the majority of the drive across London to my parents' flat, I didn't make any comment except whenever he did; being careful to gauge my responses so that I wouldn't upset him more.

I wanted everything to be perfect for the start of our life together, and I've never been one to make waves. Besides, my father was convinced that Peter was bad news, and I had been having a hard enough time trying to convince him otherwise.

It's my fault, really. Like I said, my parents are traditional Christians of the Lutheran faith and don't think I should have even started a relationship outside of my home so hastily.

What they didn't understand was that despite Peter's flaws, he was a sweet man. I mean, we all have problems, right? Just because he came from Communism didn't mean that he was a terrorist or something. Convincing them of that had been an uphill battle, and I doubted this short visit would be any different.

It started out peacefully. My mom had made us turkey and polish sausage along with lemon cake, which was Peter's favorite. But I could tell from the moment we all sat down at the table my dad was going to start putting pressure on my fiancée.

"So, Peter… have you figured out what you are going to do for work yet?"

"Dad!" I said in frustration.

"What? It's a valid question, isn't it?" he said and turned to Peter and stated, "I just want my daughter to be provided for. That's all."

My fiancée wiped his mouth before answering as articulately as possible. English was not his best attribute.

"I still await… confirmation for visa…" he answered.

"That's been a few months back. Since your last visit," my dad pointed out.

"That's the government for you… always more hurdles," mom said. I could tell the questions were bothering Peter, so I tried to steer the conversation a different way.

"I helped a homeless man today," I offered.

But my attempt didn't work.

"I am not… what is the word? Lazy. I want to work. But… hands tied," Peter insisted.

"I understand. I know you love her. I can see that. But… can I be real with you Pete?" dad asked.

I swallowed, unsure what my father would say. My fiancée gestured for him to continue.

"Bernice is our only daughter. And all of this is so rushed. Getting you here, trying to get things settled for a wedding and then on top of that, the property she is trying to fix… it feels like something out of reality tv," he said.

My fiancée didn't actually know some of those words, so I softly translated. This time, it seemed like he was angry with me.

"Why you tell father about property? That our decision," he muttered.

"Babe, they helped us get the loan! We're investing for the long term!" I told him.

"It was stupid," Peter barked back. "Hey now, no need for name calling," Mom said.

"No mom, it's fine. Peter just means that he doesn't know why I couldn't get the money myself," I said as I squeezed his hand. "I told you my credit was bad babe," I said.

"And this is exactly what I'm talking about. Putting the cart before the horse…" dad said.

I glared at him, upset that he was provoking a reaction. The only saving grace was my phone buzzing, and I saw it was the shelter calling me back.

"Berni, you know the rules. No cell phones at the table," mom chided.

"Sorry, I need to take this," I responded, getting up and moving to the hallway.

"Hello? Bernice Manchester speaking," I said softly.

"Yes. Evening, mum. This is the Saint Alphaeus Homeless Shelter you called earlier about a man needing assistance in the Highbrooks?" the answer came.

I paced toward the window as I refrained from hearing my dad lecture Peter some more. It was making my blood pressure rise.

"Yes, yes that's right. Did you get him help?" I asked.

"Well that's the thing mum, we checked the entire property top to bottom as best as we could… couldn't find me anywhere. Could you give a description?" the employee asked.

I pursed my lips, realizing that the old man had likely decided to leave after our encounter. Some people just don't recognize they need help, I thought to myself.

"No… I'm sorry I probably made a mistake. I'm sorry to waste your time," I told them as I heard Peter shout something in Russian and my front door slam.

I ended the phone call there and went into the kitchen to see what had happened.

"What did you say?" I asked my father angrily.

"Nothing that didn't need to be said," he said.

"Dad seriously. Why can't you be happy for me? Every time Peter has traveled, it always feels like an interrogation!" I muttered.

"Your father just wants what is best for you," mom insisted.

I sighed in frustration. "What I need right now is for you to let me live my own life! Make my own mistakes!"

"Oh, you're gonna be making plenty of those with Putin out there," dad muttered.

"Dear!" Mom snapped.

I sighed.

"It's fine. I should've known coming here was a mistake too…"

I grabbed my coat and mom tried to stop me.

"Where are you going?"

"I've got a credit card. Peter and I can grab a hotel. Anywhere more hospitable than here," I answered.

"I'm sorry about your father. He means well," she whispered as she led me out to where Peter was getting a smoke.

"Tell him he can stop worrying. I'm a big girl. I can take care of myself," I told her as she hugged my neck and also apologized to Peter.

We left right around nine. "I'm sorry about my dad," I said once we were finally settled in the hotel. All I wanted to do was just cuddle in my fiancée's arms and forget about it.

But Peter was still brooding.

"Father a very stubborn man."

"Oh, and you aren't?" I teased, punching his arm.

Peter was clearly not in the mood though and muttered. "Why he not like me?"

"No, it's not that at all babe!" I said as I wrapped my arms around him and snuggled. "He just doesn't want me having another heartbreak," I explained.

He nodded, and we laid there for a moment in silence as I played with his beard.

"Hey… what exactly did you say to him tonight, anyway?" I asked.

"Hmm? Oh. Told him he could Srat' tebe v rot," Peter remarked.

"What does that mean?" I giggled.

"To crap in his mouth," he said with a smug smile. I sat up, looking at him like a scolding mother.

"Peter, that's my father! Don't talk to him like that!" I told him.

"What? I do not see the issue. He was rude to me!" he retorted.

"He wasn't rude, he was just concerned for my safety," I argued.

"And why be concerned? What is reason for concern? Tell me concern!" Peter insisted.

I stood up, flustered that he didn't see anything wrong with his derogatory remarks.

"You need to apologize to him! He was looking out for us! He has done a lot for us you know!" I told my fiancee.

Peter snuffed his nose in the air and remarked. "He help you. He no help me. I don't see reason for apology," he argued.

"Don't be like that… we want to get along with them, don't we? I mean… they are the only family I have," I told him.

"Not my family," Peter snapped back.

I did my best not to blow up. I knew that it wouldn't get any better if I kept pressing the issue.

So I grabbed my pillow and said icily, "I'm sleeping in the other room."

"Fine. Whatever," Peter said, acting like he didn't care. I was just too exhausted for any of this.

Grabbing a warm blanket from the dryer, I snuggled onto the couch and sighed, wiping away a few tears. Why was this so much harder than I ever really dreamed?

Eventually, that same tiredness overwhelmed my body into sleep.

***

Both of us slept in and missed breakfast the next morning. But our day was so full of things to do for the Highbrooks that I figured busting out tails off over there would let us forget about the arguments from the night before.

When we arrived, Peter seemed to be in good spirits, especially when he saw that the building seemed to have a certain architectural design similar to what he was used to from Moscow.

"Not all houses are homes," he said as we approached the complex. I noticed him looking at the Russian graffiti and I remarked, "I forgot to tell you about that. I wondered what it meant."

"It is… what is word? Old wives tale? Yes… something associated with domovoi in old country," he explained as we walked inside.

I squeezed his arm and remarked, "Sounds Scary. Tell me more about this domovoi…"

But Peter was otherwise distracted. I knew immediately what he was thinking as his eyes roamed the dusty banisters and the broken tiles. "It needs a little TLC…" I said as he covered his mouth and brushed off a ton of old ashes from the front desk.

"This is worse than pig sty… why did you ever get this property?" he muttered.

"It's not that bad. Besides. We can make it better!" I remarked with a smile as we walked up the stairs. I didn't want him giving up when we hadn't gotten started at all but I could tell with each corner we turned and room we explored, he was growing more and more apprehensive.

"Do AC work at least?" he asked. "No, sorry sweetie, hasn't been installed yet…" I admitted. I was getting the impression that he was not liking this arrangement one bit.

"I'm sure once we get started, we won't really notice. I can open some windows." I said as we started back to the door to go and grab tools from his truck. Peter mumbled something under his breath, but I ignored it. I could see why the place would make him in a bad mood.

He probably thought that I'm a sucker for even purchasing it, I realized.

But soon enough, I was sure he would see its true potential.

***

A few days passed by. Peter started working on fixing holes in the wall, upholstering furniture that could be saved and electrical. I focused on the basements. There was a lot of flooding down there and old equipment that needed to move; so a lot of times we hardly got to see each other.

When we were together, things didn't turn out so well. I could see that the lack of air, running water and other proper utilities was agitating him. Casual conversations would turn into arguments quickly.

"Can you help me move some of the stuff on the fourth floor? Toss it out the window?" I asked one time, squeezing his muscles. His glare told me he wasn't in the mood.

"I need to take a smoke," he said as he wiped away more sweat.

"We can't keep having breaks or we'll never get anything done!" I told him.

He whipped around to point a finger in my face. "You think I am lazy? Or did you bring me here to make me your slave?" he growled.

"What? What are you talking about? I'm pitching in too!" I told him.

"You hardly doing any heavy lifting!" Peter snapped back. I could tell his temper was rising.

"Babe, you know I can't," I teased him, placing my hands on his chest. He pushed me away a little rough. "Don't treat me like a child."

"Well, you are acting like one," I remarked. This time I was the one about to leave, not wanting this to get any more heated. But he grabbed my wrist and twisted me back toward him, shouting in my face. "Don't act like a bitch."

"Get your hands off me!" I said back, wriggling from his grasp and rubbing my arm gently. "That really hurt!" I muttered and then said, "Just leave me alone."

He mumbled an apology as I stormed back to the basement, frustrated that I had let things escalate so quickly.

I slumped down near the bottom of the stairs and held my face in my hands, trying not to be overwhelmed with emotion.

Then, from amid the shadows, I heard this strange low grunt. It made me stiffen, and I looked toward the old laundry units that were pushed against the cement walls. From in between two of the washers, a pair of glossy eyes looked in the shadows.

"Who's there?" I asked cautiously. The shape moved toward me and into the light, revealing it to be the homeless man I thought had run off.

He looked like he was in worse shape than before, his skin shriveled and rotting, his teeth hardly hanging in. And he looked like he was sizing me up for his next meal.

"What are you doing here? What do you want with me?" I asked as I stood up. The man growled like a feral animal. I knew he didn't understand what I was saying, but still I tried to reason with him.

"I can help you, let me help you," I told him, trying to reach out toward his shoulder.

He gnashed his teeth and lunged toward me, scratching my arm with his twisted nails. Then he came at me with even more ferocity as I screamed.

Suddenly I felt a firm grip on my other hand, pulling me back up the steps. Peter guarded me and swung a hammer toward the old man, causing the stranger to growl in frustration and slink away toward the shadows.

"Don't hurt him! He's just confused!" I said. "Are you crazy. He tried to attack you…" Peter insisted as he moved toward the old man.

"Let's just call the police, please," I said, holding him back. The old man squatted down back into his hiding place the way a snake would return to its hole and Peter stalled, then nodded toward my suggestion. "Fine. But I want him gone," he muttered as we walked up the stairs together. I could still hear the old naked man growl as we did.

***

Unsurprisingly when the police did arrive, somehow the homeless man had already managed to find a different hiding place.

"I don't see how that's possible. There's no other way out of the basement," I told them as they came up the stairs.

"He probably been here a lot longer than we think. Knows all the ins and outs," one officer suggested as he looked toward a bruise on my arm.

"The squatter do that too?"

I quickly covered it up and shrugged, feeling my face turn beet red.

"It's nothing. I got a few scrapes working upstairs," I told them.

The officer nodded, glancing over toward Peter, who was making a statement to his partner, and then he reached into his pocket and took out a business card.

"Well listen; if you feel like you are in any kind of trouble… this is my private line," he said, passing it to me.

"Thank you… I'll keep that in mind," I said with a nervous smile.

***

Peter and I made up to each other that night on the rooftop. I insisted that we should grab a six-pack and just look out at the stars as the night passed us by.

"Isn't this country beautiful?" I asked wistfully as we saw a shooting star.

"You are beautiful. I am so sorry for my behavior earlier. Bernice, you are… what is word? You are my world," Peter told me. I kissed him. "Let's promise not to fight anymore," I said.

We made love amid the dark.

But our love did not last for much longer.

***

Another week passed, and we started to see a change in the Highbrook. Wallpaper was in place, carpet was down, the lights were on. It felt like it was alive again.

But Peter and my arguments were getting worse. Each time, they ended with neither of us talking to the other for the rest of the day. One time, Peter even threw something at me. I knew he wanted this project to be over with, but these petty fights were getting us nowhere.

Finally, I confronted him about it in the kitchen.

"We need to talk," I said as he got under the sink to fix a leaky pipe.

"Not now," he remarked.

"Yes now," I said as I sighed and remarked, "Frankly, I need to know that we are okay. That this is going to stop."

He looked up at me, confused and agitated.

"I am not doing anything wrong," he insisted.

"We've been at each other's throats for almost a month now! We said we would stop! You promised!" I told him as I fought back tears.

"I am not liar," he growled.

"Well then I'm a fool because all you've done is treat me like I'm your property!" I said.

He slammed down his tools and got in my face.

"I didn't ask to come here and do all of this! If I wanted this servitude, I would have stayed in Russia!" he snarled.

"Well then go back there for all I care!" I shouted as I stormed out.

I went up to distract myself with cleaning.

Another day we were in the basement again, arguing over the plumbing, and Peter slammed me against the wall.

"You're hurting me!" I told him.

He apologized immediately and slammed his fist into the wall instead of my face. The act of violence made me frightened. And that night I almost called the police on Peter.

I need to give him another chance, I told myself. This is a lot harder on him, coming to a new place and adjusting. I told myself things would get better.

Then I found the old man again, this time while I was vacuuming one of the penthouses. I was dusting the closets and then when I turned, he was just… well, there somehow. He was on the carpet, hardly looking as starved as he had before, but still a bit disheveled. He was, however, wearing some clothes that I guessed he had stolen from the laundry, so at least I didn't have to see his naked body again.

"Dom… I don't want to call the police on you again. Please tell me why you are here," I insisted.

He reached toward the carpet and ran his fingers through the fabric before making a grunting noise.

"My… home…" he answered.

"But you can't stay here!" I told him.

"My home!" he said, this time with a firm voice.

"It's our home now," I told the old man as I walked past him and added, "I don't want to get you in trouble. If you agree to leave peacefully, I will pretend I didn't see you," I told him.

"Leave? I am not the one who will be leaving," Dom answered angrily. His tone frightened me and I quickly locked the door. Suddenly he was agitated again and scratching on it like he could get through.

"I'm sorry…" I said as I rushed to find Peter. This needed to end before we opened our doors to the public in a week.

I found Peter in the kitchen on the second floor, working on the cabinets. I could see that he still hadn't been cooled down from earlier, so at first, I hesitated about mentioning the return of our unwanted house guest.

He saw my frantic eyes and didn't question why I was there, instead following me up the stairs. Once at the locked room, I stood at a distance and watched as my fiancée burst through, only to find an empty suite.

"Bernice, what is this about?" he asked in frustration.

"It was the old man… he was here!" I insisted, shocked that he was gone again.

"I do not have time for games," Peter said, pushing past me.

"I'm telling the truth! Don't walk away from me!" I said, grabbing his hand the same way he had that first day.

He turned around and smacked me in the face, sending me tumbling to the floor.

"Don't lay your hands on me, woman," Peter shouted back.

"What the fuck? You son of a bitch!" I said, getting up and then shoving him back. His body hit the wall and this time I could tell that I had taken things too far.

With a wild look in his eye, Peter came toward me and grabbed my hair, tossing me to the bed.

"Sick and tired of your childish tantrums!" he snapped as he pinned me down. I struggled as he grabbed and fondled me, making my body feel exposed and uncomfortable. "Get off me!" I snapped back.

"Shut your mouth, you want this," he said as he ripped my clothes off, acting like a sexual sadist.

"No I don't! Stop! I said stop, you bastard!" I said, slapping him and kicking.

His face got hotter with fury and his hand gripped my neck, making it hard to breathe. "You're such a bitch!" he shouted.

Then from behind us we heard a low thrum, a growl emerging from the hall.

Peter released his grip on me and turned to see the old man there, his gaze feral and angry toward the two of us. I gasped for breath as Peter went toward the old man and yelled, "Mind your business, Codger."

He raised his hand to hit the old man, and I rushed to stop him, causing Peter to slam his fist against me instead.

"You little bitch!" he said, as I scratched my nails against his face.

"Stop it!! You monster!" I shouted back.

Suddenly the old man struck, acting like a cobra. He grabbed ahold of Peter and pulled him to the floor.

"What the fuck?" My fiancée snarled as he tried to get away from the old man's grasp, but surprisingly, he was stronger than he looked.

Then something beyond belief happened.

The old man began to sink into the floor, his body slowly melting into the carpet. "Bernice… help…" Peter said as the stranger grabbed his neck and tightened his hands on his throat. The old man's fingernails transformed into claws, his teeth into fangs, and suddenly I realized he was consuming Peter. Taking him into the floor as well.

Peter screamed as his legs broke, trying aimlessly to fight the creature that had a death grip on him as they sunk into the floor. Then his back snapped, and he shouted obscenities and looked to me for help, desperate to escape.

I stood there and watched, paralyzed with fear. But also thankful as a sudden realization came over me. The stranger was helping me, protecting his home.

Peter's skin began to slide off, pushing his muscles and bones to different directions as he was now against the carpet himself, the old man's mouth widening until it was large enough to swallow him whole.

Peter kept shouting at me, calling me all kinds of names in English and his native tongue until both he and the creature were completely gone, one vanished, the other devoured. Then the carpet morphed and settled like a rippling lake.

***

I told my parents that Peter had left and returned home; they didn't ask any other questions.

The next week, people started moving in.

New couples like me and Peter had been meant to be. A few even reminded me of our dynamic and that worried me.

I still see Dom sometimes, slinking amid the shadows, but I don't bother him anymore. We understand each other. I bring him a small tray almost daily, a gift to thank him for what he did for me.

And sometimes, when I see those young couples that remind me of Peter and I a little *too* much, I give him something else.

THAT ABOMINABLE SOUND

I arrived at the Kotirc Outpost at approximately 3:30 in the afternoon alongside three senior officers from HQ.

We had been told nothing about the state of the facility itself or its staff, simply that we had lost all communication with them about three days before our arrival.

Russell, the head of our group, explained the situation as best as we understood it.

"There is room for ten members here at the outpost, but I believe one group left about a month back and now there are only four scientists left."

I checked the list, knowing these were the people we were meant to interrogate to the best of our ability.

Lucas Wharton, Chief Astrophysicist

Patrick Barnes, Chief Astronomer

Felicia Colt, Secondary Astronomer

Lily Chen, Chief Mathematician.

Something had happened here at Kotirc, and one of them had the answer.

It was up to us to determine what.

Russell led the way into the facility, instructing me to find the power box as soon as possible to restore electricity. I couldn't help but notice a strange red vine growing all across the once pristine tiles.

"How long have they been isolated here?" I asked Mira.

"Their mission was meant to monitor the Halter Vine M30 burst for the past three months, but we didn't know for sure when that was going to happen to be honest," she explained.

I didn't bother asking about the technical stuff. That wasn't my job. I was just here to find the truth.

Going further into the facility, I noticed that some of the vines seemed rich with stains of blood, as though someone had died on this floor and the plant life had swallowed them up and fed off their lifesource the way an orchid would raindrops.

"Guys… I think you need to see this," I heard Mira shout down the corridor. Russell and I were there in a second, staring down at the half-decayed body of one of the scientists.

"What the fuck…" I whispered softly. It looked like he had been wearing some type of protective suit that was normally used for astronauts in space, and his entire upper body had been cut off in one single motion, the way a guillotine chops off a head. There was no sign of any further blood anywhere nearby.

But then we heard the sound of feet shuffling in the shadows.

It was another crew member, this one wearing a red jumpsuit with Korean letters on the name badge. It was approaching us like a feral animal.

As it got closer, I realized that instead of hands, long red tendrils shaped its upper body and distorted its skeletal structure, making the astronaut scuttle toward us like a crab.

None of us had a clue how to respond and for a moment I was sure that we were about to be attacked as the strange human—like creature shrieked. It was a mixture of pain and anger.

Then a shot rang out across the void, filling the creature's shadowy face with lead.

It stumbled backward, shrieking again defiantly as we saw a black-haired Asian woman step out of the next room and blast it over and over until at last it crumpled over in agony.

"Thank the lord," Russell began, but then the woman turned the weapon toward us. Her eyes were full of suspicion and fear. Like she had just seen the worst nightmare of her entire life.

Given what we just saw trying to attack us, I didn't doubt it.

"Who the hell are you?" she asked, keeping herself gun raised.

"Please… Lily? Calm down, HQ sent us," Mira said softly.

"Headquarters? That's a lie. They don't give a damn about us," the woman stuttered, trying to figure out how the hell we were there. Did she think we were figments of her imagination?

"We received Commander Willard's message fourteen days ago, an SOS alerting us that your outpost was in need of emergency supplies. Then we lost contact with you and your team three days ago…" Russell paused and showed her the clip of Willard explaining how team 1 was choosing to leave the facility and asked, "Do you recall sending these messages?"

She looked at her commanding officer and then became frantic again, backing away and screaming, "Turn it off!!! Turn it off now!"

Russell did as she requested and all of us stood there in silence for a moment as we tried to determine what to do next.

"Lily… where are the other members of team two…?" Mira whispered.

Her eyes twitched as she tried to hold back tears.

"Dead… I… I killed them," she explained.

"Killed them? What happened here?" I asked.

"It wasn't me!! No. It was the noise. It got inside my head… I could feel those tentacles winding straight into my mind… it felt like I was going to explode. Burst from the inside out!!" Lily screamed.

She was hardly cohesive, or able to form a simple thought. I knew if we didn't act soon, she might decide to attack us the same way she had her other crew members.

"Lily, we want to take you home. But first, we need to determine what happened here at Kotirc. Let's get somewhere safe and then we can talk, hmm?" Mira said.

But it was clear the woman wasn't going to just comply with what we wanted. Russell gave me the most imperceptible of nods to tackle her the next moment we got.

When I saw her hesitate again, I rushed toward her and grabbed at the weapon. We struggled for a moment, both trying to overpower the other.

Then the weapon went off by accident and I heard Mira make a soft gurgling noise.

"Holy shit. Do you have a Med kit??" I asked as I pushed Lily away.

"I… I don't know. I didn't mean to. No… no, I did. It was the malevolence inside me. Forcing me to. I can't stop it… I can't…" she muttered as she dropped the weapon. Russell took the chance and pinned her to the wall, shouting to me to find a sedative.

I scanned the facility and ran to another room for supplies. Climbing over more of the strange tentacled vines, I opened the cabinets and grabbed the syringe, freezing in place as I saw another dead colleague of hers, his entire upper body literally collapsing on itself from the waist down.

What the hell had happened here?

I ran back to where Russell was doing his best to keep her still and plunged the needle into her neck as she continued to beg for us to just kill her.

As much as I didn't trust her sanity, I knew we still needed to get clear answers.

I checked on Mira next. She was saying a soft prayer as she patched herself up.

"I'm fine… she got me in the ribs. I think I will be fine," she told me as I helped her to the next room.

Russell instructed us to check the remainder of the facility to be sure that Lily was telling the truth.

"And take a sample of that monster too… I'm suspicious of whether or not it might be connected to what happened to the crew," he instructed.

***

About fifteen minutes later, we had set up the Rec room to act as our interview booth for Lily, with her chained to one of the tables. She was still agitated despite the sedation and standoffish, so Russell decided to begin the questions with details about their research.

"Get her to talk about what interests her," he insisted as he began sampling the vines and the blood we had found throughout the outpost.

I've transcribed the interview below to the best of my ability. Some of her ramblings were difficult to catch even after reviewing the audio, so I apologize for that. For the sake of the notes, I have only designated her speech as bold.

"Do we have to record this?"

"It helps to keep everything from being jumbled for the record."

"Is this audio on a private frequency?"

"It's not connected to any network."

"All right. Good. That's good. Fine. We can begin."

"According to Commander Willard's notes, your team was researching a newly discovered fast radio burst. For the sake of clarity, can you explain what that is."

"A fast radio burst is a transient radio pulse of length ranging from a fraction of a millisecond to a few milliseconds, caused by some high—energy astrophysical process not yet understood. Or at least, that's what we thought, anyway. The Halter burst was not immediately a threat to us after all."

"A threat…?"

"We were trying to determine the regularity of the burst. To discover its source. Comprehend what it was trying to say. Did you know that one such burst lasted for nearly 16 days, doctor? 16 fucking days."

"So there is a pattern to these bursts?"

"Lucas was the first to theorize it was some kind of code. Coming from beyond the scope of the Milky Way. He believed it was an attempt by an alien life form trying to communicate with us… and so he made the fatal mistake that corrupted us all."

"Commander Willard noted that the source of the burst was likely coming from somewhere 3000 million light years away. How could anything like that be a danger to mankind?"

"We didn't see the pattern. Or what it was doing to us at first. Didn't understand that the sound was infecting our minds. It was just research at first. But for Lucas and Patrick it soon became an obsession. To unlock what these alien messages were transmitting."

"So you started to record every burst from the Halter source? What did you find?"

Lily began to laugh nervously. It was the sort of laugh that sounded like a woman had gone mad.

She refused to continue questions for the time being, so I checked on the samples from the bodies we had found so far.

"This is… both unsettling and remarkable," Russell explained as he passed me one of the tubes and a microscope to see for myself.

"This looks just like human blood," I realized.

"That's because it is. There is no mutation here. Just an evolution. Everything about that thing we killed is entirely human, down to the microscopic level."

"But how is that possible?" I asked.

"What has Miss Chen told you?" he asked.

I glanced back toward the Rec room, feeling Lily's eyes burning on me.

"I don't think she is telling us the whole truth. But then again, I don't believe she trusts us."

"Big Surprise. I don't trust her either," Mira said, walking into the room and waving what looked like a security tape.

"What is that?" I asked.

"Recording of the past 24 hours. I was just reviewing part of the footage that wasn't corrupted. Looks like our friend in the Red

Jumpsuit over there killed her crewmates one by one over the past few hours before we arrived," she explained.

"Jesus Christ," Russell exclaimed.

"So then all of the crew had been mutated or whatever into those things," I realized.

"Not precisely. Maybe you should check it out yourself rather than me explaining it," Mira told us.

"I should get back to questioning her. We can't leave her alone for long," I said.

"I can review that material, perhaps discover at what point Officer Chen lost her sanity," Russell decided.

When I returned to Chen, there was only one question on my mind. I figured we could kill two birds with one stone.

"Lily… can you tell me what went wrong during your research?" I asked.

"Everything. But if you mean where it all started. I think it was about a week ago. Patrick and Felicia agreed to stay up all night and try to decipher the burst. They figured a pattern had to be there and we could make a breakthrough. But then the next day they still hadn't eaten. Hadn't slept… they were acting like zombies…"

"What did they find?"

"It… it was that noise. That abominable sound! It was inside them already. The others didn't realize it, but it was corrupting them. Changing their brainwaves. Transforming them. Like tendrils spreading through their mind… they were becoming its first victims."

"The sound of the burst altered their molecules? That's how their body started to mutate?"

She was becoming angry again, her body flailing as she tried to break loose from the bonds Russell had put her in.

"You can't listen to it. It spreads now through all the noise. It's a living sentient sound that won't stop until it engulfs all of us…"

I saw Mira signal for me to come over to her and I paused the interview to check out the security footage.

I saw Lily immediately on camera, using what looked like a simple kitchen knife to protect herself from harm. Then Patrick came on screen, or whatever was left of him. His body was already undergoing the strange changes, hardly able to function the way it normally would. His bones and skin distorted like a burst of noise walking and crawling down the hall.

Lily attacked him immediately as he got close, stabbing him over and over until his monstrous body stopped quivering.

"So it's exactly like she said… the crew mutated and she fought for her life," I realized.

"Keep watching," Mira ordered me.

Lily pushed off Patrick's body and then crawled into the nearby air vent, perhaps as a hiding place from the other survivors. She was watching two of her unidentifiable crewmates in another room, both of which were wearing blue jumpsuits, and listening as they consulted among themselves about a possible suspect.

"No audio?" I asked.

But I soon found that I didn't need any.

As Chen stayed in the vent, I watched her body begin to shape shift as well. Long, thin skin tendrils pushed from her hands and came out of the vent, grabbing ahold of the first crewmate and slamming them against the wall.

Mira stopped the tape and remarked, "There's more, but I figured that was enough for now. She's lying. She can control the mutation and she doesn't want us to know."

We went to Russell to consult with him about what to do, but he was distracted listening to some of the audio recordings the crew had kept on the facility.

"It's just a bunch of noise… but it's… it's so beautiful," he admitted as we arrived. I couldn't help but to notice blood trickling from his ear.

"Are you okay?" I asked.

His eyes looked dilated for a moment, and he smiled. "I'm fine, of course. Yes. What did you find?"

We showed him the tape, and he agreed that we needed to confront Lily about it.

"She may be human on the outside… but I think she is just pretending," Russell decided as we went back to the Rec room.

Only to find that our suspect was no longer there.

"Lock down the facility if you can," Russell told Mira as I rushed to check the current security feed. She couldn't have gone far, I told myself.

As I entered the room, I felt a gun against my head and raised my hands defensively.

"Close the door," Lily ordered.

"You don't want to do this, Officer Chen. We just want to help you. You can overcome this infection."

She laughed again. But this time, it sounded like she was pitying me.

"I have already done that without your help. I'm more than you will ever be."

She shoved me against the control panel, and I got a good look at her face. Already there were more distortions in her features, bursts of noise struggling to destroy what was left of her humanity. She was just a shell of her former self.

"Lily, you aren't well. The noise, it's controlling you. Forcing you to kill and destroy anything in its way!!" I said. I knew some part of her former self was still in there, struggling to regain control.

"I may not look like the self, you know, doctor. But I can't lie to myself anymore. There is no escape from the noise. It's everywhere, don't you see that? We have opened Pandora's box and released it into the world. It used me to lure you here for a reason… to spread beyond this facility and into the sounds of the world!! Now your screams will be contagious. Your skin it's host. I'm doing you a bloody favor by killing you now," she snarled.

"Lily… fight this. I know you can."

I reached behind me and searched for something to protect my-self with. And then I touched the fire alarms and instinctively pulled them, hoping to alert my colleagues.

I immediately saw her human face melt away and tentacles burst from her skull. They were formed of membrane and bone and teeth, shrieking at a thousand decibels hatred of a million stars as they lunged for me.

To my left, Russell entered and slammed the door against Lily, urging me to run. I leapt over her transforming body and didn't look back.

The alarm got louder with each passing moment as the humanoid creature struggled to maintain form, to hide in Lily's body like a parasite. It wouldn't stop until it had killed her. And us… and was free. Just like she had warned.

It slammed Russel against the wall and swarmed down the hall like a blob, a mass of skin and tissue that shrieked of pain and evil. Yellow and leaking bodily fluids of all kinds as it shed its human form and revealed the devilish abomination beneath.

I collided with Mira in the electrical room and pushed her to the other side, the creature not hesitating to follow. Then we both pushed down on the kill switch and watched as the frayed wires caused the room to go up in flames.

The strange noise that had infected our colleagues from across the universe screamed as it tried to fight. But it had adapted too perfectly to Lily's human body.

The fire was its undoing and soon all that was left was a smoldering crispy heap of skin, muscle and bone and decay.

***

We concluded our investigation of the Kotirc Outpost at 1700 hours that same day and reported to Hq we requested transport. We all agreed that we would not disclose the findings of the radio burst to anyone else.

"This was isolation and insanity, nothing more," Russell told us.

As part of our extraction, we did, however, determine to bring with us samples of the strange red plant that had grown during the team's time here. We believe it is somehow also a part of this strange transformation that the entire area went through after the transmission from the distant stars became sentient.

"At least the first team made it out safe," I told my colleagues as we boarded the helicopter to leave.

"I've been thinking about that. Trying to figure it out. Why would this sound go through all this trouble to broadcast itself to escape this facility? Weren't team one already possible carriers?"

"The second team must have realized there was a way to trigger the outbreak. To activate the latent infection and mutate their bodies," I realized as we sat down, and I saw Russell itch at the back of his ear. I could see strange pores digging their way into the back of his eardrum.

"Lily believed that the sound wanted us to come here so it could infect us, hide in plain sight and leave to find a new nest…" I said as I watched him nervously.

"What do you think, Commander? Is there an imposter among us?"

Russel's eyes dilated for a second and he smiled softly.

"I'm sure if there was… by now, it would probably be too late for the others."

I chuckled nervously as we left the facility. And then as we lifted off, I heard this strange ringing in my own ears.

It was like a thousand screams in the night sky. Vivid and deadly.

Somehow, I knew it was the same damned noise that the others had been controlled by.

My god, it was inside me.

That abominable impossible sound!!

Transforming me into a wicked little trickster.

Making me into a perfect liar.

Russell shared a knowing look toward me, and I felt a shudder roll down my back.

We both knew before this flight was through, there was about to be one more causality.

ALL IN OUR HEADS

Everyone knew Sebastian Clarke.

Hailing from Ireland. He was a Famed psychotherapist, philanthropist to the community, motivational speaker and devoted husband.

So when word got out that he would be offering a free seminar on taking charge of your life again, the seats were full in less than a day. Rumor was that Clarke had set up a new office in the city and was also allowing any who attended to fill out applications.

Supposedly though, he only tackled the extremely difficult and unorthodox cases; the ones that other therapists simply couldn't handle. The ones that some shunned or turned a blind eye to.

On the afternoon of September 19, 2019; what Doctor Clarke didn't know was that by opening his door to the unknown he would never be able to shut it again.

And that was thanks to Adrian Brenner.

Brenner sat in the back of the auditorium, listening as the therapist began his speech.

The entire audience hung on every word that was said, Brenner included.

"I want you to take a moment and look around the room, go ahead. Pause for a second and think about how many people are here trying to regain their sanity. They are your neighbors, your friends, your coworkers, your lovers, your family. Until you got into this room, you were strangers. But now you are a part of something bigger than yourself. This place is a place of safety, of healing, of rebirth. You aren't alone anymore in your problems. And it's only by working together that we can overcome them!" Clarke declared.

A round of applause got things underway as Sebastian continued to explain how our human mind can trick us.

"We like to believe we are in control of our lives. It's that sense of self that helps us to wake up in the morning, go to work everyday. But there is so much beyond our grasp that we can't fathom, and that can be frightening. We didn't get to choose our parents. We didn't get to decide our culture, our race. There are literally hundreds of these decisions made for us before we can even take a breath of fresh air. So truly, the only sanity we can manage is the kind we make. We have to have some mastery over our fates. And we can, once we accept this fundamental truth," the man said.

The seminar went on to explain how that feelings of rage and anger were just our bodies' ways of fighting for freedom, and how that once we learn to live within our means, and to aspire for realistic goals, we can have peace. Adrian loved every minute of it.

But he didn't think that it would cure his own restless mind.

Once the three-hour event was over, people lined up to get a signature of Doctor Clarke's book, *All in your Head,* and Brenner couldn't help but to smirk at the title. Given what he was afflicted by, he thought it to be ironic.

The thirty-year-old stood in line patiently like the rest of them, but he was already convinced that Clarke would be able to help him when others could not. This was his last chance at a sane life.

Finally, he stood face to face with the great man who quickly autographed one of the leather-bound books and passed it to him.

Brenner nodded in thanks and stood there for a moment, struggling to find the right words to say.

"Is there something else?" Clarke asked pointedly.

Suddenly he froze up. Unable to speak or react, he grabbed a pen from the table and scrawled a note into the book before passing it back to the doctor.

It was his hope that this unusual behavior would spark the therapist's interest, and once he finished with the note he ran off to the bathroom to calm down.

"It's going to be fine. The doctor is going to help you," he insisted as he gave himself a pep talk in the mirror.

His reflection didn't look as confident as he was attempting to sound.

For a long moment, he stared at his own image, trying to figure out which side of the glass he was actually on.

Then he saw it. Just out of the corner of his eye.

Immediately he smashed his fist against the glass, panicking and shattering the shards into his skin as he ran from the restroom.

Outside, Clarke was waiting. He nearly collided with the doctor, who had actually been in the process of trying to find Adrian.

"What is the meaning of this?" he asked, pointing to the note in his book and then noticing the broken and bruised hand that Brenner was cradling.

"Please… you're the only one I know that can help," Adrian insisted.

Sebastian called out to a few of his staff to come help the man and bandage him up.

Clarke didn't confirm anything about whether or not he would schedule the man a session, but Brenner could see it in his eyes. The doctor needed to know more.

It would eventually consume him until he had no choice but to arrange a meeting.

***

Sebastian Clarke did not have many friends.

His career was his life. He would spend long hours in the office compiling notes, trying to help the people that came to him, but often forget about himself.

Having empathy for others often comes with a great expense to one's self and Doctor Clarke paid that price tenfold.

First and foremost with his marriage. His wife became distant and despondent, angry that he would often work late to try and finish up a thesis or he would have to volunteer for a suicide watch. But she would also always claim that she understood. It was a sacrifice they had to make.

Eventually though, time eroded her forgiveness, and she requested a legal separation. Their marriage needed more fixing than any of his mentally broken patients. It caused him to nearly give up, but Clarke chose to give in and try the separation. Maybe the old adage of distance makes the heart grow fonder would work in their case.

This is why he came to the city. To try and rekindle whatever he had lost with Elaine, and to figure out what was going on in his own head.

It wasn't working, though. He was beginning to lose sleep and not eating properly. Sometimes he also forgot to bathe, and some would whisper that he had gone mad. And maybe they were right, because when he came to the city, that was when he started to have the nightmares.

At first, he thought maybe they were just a sort of his subconscious dealing with the separation from his wife, or handling the move. But as they became more vivid, he began to dispatch that maybe he was wrong about that. Maybe the dreams meant something else entirely.

This is how things would play out when his insomnia took shape:

Sebastian would be a child again, perhaps six or seven. He would wake up in his grandfather's vineyard; the one he would often spend his summers at in Ireland. The smell of the grapes and the butterflies would instantly attract him and before he knew what was happening, young Sebastian would be chasing them here and there across the fields.

It would always start off so pleasant. But it would never stay that way. Often, as he got closer to his grandfather's house, he would see storm clouds. A crack of thunder would stop him in his tracks and force him to look at the sky. A brilliant bolt of lightning would smash down from the heavens and split apart the tree he often climbed.

And in the midst of the destruction, he would see a shadow. An ominous figure that ha fro be at least ten or twelve feet tall. The figure would move slowly from the destruction of the tree, almost as if it were hunting for something or someone.

It was hard to describe precisely what the figure looked like, for the mists often made it difficult for young Sebastian to see, but one thing was certain. This was a monster of every sort of nightmare. With iron claws that could easily rip him apart and a metal axe that could sever him in two, the creature's only purpose was clearly destruction.

Perhaps most hideous of all, the beast had no head and the blade it used to cast judgment upon others was sharp and bloodied; a clear indication that it had purposefully dismembered itself. Why the young Sebastian could not be sure, but it did seem to give the monster a sense of its surroundings more than any normal vision might. As though this act of self-harm had embued it with magical strength.

Fear seized him in that moment. To run and to hide was an impossibility, but he still tried. And even though the nightmare did not move with speed, he always felt its presence. It was always going to find him. And every pace he made to escape only caused his own body to age and deteriorate until at last the inevitable occurred. The axe would be upon his neck, and the creature would swing it high to finish him off.

Only the shriek of his alarm would keep him safe, and he would wake with cold sweats.

What if one the blade fell down on him? Was it possible to die if he didn't wake?

At first, he thought that couldn't be possible, after all, it was just a figment of his imagination.

But that changed when he met Adrian Brenner.

It was after a seminar, and he was signing books dismissively; thinking little of the events of the day. He was eager to return to his hotel and to spend the night drowned in bourbon and paperwork.

But then this stranger took his attention. He wasn't there for an autograph. He needed help. Ordinarily Sebastian would always let his secretary handle these appointments, but since the office was still new, he thought having an open invitation would work best.

And it did. By the end of the day, he had nearly three hundred new applications. But none caught his interest as quickly as Adrian Brenner.

All it had taken was one word scrawled hastily on the book that Adrian had passed back.

Dullahan.

The name of the ghost that he had been trying to ignore.

The name he could never remember, but always lingered at the edge of his mind.

And Adrian Brenner knew about it.

And Sebastian Clarke had to know why.

*** ***

Their first session was on a Thursday. Doctor Clarke had cleared out his entire afternoon to talk with Adrian.

He got there around 3:30, a little later than expected, but it was clear that the middle-aged man was nervous about how everything would go.

The doctor tried to make his office as serene and calming as possible, having worked with other patients that were far more manic than Adrian; he figured it would be enough.

"I don't really know where to begin, other than I wish it had never started. It's been a part of me for almost a year now, constantly harassing me in my dreams and even while awake. Always looming and getting closer," Adrian told him as he settled down on the couch.

"You haven't been sleeping properly?" Clarke guessed, and the other man only nodded.

"I used to have a life. A career. A family. Heck doc, I guess I was just like you. Working at a big law firm, helping the less fortunate. I didn't figure I needed anything from anyone. I made my own luck and climbed that corporate ladder all by myself. So why would I even think that anything would slow me down? Guess that goes to show exactly how much a fool I am. A pompous, idealistic one at that!"

The doctor could tell already that Adrian preferred to talk to himself, so he carefully chose which moments to interject.

"I was an account. I had a good amount of clientele that came to me for advice over the years. It paid good too. I used so much of my time to devote to that job, I thought that I was making an impact. But then the Dullahan showed up, and everything changed," Brenner explained.

"Tell me when you first started having the dreams," Sebastian told him.

"Dreams? Oh no, sir. These are experiences I have while I wake. Vivid hallucinations of that headless monstrosity that follow me everywhere I go!" Adrian blurted out.

The therapist steepled his fingers together, clearly intrigued by this concept and asked for more details.

"I wish I could rightly say what started it or even when. It's been happening so frequently that I haven't been able to rightly focus. To give these muddled thoughts the attention they deserve. But I will try. I can at least trace back to the first instance I recorded," Adrian offered.

Sebastian was taken aback to see that the man had compiled at least four months' worth of reports on the hallucination, including locations and time of day.

"This is an impressive catalogue," he said.

"I just want to make them stop. I don't care what it takes. Hypnotism, radical experiments, drug trials. I just want my life back." Adrian reiterated.

"This is going to take some time for me to go over… maybe we should have a sit down in a week to go over this?" Doctor Clarke suggested.

Brenner was already feeling relieved for coming and thanked the therapist for taking the matter so seriously.

He even went home that evening and got a peaceful night's rest.

Unaware of the fact that he was passing on a curse to another unsuspecting party.

***

Clarke scoured the notes once he returned to his hotel room, looking over the different places that Adrian had been visited by the specter and then chose to draw up a map.

Slowly and carefully, he was seeing a pattern emerge and noticed that the Dullahan was using traditional structures almost as if it were studying and methodically hunting the younger man.

As a hallucination, it was very intuitive and strategic, for Brenner's notes would highlight ways that he thought he could outwit the ghost. Only for the Dullahan to again find a way to become a looming persona in his life.

Doctor Clarke assumed, of course, this was merely an aspect of the poor man's delusion. He has made this fantasy so elaborate it's become impossible to distinguish from reality, Clarke thought sadly.

As the hours wore on, he couldn't help but to also visualize the encounters with the monster himself and he decided despite the hour to try an experiment.

Three times in the journal Adrian reported that he saw the Dullahan near to the park at night. Somehow Clarke was sure that the reoccurring location was a subconscious way of projecting some past trauma, so he grabbed a coat and wrent to investigate.

The park wasn't far from the shoddy hotel Clarke had been calling home, perhaps a nineteen-minute drive. Since traffic was light that night, he made it there in only thirteen.

According to Adrian's journal, the Dullahan approached him near to the bridge that separated the eastern part of the park to the west. The encounters were always at night and the creature would often attempt to kill the poor man while he was trying to catch a smoke.

Clarke was already forming theories in his head about what was causing these delusions as he walked briskly against the winter breeze.

Perhaps Brenner was experiencing guilt over the addiction to nicotine, and the Dullahan was a symbol of his subconscious desire to break the nasty habit. Or it could have stemmed from the stress the accountant was undoubtedly experiencing due to the myriad of business deals that he was likely in charge of.

As he stood there and looked across the park toward the bridge, Sebastian second guessed even coming. The waking vividness of the nightmares that Adrian was experiencing couldn't possibly occur simply because of a set time and place, and certainly the phenomenon wouldn't happen to him.

Still though, the therapist wanted to see for himself if anything would actually happen, so he stood there against the bridge and kept waiting.

The night was quiet. Not even the insects made a sound as he searched the empty park for any sign of life. It almost felt supernatural.

But the Dullahan did not come. And Doctor Clarke became certain that the creature was nothing more than the sad, fractured hallucinations of a broken man.

***

The next time Adrian came for a session, Doctor Clarke had prepared notes on possible treatment plans that could assist the young accountant with the delusions. Medications that he planned to prescribe were at the top of the list, along with printouts and notations on alternative routes they could explore.

"I want you to review all of this with an open mind, Mister Brenner. We can make real progress to treat this disorder head on, if we work together. We have to be on the same page," Sebastian insisted.

Adrian said nothing as he took the notes and reviewed them. His hands were having slight tremors, which at first the doctor assumed was being caused by the pain or insomnia that his patient clearly felt.

A moment later, though. Brenner surprised him and started to rip up the documents.

"What are you doing?" Doctor Clarke asked in shock.

"I thought I had a chance coming to you. I thought you would be different than all the rest!" Adrian snarled, tossing the papers in the therapist's face.

"This is nothing but a farce. You think I came to you for pills and to be coddled? My life is on the line here! I'm being pursued by something far worse than any normal treatment can possibly help! I need to kill the thing, not pretend it doesn't exist!" Brenner snapped.

He stood up, prepared to leave; and Clarke tried to calm him down.

"Surely you recognize how utterly ridiculous that sounds, Adrian! First off, I am a man of medicine, not some mystic. My methods are practical. I've helped hundreds, perhaps even thousands with disorders just like yours!"

"I thought you, of all people, would understand that this isn't merely a disorder!" Brenner spat back.

Sebastian balked at that, tilting his head slightly and commented, "What do you mean by that statement?"

The accountant looked at him with only contempt and remarked, "Don't try and deny it, I knew from the moment that I saw you… you've had the same vivid nightmare haunt you."

Sebastian held back a retort even as Adrian nodded with confidence.

"You can't hide from it, Doctor. We're connected somehow. The Dullahan has chosen us for a reason…"

Clarke's mind was spinning, trying to bring the conversation back to reality.

"I'll tell you what. Let's make an agreement. You say that the Dullahan is in pursuit of us. For whatever reason, there must be some merit to confrontation of the beast. Then let me propose this. We meet tonight at my hotel and together attempt to make contact with this headless monster. If it's as threatening as you claim, then we should seek a way to dispose of it together. What do you say to that?" the doctor responded.

He was expecting Adrian to back down from the preposterous idea. But the therapist should have known better than to wager with a man that had nothing to lose.

"What's the address?" Brenner asked.

It was too late to back out now, Sebastian realized.

But perhaps this could finally give the poor man some way to find relief from this delusion, he reasoned.

"I'll email it to you shortly. Be there around eight… and we can face our demons together."

***

During the interim hours of their next casual appointment, Sebastian decided to research about the history of the legendary Dullahan.

By finding all the different theories and origins of this myth, perhaps I can discover a way for both Adrian and myself to rid our minds of these vivid monsters, he reasoned.

The Celtic tales varied from website to website, but a few general features stuck out.

Perhaps what was most well known was his headless appearance and there were many stories that suggest how he lost his head. One of which being that he was a soldier in his previous life and had his head taken from him in battle.

His roaming has been depicted as him searching for his lost head for all of eternity.

However, some stories suggest that he already has his head and that he rides with a darker purpose, believed to be so bitter about his own death that he searches for other souls to take with him to the afterlife.

Sebastian remembered that the creature was commonly portrayed as either riding on the back of a black horse, also headless, or riding a black carriage that is pulled by 6 black horses.

But neither of those seemed to feature in the nightmares he and Brenner were experiencing, so he moved on.

Many of the legends circled around how the monster was meant to be a warning of some kind, telling all to stay out of The Dullahan's path.

No locked gate stays closed when he approaches, bursting open to let the Dullahan through.

As he makes his way through towns and villages after dark, the people hide behind their curtains because if anyone were to look at him, they would be immediately blinded or far worse.

This he causes by slashing their eyes out with a whip made from a human spine, or by throwing a basin of blood into their eyes.

The site said that the nightmare had the ability to speak only once on a journey and that is to say the name of the person whose life he wishes to take.

Once the Dullahan states this name, that person's soul is called to death and there is no defying this call.

Sometime during the wait, Doctor Clarke nodded off; imagining this ferocious creature chasing after him fervently. As much as he wanted to confront it, the terror he felt any time the Dullahan was near was too great to ignore.

A knock on his door startled him awake and he let Adrian into the messy apartment, wishing that he had never even researched all of the grisly details of the monster.

"You've seen him recently?" Adrian asked. Sebastian didn't really bother to deny it, and instead encouraged the stranger to sit and got them both a bottle of wine.

"I think we need to figure out exactly how we can summon it," he remarked.

"And how to kill it?" Adrian suggested.

"The research I found is unanimous of that. Destroy the head," he said dismissively as he opened the curtains to the hotel balcony to let in the cool night air.

"I've never seen the creature carrying a head. Have you?" Brenner whispered.

"No. But again, I have never entertained the idea that the monster might be real."

"Then you will be his victim," Adrian said decisively.

Sebastian chuckled at that as the two men shared wine and some snacks.

Clarke was thinking about his wife. How he could be with her now instead of here.

"I've done a lot wrong in my life," he admitted as they let the night pass them by.

"Do you believe the Dullahan is aware of our sins?" Adrian asked.

"I think it's a manifestation of our guilt," Sebastian admitted.

"My wife Olivia warned me this job would take me over. Eat away at my soul. It's become my every waking moment for so long, I honestly don't know what I would do without it," Clarke explained.

"But you seem so well put together. Calm and conservative," Brenner said.

"I think your coworkers likely said the same of you before you let this obsession get the best of you," Doctor Clarke remarked.

The young accountant smiled and looked toward the window. But then his expression changed to one of horror.

"Don't look. He's here," Adrian said in a faint whisper.

Sebastian resisted the impulse and decided to play along. This was, after all, what he hoped would solve the problem.

"What does he look like?" the therapist asked.

"Tall. Dark. Very strong. A cloak as black as night. An ax that is ready to rip you limb from limb," he shivered. Adrian stood, frightened and was about to run when Clarke snapped. "No. We said we would confront it together. And that's what we will do!"

"I can't. No… no, please," Brenner said as he began to sob.

"He… he has chosen you. Sebastian Clarke. He demands your soul tonight," Adrian said.

"My soul? If it even exists, I gave it up for this job long ago," he said dismissively

Sebastian finally turned around, unsurprised to see the balcony was empty.

Then suddenly Adrian tried to push him toward the edge.

The doctor let out a help as he twisted about and tumbled, narrowly avoiding the ledge.

Adrian Brenner was not so lucky. He fell over, crying out in surprise as he gripped the balcony and hung on for dear life.

"What the hell is wrong with you?" he asked in shock.

But something else had gone terribly wrong in the short burst of aggression. Adrian's shirt was wrapped tightly around his neck, suffocating him as he clung to the rails.

"I'm sorry Clarke… I'm sorry. I didn't want it this way… but it's fate. We are destined to meet…" the accountant sputtered, even as his doctor tried to save him.

Then, Sebastian saw something else in the man's eyes. An evil that lived there, a need to kill. And he hesitated.

"This was all for show. You never saw the Dullahan at all. You want to take on its charge… and take the souls of those you don't think deserve them," Clarke realized.

Then another darker thought crossed his mind. "Who are you really?"

"Olivia told me how you treated her. Casting her aside like garbage. I couldn't let that continue. Not while you sat here in your penthouse drinking wine and ignoring her," Brenner said as the strangulation got worse and he couldn't breathe.

Of course, only Olivia knew about the dreams, Clarke thought.

He knew he could press charges. Perhaps even convict his wife if he could prove the two were involved.

But instead, Sebastian Clarke made a human mistake. He watched as the life faded from Adrian Brenner's eyes and his neck snapped from the tightening noose of clothes.

Then, as his body became limp, the noose became so tight that the man's head was severed from his body, causing it to tumble toward the swimming pool below first.

It all seemed to happen in slow motion as Doctor Clarke watched, stunned to see that in a bizarre way Adrian had become the Dullahan, his separated body and head floating eerily in the water below.

***

The next morning Sebastian filed a report, claiming an assault by Adrian and also called his wife.

"It's finally time to sign those divorce papers," was all Clarke said. It made him feel like his spirit was being crushed at the finalization of all of it.

To think that she hated me this much to finish me off, he thought as he came into the office the next day.

"Doctor Clarke, I was just about to call you. You have a patient waiting," his secretary said as he arrived.

"My schedule was clear today. Did you tell them to come back?" he asked.

"I think he was here before I was. I didn't bother him sir, I just saw him sitting in there," the secretary said as she gestured toward the office door.

Sebastian sighed and entered, wondering who was bothering to interrupt his off day.

Then he froze as he saw the familiar face of Adrian Brenner.

Except that this time, the face was no longer attached to a body; but merely cradled at the side of the man's torso.

The severed head had a terrible appearance, covered in rotting flesh that gave off the strong odour of rotting cheese, with the complexion of stale dough.

His mouth was split into a terrifying grin, almost as if Adrian was finding joy in becoming the Dullahan. In taking the life of others like Clarke.

His eyes lit up with an evil fire as his body stood and his free hand pointed a gruesome, broken finger at Clarke.

"It's all in your head… it's all in your head… it's all in your head…" the doctor mumbled again and again as he tried to not tremble in fear.

But even the most imaginary of evils can cause the most real harm.

THE WANDERING CAMPFIRE

There are times in our life that can define us. Tell us who we are. We go around thinking we know how the world works, and then these moments hit us like a freight train.

Suddenly we realize that we know nothing at all.

This is one of those instances. And it's something that you won't be prepared for, no matter how much you think you could be. I thought I was. I thought I knew what to expect. I was wrong.

But maybe your experience will be different than mine? Maybe you can press your luck.

If so, listen closely. What follows may save your life, should you see the Wandering Campfire…

***

It likes the dark. This fact has been confirmed by all eyewitnesses. Some say that it's the shadows which attract the flickers of the blaze. Others claim the light of the embers comes first, and the darkness follows. One thing is for certain: only at night will you see it.

Not an ordinary night, of course, otherwise every Tom, Frank and Harry would see the damned thing. That would be making things easy… and that's not how it works. It needs to be on the blackest night of the year, the kind of night where you can't even see your hand in front of your face without a flashlight. You need to be stumbling. You need to be lost so it can be found.

A map won't help you, but going deeper into the woods definitely will. In the forests it can stay hidden, it can trick you. This is its turf, and you're just an intruder, after all.

So find a place that makes you feel uneasy. Where there are no signs of life for miles. It may take some time, days perhaps. But then, if you're taking this journey, you know that what lies ahead isn't meant for the faint of heart. Your time is already stolen from you the moment you start to look.

By then it's already too late, once you have passed the last known memories of civilization. You'll keep going, of course, deeper into the forest to listen to nature, but you shouldn't expect to come back.

Those that do come back are changed. One woman said she was enlightened. The universe suddenly turned upside down and yet it all made sense, she said. More than it ever had. The unknown is tangible, if but for a moment, but don't expect it to suddenly be understood.

Expect only your world to be transformed as well.

I had already seen my fair share of bad luck before I went into the woods that day, having just come out of rehab but a week before. The accident had changed me. Rotted my insides and made me bitter. My wife, gone, the children too. No longer was the stable rock they knew.

I needed purpose again.

Find the fire, my best friend Trudy told me. Trudy had been in and out of rehab several times before I showed up, so much so that the staff there called him a regular customer.

We bonded because we were broken, and I could see glimmers of myself in him. A man that lost everything, struggling to keep going for no reason at all. Trudy admitted that he had tried suicide several times, but the world kept pulling him back.

He was the one that told me about the wandering campfire, during a therapy session of all places. The interventionist had asked, was there anything in this world that could give him a reason to go on?

Trudy paused, thoughtful. Reflective. There was hurt in his eyes. Like he was trying to suppress an old wound and at the same time, someone was pouring salt into it.

I'll never forget what he said.

Nobody has a reason to go on, not really. We tell ourselves we do, and we keep suffering. Life is pain, I've accepted that. Death is a release, but it's a give and take. You won't get that freedom unless you give up everything. And that last bit of suffering… it can be hard to let it go. Because it's final, it's absolute. And that is terrifying…

Then he took a sip of water and I swear no one could hear a pin drop. He had more to say.

There's a story I heard, he said, looking at me with dead eyes, about a campfire that moves in the darkest forest on earth. It's a legend, probably older than all of us combined, but it's one that has always stuck with me. This lonesome burning signal, beckoning anyone who dares to come find it. Offering something more freeing than death.

And what does it give? I can't believe the staff asked this. Maybe they hoped that Trudy would break from the story and realize he was speaking gibberish. Or maybe they were genuinely intrigued. I think that's the beauty of it. When you hear about something more exhilarating than life or death. Something unknown is the only force more powerful than that.

He said he didn't know; he never had the guts to go look. Something told him that if he did… it would be beyond his comprehension to even explain. And that was more terrifying than anything he had ever experienced in life or in death.

After the session, I pulled him aside. Asking more about the strange wandering fire. Something like that couldn't be real? And if it was, what would make it so tantalizing to risk everything for?

Trudy smiled. He knew I was thinking of searching for it once I was clean. The world is made of more than what's real and what's not. We both know that, he told me.

And then he admitted how he really knew about the campfire. He has seen it, in his near-death experiences. A flickering blaze that was tugging at his soul.

The fire could be the end. The end of everything. Or it could be the beginning. We don't know, he admitted. And I still don't, of course. Not even after what I have seen.

That night when I went, I brought with me supplies for three days. A bedroll, some water, some food, a hunting rifle to scare off wildlife. Nothing that would slow me down. Trudy had told me that once I found it, the chase would be on. The fire would draw me further away from reality and closer to the truth. The closest thing to the truth I would ever experience.

I kept my senses about me at first; I think that's part of the way it draws you in. There was nothing about the woods that made me feel comfortable. It had been ages since I actually went for a hike of any kind, not since before my accident. The world hasn't felt safe to even dare to explore. And I haven't had the energy to consider going out. But the stories of the campfire made me have that desire again.

A reason to keep going. I've never been one to believe in ghosts… never even believed in God. So what made the campfire different?

It was the way people described their experiences. It felt authentic. It felt real.

I knew some of them were fake, those were easy enough to sift through. When you feel the leaves crunching under your feet and you don't know where you are, and the stars and the sky start to all blend together… there is no faking that.

And that was what I was beginning to feel as the night got darker. The forest was closing in. The instructions told me to draw symbols on the forest floor. Not to help me find my home… but to help the campfire.

The first sign you will get is a smell. Most campfires have an earthy scent to them. Something that makes you feel connected to nature. A soothing aroma that makes you feel comfortable.

When you stand in the darkness and you etch those ancient runes in the dark, you aren't inviting anything that could be remotely considered pleasant.

The smell will hit you the same way you feel when you have seen a dead body, animal or human, making you want to turn your head and vomit. I made the mistake of eating before I even left the roads, so as it wafted over me, I began to hurl up my guts. Feeling dizzy and faint, I could hardly keep myself standing. The world was spinning, and I felt that I was going to fall off.

This can last a few minutes or even a few hours, but the important thing is to go toward the smell. That repugnant odor is the only evidence you have so far that will connect you to the beyond. It's the first step to recognizing this reality you experience isn't so easily understood.

As you keep moving, your first encounter with the campfire will be the most difficult. You'll see a flicker of fire that is gently nudging itself in and out of the darkness. Between the trees, it's hardly visible at all, and you may tell yourself that your eyes are playing tricks on you.

Because it will seem as though each time you look away, the campfire will move.

The key is to stay focused. No matter how much your eyes burn, or how difficult it will feel to walk.

Your legs will be heavy. Your hands might be numb.

But it will be a black hole drawing you toward it. The closer you get, the faster it will come to you.

There will be something different for everyone at that first sighting. But there will always be a place to sit down. The fire will fill you with anxiety as you get close. I felt the hairs on the back of mt neck stick up as I stood there, facing it and realizing that the legends were all real.

Part of me wanted to turn and run away. How far would it take me to return to the real world? An hour? A day? Could I ever return at all?

The mesmerizing flames told me that it wouldn't be possible. Instead, I would need to wait and watch and see where the campfire took me.

My journey into the beyond was starting here.

You must offer the campfire something that you can't afford to lose. That is a part of the ritual that never wavers. It can be anything that was a part of your life. Perhaps an important item given to you by a loved one. Something that you didn't want to leave behind. A picture or a piece of jewelry. The instructions tell you that if the offering isn't good enough, the campfire will simply diffuse, and the forest will return. You only get one chance.

I didn't want to risk losing this opportunity.

I took out the Swiss Army knife and held my hand near the log that was closest to the fire. The blade touched my ring finger, and I closed my eyes, wondering if it would make any sense to even pray.

I pressed down as hard as I could, blood spilling out as flesh was torn away. The blade made a quick cut; it was final and couldn't be taken back. The finger was severed from my body. At the same time, I pressed my bleeding hand toward my jacket, trying to hold back a scream.

This was my offering, and I knew the fire would realize its meaning, because attached to the flesh was my last memory of my wife. That golden ring that I vowed to keep, no matter what.

My last tangible connection to this world and my first big step to the world beyond.

The bleeding was still throbbing through my body as I picked up the raggedly piece of flesh and tossed it into the fire.

The inferno blazed up, clouding my vision as I covered my eyes instinctively.

Then the fire began to move. It had accepted the finger and was taking me somewhere else.

I had only but a moment to grab my things and rush through the woods toward it.

I wish I had hesitated. I wish I hadn't taken this insane journey. But I knew there was no turning back, more so than ever before.

Past the point of no return, the wandering campfire was guiding me to the ultimate truth of existence. And I was dragged toward it like a fish with a hook in its mouth.

As you move forward, it will feel as though you have gone nowhere. Have you ever driven through a long, dark tunnel? The kind that shows a glimmer of light, but the walls blend together over and over as you go further down it?

This is what the forest will do to you. The trees will seemingly push themselves apart and then fall back into place as the campfire moves. At first it will be a gentle flow, the ground itself won't move, or at least it won't seem to. The closest way to describe it is walking on a treadmill. You go down that same path over and over, a carrot dangling in your face that tells you that you will reach the finish line. And yet with each step you make toward the campfire, it's a little further away.

Then the fire will start to feel further away. Again, nothing will change around you, but as you begin to walk toward it, it may feel as though the forest is going in reverse. Except every part of you knows that you are going forward. Trying to reach for that inescapable feeling of purpose that it is tantalizingly offering to you. And then the forest will continue to fall away, the trees, the sky, the stars. Eventually, nothing will be left except for the campfire itself. The darkness of the ground will make you think that you are falling. And you can't stop it now. It's rushing toward you again, and you feel that you are going to fall into the blaze.

Finally, you are exactly where this force of nature wants you. The fire is larger now, almost as if it's encompassing the entire forest.

And then you will need to sit and wait. There is nothing to sit on of course, only darkness. You must close your eyes and trust that you don't fall. The rest will happen automatically. You will feel that you are sitting in a cold hard chair, and the fire will flicker and invite you to touch it.

There won't be any warmth. You will feel colder than you have ever felt in your entire life. This sense of dread will wash over you.

And you will feel that you are constantly waiting for something. All sense of time, night and day, or anything you once were clinging to us is going to be gone.

Then, across the fire… you will see a figure.

A darkness that stands tall and silently across the fire, an evil that you know is from beyond any hell you could ever conjure up.

I felt something heavy on my chest, a hot coal burning my skin. I couldn't speak and I knew that the instructions told me I shouldn't. This was time to listen. The shadow would do the talking.

It uttered my name first, as it seemed to sit down. I numbly nodded, a breath of icy air hitting my bones.

"Do you understand where you are?" it asked.

I couldn't help but to be surprised. It was offering me the chance to answer. Something I was sure I wasn't supposed to do. Instead, I kept quiet as it repeated the question several times, until at last it became angry and tossed embers toward my face.

"If you don't know; then what brought you here?"

The fires hit me, and I instinctively screamed. I thought that moment was my last in this life, instead the shadow simply lingered. Waiting for me to actually tell my story.

"I… I was in an accident… about 18 months ago," I said, hardly recognizing my own voice. Was I really doing the talking, or was it still the shadow? It felt as though we both shared the same resonance in that moment.

"My wife and I… we were… going to this function. It was a horrible storm. I told her we shouldn't go. She insisted that it mattered. But the ice on the road… black ice. I couldn't see it. I hit it hard, and my reflexes got the better of me… The car tumbled end over end down the highway. We collided with four other cars. I felt everything. The intense pain shook through my body, and it kept me awake as I saw bodies piling up around me…"

"Eight cars… at least thirteen dead. Several children included… Along with my wife. The news called it the worst accident in the history of the state in the past ten years. I don't know if that's true. But… I died that day. I saw everything that I ever loved taken from me and I was one of the few still standing. One of the few that crawled out with hardly anything but bruises…"

"People told me it was God, a miracle to help me appreciate life. I turned to drugs. I turned to suicide. But none of it has left me satisfied. I don't believe any of those answers. I think I had to come here… to find this fire… to see the beyond… so that I could understand…"

As I finished my story, silence loomed between us. The figure stood there, staring either at me or the campfire, saying nothing. Was it trying to determine if I should live or if I should die? I wanted my suffering to end. I wanted absolution.

Instead, a cold, dead laugh rumbled through the darkness.

It made me feel like nothing.

It made me suddenly aware that my suffering, my very existence was meaningless. In the grand universe, my problems, my heartbreak… it would all be eventually consumed by a fire, much like the one sitting in front of me.

"Nothingness is eternal, misery and pain are life, and endlessness is the only absolute serenity that anyone can obtain. When you kept living, you thought it meant you had purpose. You thought it might mean your life would have a reason. But no life does. Nothing does. Existence is chaos," the shadow told me as it grew taller. Long slender arms reached up and beyond the view of the fire, like a spider's legs reaching for a prone fly that was caught in a web.

Then those arms morphed into claws, razor sharp tendrils that began to snake their way toward me.

"Let me offer you the freedom of nonexistence," the shadow rumbled as the entire forest began to push its way back toward us. It felt that I was being swallowed whole by the woods.

The trees were melting into twisted and rotten flesh, sliding down to the ground and becoming blackened, burnt fingers that were reaching to drag me to the inferno.

The branches snapped and turned toward me, the hollow wood morphing into faces of people that I had hurt. That I had harmed. All snarling and snapping their jagged teeth toward me.

Suddenly I felt the urge to run. To live. No matter the moment of suffering that I was enduring, I couldn't end my life here.

The reflection of my wife's face came into the campfire. Her soft eyes urged me to action. Then those same comfortable eyes turned dead, color drained. This was the end of everything. This was all that the campfire would ever offer me.

It was all that anyone could ever grasp or understand.

The shadow was covering the entire sky, its laughter echoing throughout the forest. Sharp spikes rippled across the floor, and the canopy became filled with falling knives. My back was torn to ribbons. My running soon became a crawl. I was falling into the earth, into this eternal wandering blaze.

All it wanted was my suffering to fuel the flame.

My legs hit the fire, scarring my back ankles and feet first as I screamed and fought. The shadow kept lurching forward, towering over me as molten fire dripped onto my face.

This is what I wanted, to suffer for my life. To pay for what I felt was my fault. But was this hell my freedom? Was my life null and void?

Something stirred deep inside me, and I pushed my way toward the flame even further. I recognized this was the sacrifice I should have offered. My very soul. Only then would I get the absolution I sought.

Flames engulfed my body as I struggled to cover my eyes. The campfire grew larger, and the laughter was covered over by the roaring fire.

I was falling deeper to the depths of darkness that would melt away all of reality. Then I was rising, pushed up back to the ground. Spitting and sputtering like a newborn, I was hardly able to move as the fire disappeared and my charred and blackened body lay prone on the forest floor.

I was dead. I felt nothing. I was nothing. And then, I was opening my eyes and looking at my beautiful wife.

She looked so much younger, so kind and caring. She was standing at the campfire. About to jump in. And she was telling me that it was going to be okay.

Move on, she said. Live, love and suffer. That was what my existence needed to be. I promised her I would. I promised I would make sense of the chaos that we are given.

Then the forest sky came back, the lonesome woods. I lay there for days maybe before other hikers found me. They didn't even know if I was still human. Maybe I wasn't anymore.

I was taken to heal, but part of me has stayed there even now. I still feel the fire everywhere I go. It burns inside me. My soul is part of this eternal, endless chaos. It is consuming others, giving them a peek into the unknown.

I saw it there, beyond death. This endless madness that will devour us all. It was waiting in the fire. It was in the shadow, and it is now inside me. For I am death, walking on this earth and carrying the fire where I go. Sharing my experience to others who hunger for that freedom. Enticing them to seek out the unknown.

The campfire will grow, it will always move and make use of the weak and the fragile.

But most importantly of all. It will burn.

It will burn the world.

FULL MOON FLIGHTS

Last year BloodyDisgusting gave it 4 out of 5 screams.

Fangoria Magazine touted it as "the most original haunted concept on the market."

But you shouldn't believe the reviews. No, really; don't. Full Moon Flights is not what it seems.

According to the brochure, they are a modern haunted house for fans of fear, a departure from the ordinary and a journey into the unknown, where nightmares are inescapable.

"We don't allow guests to book flights, instead; we let those who have the courage and curiosity to come find us," the blurb read.

Everything about it screamed a publicity stunt to me. A private jetliner filled with costumed actors and jump scares designed to give people an adrenaline rush all night long.

The latest event was this Halloween near me; and since I couldn't think of a better way to spend the evening, I decided to take a drive out to the provided coordinates where the plane was said to land.

Departure time was scheduled for precisely 12:01am so I got there early, intent on documenting each and every aspect of the experience.

Besides myself, there were about 6 other cars parked at an old airstrip, a fitting place for the spooky flight to land, I thought as I looked about the dilapidated buildings. No one had used this place in a very long time, if ever.

I grabbed my cell and small backpack filled with emergency supplies and gear, everything that I thought I would need for the night; but then, from the looks of some of the other patron's gear, it seemed I was the one underprepared.

"First time?" a woman wearing a Freddy Krueger shirt asked as she offered me a small capsule.

"Yeah… what's this for?" I asked.

"Helps keep your head in the game… for a little while anyway," she said as she stared up at the sky. "Guess they want to be fashionably late, like usual."

"How many times have you been a passenger?" I asked.

I remembered reading that some claimed the event had staff hidden among the guests to try and boost interest, so everything she told me I took with a grain of salt at first.

"Five times, maybe six? It's a helluva ride, I tell you what," she answered as she extended her hand and added, "I'm Isabella. Nice to meet you."

"Max… Same here. When are they supposed to arrive?" I asked, noticing the other passengers were getting antsy.

I couldn't see any signs of a plane in the sky, and I wondered what sort of showy entrance the proprietors had in mind to dazzle us.

"Don't know. These things are unpredictable." She lit a smoke, and I wandered toward the other passengers.

"She try to sell you one of those pills too, eh?" a man with an Australian accent asked as I looked down at my palm where the red and white tablet was at.

"Is it some kind of hallucinogenic?" I whispered.

"Don't know mate, but I personally wouldn't risk it. This night is probably going to be crazy enough as is," he told me.

"You came all the way from around the world, just for this?" I asked. He didn't respond, but his eyes showed a story of pain and heartache. He was searching for something but wouldn't dare disclose what.

The others were not as fascinating. Two twins from Manchester were here for a birthday present to each other, and a couple of young reporters finished up our group. Considering the price of tickets for the event, I knew that to get their money worth, they all expected an extreme fright.

Twenty minutes passed and the flight still hadn't arrived, so the taller twin, Tania, started to make a fuss.

"This is so unprofessional!" she said as she walked toward the wide hangar bay. I gathered she was hoping to find someone to complain to and it was the first time that I noticed we were the only ones here. I had read online the flights were always packed to the gills, so why were there only 6 of us?

"What do you suppose is going on?" Isabella asked. She wasn't as chatty either, in fact, the whole group seemed on edge as we followed Tania to the other side of the airfield. Even the wind had stopped blowing. Something about the night just suddenly seemed more sinister.

As we turned to go back toward where we had parked, a sharp burst of air pierced the darkness and all of us felt it nearly knock us down. Tom the Aussie lost his hat and actually tumbled over as I looked up and saw the large passenger plane seemingly appear out of nowhere.

It was about the size of a Delta airline jetliner, with at least the capacity for 150 passengers or more and painted entirely black to match the dark sky. A rumble of thunder crackled across the backdrop of the plane as I noted that there were only a few windows and only one entrance, further showing that they intended for you to have an immersive experience once aboard.

I knew it hadn't been there moments ago, and now all of the sudden it had landed. The ramp to the first-class seating area was already lowered as though they had been the ones waiting for us rather than the other way around.

Isabella gave me a nudge and said nervously, "I told ya they know how to make an entrance."

I nodded and grabbed my things, heading toward the plane as I spotted one of the stewardesses gathering luggage from the other passengers. Tom was the first in line, eager to be aboard.

"Welcome back Mister Bradley. Always a pleasure to have you flying with us," the pale blonde employee said. Her face looked so perfect I half thought she was a robotic of some kind. So pristine and exact.

Tom became red in the face, apparently not anticipating that they would give away his apparent frequent flyer status, and then dashed up the steps to find a seat before any of us had a chance to open a conversation about it.

"Do you have your tickets?" the stewardess asked, focusing on the twins next.

Rylee, the shorter one, took them out of her pocket and both of them eagerly entered without much fanfare.

I was next.

"Welcome back Mister Declan. I see you came prepared this time," the stewardess said as I took out my ticket. I gave her a look of confusion.

"This is my first time," I told her.

The stewardess didn't blink as she ripped the ticket and told me, "Of course it is… yes. I must have confused you with someone else…"

I didn't bother asking any other questions as I figured it was probably part of the show and boarded the plane as well.

At the front before the first-class cabin area, two more blonde stewardesses that looked almost identical to the one I had seen outside greeted me outside of the pilot's chambers and offered me a warm drink which resembled some kind of raspberry tonic.

"Before takeoff, we recommend all passengers drink this mixture. It will prevent any sort of nausea or displacement," the first woman told me.

I knew it was likely they wouldn't let me board unless I downed the concoction, so I downed it hurriedly and then pushed open the curtains to look at the interior of the cabin.

Much to my surprise, it looked like an ordinary jetliner would, with rows of compartments above the seats for luggage and about 5 seats on either side of the aisle, most of which were empty.

I checked my stub to see where I was supposed to seat.

Economy row C, seat 3.

The Aussie was the only one of us in first class, and I almost envied his deep pockets, wondering if his experience would be entirely different from our own.

Back in economy, I immediately felt a bit more cramped and claustrophobic, especially due to the dim lighting. Was that for aesthetics? I wondered as I moved to my seat and noted I was near a window. A window that appeared to be sealed shut.

A moment later, anbusinessmaness man appeared from the curtain and nodded, sitting down next to me.

"Did you get here late?" I asked, not recalling him in the crowd outside.

He responded in his native tongue and took the seat beside me, nervously fidgeting with his wedding ring as more passengers boarded.

"Bloody hell, where are all these people coming from?" I asked, noticing a whole family pass us to go to third class.

I reached over to my window to try and see if maybe a large group had shown up at the last minute, but then Isabella reached from the row behind me and kept me from opening it.

"I wouldn't do that if I were you," she warned.

I snatched my hand away, tired of her games, and pulled the shudder on the window up, anyway.

But the airfield didn't look familiar anymore. Instead, it seemed as though we were landed somewhere in a busy city district, like Hong Kong or Seoul. Nowhere near the same rustic countryside of Midwest America.

"What the hell…?" I whispered as Isabella shut it back.

"We're about to take off, and trust me, you want these closed," she warned again. This time I decided to listen.

Another stewardess appeared near the front of the cabin and grabbed a small speaker connected to the compartment beside her to give us a few guidelines. I couldn't help but notice now that the plane was seemingly packed full of people.

"Good evening. On behalf of all us here at Full Moon Flights, we want to thank you again for joining us on this amazing journey. The Captain has turned on the fasten seatbelts sign at this time as we go over a few instructions in the event of an emergency," she said in a singsong voice. Honestly, she seemed a bit too chipper given the information she next presented.

"As you might have noticed during your arrival, there are no emergency exits or equipment aboard the flight. We have optimized the cabin to be entirely for the experience into the unknown. That being said, should we encounter any unanticipated turbulence, we ask all passengers to remain seated. The safest bet for us to reach our destination will be your full cooperation in these circumstances."

I couldn't believe what I was hearing, especially how dangerous it sounded. I heard one man behind me cuss profusely as the stewardess next explained there was no emergency oxygen on the airliner either.

"Rest assured that what you will be dealing with tonight will take your breath away, but if you can face it… you will get to your destination as intended," she said as she finished her announcement and then disappeared to the front of the plane. Something about the way she spoke made me very uneasy. Her choice of words felt intentionally vague.

A clamor of gossip stirred as we all wondered what the hell we had signed up for.

"This must be just to get us nervous," a younger girl said a few rows up.

"I heard they intentionally make it this intense before the show starts," another man said.

It made me a little calmer to hear these rumors swirl about, but I still had no idea what to expect. Behind me, Isabella squeezed my shoulder and muttered, "Buckle up Max."

I obeyed her and listened as a new voice came over the intercom. This one was gruff and sounded distorted. Almost inhuman.

"This is your Captain speaking. We are T—minus 3 minutes to take off."

I'm not sure why but the succinct way he spoke, coupled with the way my stomach was twisting into a knot; made me very uneasy. There was no turning back. No escape, I realized.

Then the plane began to move.

Instinctively I gripped the seat cushion as I felt the engines begin to roar and the plane shake and pick up speed.

The Asian businessman next to me did the same, closing his eyes and seemingly chanting. Was he praying?

I could hear the wheels skid against the runway and the noise grew louder as I was pushed into the seat a bit by the thrust of the engines. Then we began to ascend.

The roar got louder as I looked about at some of the other passengers to see their reaction. Some were grabbing bags to puke in, clearly new flyers, while others were excitedly counting the seconds as we kept going higher. I wasn't sure which category I fit in, but I was ready for the flight to stop its rush into the heavens.

The plane shook again as we reached what I assumed was highest altitude, and the light above my seat told me I could move about the cabin freely.

Immediately I turned to Isabella to get some clear understanding of what to expect. Only to find she had already unbuckled and left to the third-class cabin. I sighed in frustration, trying to get the attention of a stewardess. But the women were now standing toward the front, like statues unblinking and looking on toward us. It was bizarre, but exactly what I expected for this sort of thing.

I took a few breaths and calmed down, reminding myself that I should be trying to enjoy the experience as I saw the curtain behind the stewardesses open and a woman wearing a geisha dress and kabuki mask enter, dancing amid the aisle toward my row.

Immediately the Asian man next to me tensed up. I saw his face had a look of panic. Was this someone he knew? Had the flight personnel secretly allowed them to board? Was he in danger? The woman got closer and then bowed respectfully toward me, clearly wanting to sit beside the businessman. I'm not sure why, but I felt obliged to let her in and moved out toward the aisle.

The businessman started to shout something in alarm and tried to unbuckle, then the woman straddled his lap. It almost looked like she wanted to make out with him as I watched her gently touch his face. He started to shout louder, and I watched as the woman leaned in for a kiss.

Someone squeezed my shoulder again, and I turned to see Isabella standing there. "Come with me," she ordered. I half wanted to see what would happen to the man I was sitting beside, but still obeyed. Clearly, she knew more about this flight than me.

As we entered third class, I found myself taking a moment to adjust to the darkness in the room. There weren't any windows back here. And the only dim lighting was coming from the screens on the back of each of the seats. Miniature flat screen televisions that all of the passengers were glued to like zombies.

"What is this?" I whispered, worried that our voices would break some of them from a trance.

"I believe they are doing something to them, brainwashing... or something. I'm not sure. I was hoping you could help me get into the luggage compartment overhead," she said as we made it to the middle of the aisle.

I noticed that the expressions on the people's faces seemed contorted with terror or dread. As though whatever they were watching were driving them mad.

"Sure... but before I do that, you need to be honest with me. Why are you really here?" I asked.

Isabella bit her lip and glanced toward the door.

"We don't have time for that. The stewardesses will be here any moment. So can you help break this open or not?"

I huffed and looked at the lock, realizing that I actually did have something that could open it up.

"Yeah... sure. Let me go back to my luggage."

Isabella told me to hurry as I returned to economy class, and I saw the stewardesses were now removing... something from the seat near me.

It looked like the shriveled up remains of the businessman. It looked like a corpse.

"Mister DeClan, your in-flight movie is about to start," the first stewardess said, as I noticed that now there was a mini tv in front of my seat as well. Had that always been there?

"What happened to the man sitting beside me?" I asked. I now noticed there seemed to be red dark stains on the seat. Blood.

"It's best if you keep your journey to yourself and not worry about others," the stewardess said with a pleasant smile. She stood there waiting for me to comply with her instructions.

Hesitantly, I sat down and put on the headphones. Everything about this was beginning to grow increasingly stranger and stranger, not what I signed up for at all.

As I activated the screen in front of me, a burst of white noise pierced my ears, and I nearly knocked the headphones off. Then crashing waves filled the screen, and I froze.

What I was seeing didn't seem possible. It was showing me memories of my time as a child near the beach. Memories I've never shared with anyone.

I watched in amazement as I saw my own mother in the waves. This was the moment that she had taken her own life, I thought. A secret that I had wanted to take to my grave.

How could this flight know?

The noise got louder as I heard whispers amid the waves. Something was speaking to me, telling me its own secrets. Chills ran down my spine as every moment played out exactly as I remembered it. My mother was just walking into the water, unconcerned with my cries as the waves crashed over her body. The whispers got louder. It sounded *just* like her.

"Join… me…" it croaked.

Then, shots rang out amid the cabin.

I jolted back to reality and saw Tom entering economy class waving a pistol about. The stewardess was his victim. Her lifeless body sprawled on the aisle in front of me. Except there was no blood. She just looked like a mannequin now.

"What the hell, man?" I shouted, standing up as he neared my seat.

"Don't let 'em harvest ya Max. You are too good for that. We can make it through this together. But you have to help me, you hear?" he said.

Other passengers were screaming as he waved the gun around, warning them to stay back.

"What the hell is wrong with you? They are bloody frightened of you," I shouted.

"That's exactly what they want you to think. Now take me to that stupid chick you talked to earlier, the frequent flyer," he ordered.

I raised my hands up defensively and we walked together toward third class.

"Look; whatever you think this is… it's not. These are just actors," I told him as we entered the dark room. Even when I said that, I didn't fully believe it. Something deep in the pit of my stomach told me that none of this was normal.

I planned to use the sudden shift in light to take advantage of him, but I never made it that far.

Instead, the entire plane started to shake due to turbulence, and he lost the gun. It slid across the floor as he fell on me, and I shouted to Isabella to find it.

She obeyed, and I turned to punch Tom straight in the jaw as the lights in the cabin began to flicker.

Then all of the passengers around us started to convulse and go into shock, seemingly being given a stroke due to the sudden loss of power.

Amid the chaos, somehow Isabella found the weapon and aimed it toward me. Tom had already produced a knife, and I shouted for her to shoot him.

Instead, she aimed at the luggage compartment over our heads. A single bullet caused the lock to blast off and several small bags fell, causing Tom's knife to become lodged in my shoulder.

"Shit!!" I said as I looked across at some of the passengers, begging them to help. Instead, they were beginning to attack each other. One man was mauling out his son's eyes and eating them. A woman was digging straight into her face, trying to rip skin off. And two children were smashing each other in the stomach constantly with sharp forks.

Any hope I had that this was all an act died at that moment.

Isabella scrambled to search amid the bags as Tom got his bearings. Then she found what she was looking for. It looked like a small briefcase.

"Don't!!" Tom shouted.

I frowned, trying to figure out what the hell was happening as she put in the correct key code and the latches unbolted. Inside, there were six coals filled with a glowing yellow serum. She grabbed one and rushed toward the Aussie.

I crawled out of the way into one of the seats as she lunged and pierced his neck, forcing the needle in all the way. I saw Tom's eyes dilate and then go completely black. Then he fell to the floor, unconscious. I snatched up his knife, just in case things got crazier from here.

It was a smart call.

Before I got a chance to even ask Isabella what the hell she was doing, she was through the curtain to economy class. I slowly stood up, trying to catch my breath, when one of the mutilated passengers grabbed ahold of me, forcing me to stare into their hollow, sunken face. There wasn't even a face there anymore, just a maw with endless teeth. Somehow, they had transformed into nightmarish beings.

I pushed it away and tumbled over Tom to get back to economy class, pausing in between the two cabins to go into the restroom.

The small room felt so much more claustrophobic than usual as I locked the door and looked at my reflection in the mirror. Splashing water on my face, I tried to get ahold of myself and chanted, "It's all in your head, Max… it's all in your head…"

I gripped the sink for a minute and felt my breathing return to normal, hoping that maybe I was able to come back to normalcy.

Then I noticed something shimmer in the mirror. I looked at it for a short moment, frowning in concern.

Then my reflection smiled wickedly toward me. A second later, a strong icy hand emerged from the mirror and gripped my neck.

I was gasping for breath as I felt my reflection strangle me and I reached into my pocket where Tom's knife was still hidden away.

I sliced it across the doppelgänger's arm, causing strange black slime to bleed out from him as he loosened his grip and I escaped to the main cabin.

I was still trying to make heads or tails of what was happening when I caught sight of the twins. After all that had just happened, I could hardly remember their names. Rylee? Tania?

All I knew for sure was they were both covered in blood, hobbling toward me with heads. Knives in their hands, having carved off each other's skulls, blocking my way to first class. I could hear Isabella shouting something to a stewardess as I looked back toward third class. The jetliner was shaking violently again, and I heard the captain announce something overhead.

"Attention esteemed guests, we are entering a rough patch and advise you to buckle up," he said in a voice that sounded too excited for the coming maelstrom.

Suddenly I was thrust to the ceiling. The twins fell upward as well, their bloody bodies toppling like ragdolls as I found myself unable to avoid sliding into them.

The airliner shook, and I slowly moved toward the aisle where this all began, trying desperately to regain my footing.

Then I heard a loud growl from the third-class cabin.

I shouldn't have looked. Tom's head peered out of the curtain, but what followed it was not human.

It had a long neck, like a giraffe without skin. And legs that were as wide as the entire cabin, stretching out toward passengers and stepping on them like ants. The legs had mouths like a Venus flytrap shrieking as the strange creature twisted its body like a contortionist. It clung time the ceiling, Tom's pure black eyes looking straight at me as his chest opened up and hundreds of miniature spidery creatures skittered toward me.

"Holy shit..." Isabella shouted as she entered the room. Tom leapt toward her, shrieking as his mandibles ripped into her chest. The plane started to level again, and I moved down to my seat, desperately trying to find some way off.

All I could think to do was break the window. I still had Tom's knife and my rattled brain told me to give it a try. Reaching toward the window, I raised it up even as I heard Isabella scream for me to stop.

I was expecting to see just the darkness of the night. Instead, it was blinding light, hitting me right in the face as I covered my eyes and tried to hit the window.

I heard the glass crack, and I kept going as hard as I could.

Suddenly the screams in the cabin were replaced with the roar of a void. Whatever was beyond the window, I had managed to reach it. And now we were all about to be sucked out. I gripped my seat as hard as I could as alarms began to blare.

Tom's gargantuan body was the first to go. It was like watching a camel be shoved through a needle hole. His face contorted, and I heard the breaking of bones. He tried to grab a hold of me, his tongue lapping out and sliding against my face as I heard him mindlessly groan.

His front claw grabbed at my hand and I lost my grip, my legs hitting the shattered glass as I felt the roar of the plane against my body. It felt like I was a puppet, being dragged by a massive child. I was gripping the window, looking toward the heavens.

I can't describe the impossible things I saw in that sky. This was not our Earth. Not our reality. It was a kaleidoscope of universes crashing into one another, exploding in rainbows of colors that I couldn't comprehend. From the endless ethereal streaks of light and dark, massive tentacles wrapped around the plane like vines. Suffocating it.

I could see something just beyond the horizon. A maw. The jaws of eternal damnation themselves. Ready to swallow me whole.

Isabella reached out of the window to grab my hand and struggled to pull me in. I was lost in the gaze of the eyes of the demonic entity that awaited us.

As soon as I was inside, I saw that she had another serum prepared, this time for me.

"You really should have taken that pill, bud," she warned as she stabbed in my arm before I could get a chance to react.

The world spun.

I saw her face begin to melt away. In its place first were the twins, growing two necks and forming a single monster to grin devilishly at me.

Then they faded and showed the geisha woman, except this time her kabuki mask was made of flesh. The remains of her husband.

Her long, clawlike fingernails dragged at my chest as she removed the mask. And I saw my own mother. Her lifeless eyes locked with my own as I fell into an ocean of sleep.

I can't remember what happened next. It felt like I was having an out-of-body experience. I was above the plane now, watching as the tentacles of the monster crushed it and swallowed it whole. The shrieks of passengers. Not just hundreds, but millions from all across reality. Being fed into this hungry monster's jaws.

Then I was back in my seat.

The unfasten your seatbelt sign flashed on and I gripped my cushion, looking toward the Asian businessman who was now seemingly alive.

How was I alive? I looked down at my arm, rubbing the place where Isabella had injected me. It still felt sore.

This hadn't been a dream… I realized as I looked around the cabin. The overhead intercom came on again.

"Attention passengers, we are about to arrive at our destination… please remain seated to enjoy the full experience."

I felt a squeeze on my shoulder and then Isabella whispered into my ear. "Everything you just experienced was real. It just happened *here* yet. You need to find Tom and get off this flight. Now."

I was about to turn to her when she squeezed my sore spot harder and snapped at me. "Don't look back, don't hesitate. Just run." Then she passed me a gun. Was it the same one that Tom had used before? I wasn't sure.

My heart started pumping fast as I unbuckled and moved toward first class. The stewardesses were there, blocking my way. For some reason I knew they would try to stop me. So I swung the hammer of the weapon straight toward the left one. The two of them slammed into each other and it sounded like two dummies collapsing against one another in a store.

I pushed past them to enter the first-class seating area. Most of the passengers here were rich upper class, just like any other normal flight. But as I moved down the aisle, I couldn't help but to notice the color was drained from their faces. They were trapped in their seats. Unable to move. I reached toward one man to try and wake him, and his skin became as brittle as ash.

"They are husks," a voice said in front of me.

I turned and looked to see a man standing there wearing a pilot uniform. But nothing about him made me feel that he was human. He might have once been. But now all that remained was this memory.

"What are you doing to them?" I asked, my voice trembling as I searched the cabin for Tom. Isabella's warning was ringing in my head. But I still needed to *know* more.

"Only what they signed up for. What you've already experienced. You've cheated, Max. Seen the end of the journey and managed to make it back. But it doesn't matter. The fear we can harvest from your soul is endless. You will never truly leave this flight," he said, taking a step toward me.

I clenched my fists and cocked the weapon toward him, letting loose a few rounds into his body. It didn't deter the specter. I'm not even sure why I tried after all I had seen.

But it did grab Tom's attention. He stood up and moved toward me.

"What are you doing, man? Do you want to get us both killed?" he shouted.

I looked toward the gun, my hands shaking as I saw a scar was beginning to form on my arm. How had it gotten there?

"I think we might already be dead," I said, passing him the weapon. The ghost pilot was gone temporarily but Tom warned it wouldn't matter.

"God, my head hurts. That drug really did a number on me," he said, rubbing the spot where Isabella had injected him.

"How is any of this possible?" I said, my mouth dry as he led me back through economy class.

This time I saw my doppelgänger again, sitting there staring out the window and watching as the jetliner began to shake again. Tom was rattling off an explanation, or an interpretation of events to me as we moved on.

"From what I understand, the plane moves beyond the realm of space and time that we know. Past the horizon into a new endless dimension. One where pure chaos is born. The people, if they are that; who run this contraption… they are feeding a creature. Trying to birth it into the reality… this reality that we know of. It's growing stronger, Max. Every new flight is harvesting more memories of reality and fear into it," he said.

We were almost to the back of the plane now. No one had stopped us. His explanation made some sense to me as we stood there and he started to look among the things before commenting, "You probably have a dozen other questions about this mess, like how I know all this and why Isabella, if that is her real name; is helping us. I don't know. I came onboard for my wife. She boarded a flight 3 years ago. And I'm gonna find her."

He paused and passed me the weapon, along with a parachute. "But that isn't how your journey ends, Max. You've got a chance to get out. Warn the world if you can. Just don't worry about me."

"If your wife is trapped here; you'll need to give her the serum that we both took…"

He nodded, nodding me adieu as he left to search the plane.

The luggage compartment was oddly silent as the jetliner shook again and I put on the backpack. I slowly walked toward the back of the plane, near to where the landing gear was stored. It would be the safest place to jump, I realized.

I crouched down and gently kicked at the shutters beneath the gear, wondering how strong they were.

Then I heard a faint whisper. Someone was there with me.

Instinctively I jolted up and cocked the weapon. "Show yourself."

From amid the luggage, I saw a shadow move and slither toward me. Eventually, it formed a shape.

The ghost pilot?

No, it was a doppelgänger of my own mother, I realized.

"Don't come any closer," I warned her. Her eyes looked so watery and full of pain.

"Max… it's me. I'm real. This is real, all of it," she whispered to me.

"It can't be. You're dead," i shouted back. "I saw you die!"

"That was just one way my journey ended. It doesn't have to be that way anymore," she said with a gentle smile.

"The Journey has shown me so much. We can have a life together. Endless amounts of lives…"

I heard another rustle amid the luggage. It was Isabella coming to check on me.

"Max, don't listen to her. You have to leave."

"You can't leave Max. No one can. Board the flight, you are part of the ship…" another voice cackled amid the rafters.

My mother raised a welcoming hand toward me. "This can be the life we never got together," she pleaded with me.

I knew it was a trap. But it felt so inviting. To be able to escape into an endless cacophony of realities where I could experience the love of a mom I never knew.

But none of it would be real, I realized.

I steadied my aim, and fired straight at her head.

The shadow screamed and blurred into a thousand slithering eels as Isabella shouted for me to go.

I turned and slammed my foot against the landing gear, again and again. The black slime oozed toward me, the screeching eels rapidly closing in for a choke hold.

Then finally the metal gave way and I saw clouds beneath my feet.

"Come with me!!" I shouted to Isabella. After all she had done to help me, it felt like helping her was the right thing to do.

"It's too late for me. I'm part of the ship already, but I'll be here to help people get off every damn time," she responded.

I reached for her, ignoring her insistence that she was doomed. But instead, the shadows ensnared her, and I watched as black slime poured into her eyes and mouth, the shadow began to eat away at her body. And I knew I had to leave.

Crawling down to the landing gear, the rush of air beneath the plane was overwhelming. I heard the screams from the flight roar and didn't hesitate this time.

I jumped.

Spiraling into the air, I heard the roar of white noise and looked up to see an empty sky. Like it had never been there at all. The force of my fall began to increase, and I pulled at my parachute cord, feeling it tug and jolt me up in the air. Then everything began to slow. I was drifting amid the atmosphere.

Gradually I made my way to the surface, tumbling about on the soft ground as I got my bearings. I was back at the airfield.

Standing up, I checked my watch and realized that not a minute had passed since I boarded.

I shook off the parachute and stumbled toward the road, watching as some cars approached.

I covered my eyes as one car parked in front of me, and a man dressed as a British explorer stepped out.

"What in the devil have you just been through, my good man?" he asked, clearly startled by my appearance. I saw a couple behind him holding tickets, apparently awaiting an upcoming flight.

I opened my mouth to tell, to warn him, then I saw a familiar face in the crowd. Isabella.

I moved toward her, grabbed a hold of her arm and muttered, "Are you real? Is this… real?"

"Hey! Hands off! What's gotten into you, bud?" she said, shaking me off like she didn't know me.

I still felt like my head was spinning.

"You're here for the Full Moon Flight?" I asked, trying to understand and carefully choosing my words.

"Yeah… first time. I heard they are a scream. You been on one yourself?" Isabella asked.

I didn't see a hint of deception in her eyes.

Slowly I nodded, reaching into my pocket and passing her the pill she had given me right before I boarded. Only she hadn't done that yet.

"You'll need this for the trip," I told her. She gave me a look of puzzlement and I walked off without another word. I knew there was nothing I could say to even explain how I understood her role now for this.

A moment later, I felt a rush of wind and the dark jetliner appeared right behind the hangar bay like it had before. A journey into the unknown, an experience like no other; that's what the reviews say.

But that isn't what mine is going to say.

This is my review for Full Moon Flights.

Don't believe the hype.

This event is a killer.

And you don't want to become a frequent flyer like me.